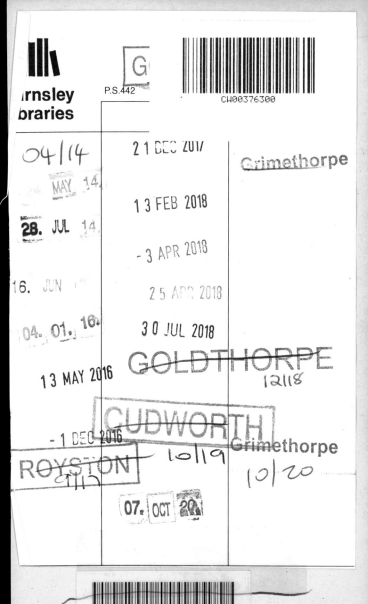

Maisey Yates was an avid Mills & Boon® Modern™ Romance reader before she began to write them. She still can't quite believe she's lucky enough to get to create her very own sexy alpha heroes and feisty heroines. Seeing her name on one of those lovely covers is a dream come true.

Maisey lives with her handsome, wonderful, diaper-changing husband and three small children across the street from her extremely supportive parents and the home she grew up in, in the wilds of Southern Oregon, USA. She enjoys the contrast of living in a place where you might wake up to find a bear on your back porch and then heading into the home office to write stories that take place in exotic urban locales.

Recent titles by the same author:

HIS RING IS NOT ENOUGH
THE COUPLE WHO FOOLED THE WORLD
HEIR TO A DARK INHERITANCE
(Secret Heirs of Powerful Men)
HEIR TO A DESERT LEGACY
(Secret Heirs of Powerful Men)

Did you know these are also available as eBooks?
Visit www.millsandboon.co.uk

FORGED IN THE DESERT HEAT

BY
MAISEY YATES

MILLS & BOON

Published in Great Britain 2014
by Mills & Boon, an imprint of Harlequin (UK) Limited,
Eton House, 18-24 Paradise Road, Richmond, Surrey, TW9 1SR

© 2014 Maisey Yates

ISBN: 978 0 263 91108 4

Harlequin (UK) Limited's policy is to use papers that are natural, renewable and recyclable products and made from wood grown in sustainable forests. The logging and manufacturing processes conform to the legal environmental regulations of the country of origin.

Printed and bound in Spain
by Blackprint CPI, Barcelona

FORGED IN THE
DESERT HEAT

To my daughter.
Never be afraid to stand up for yourself,
or to stand for what's right.
You're the hero of your story.

CHAPTER ONE

SHEIKH ZAFAR NEJEM scanned the encampment, the sun burning what little of his skin was revealed. He was as covered as he could possibly be, both to avoid the harsh elements of the desert, and to avoid being recognized.

Though, for most, the odds of that would be low out here, hundreds of miles from any city. But this was his home. Where he'd been raised. The place where he'd made his name as the most fearsome man in Al Sabah.

And considering his competition for the position, there was weight to the title.

Nothing seemed out of the ordinary here. Cooking fires were smoldering, and he could hear voices in the tents. He stopped for a moment. This was no family encampment, but that of a band of highway men. Thieves. Outlaws, not unlike himself. He knew these men, and they knew him. He had a tentative truce with them, but that didn't mean he was ready to show himself.

It didn't mean he trusted them. He trusted no one.

Especially not now.

Not now that there was certain to be unrest. Anger, backlash over his installation in the palace. On the throne.

Back to his rightful position.

The Gypsy Sheikh's return had not been met with delight, at least not in the more "civilized" corners of the country. His uncle had done far too efficient a job in destroying his reputation for anyone to be pleased at his coronation.

If only he could dispel the rumors surrounding his exile. But he could not.

Because they were true.

But here, among the people who felt like his own—among the people who had suffered most at his uncle's hand—there was happiness here at least. They knew that whatever his sins, he had been working to atone.

Zafar looked out toward the horizon, all flat and barren from this point to Bihar. There was one more place to stop and seek shelter, but it was another five hours' ride, and he didn't relish the idea of more time spent in the saddle today.

He dismounted his horse and patted the animal, dust rising from his black coat. "I think we'll take our chances here," he said, leading him to a makeshift corral, where other horses were hemmed in, and opened the gate.

He closed it, making sure it was secure before walking back toward the main tent.

One of the men was already coming out to greet him.

"Sheikh," he said, inclining his head. "A surprise."

"Is it? You had to know I was heading back to Bihar." A growing suspicion. The desert was vast and it seemed strange to intersect with Jamal's band of thugs at this particular moment.

"I may have heard something about it. But there is more than one road to the capital city."

"So you had no desire for a meeting with me?"

The other man smiled, dark eyes glinting in the golden light. "I didn't say that. We were hoping to run into you. Or, at least, someone of your means."

"My means are still limited. I haven't yet been back to Bihar."

"And yet, you do find ways to acquire what you need."

Zafar looked the man over. "As do you. Will you invite me in?"

"Not yet."

Zafar knew something wasn't right. His truce with Jamal and his men was tentative. It was probably why they wanted to see him. He was in a position to put a stop to what they did out here in the desert, and he knew the places they liked to hit.

They weren't dangerous men; at least, they weren't entirely without conscience. And so they were on the bottom of a long list of concerns, but, as was human nature, they clearly believed themselves more important in his world than they were.

"Then have you gifts to offer me in place of hospitality?" Zafar asked dryly, a reference to common custom out in the desert.

"Hospitality will come," Jamal said. "And while we don't have gifts, we do have some items you might take an interest in."

"The horses in the corral?"

"Most are for sale."

"Camels?"

"Them, as well."

"What use have I for camels? I imagine there is an entire menagerie of them waiting for me in Bihar. Cars, as well." It had been a long time since he'd ridden in a car. Utterly impractical for his lifestyle. They were a near-foreign thought now, as were most other modern conveniences.

The other man smiled, his teeth brilliantly white against his dark beard. "I have something better. An offer we hope might appease you."

"Not a gift, though."

"Items this rare and precious cannot be given away, your highness."

"Perhaps you should allow me to be the judge of that."

Jamal turned and shouted toward the tent and Zafar watched as two men emerged, holding a small, blonde woman between them. She looked up at him, pale eyes wide, red rimmed. She wasn't dirty, neither did she look like she'd been handled too roughly. She wasn't attempting an escape, either, but given their location...there would be no point. She would have nowhere to go.

"You have brought me a woman?"

"A potential bride, perhaps? Or just a plaything."

"When have I ever given the indication that I'm the sort of man who buys women?"

"You seem like the sort of man who would not leave a woman in the middle of the desert."

"And you would?" he asked.

"In no uncertain terms, Your Highness."

"Why should I care about one Western woman? I have a country to consider."

"You will buy her, I think. And for our asking price."

Zafar shrugged and turned away. "Ransom her. I'm sure her loved ones will pay much more than I am willing or able to."

"I would ransom her, but it is not my intention to start a war."

Zafar stopped and turned, his muscles locked tight, his heart pounding hard. "What?"

"A war, Sheikh. It is not in my best interest to start one. I don't want those Shakari bastards all over my desert."

Shakar was the closest neighboring country to Al Sabah and relations between the two nations were at a breaking point, thanks to Zafar's uncle. "What does Shakar have to do with this woman? She's Western, clearly."

"Yes. Clearly. She is also, if we believe her ranting from when we first took her, American heiress Analise Christensen. I imagine you have heard the name. She is betrothed to the Sheikh of Shakar."

Yes, he had heard the name. He was largely cut off from matters of State but he still heard things. He made sure he did. And clearly, Jamal made certain he heard things, as well. "And how is it I play into this? What is it you want with her?" he spat.

"We can start a war here, or end one, the choice is yours. Also, with the wrong words in the right ear, even if you take her, but threaten us? We can put you in a very bad position. How is it you ended up with her? The future bride of a man rumored to be the enemy of Al Sabah? Your hands are bound, Zafar."

In truth, he would never have considered leaving the woman here with them, but what they were suggesting was blackmail, and one problem he didn't need. One problem too many.

So, buy her and drop her off at the nearest airport.

Yes. He could do. He didn't have very much money on him, but he didn't think their aim was to get the highest price off the beauty's head so much as to seek protection. Zafar was, after all, ready to assume the throne, and he knew all of their secrets.

He looked down at the woman who claimed to be an heiress, betrothed to a sheikh. Anger blazed from those eyes, he could see it clearly now. She was not defeated, but she was also smart enough to save her energy. To not waste time fighting here and now.

"You have not harmed her?" he asked, his throat getting tight with disgust at the thought.

"We have not laid a finger on her, beyond binding her to keep her from escaping. Where would her value be, where would our protection be, if she were damaged?"

They were offering him a chance to see her returned as if nothing had happened, he understood. If she were assaulted, it would be clear, and Al Sabah, and by extension the new and much-maligned sheikh, would be blamed.

And war would be imminent.

Either from Shakar or from his own people, were they to learn of what had happened under his "watch."

He made an offer. Every bit of money he had. "I'm not dealing," he said. "That is my only offer."

Jamal looked at him, his expression hard. "Done." He extended his hand, and Zafar didn't for one moment mistake it as an offer for a handshake. He reached into his robes and produced a drawstring coin purse, old-fashioned, not used widely in the culture of the day.

But he'd been disconnected from the culture of the day for fifteen years so that was no surprise.

He poured the coins into his hand. "The woman," he said, extending his arm, fist closed. "The woman first."

One of the men walked her forward, and Zafar took hold of her arm, drawing her tight into his body. She was still, stiff, her eyes straight ahead, not once resting on him.

He then passed the coins to Jamal. "I think I will not be stopping for the night."

"Eager to try her out, Sheikh?"

"Hardly," he said, his lip curling. "As you said, there is no surer way to start a war."

He tightened his hold on her and walked her to the corral. She was quiet, unnaturally so and he wondered if she was in shock. He looked down at her face, expecting to see her eyes looking glassy or confused. Instead, she was looking around, calculating.

"No point, princess," he said in English. "There is nowhere to go out here, but unlike those men, I mean you no harm."

"And I'm supposed to believe you?" she asked.

"For now." He opened the gate and his horse approached. He led him from the enclosure. "Can you get on the horse? Are you hurt?"

"I don't want to get on the horse," she said, her voice monotone.

He let out a long breath and hauled her up into his arms, pulling her, and himself, up onto the horse in one fluid motion, bringing her to rest in front of his body. "Too bad. I paid too much for you to leave you behind."

He tapped his horse and the animal moved to a trot, taking them away from the camp.

"You…you bought me?"

"All things considered I got a very good deal."

"A good…a good deal!"

"I didn't even look at your teeth. For all I know I was taken advantage of." He wasn't in the mood to deal with a hysterical woman. Or a woman in general, no matter her mental state. But he was stuck with one now.

He supposed he should be…sympathetic, or something like that. He no longer knew how.

"You were not," she said, her voice clipped. "Who are you?"

"You do not speak Arabic?"

"Not the particular dialect you were speaking, no. I recognized some but not all."

"The Bedouins out here have their own form of the language. Sometimes larger families have their own variation, though that is less common."

"Thank you for the history lesson. I shall make a note. Who are you?"

"I am Sheikh Zafar Nejem, and I daresay I am your salvation."

"I think I would have been better off if I were left to burn."

Ana clung to the horse as it galloped over the sand, the night air starting to cool, no longer burning her face. This must be what shock felt like. Numb and aware of nothing, except for the heat at her back from the man behind her, and the sound of the horse's hooves on the sand.

He'd stopped talking to her now, the man who claimed to be the Sheikh of Al Sabah, a man whose entire face was obscured by a headdress, save for his obsidian eyes. But before she'd been kidnapped…and it surely had only been a couple of days…Farooq Nejem had been the ruler of the country. A large and looming problem for Shakar, and one that Tariq had been very concerned with.

"Zafar," she said. "Zafar Nejem. I don't know your name. I can't…remember. I thought Farooq…"

"Not anymore," he said, his voice hard, deep, rumbling through him as he spoke.

The horse's gait slowed, and Ana looked around the barren landscape, trying to figure out any reason at all for them to be stopping. There was nothing. Nothing but more sand and more…nothing. It was why she hadn't made an escape attempt before. Going out alone and unprepared in the desert of Al Sabah was as good as signing your own death certificate.

They'd been warned of that so many times by their guide, and after traveling over the desert in the tour group on camelback for a day, she believed him.

So much for a fun, secret jaunt into the desert with her friends before her engagement to Tariq was announced. This was not really fun anymore. And it confirmed what she'd always suspected: that stepping out of line was a recipe for disaster.

She was so fair, too much exposure to the midday sun and she'd go up in a puff of smoke and leave nothing but a little pile of ash behind.

So bolting was out of the question, but the fact that they were stopping made her very, very uneasy. She'd been lucky, so lucky that the men that had kidnapped her had seen value in leaving her untouched. She wasn't totally sure about her new captor.

She took a deep breath and tried to ignore the burn in her lungs, compliments of the arid, late-afternoon air. It was so thin. So dry. Just existing here was an effort. More confirmation on why running was a bad idea.

But she had to be calm. She had to keep control, and if she couldn't have control over the situation, she would have it over herself.

Her captor got down off the horse, quickly, gracefully, and offered his hand. She accepted. Because with the way she was feeling at the moment, she might just slide off the horse and crumble into a heap in the sand. That would be one humiliation too many. She had been purchased today, after all.

"Where are we?" she asked.

"At a stopping point."

"Why? Where? How is it a stopping point?" She looked around for a sign of civilization. A sign of something. Someone.

"It is a stopping point, because I am ready to stop. I have been riding for eight hours."

"Why don't you have a car if you're a sheikh?" she asked, feeling irritated over everything.

"Completely impractical. I live in the middle of the desert. Fuel would become a major issue."

Oh yes. Fuel. Oil. Oil was always the issue. It was something she knew well, having grown up the daughter of the richest oil baron in the United States. Her father had a knack for finding *black gold*. But he was a businessman, and that meant that the search was never done. It was all about getting more. Getting better.

And that was how she'd met Sheikh Tariq. It was how she'd ended up in Shakar, and then, in Al Sabah.

Oil was the grandaddy of this entire mess.

But it would be okay. It would be. She thought of Tariq, his warm dark eyes, his smile. The thought of him always made her stomach flip. Not so much at the moment, but given she was hot, tired, dusty, and currently leaning into the embrace of a stranger, thanks to her klutzy dismount, it seemed understandable.

She straightened and pushed away from him, heart pounding. He was nothing like Tariq. For a start, his eyes were flat black, no laughter. No warmth. But so very compelling…

"Where are we?" she asked, looking away from him, and at their surroundings.

"In the middle of the desert. I would give you coordinates, but I imagine they would mean nothing to you."

"Less than nothing." She squinted, trying to see through the haze of purple, the sun gone completely behind the distant mountains now. "How long until we reach civilization? Until I can contact my father? Or Tariq?"

"Who says I'll allow you to contact them? Perhaps I have purchased you for my harem."

"What happened to you being my salvation?"

"Have you ever lived in a harem?" He lifted a brow. "Perhaps you would like it."

"Do you even have a harem?"

"Sadly," he said, his tone as dry as the sand, "I do not. But I am only just getting started in the position as sheikh, so there is time to amass one."

She nearly choked, fear clutching at her. "I am…stranded in the middle of a foreign desert…."

"It's not foreign."

"Not to you!" she said.

"Continue."

"I am stranded in the desert with a stranger who claims he's a sheikh, a sheikh who bought me, and you are joking about my future! I have no patience for it."

She had no patience left in her entire body. At this moment, she had two options: get angry, or sink to the ground and cry. And crying was never the preferred option. No, the schools she'd attended, the ones she'd been sent to after her mother left, had been exclusive, private and very strict. She'd been taught that strength and composure were everything. She'd been taught never to run when she could walk. Never to shout when a composed, even statement would do. And she'd learned that tears never helped anything in life. They didn't change things. They hadn't brought her mother back home, certainly.

So she was going with anger.

His manner changed, dark brows locking together. His black eyes glittering with dark fire. He tugged at the bottom portion of the scarf, which had kept most of his face hidden until that moment, and revealed his lips, which were currently curled into a snarl.

"And you think I have the patience for this? These men are playing at starting a war between two nations simply to keep their petty ring of thieves intact. They are trying to buy my loyalty with blackmail. Because they know that if your precious Tariq finds out you were taken by citizens of Al Sabah, or God forbid, they find out the Sheikh of Al Sabah possessed you for any length of time against your will, that the tenuous truce we have between the countries will shatter entirely. How do you suppose my patience is?"

She blinked, feeling dizzy. "I...I'm going to start a war?"

"Not if I play it right."

"I imagine putting me in your harem wouldn't defuse things."

"True enough. But then...perhaps I want the war."

"What?"

"I am undecided on the matter."

"How can you be undecided on the matter?"

"Easily," he said. "I have yet to have a look at any of the papers left behind by my uncle. I have had limited contact with the palace since finding out I was to be installed as ruler."

"Why?"

"Could have something to do with the fact that my first, albeit distant, act was to fire every single person who worked for my uncle. Regime changes are rough."

"Is this a…hostile takeover?"

"No. I am the rightful heir. My uncle is dead."

"I'm sorry." Her manners were apparently bred into her strongly enough that they came out even in the middle of a crisis of this magnitude.

"I'm not. My uncle was the worst thing to happen to Al Sabah in its history. He brought nothing but poverty and violence to my country. And stress between us and neighboring countries." His dark gaze swept over her. "You are unfortunate enough to have become a pawn in the paradigm shift. And I have yet to decide how I will move you."

CHAPTER TWO

FOR ONE MOMENT, Zafar almost felt something akin to sympathy for the pale woman standing in front of him. Almost.

He had no time for emotions like that. More than that, he was nearly certain he had lost the ability to feel them in any deep, meaningful way.

He'd spent nearly half of his life away from society, away from family. He'd had no emotional connections at all in the past fifteen years. He'd had purpose. A drive that transcended feeling, that transcended comfort, hunger, pain. A need to keep watch over Al Sabah, to protect the weakest of his people. To see justice served.

Even at the expense of this woman's happiness.

Fortunately for her, while he imagined she would be delayed longer than she would like, he had a feeling their ultimate goals would be much the same. Seeing her back to Tariq would be the simplest way to keep peace, he was certain. But he had to figure out how to finesse it.

And finesse was something he generally lacked.

Brute force was more his strength.

"I don't like the idea of that at all," she said. "I'm not really inclined to hang around and be moved by you. I want to go home." She choked on the last word, a crack showing in her icy facade. Or maybe the shock was wearing off. It was very likely she'd been in shock for the past few days.

He remembered being in that state. A blissful cushion

against the harsh reality of life. Oh yes, he remembered that well. It had driven him out into the desert and the searing heat had hardly mattered at all.

He hadn't felt it.

He was numb. Bloody memories blunted because there was no way he could process them fully. Deep crimson stains washed pink by the bone-white sun.

If she was lucky, she was being insulated in that way. If not…if not he might have a woman dissolving in front of him soon. And he really didn't have the patience for that.

"I'm afraid that's impossible."

"Right. War. Et cetera."

"You were listening. Now, hold that thought while I go and set up a tent. Can you do that? And can you also not wander off?"

"I don't have a death wish," she said. "I'm not about to wander off into the desert at night. Or during the day. Why do you think I haven't escaped?"

"That begs the question how you were taken in the first place." He took the tent, rolled up and strapped to the back of his horse, and walked over the outcrop of rock. He would hide them from view as best as he could.

Jamal and his men were hardly the only thieves, or the only danger, they could face out in the desert.

"I was on a desert tour. Of the Bedouin camps in Shakar. On the border."

"So my people went into Shakar to take you?"

She nodded. "Yes."

"You are damned lucky they knew who you were." He didn't like to think of the fate she might have met otherwise.

"My ring," she said. "It gave me away. It was part of the Shakari crown jewels." She flexed her fingers, bare now. "They kept that. But then, they would be pretty bad thieves if they didn't."

"Fortunate you had it," he said. "Odd they did not produce it as proof."

Pale eyes widened, panic flaring in their depths. "But you must know about me," she said. "You must know that Tariq planned to marry soon. I would imagine even base intelligence would have brought you that bit of information."

"An alliance that pertains to the political, I believe," he said.

"Yes. And he loves me."

"I'm sure he does," Zafar said dryly.

"He does. I'm not fool enough to think that my connections have nothing to do with it, but we've been...we've been engaged for years. Distantly, but we have spent time together."

"And you love him?"

"Yes," she said, tilting her chin up, blue eyes defiant. "I do. With all my heart. I was looking forward to the marriage."

"When was the marriage to take place?"

"A few months yet. I was to be introduced to his people, our courtship to be played out before the media."

"But your courtship has already taken place."

"Yes. But you know...appearances. I mean, that's the whole point of not taking me straight back to Shakar, isn't it? Appearances. You don't want Tariq to know your people, or by extension, you were involved in this. And you don't want to appear weak. You don't want people to know it happened on your watch." She nodded once, as if agreeing with herself. "That's a big part of it, isn't it?"

"I haven't had a single day in the palace yet. I don't want to be at the center of a scandal involving a kidnapped future sheikha of a neighboring country, so yes, you're right."

"I see."

"What is it you see, *habibti*?" he asked, the endearment flowing off his tongue. It had become a habit to call women that. Because it was easier than remembering names. Safer, in many ways. It kept them at a distance and that was how he preferred it.

Life in the desert, on the move, made it difficult to find lovers, but he had them in a few of his routine stops. A couple of widows in particular Bedouin camps, and a woman in the capital city who was very good at supplying him with necessary information.

She squinted, pale eyes assessing him. "That this is a threat to you personally."

"I am not the most well-liked man in Al Sabah. Let's just say that. This is an issue when one means to rule a country."

It was the understatement of the century. If he had been recognized anywhere in the city while his uncle was in command, his life would have been forfeit. His exile had been under the darkest of circumstances, and since then, he'd hardly done anything to improve his standing, particularly with those loyal to his uncle.

His loyalty was to the Bedouins. To ensure they never suffered because of his uncle's rule, and without him, they would have. No medical, no emergency services of any kind. His uncle had put them at the mercy of foreign aid while taxing them with particular brutality.

They had become Zafar's people.

And now...now somehow he had to assume the throne and unite Al Sabah again, redeem himself in the eyes of the people in the cities while not losing the people in the desert.

And without incurring the wrath of the Sheikh of Shakar.

Not a tall order at all.

"It doesn't really make me feel all that good about being out here with you."

"I'm certain it does not. I'm also certain that's not my problem. Now, I have a tent to pitch so that we don't have to sleep in the open."

"You expect me to sleep in a tent with you?"

"I do. The alternative is for one of us to sleep without any sort of protection and I'm not going to do that. I assume you won't, either. You should see all the bugs that come out at night."

Ana shuddered. The idea of sleeping in the vast openness of the desert with no walls around her at all was completely freaky, and she didn't want any part of it. But the thought of sleeping next to this man…this stranger…was hardly any better.

Her one and constant comfort was the fact that he didn't want to start a war.

Maybe she should tell him she was a virgin. And that Tariq knew it. So if he tried anything he shouldn't there would be no getting out of it. War would be upon him.

A war over her hymen. Yuck. But potentially true.

And if it would help protect her, well, she wasn't above using it as an excuse. But she would save it. Because… yuck.

"How long do you intend to keep me with you?" she asked, watching as he began to work at setting up what looked to be a far-too-small tent.

"Until I no longer need to." He was wearing so many layers, robes to keep him protected from the sun, that it was hard to tell just how his body was shaped, and yet, because of the ease of his movements and the grace in them, she got a sense that he was a man in superior physical condition.

Not that she should notice or care.

"That's not very informative."

"Because I have no more information to give. I will

have to evaluate the situation upon arrival at the palace, and until then, we are stuck with each other."

He continued to work, his movements quick and agile, practiced.

"So…you do this a lot?"

"Nearly every night."

"You buy kidnapped women and then carry them off on your horse every night?"

"I was just referring to the tent."

"I know," she said, looking up at the sky, vast and dotted with stars. "Just trying to lighten the mood." Otherwise she really would cry. She didn't have enough energy for anger anymore. Lame jokes were her last line of defense.

And she couldn't fall apart. Not now. Her father would need her to keep it together, to make sure she made it back to him. Back to Tariq. She'd done everything right, had spent so many years doing her best to be helpful. To not be a burden.

Falling down in the home stretch like this was devastating.

"Technically," he said, tying a knot in a rope at the top of the tent. "I didn't buy you. I ransomed you."

"That does sound nicer."

"Think of it that way then. If it helps."

"A small comfort, all things considered, but I'll take it."

"There, it is done. Are you ready to sleep?"

No and yes. She didn't want to get into the tent with him and sleep on the ground. It was demoralizing. More than that, it was scary. The idea of being so close to him made her heart pound, made her feel dizzy. But she was also ready to collapse with exhaustion. No matter that Zafar was a stranger, he wasn't her kidnapper. He wasn't the same as the men who'd been holding her these past few days.

No matter how austere and frightening he was, he had saved her from her kidnappers.

"Oh…thank you," she said, a tear sliding down her cheek. "Thank you so much."

And something in her broke that she hadn't even realize had been there. The dam on her emotions that had been keeping her strong, keeping her from falling apart since she'd been taken from the camp all those days ago. Or maybe the same dam that had been in place for years, holding back tears for ages, and unable to withstand this new onslaught of life's little horrors.

And control was suddenly no longer an option.

A sob shook her body, emotion tightening her throat. And then she broke down completely. Great gasps of breath escaping, tears rolling down her face.

He didn't move to comfort her; he didn't move at all. He simply let her cry, her sobs echoing in the still night. She didn't need his touch. She just needed this. This release after days of trying to be strong. Of trying not to show how scared and alone she felt.

And when she was done she felt weak, embarrassed and then angry again.

"Done?"

She looked up and saw him regarding her with an expression of total impassivity. Her outburst hadn't moved him. Not at all. Not that she really wanted comfort from this big…beast man. But even so. A little reaction would have been nice. Sympathy. Offer of a cold compress or smelling salts or…something.

"Yes," she said, her throat still tight, her voice croaky. "I am done. Thank you."

"Ready to sleep?"

"Yes." The word escaped on a gust of breath. She was completely ready to collapse where she was standing. She didn't know how that had happened. How exhaustion had taken over so completely.

And then she realized she was shaking. Shivering. She couldn't do this. She had to be strong and keep control. She had to hold it together.

"I don't know why," she said through chattering teeth.

He swore, at least she assumed it was a swearword, based on the tone, and took two long strides toward her, gripping her by the arms and drawing her into the warmth of his body. It wasn't a hug. She knew that right away. This was no show of affection; it was just him trying to keep her from rattling apart.

She trembled violently, his strong arms, his chest, a wall of support. It was amazing that he smelled as good as he did. Yes, it was a weird thought, but it was simple, basic and one she could process.

All those layers in the heat and she would have imagined he might smell like body odor. Instead he smelled spicy, like fine dust and cloves. And he did smell of sweat, but it wasn't offensive in any way. He smelled like a man who had been working, a man who had earned every drop of that sweat through honest effort.

That, somehow, made it seem different than other sweat.

Not that she could really claim to be an expert in the quality of sweat, male or otherwise, but for some reason, that was just how it seemed to her.

This current train of thought was probably a sign of a complete mental breakdown. Highly likely, in fact. Yes, very likely, because she was still shaking.

And adding to the signs of a breakdown, was the fact that part of her wanted to curl her fingers around his robe and hold him tightly to her. Cling to him. Beg him not to let her go.

"The nearest mobile medical unit is…not very near,"

he said, his voice rough. "So please don't do anything stupid like dying."

"If I were dead, how much help would a mobile medical unit be anyway?" she asked, resting her head on his chest, something about the sound of his heartbeat making her feel more connected to the world. To living. She was so completely drained; it felt like it was the reminder of his life that kept her connected with hers. "Besides I don't think I'm dying."

"Does anyone ever think they're dying?"

"I'm not hurt."

"How long has it been since you had a drink?"

She thought back. "A while. I'm not even really sure how many days it's been since I was kidnapped."

"I'm going to put you in the tent."

She nodded, and at the same time found her feet being swept off the ground, as her body was pulled up against his, his arms cradling her, surprisingly gentle for a man with his strength.

He carried her to the tent and set her down on a blanket inside. Then he left her, returning a moment later with a skin filled with water.

"Drink."

She obeyed the command. And discovered she was so thirsty she didn't think she could ever be satisfied.

She pulled the skin away from her lips and a drop ran down her chin. She mourned that drop.

"I hope you weren't saving that," she said.

"I have more. And we'll stop midmorning at an oasis between here and the city."

"Why didn't we stop at the oasis tonight?"

"I'm tired. You're tired."

"I'm fine," she said. His tenderness was threatening to undo her, if you could call the way he was speaking to her now *tenderness*.

"You must be realistic about your own limitations out here," he said. "That is the first and most valuable lesson you can learn. The desert can make you feel strong and free, but it also makes you very conscious of the fact that you are mortal."

She lay down on the blanket and curled her knees into her chest, her back to Zafar. She heard the blanket shift, felt it pull beneath her as he lay down, too.

"The wilderness is endless, and it makes you realize that you are small," he said, his voice deep, accented, melting over her like butter. She felt like the ground was sinking beneath her, like she was falling. "But it also makes you realize how powerful you are. Because if you respect it, if you learn your limitations and work with them, rather than against them, you can live here. You will never master the desert…no man or woman can. But if you learn to respect her, she will allow you to live. And living here, surviving, thriving, that is true power."

Her eyes fluttered closed, and the world upended. "I'm cold," she said, a shiver racking her.

A strong arm came around her waist, and she was pulled into heat, warmth that pushed through to her soul. It was a strange comfort. It shouldn't even be a comfort, and yet it was. Being held by him felt good. Human touch, his touch, soothed parts of her she hadn't known had been burned raw by her nights in the desert.

His fingertip drifted briefly along the line of her bare arm. A soothing gesture. One that stopped the chill. One that made her feel like a small flame had been ignited beneath her skin.

Her last thought before losing consciousness was that she'd never slept with a man's arm around her like this. And the vague sense that she should be saving this for the man she was marrying.

Except that didn't make sense. This was just sleeping.

And she badly needed sleep.

So she moved more tightly into his body and gave in to the need she'd been fighting against ever since she'd been kidnapped.

And slept.

CHAPTER THREE

"YOU NEED TO wake up now."

Zafar looked down at the sleeping woman, curled up on the floor of the tent like an infant.

The sun was starting to rise over the mountains, and in a moment, the air became heated. Enough that if you breathed too deeply it would scorch your lungs. And he didn't relish riding through the heat of the day. He wanted to get to the oasis, wait it out, then continue on to the city.

He didn't want to spend another night out here with this fragile, shivering creature. He needed to be able to sleep, and he could not sleep beside anyone.

Plus, she was far too delicate. Far too pale. Her skin an impractical shade of pink, her hair so blond it was nearly white, her eyes the same blue as the bleached sky.

She would burn out here in the desert.

She stirred and blinked, looking up at him. "I…" She pushed into a sitting position. "Oh, no. It wasn't a dream."

"No. Sorry. And are you referring to me or the kidnapping? Because I should think I am preferable to a band of thieves."

"The kidnapping in general. This entire experience. Ugh. My whole body hurts. This ground is hard."

"I'm sorry. Perhaps you should talk to the Creator about softening it for you."

"Oh, I see, you think I'm silly. And wimpy and whatever." She pushed a hand through her hair, and he noticed her fingers got hung up in it. He wondered how long it had been since she'd been able to brush her hair. He imagined she hadn't been given the opportunity to bathe or take care of any necessities really.

And he wondered if they had gone with her when she'd had to take care of certain biological needs. If they had stood guard. If they had made her feel humiliated. It heated the blood in his veins. Made him feel hungry for revenge. But he couldn't follow the feeling. Emotion didn't reign in his life. Not now. Emotion lied. Purpose did not.

And it was purpose he had to follow now, no matter the cost.

"I think very little about you, actually. At least, about you as a person. Right now, you are an obstacle. And one that is making me late." He'd been contacted by one of his men. There was an ambassador Rycroft, a crony of his uncle's who was anxious for a meeting. Zafar was about as anxious for it as he was for a snakebite, but he supposed that was his life now.

Meetings. Politics.

"Excuse me?" She stood now, her legs shaky, awkward like a newborn fawn's. "I'm making you late? I didn't ask to be kidnapped. I didn't ask for you to buy me."

"Ransomed. I ransomed you."

"Whatever, I didn't ask you to."

"Be that as it may, here we are. Now get out, I need to take the tent down."

She shot him a deadly glare and walked out of the tent, her chin held high, her expression haughty. She looked like a little sheikha. A pale little sheikha who would likely wither out here in the heat.

"I have jerky in my saddlebags," he said.

"Mmm. Yay for dry salted meat in the heat," she said,

clearly not satisfied to look at him with venom in her eyes. She had to spit it, too.

For all her attitude, she went digging through the bags, and as soon as she found the jerky she was eating it with enthusiasm. "More water?" she asked.

"In the skin."

He continued deconstructing the tent while she drank more water and ate more food. For a woman who was so tiny, she didn't eat delicately.

"Did they feed you?"

"Some," she said, between gulps of water. "Not enough, and I was skeptical of it. So I only ate when I couldn't stop myself."

"Poisoning you, or drugging you would have served no purpose."

"Probably not, but I was feeling paranoid."

"Fair enough."

"But you won't hurt me, will you?" she asked, almost more a statement than a question, pale eyes trained on him.

"You have my word on that."

He would not harm a woman. No matter her sins. Even he had his limits. Though he might see a woman thrown in jail for the rest of her life, but that was an entirely different woman. A different matter.

"I didn't think you would. That's why I slept."

"How many days?"

She shook her head. "I don't know. I was afraid to close my eyes because who knew what might happen. But it only makes things worse. It makes you...think things that aren't real, makes it all blur together and then...it's all scary enough without the added paranoia. I thought I was going crazy."

"Understand this," he said. "I'm not holding you for fun. I am not holding you to harm you in any way. I need to get a better read on the situation. I know this isn't ideal for you, but war during your courtship would be even worse."

"War would be worse in general," she said. "But maybe I can talk to Tariq…."

"Maybe. And maybe it would matter. But there are times when a man must show his strength to protect what is his. There is a time for peace, but when your fiancée has been kidnapped, I am not sure that's the time." He paused. "And then there's how my people will react. It is the sort of thing they expect of me. I will be implicated, make no mistake. Jamal will ensure it. And you know, for many leaders, it wouldn't matter. They could crush the rumors, destroy the rebellion. Me? There is no loyalty to me here. It is not the love of my people chaining me to the throne, but law. If they could see me relieved of the position, many of them would, do not doubt it."

"But you need to rule?"

"I was born to rule. It is my rightful place, stolen from me. I was exiled, banished, and I will not live the rest of my days that way. The throne of Al Sabah is mine now, and I mean to take it."

"Even if you have to hold me to do it?"

"You will be kept in a palace, surrounded by luxury that rivals anything your darling fiancé could produce for you, so I doubt you'll feel to put upon. Consider it a spa retreat."

She looked around them. "Shall I start with sand treatment? Good for the pores, or what?"

"All right, the retreat portion of the vacation starts tonight. For now, consider yourself still on the desert tour. Only this is one-on-one. And you're now with a man who knows the desert better than most people know the layout of the city they grew up in."

"I don't know whether to ask questions about the rocks or the dirt. The beauty is so diverse out here."

"The landscape in Shakar is similar. Perhaps you should

rethink your upcoming marriage if the best you can muster for your surroundings is a bit of bored disdain."

"I'm sorry to have insulted your precious desert. I'm in a bad mood."

"Your mood is the least of my worries, *habibti*. Now—" he put the bundle of tent back onto the horse, took the skin from her hand and refixed it to the saddlebags "—get on the horse, or I shall have to assist you again."

She looked up at the horse and then back at him, genuine distress in her blue eyes. "I can't. I wish I could. But my legs feel like strained spaghetti. It's not happening."

"It's no matter to me. I held you all night. Putting my arms around you again isn't exactly a hardship." Her cheeks turned a brilliant shade of red and it had nothing to do with the sun. He didn't know why he'd felt compelled to tease her that way. He didn't know why he'd felt compelled to tease her at all. He couldn't remember the last time he'd ever felt the least desire to engage in humor or lightness of any kind.

But beneath that was something darker. Something he had to ignore. A pull that he couldn't acknowledge.

"Do what you must," she said, defeated.

He locked his fingers together and lowered his hands, creating a step for her. "Come on," he said.

She looked down and squinted. "Oh, fine." She put one hand on the horse's back and one on his shoulder, placing her foot into his hands and pushing up. He lifted her as she swung her leg over the horse and took her position.

"Front or back, *habibti*, it's no matter to me."

She looked genuinely troubled by the question. And then as though she was calculating which method would bring her into the least contact with his body.

"I...front."

He found the position a bit more taxing, but the alternative was to have her clinging to his back, thighs shaped

around his, her breasts pressed to his back. The thought
sent a strange tightening through his whole body. His
throat down to his stomach, the muscles in his arms, his
groin.

No. He had no time for such distraction. She would remain untouched. Protected. He swore it then and there. A
vow made before the desert that he would not break.

Fiancée or not, a man who would take advantage of a
woman in her position was the basest of creatures.

*And are you not more animal than man after your time
out here?*

No. He knew what was right. And he would see it done.

Right was why he was returning now. Back to a palace that was, in his mind, little more than a gilded tomb.
A place that held ghosts. Secrets. Pain so deep he did not
like to remember it.

But this had nothing to do with want. Nothing in his
life had to do with want; it was simply duty. If doing right
meant riding into hell, he would. While the palace wasn't
hell, it was close. But there could be no hesitation. No
turning back.

And no distractions.

He got on behind her, gripping the reins tightly. "Hold
on." He wrapped an arm around her waist. "If we're going
to make it back to the palace today, we have to go fast."

Fast was an understatement. They made a brief stop at the
oasis, a pocket in a mountain that seemed to rise from the
earth, shielding greenery and water from the sun, providing shade and relief from the immeasurable heat.

Sadly, they didn't linger for very long and they were
back in the sun, the horse's hoofbeats a repetitive, pounding rhythm that was starting to drive her crazy.

By the time the vague impression of the city, hazy in the
distance, came into view, Ana was afraid she was going

to fall off the horse. Fatigue had set in, bone deep. She felt coated in a fine layer of dust, her fingers dry and stiff with it.

She needed a bath. And a soft bed. She could worry about everything else later, as long as she had those two things as soon as humanly possible.

This was not her life. Her life was cosseted in terms of physical comforts. A plush mansion, a private all-girls school with antique, spotless furniture and women's college dorms that rivaled any five-star hotel.

Hot baths and soft beds had been taken for granted all of her life. Never again. Never, ever again. She was wretched. She felt more rodent than human at the moment. Like some ground-dwelling creature rooted out of her hole, left to dry out beneath the heat.

As they drew closer she could see skyscrapers. Gray glass and steel, just like any city in the United States. But beyond that was the wall. Tall, made of yellow brick, a testament to the city that once had been—a thousand years ago.

"Welcome to Bihar," he said, his tone grim.

"Are you just going to ride in?"

He tightened his hold on her. "Why the hell not?"

He was a funny contradiction. A man who was able to spout poetry about the desert, soliloquies of great elegance. And yet, when he had to engage in conversation, the elegance was gone. On his own, he was all raw power and certainty, but when he had to interact…well, that was a weakness for sure.

"Seems to me a horse might be out of place."

"In the inner city, yes, but not here on the outskirts. Not on the road to the palace. At least not the road I intend to take."

They forged on, through the walls that kept Bihar separate from the desert. They went past homes, pressed together, stacked four floors high, made from sun-bleached brick. Then on past an open-air market with rows of baskets filled to the brim with flour, nuts and dried fruit. People were milling about everywhere, making way for Zafar without sparing a lingering glance.

She turned and looked up at him. Only his eyes were visible. Dark and fathomless. His face was covered by his headdress. No one would recognize him. It struck her then, how funny it was.

The sheikh riding through on his black war horse, a captive in the saddle with him. And no one would ever know.

They continued on, moving up a narrow cobbled street, past the dense crowds, and through more neighborhoods, the houses starting to spread out then getting sparser. The cobbles turned to dirt, a path that followed the wall of the city, in an olive grove that seemed the stretch on for miles. Then she saw it, a glimmer on the hilltop, stretching across the entire ridge: the palace. Imposing. Massive. Beautiful.

White stone walls and a sapphire roof made it a beacon that she was sure could be seen from most points in the city. Bihar might have thoroughly modern buildings that nearly touched the sky, but the palace seemed to be a part of it. Something ethereal or supernatural. Unreal.

Zafar urged the horse into a canter and the palace rapidly drew closer. When they arrived at the gate, Zafar dismounted, tugging at the fabric that covered his face, revealing strong, handsome features. Unmistakable. No wonder he traveled the way that he did. There was no way he would go unrecognized if he didn't keep his face covered. No way in the world.

He reached into the folds of his robes and pulled out…a cell phone. Ana felt like she'd just been given whiplash. Everything about Zafar seemed part of another era. The man had ridden a freaking black stallion through the city streets, and now he was making a call on a cell phone.

It was incongruous. Her brain rejected it wholly, but it couldn't argue with what she was seeing. Her poor brain. It had tried rejecting this entire experience, but unfortunately, the past week was reality. *This* was reality.

"I'm here. Open the gates."

And the gates did open.

She was still on the horse, clinging to the saddle as Zafar led them into an opulent courtyard. Intricate stone mosaic spiraled in from the walls that partitioned the palace off from the rest of the world, a fountain in the middle, evidence of wealth. As were the green lawns and plants that went beyond the mosaic. Water for the purpose of creating beauty rather than simply survival was an example of extreme luxury in the desert. That much she knew from Tariq.

As if the entire palace wasn't example enough.

She looked at Zafar. His posture was rod straight, black eyes filled with a ferocity that frightened her. There was a rage in him. Spilling from him. And then, suddenly, the walls were back up, and his eyes were blank again.

They were met at the front by men who looked no more civilized than Zafar, a band of huge, marauder-type men. Desert pirates. That's what they made her think of. All of them. Her escort included. One of the men, the largest, even had a curved sword at his waist. Honestly, she was shocked no one had an eye patch.

Fear reverberated through her, an echo along her veins, a shadow of what she'd felt when she was taken from the camp and her friends, but powerful enough that it clung to every part of her. Wouldn't let her go.

She was in his domain. Truly, she had been from the moment she'd been hauled across the border from Shakar to Al Sabah, but here, with evidence of his power all around, it was impossible to deny. Impossible to ignore.

His power, his strength was frightening. And magnetic.

It drew her to him in a way she couldn't fathom. Made her heart beat a little faster. Fear again, that was all. It could be nothing else.

"Sheikh," one of them said, inclining his head. He didn't even spare her a glance.

"Do you need help dismounting?" Zafar asked.

"I think I've got it, thanks." She climbed down off of the horse, stumbling a little bit. So much for preserving her pride. She looked over at Zafar's sketchy crew and smiled.

"We shall need a room prepared for my guest. I assume you saw to the hiring of new servants?"

She nearly laughed. Guest? Was that what she was?

The largest man nodded. "Everything has been taken care of as requested. And Ambassador Rycroft says he will not be put off any longer. He insists you call him as soon as you are in residence."

"Which, I suppose is now," Zafar said, his voice hard, emotionless. "Take the horse."

"Yes, Sheikh."

If any of his men were perturbed by the change in status they didn't show it. But then, she imagined that Zafar had always been the one in charge. That he had always been sheikh to those who followed him.

Questioning him wasn't something anyone would do lightly. He exuded power, strength. Danger. Everything that should have repelled her. But it didn't. It scared her, no mistake, but it also fascinated her. And that scared her on a whole new level.

"Your things?" the other man asked.

"I have none. Neither has she. Remedy that. I want the woman to have a wardrobe of new clothing before the end of the day. Understood?"

The man arched one brow. "Yes, Sheikh."

Oh, good grief. They were going to think she was the starter to his harem. Or at least they would think she was his mistress. But there was no way to correct it now. This was an unprecedented point in Al Sabah's history. Zafar was taking over the throne, and the entire palace clearly had new staff. Zafar would be an completely different sort of leader to the one they'd had before, that much was true.

And it would be such a relief, not just to the people here, but to Tariq's people. She knew that things had been strained between Shakar and Al Sabah, that Tariq had feared war. He'd called her late one night and expressed those fears. She'd valued that. Valued that he cared enough to tell her what was on his mind, his heart.

It was part of why she'd fallen in love with him. Part of why she'd said yes to his engagement offer. Yes, her father had instigated it. And yes, he was a driving force behind it, but she wouldn't have said yes if she wasn't genuinely fond of Tariq.

Fond of him.

That sounded weak sauce. She was more than fond of him. *Love* was the word. No, theirs wasn't a red-hot relationship. But so much of that was to be expected. Tariq was old-fashioned and he'd courted her like an old-fashioned guy. It was respectful.

Plus, he was so handsome. Smooth, dark skin, coal eyes fringed with thick lashes, strong black brows…

She looked back at Zafar and the memory of Tariq and his good looks were knocked completely from her head.

Faced with Zafar, the sharp angles of his face, black beard covering most of his brown skin, obsidian eyes that were more like a dark flame and his lips…she really was quite fascinated by his lips…well, it was hard to think of anything else.

He wasn't smooth. His skin was marked by the sun, by wind. There was nothing refined about him. He was like a man carved straight from the rock.

She wasn't sure *handsome* was the right word for it. It seemed insipid.

"Shall we go in? It is my palace, though I have not been back here in fifteen years. I was born here. Raised here."

Which meant he'd come into the world like everyone else, rather than being carved from stone, so there went that theory.

"Must be...nice to be back?" She watched his face, saw no expression change. If she hadn't caught that moment of intense, dark emotion at the gates, she would think he felt nothing at all. "Strange? Sad?"

"It is necessary that I'm back. That is all."

"I'm sure you feel something about being back."

"I feel nothing in general, Ms. Christensen," he said, addressing her by her name, any part of it, for the first time. "I should hardly start now. I have a country to rule."

"But you're...human," she said, though it sounded more like a question than a statement. "So, I'm sure you feel something."

"Purpose. Every day since my exile there has been one thing that has enticed me to open my eyes each morning, and that has been the belief that my people need me. That it is my duty and my right to lead this country, to care for these people, as they should be led and cared for. Not in the manner my uncle did it. Purpose is what has driven me for nearly half of my life, and purpose is what drives me now. Emotion is unnecessary and weak. Emotion lies. Purpose doesn't."

In so many ways, he echoed a colder, harsher version of what she'd always told herself. That doing right was what mattered. That when people stopped doing right and started serving themselves, things fell apart. Utterly and completely.

She'd seen it in her own family. She'd never wished to bring the kind of destruction her mother had, so she'd set out to be better. To be above selfishness. To do the right thing, the thing that benefitted others before it benefitted her.

To take care, instead of destroy. To be a blessing instead of a burden.

But hearing it from his lips, it seemed...wrong. At least she acknowledged emotion; she just knew there were more important things in life than giddy happiness. Giddy happiness was fleeting, and selfish. She felt it was just her mission to make sure she didn't put her feelings above the happiness of others. There was nothing wrong with that.

"You know what else doesn't lie? My muscles. I'm so stiff I can hardly move."

"A bath then. I will have one drawn for you."

"Th-thank you."

"You sound surprised."

"You're giving me nicer things than my last kidnapper."

"Savior, Analise. I think the word you're looking for is *savior.*"

She looked into his midnight eyes and felt something tug, deep and hard inside of her. Something terrifying. Something that touched the edge of the forbidden. "No, I really don't think that's the word I'm looking for."

"Come," he said, walking toward the doors of the palace.

Zafar didn't wait for the double doors to open for him. He pushed against them with both palms, flinging them wide, the sound of the heavy wood hitting the stone walls echoing in the antechamber.

He simply stood for a moment, and waited. For what he did not know. Ghosts, perhaps? There were none. None that were visible, though he could almost feel them. The pain, the anguish this place had witnessed seemed to echo from the walls and he felt it deep down in his bones. If he listened hard enough, he was certain he could still hear his mother screaming. His father crying.

The air was heavy. With memory, with a cold, stale scent that lingered. Probably had more to do with the stone walls than with the past.

He'd spent years living in a tent. Hell, it had been over a year since he'd actually been in a building that wasn't made from canvas. The walls were too heavy. Too thick. Making the air even harder to breathe.

He wanted to turn and run, but Ana was behind him. He felt like an animal being herded into a cage, but he wouldn't show that weakness. He couldn't.

So he took another step inside. Into darkness, into the place that had seen so much death and devastation. It was a step back into his past. One he wasn't prepared to take, but one that had to be taken.

"Zafar?"

He felt a small hand on his arm and he jerked away, looking down at Ana. She didn't shrink back, but he could see something in her wilt. Unsurprising. She must think him more beast than man, but then, there was truth in that.

"We shall have your bath run for you," he said, his voice tight, cold, even to his own ears.

He had no choice but to move forward. To embrace this because it was his destiny. And his penance. He gritted his teeth and walked on.

Yes, this was his penance. He was prepared to pay it now.

CHAPTER FOUR

It was Zafar's great misfortune that Ambassador Rycroft was near and insisted on a meeting immediately. With Zafar in his robes, filthy from traveling. He had no idea how he must appear to the immaculately dressed, clean-shaven man who was sitting in his office now. He had very little idea of how he appeared at all. He didn't make a habit of looking at mirrors.

The man was, per the paperwork he'd seen of his uncle's, important to the running of the country. At least he had been. Zafar suspected that many of the "trade agreements" ran more toward black market deals. But he lacked proof at the moment.

They'd been making tentative conversation for the past few minutes, and Zafar felt very much like a bull tiptoeing through a china shop.

"This regime change has been very upsetting to those of us at the embassy."

"I am sorry for that," Zafar said. "My uncle's death has inconvenienced you. I'm not certain why he couldn't postpone it."

Rycroft simply looked at him, offense evident in his expression. "Yes, well, we are eager to know what you intend to do with the trade agreements."

"Your trade agreements are the least of my concern." Zafar began to pace the room, another move that clearly

unnerved his visitor. He supposed he was meant to sit.
But he couldn't be bothered. He hated this. Hated having
to talk, be diplomatic. He didn't see the point of it. Real
men said what they meant; politicians never did. There
was no honor in it, and yet, it was how things worked. "I
have stepped into a den of corruption and I mean to sort it
out. Your trade agreements can wait. Do you understand?"

Rycroft stood, his face turning red. "Sheikh Zafar, I
don't think you understand. These trade agreements are
essential to the ease of your ascension to rule. Your uncle
and I had an understanding, and if you do not carry it out,
things might go badly for you."

Anger surged through Zafar, driving his actions before
he had conscious thought. All of his energy, seemingly
magnified by the feeling of confinement he was experiencing in this place, broke free. He grabbed the other man
by the shoulders and pushed him back against the wall,
holding him firmly. "Do you mean to threaten me?"

Politicians might use diplomacy. *He* would not.

"No," the ambassador said, his eyes wide. "I would
not…I would never."

"See that you do not, for I have erased men from this
earth for far less, and don't forget it."

He released his hold on Rycroft and stepped back, crossing his arms over his chest.

"I will go to the press with this," the other man said,
straightening his jacket. "I will tell them that they have
put an animal on the throne of Al Sabah."

"Good. Tell them," he said, anger driving him now, past
the point of reason. Past whatever diplomacy he might have
possessed. "Perhaps I will have fewer pale men in suits to
deal with if you do."

As she sank down into the recessed tub, made from daz-
zling precious stone, and the warm water enveloped her
sore, dusty body, Ana had to rethink the savior thing.

These bubbles, the oils, the bath salts…it all felt like they, and by extension, Zafar, might very well have saved her life.

She would have liked to stay forever and just indulge, but she knew she couldn't. She didn't just relax and indulge. It wasn't in her. She had to be useful. There was always something to do. Except, right now there wasn't really anything.

Such a strange feeling. She didn't like being aimless. She didn't like feeling out of control. She needed purpose. She needed a project. Something to keep her mind and hands busy. Something to make her feel like she was contributing.

Being kidnapped wasn't engaging much, except the constant war between her fight-or-flight response. It was terrifying, all of it, and yet she didn't know the right thing to do.

She'd been working so hard for so many years. The desert trip was her last and first hurrah. Post-graduation, pre-public engagement. She'd wanted a touch of adventure, but nothing like this.

She pushed up from the bench and stepped out of the bath. There was a plush towel and a robe waiting for her. And she would be lying if she wasn't enjoying it all a little bit. Premature princess points being cashed in now.

Glamorous in theory. And yet, it would be a lot like an extension of the life she already had. Living for appearances. That was all normal to her. She felt like she was always "on." Even with her friends. The elite women's college they'd gone to had encouraged them to be strong, studious and polished. To conform to a particular image. And even when they had personal time, even when they laughed and let the formality drop a bit, that core, that bit of guardedness, still ran through the group just beneath the surface.

She'd always been afraid to show too much of herself.

Those tears in the desert had been some of the most honest emotion she'd let escape in years.

She wrapped herself in the robe and wandered back into the bedroom. "Oh, you are kidding me," she said, looking down at the long, ornate table along the nearest wall. There was a bowl filled with fruit on it. Figs, dates, grapes.

"All I need is a hottie cabana boy with palm fronds standing by to fan me," she muttered, taking a grape from the cluster and popping it into her mouth.

"I see you're finding everything to your liking."

She whipped around and saw Zafar striding through her bedroom doors. He looked…different. He had lost the headdress and heavy traveling robes, in favor of a white linen shirt and a pair of pale dress pants. His long hair was wet, clean and tied back. He had kept the beard, but it was trimmed short.

Somehow, he looked even more dangerous now, with this cloak of civility. Because at least before, he was advertising that he was a hazard. He had danger signs and flares all over him before. This great hairy beast with a full beard and flowing robes. With windburned skin and a thin coating of dirt. And the sweat smell. Not forgetting that.

But now she felt she could see more of him, and it displayed, to her detriment, just how handsome he truly was. Square jawed with a strong chin, and yet again, the lips.

Why was she so fascinated by his lips? Men's lips weren't that big a deal.

"Everything is lovely, all things considered."

"What things considered?"

"Does the phrase 'gilded cage' mean anything to you?"

He shook his head. "No. You are comfortable?"

She let out an exasperated sigh. "Yes. More or less. But I would feel more comfortable if I could let my father or Tariq know I was safe."

"I'm afraid that isn't possible." He started pacing over

the high-gloss obsidian floor. A caged tiger. That was what he reminded her of. The thought sent a little shiver of fear chasing down her spine. "I was hardly exaggerating when I said this incident could push us into war. Neither of us want that, am I right?"

"They must be frantic!" she said. "Honestly, can you… can you channel what it might be like to feel, just for a second? They probably think I'm dead. Or sold. Which I was. But…but they probably think I'm in grave peril. I could talk to Tariq. At least give me a chance."

He shook his head. "Things are far too tenuous for me at the moment. Let me tell you a story."

"I hope it has a happy ending."

"It hasn't ended yet. You may well decide how it does end, so listen carefully. There once was a boy, who grew up in an opulent palace, fully expecting one day to be king. Until the castle was invaded by an enemy army, an enemy army who clearly knew how to get direct access to the sheikh and sheikha. They were killed. Violently. Horribly. Only the boy was spared. He would be king; at sixteen, he could very well have ruled. But there was a problem. An inquiry, suggested by the boy's uncle, which indicated he was to blame for the death of his parents. And he was found guilty."

There was no emotion in Zafar's voice. There was nothing. It was more frightening than if there had been rage, malice, regret. Blank nothingness when speaking of an event like that, total detachment when she knew he was talking about himself…it was wrong. It was frightening, how divorced from it he was.

It made her wonder if she was as safe with the dynamic ruler as she'd initially imagined.

"Exiled to the desert for fifteen years under a cloud. The uncle ruled, the people fell into despair, the country to near ruin. And who was to blame? The boy, of course. A boy who somehow survived those years alone and is now a man. A man who must now assume the throne. You see what is stacked against me?"

"I understand," she said, shifting, the stone floor cold beneath her bare feet. She suddenly became very conscious that she was wearing a robe with nothing beneath it. "But let me tell you a story about a girl and…and…no, let me just say, I disappeared some six or seven days ago from a desert tour I wasn't supposed to be on. My friends are probably frantic. My fiancé is probably…concerned." Devastated might be a stretch. Tariq was a very even-tempered man. "My father…" She nearly choked then. "My father will be destroyed. I am all that he has…you have to understand."

Even as she said it, she hoped it was true. Strange that she was wishing for her father to be distressed, but…but she was always so afraid that his life was easier without her. It had been for her mother. No child to take care of. No one to break her lovely things.

"And *you* have to understand this. Inquiries are being made about you. Discreet ones, but it is happening. Kazeem received a phone call with a very clear threat. That the future Sheikha of Shakar was missing, and should she be found on Al Sabahan soil my reign will hold a record for brevity."

"Oh," she said, feeling dazed.

"I am all this country has," he said, his voice hard, echoing in the room. "If there is to be a future for my people, I must remain on the throne. There is no room for negotiation."

"So, what if I try to leave?"

"You will be detained. But I seriously doubt you will try to leave."

"Why?"

"Because you're a sensible woman. A woman who wouldn't want blood on her hands." He looked at her, his eyes taking on a strange, distant quality. "Take it from a man who knows, *habibti*. Whether you spill it with your own hand or not, blood won't come clean."

She believed him. Believed it was true. Believed that he knew what it meant to have blood on his hands. Not for one second would she doubt it.

Could she do it? Could she risk it?

The entire thing made her uneasy, but she hardly had a choice. She could try and run, she could try to find her way back on her own, try to call Tariq, who would storm the castle and…and…oh dear.

She looked at Zafar. Did she really trust this man? That he would release her? That he would do what he said?

She did. Because she'd been alone with him in the desert overnight, and he'd slept with his arm curled around her waist to keep her from shivering. Because when she'd needed touch, no matter whether he understood it or felt it or not, he had provided it. He hadn't taken advantage of her, had never once touched her inappropriately or in a way that would harm her.

In short, he treated her exactly like a man in his position should treat her, provided he was telling the truth.

"I require an exit strategy, Sheikh," she said.

"What do you mean?"

"When will you release me? Regardless of what is happening. There has to be a set end date. A sell-by."

"I'm not certain I can give you that."

"I require it," she said. "No more than thirty days."

"It shall be done." His agreement, the heavy tone in his voice, did nothing to ease her concerns. Thirty days. Thirty days in this palace, a captive of this man. But with that thought the oddest burst of lightness came through.

More of this solitude. These moments of utter indulgence that weren't for anyone but her.

"I am not holding you prisoner," he said.

"Oh really. So, I'm free to go?" The lightness faded, because the fact remained, she was, essentially, Zafar's prisoner.

"No," he said, crossing broad arms over his chest. "Under no circumstances."

"Then how am I not a prisoner?"

"Have I tossed you in the dungeon? Is that bread and water on your table there? No. I gave you a bed. Fruit."

"So, I'm a well-fed prisoner with a down pillow."

"If you like. The difference between this and *prisoner* is in many ways the same as the difference between…purchased and ransomed. Whatever makes you feel better."

"A nap, I think."

"Excellent. A nap. And then you will join me for dinner."

"What? Why?"

"Because, *habibti*, I can hardly have you staying here at the palace looking like a prisoner, now can I?"

"Why not? Goes with the fearsome desert-man thing you're rocking."

"A compliment?"

"Not really. Why not?" She reiterated her earlier question.

"Because, it simply won't do. A little investigation on your part and you could find out a lot of very terrible things about me. Most of them very true. And the last thing I need is any suspicion that I am keeping an American woman here against her will."

"Harem rumors shall abound."

He arched a dark brow. "Indeed."

"So what do you want them to think? Because, all

things considered, later, I will be recognized, so I can't
be here as…well…a girlfriend."

He laughed, a strange, rusty sound. Clearly not an expression of emotion he'd used in a while. "I do not have
girlfriends, Analise."

"Ana," she said. "No one calls me Analise."

"Ana," he amended, "I have lovers, if you can even call
them that. Bed partners. Mistresses. Women who satisfy
me physically as I satisfy them." His words, dark, rough
and uncivilized, like the man himself, should have appalled
her. Just as the man himself should have appalled her. But
he didn't. And they didn't. Instead they brought to mind
lush scenes of him, more golden-brown skin on display
than was decent, his arms wrapped around a woman. A
rather pale woman with blond hair. She blinked rapidly
and tried to dispel the image.

Zafar continued. "I do not have girlfriends. That brings
to mind flowers and chocolates. Trips to the cinema. I
haven't been to a cinema in…ever. And I have not even
seen a movie in at least fifteen years."

A movie theater was a much-less-challenging image.
"That's…that doesn't seem possible."

Zafar was a magnified, twisted version of her in some
ways. Never taking the time to do normal things because
he was so burdened with purpose.

But really, never going to a movie theater? Not seeing a
movie in fifteen years? He wouldn't get half of her jokes.
But then, she wondered if Tariq watched movies. They'd
never talked about that. They'd talked about weighty things
like duty and honor and oil.

But not movies. And she actually liked movies.

"I was a bit consumed with daily survival and making sure the Bedouin tribes weren't completely marginal-
ized, but yes, perhaps I should have made more time for
taking in films."

"Oh…like you've never had any downtime. You *do* have mistresses," she said, feeling her face get hot. Because those same images were back. And the woman in the vision was a lot clearer this time. And *oh my*. There was no way she should be entertaining that thought. She was too practical to have vivid sexual fantasies.

"Yes, indeed, but I find sex much more interesting than watching television."

Her mouth dropped open, and she really wished she hadn't let it, but she hadn't known it was going to drop open until it did. She closed it slowly. "Well, all right. There's something I'd like to do in bed right about now. Have a nap. So…goodbye."

He inclined his head. "Until dinner. A dress will be sent."

"Good, I was worried. I would hate to look less than my best for you."

He laughed again, that same uneasy, clearly not oft-used sound. "That would be a tragic occurrence."

"Yeah. I know, right? Now out."

"You give an awful lot of orders for a…"

She crossed her arms. "Yes, that's a question…what am I?"

He regarded her closely, his dark eyes searching. "Well, you do have a lot of opinions on how I ought to do things. And you are certainly trained in the art of being royal… when you aren't letting your tongue run away with you."

"You can see my royalty training coming through?" she asked, only half joking.

"Yes. It is in the way you stand, the way you sit. Your composure, even in a difficult situation. And considering I have just had a meeting with an ambassador that has gone very poorly…"

"Have you?"

"I might have threatened to erase him from the earth."

"Oh, dear," she said.

"And he may have threatened to go to the press."

"Indeed."

"Yes, indeed. So it will come as no surprise to anyone that I am in need of a bit of help. Especially since I am due to make a showing in public very soon."

She eyed him critically. "Oh."

"And I gather you're starting to see the problem. And I think you can help me."

She swallowed. She didn't like the sound of this. A slow smile spread across his face, and that made her even more nervous.

"Ms. Christensen, I believe you are here to teach me to be civilized."

Ana had to wonder what the hell he was talking about while she put on her dress, and still while she wandered down the hall.

The palace was on bare-bones staff and eerily quiet. Not like the times she'd stayed at Tariq's palace in Shakar.

There, the palace was constant motion and sound—people moving everywhere, administrative staff, cleaning staff, serving staff, tours often being given in portions of the palace. There was always activity.

Things seemed dead here. Frozen in time. It reminded her of a fairy-tale castle, where all the inhabitants were sleeping. Or maybe turned into furniture and small appliances by a wicked enchantress.

Or maybe just that a new leader had been installed who had no subjects loyal to him beyond the broad expanse of the desert.

That was more likely.

She walked through the empty corridors and she had a sudden thought. A phone. What if she could find a phone?

She hurried through the hall, looking in opened rooms

and in nooks. And there, she found one. An old-fashioned, gilded, rotary phone sitting on a pedestal. Just waiting. She walked over to the table and stood in front of it, her palms sweaty.

She could call Tariq. She knew his personal number by heart. Not because she'd used it so much, but because she'd felt a woman ought to know her fiancé's phone number.

She stood there and imagined what she would say. And what his response would be. What if he mobilized the helicopters? And ground troops. And they swarmed the castle. And everything Zafar was working toward would be utterly destroyed because she'd had to take action.

And worse—a small voice inside of her had to say it— what if he did nothing? What if he waited? What if he too just sat back and did the thing that was most politically expedient?

That thought made her ill. And as much as she'd like to forget she'd ever had it, it was impossible to do. It was insidious, a small worm of doubt that had been burrowing its way into her for days and days now.

What if he didn't care? Sure, threats had been made. Contact established with Zafar on the matter, but this was all so political in nature. What if, when she was now more inconvenient than convenient, Tariq wouldn't really want her at all?

She backed away from the phone, her heart pounding hard. Later. She knew where the phone was now, and if she needed to make a call, she could do it later .

She wandered down a corridor, trying to ignore the sick feeling in her stomach, trying to stop her hands from shaking. She wandered until she heard movement. The kitchen. She could hear dishes and water. Voices. Finally things felt a little less haunted. And from there, she found the dining room. A serving girl was there, pouring a glass of something for Zafar, who was sitting on the floor on pillows in a semi-reclined position, a low table in front of him.

His shoes were off, no regard given to posture or manners. He had, in fact, started eating without her. He was using his hands, as was the custom, and yet somehow it just looked…shocking when he did it. Wholly sensual. He was eating too fast, like a man who had been without food for too long.

She thought of the jerky in his saddlebags. He had at least been without good food for too long.

He scooped a bit of rice in his hand and ate it, then licked his fingers. She felt a sharp, hard tug low in her stomach, one she couldn't pretend she hadn't felt. No matter how much she wished she could.

Dear heaven, if a fine was charged for looking completely disreputable, he would be forced to sell the castle to pay his debt. He just looked…dangerous and wicked, and for some reason none of it was unappealing. None of it at all. His poor table manners, the fact he was eating without her, should have offended and blotted out all the…the dark magnetism she was feeling.

But it wasn't. Why oh why wasn't it?

"Ana," he said, smiling, for the benefit of the serving girl she imagined, because she'd never seen him smile before. He still looked both wicked and dangerous. "Please come in and sit down."

She obliged, positioning herself across from him on a long, cream-colored cushion.

"Dalia, I will need privacy with Ms. Smith for the meal. We have terms to discuss. A business arrangement."

Dalia inclined her head and set the pitcher on the table. "I'll leave this for you, Sheikh. I wouldn't want you to be thirsty." She gave him a look that could only be described as adoring.

"Thank you." He took a long gulp of his drink and waved her away. She went quickly, her head bent down.

"Firstly," Ana said, when they were alone in the cavernous room, "Smith? Ms. Smith?"

"Ana Smith, much less damning than calling you by Analise Christensen, don't you think? No doubt your name will be appearing in the media, if it hasn't already. Though, I have heard nothing so I would venture to say your sheikh is conducting a covert search for you. Even more dangerous in many ways, because I have no way of knowing where he's looking."

"You mean he hasn't mobilized the military and the press and the…Coast Guard?"

"Not that I have seen, no."

"Oh." She knew there was probably a reason, and it wasn't that he didn't care, just that it was strategy. Like the strategy Zafar was employing. Greater good and all. She was just one girl. She wasn't worth uprooting national security over or anything. And stuff.

"You will be kept here at the palace. Public events would be too risky. Really, any showing in public would be. You will be known as Ana or Ms. Smith, as previously stated, and you are here to teach me…manners."

She looked at him, half-civilized and seemingly unconcerned with it. "Manners?"

"That is oversimplifying, perhaps, but that is one thing you will help me with. I am a man too long out of society, and now I must come in as a king people can stand with. They will not stand with a barbarian."

"But your serving girl…Dalia, she seemed to be a fan."

"Dalia is from one of the desert tribes. Her family owes me a debt of gratitude, and she came to serve in the palace until I could secure loyal staff."

"She likes you," she said.

"She's young. She'll get over it."

"You aren't interested?"

"Sweet young virgins are fine for some, but not for me. I don't have any interest in seducing women and breaking hearts. It's not how I am."

Sweet young virgins.

Well, indeed.

"Good. I feel better knowing she's safe." *And knowing I'm safe.*

Like she'd ever really had anything to be worried about. He wasn't a going to force himself on her, that much was obvious.

Yeah, but the seducing was worrisome....

No. Nope. No. She wasn't worried about him seducing her. That implied that she was seducible, and she was not. She so was not. But she was a sweet, kind of young…relatively. Virgin—yeah, she was that for sure—so he wasn't going to be interested. But even if he was it wouldn't matter.

Good grief, Ana, you have lost your fool mind.

He was holding her against her will, kind of, and making her play the part of Miss Manners. She had no reason to feel fluttery about him, and yet she did. Because it was easy to remember what it had felt like to fall asleep with his arm around her. How the weight of it had been warm, his body solid and comforting behind her.

How she hadn't disliked it at all, but had actually wanted to stay there in his embrace. And when she'd woken and he was standing above her, rather than lying with her, she'd been confused. She'd missed his presence.

Because she'd been half-asleep and confused, but still. It was inexcusable.

Feelings like that were a betrayal. A betrayal of the man who had…probably mobilized special forces…quietly…to find her.

In the cold light of day, she feared Zafar. His power over

her, the fact that she didn't have the control. She didn't miss having him sleep next to her. So there.

"What is it you expect me to do? Aside from telling you not to threaten dignitaries with bodily harm" she said. "Teach you which fork you eat your salad with?"

"Maybe," he said, and for the first time she developed a hint of something genuine beneath his hard tone. "Maybe you could teach me how to have meaningful diplomatic interaction. Or at least teach me how to avoid scaring people. Something I failed at today, although, I think he very likely deserved it."

"Wait…are you…serious? You mean you really want me to give you royal lessons?"

"You've passed yours so proficiently. And it would be a way to while away the time. I am officially being crowned in less than a month, and look at me," he said, sweeping a hand over his reclining figure. A fine figure it was, too. And she did look. For a little longer than she probably should have. "I am not the man that these people would want to have lead them."

"Why not? You're…strong and you are able to ransom damsels in distress when the situation calls for it, so… leadership qualities in my opinion."

"And yet, I lack charm, you must admit."

"Yeah, okay, you lack charm a little bit."

"And that cannot be."

"Just…be friendlier."

"I don't know how," he said, the words scraping his throat on the way out. "I spent…countless days in the desert alone. Speaking to no one. Sometimes I traveled with men, but then I had to be a leader, and out there…out there manners don't get things done. Diplomacy is not gutting someone when they make a mistake. I have spent the majority of the past fifteen years alone. And while my horse makes for decent company he does not talk back, which means my skills are limited."

"What is your horse's name? You never said."

Zafar's dark brows locked together. "He doesn't have one."

"How can he not have one?"

"He is the only horse. And besides that, it isn't as though he's likely to get mixed up with other horses, or that it would be unclear as to who his rider is. I travel mostly alone, remember?"

"It's just…I name my pets."

"My horse," he bit out, "is not a pet. Do you name your cars?"

"No. But I mean…people do. Some men even name their…" She trailed off, her cheeks lighting on fire. Why had she said that? What had possessed her? She didn't say things like that in front of men, or in front of trustees for charities she worked with. She knew when to keep quiet. Yeah, she got giggly with her friends, specifically the girls she'd gone on the desert tour with. They would talk about their boyfriends and their various and sundry names for their manparts, in a kind of superior way that always made Ana feel gauche. But she would laugh and blush, and generally play the part of group virgin, since that's what she was.

But she didn't just bust out the innuendo at random.

"I do not," he said, no hint of humor in his face.

"I figured as much. Unnamed horses aside—" in that moment she decided she would name the poor thing "—you really do want my help?"

"I more than want it, I need it. I need to be seen as a man and not an animal. I need to be…a king in the eyes of my people, and if I go on like I did today, it will not happen. All things considered, you might find it in you to ransom me?" he asked.

She breathed the words before she had a chance to think them through. It was a job. A project. A purpose. And she always said yes to a project. "Of course."

CHAPTER FIVE

ZAFAR WASN'T CERTAIN what had possessed him to be so honest. Except, why not? She would not be staying here; in fact, she would never speak of her being here at all. He would forbid it, and she would doubtless see the reasoning. It was all to protect his people, and her future people, after all.

Ana Christensen did not need to see him as an infallible leader, or as a fearsome warrior. Ana Christensen only needed to see him as a man, and see how she might help that man assume the throne with more ease. And preferably without being deposed by the neighboring country.

His gut kicked in at the thought of her seeing him as a man. He gritted his teeth. He did not mean it that way. He tightened the tape around his fists and repositioned himself in front of the bag he'd been pounding on only a moment earlier.

Being in the palace like this, being indoors, made him feel restless. Like he had too much energy and nowhere to channel it. That meant a lot of hours spent swimming laps in the pool, lifting weights or hitting a punching bag.

Anything that kept him from feeling like he had during his meeting with Rycroft. Like violence was a living beast just beneath the surface of his skin, waiting to tear its way out.

Anything to keep him from feeling like he was suffocating behind the walls. Or buried alive in a tomb. A tomb that held the spirits of those lives taken here.

He had spent the years since his exile in the desert. In the open. And he had not been back to the palace since he'd been driven out.

Those two made for a poor combination and created a sensation of claustrophobia he didn't like.

Fortunately, he had little time to worry about it. In a few short weeks he would become the face of the nation, and that meant he had to figure out just what face he would show the world.

Not his real one, naturally. No one wanted to engage in diplomatic discussion with a hollow, emotionless stone. A man who had left weakness and feeling behind him so many years ago he couldn't remember what it had felt like to have them inhabit his body.

Neither did he want to.

He just needed an appropriate mask. And Ana would help him fashion it.

"Kazeem told me that you were... Oh!"

He turned and saw Ana standing in the door to his workout room, her jaw slack, her blue eyes wide. Her eyes, he realized, were most definitely not on his face, but on his sweat-slicked torso. And he would be lying if he denied getting any pleasure from it.

But he would not touch her. Ever. It was impossible. A little lust was hardly worth the security of an entire nation.

And you've followed your cock down that path before, haven't you?

He banished that insidious voice. The one that would see him curled up on the floor crying like a child rather than taking action. He had no room for regret. He could only move forward.

He could not erase his past mistakes. They would always stain. The ghosts would always haunt these halls.

The best he could do was attempt to make the future better. For his people. People who had suffered for far too long at the hands of his uncle. Indirectly, his own hands.

Or perhaps not so indirectly.

"That I was what?" he asked.

"Here. But he didn't mention you were busy."

"You thought I was in here reclining, perhaps?"

"No. But…maybe fencing or something. Not…boxing…with yourself."

"This is how I keep fit. I hang the bag inside my tent when I travel."

"That tiny thing?"

"The bag or the tent?"

"The tent. The bag isn't tiny."

"The tent I had the night I acquired you is not the one I normally travel with." He turned and wiped the sweat from his forehead, then started unwinding the tape that was around his fists.

"Well, to what did I owe the pleasure of the mini-tent experience?" Her perfect, pale cheeks darkened, a pink stain spreading over them. And that blush, the acknowledgment that there was something in that night that might make her blush, threw his mind right back there.

To what it had felt like to have her in his arms. Soft. Petite.

Sweet.

So not for him. Not under any circumstances. Not even if she were just a woman he met on a city street. Even then, she wouldn't be for him. All he could ever do with a flower was bruise the petals.

A flower would wither and die out in the desert. And he wasn't just from the desert; the desert was in him. And his touch would only burn her.

A good thing, then, that she was not just a woman on the street. A fortunate thing that she was off-limits for a million reasons, because if the only reason were her well-being... Well, he simply wasn't that good a man.

But with the fate of a nation resting on whether or not he kept it in his pants? He could keep them zipped.

"I saw no point in carrying the extra weight. I traded with a man I met on the road. A smaller tent, food. And it's fortunate for you I was able to trade or I might not have had the money to buy you."

"Ransom."

"If you like."

She frowned. "I thought we agreed it was a lot less demeaning."

"It makes no difference to me."

"One makes you the hero...the other makes you a bastard."

"You say that like you think I might have a preference between the two."

"I...don't you?"

He lifted a shoulder. "Not particularly. I don't have to be good, Ana, I just have to win. In the end, Al Sabah has to win. The rest...the rest doesn't matter."

"And you'll do anything to win?"

"Anything," he said.

Ana believed him. There was no doubt. The way he said it, so dark and sure and certain, sent a shiver through her body, down into her bones. And yet it didn't repel her. It didn't make her want to run. Perversely, it almost made her want to get closer.

The shock of fear that ran through her body was electric. It sent ripples of warning through her body, showers of sparks that sent crackling heat along her veins.

She felt like a child standing before a fire. Fascinated and awed by the warmth, knowing there was something that might make it all dangerous, but not having any real concept of the damage it could do.

Even having that moment of clarity, she didn't draw back. She did take a step toward him, though. Zafar, in all his shirtless glory.

She'd thought him arresting in his robes. Handsome in the linen tunic, moisture clinging to him from his shower. Without a shirt, his long hair escaping the bonds of the leather strap that normally kept it bound, his body glistening with sweat, a bead of it rolling down his chest, down his abs, sliding along the contours of his hardened muscles...well, just now he defied reality.

He was unlike any man she'd ever seen. All hard, harsh, assaulting masculinity. There was nothing soft about him, nothing to put her at ease or make her feel safe. He bound her breath up in her body, kept it from escaping. Made a rush of feeling whisper over her skin that she couldn't identify or deny.

She knew attraction. She was attracted to Tariq. He was handsome; he gave her butterflies in her stomach. He was a great kisser, though, admittedly at his own insistence their kisses had been brief.

He was everything she could have asked for.

And yet suddenly it seemed like her eyes had just opened and she'd realized there was something more. Something more to men. To the way looking at a man could make her feel. And she wasn't sure what the feeling was exactly. Attraction or something else, because it wasn't attraction like she would have named it last week. Or even two days ago.

But it was something. Something deep and visceral and completely disturbing. And it was holding hands, tightly, perversely, with fear. Perhaps that was why it seemed so intense? Adrenaline combined with attraction, the kind any woman would feel toward a man with such...testosterone-laden qualities. It was like a biological imperative. Strong man, producer of much sperm and good offspring. It was basic high school science, was what it was.

She shook off that line of thinking and tried to focus on the conversation.

"The end justifies the means?" she asked.

"Yes. But the thing you have to understand is that I have a country to run and I must look acceptable while restoring order."

"Please tell me you aren't a crazy dictator, because I don't want to help install a man who's going to turn this country into a military state."

"I won't be any kind of ruler if I can't get my people to accept me. A head is of no use without the body behind it. In two weeks time there is a reception planned, a party celebrating the new sheikh, a show of power for the rest of the world. All brought about by my adviser."

"One of the big dusty, sand-pirate-looking guys?"

She thought he nearly smiled. "Yes."

"And what do they know about that sort of thing?"

"A lot. Before he lost his family Rahm was the leader of the largest tribe in Al Sabah. But after...he couldn't continue on. Needless to say, he is a man who understands power and how to obtain and maintain it."

"He lost his family?"

Zafar swallowed hard. "Yes. Do you know what my uncle did in his time as ruler?"

She looked away from him. "My Al Sabahan history is rusty."

"He raised taxes, most especially on the Bedouins. And trust me when I say it was collected. Even if it had to be taken from their herds. From their tents. Skins and other wares. He took it. He cut services. Mobile medical units, schools. People lost their lives because of the neglect, the poverty."

"Rahm..."

"He suffered, as well. And unlike me…Farooq did have a harem. And when possible…he stole their daughters and brought them here. Unlike me…my uncle did like sweet innocent virgins." His voice was rough, his manner filled with disgust. The rage radiating from him spoke volumes about what manner of man he really was. That at his core, no matter what he said, no matter what he claimed about the end justifying the means, he was a good man. A man who despised hurting the weak. A man who sought justice, no matter the cost.

"Did you save Dalia from that fate?" she asked, her voice choked. She was starting to understand. Zafar had a collection of the broken in his country, surrounding him tightly, acting as his helpers, his staff. And in doing that, he was holding them together.

"Yes," he said. "Thankfully. She is one I was able to help before he managed to take her too far."

"How?"

His expression turned cold. "The men who captured her did not walk away. Let us leave it at that."

She nodded slowly. "Okay."

"I told you, *habibti*," he said, "I have blood on my hands. I will fight for my people. To the death. To the end. But in order to do that…they have to trust me, and while I am confident in my ability to frighten enemies, to seek out justice and destruction for those who would seek to hurt us…I am not confident in my ability as a speaker. Or a diplomat. The guest at a nice dinner."

"If we play things right, maybe I can help you, and you can repair relations between Al Sabah and Shakar. We could have dinner together after Tariq and I marry."

"There. Vision for the future."

"Yes." Except it would be awkward. And terrible, really. Could she ever tell Tariq about this? Would they have to start their marriage out with a lie?

She just didn't like any of it.

There was always the phone. She could always call.

She looked up at Zafar, at his eyes, and she knew she couldn't yet. Not just yet.

She couldn't just leave him. She couldn't just leave him and his people the way things were. He had ransomed her. He could have left her. He could have used her. But he wasn't that man. He was the man who saved girls from being kidnapped. The man who had blood on his hands from saving those who couldn't save themselves.

And that was when she knew she would do it. She could do this. And she wouldn't feel so useless. So at loose ends. If she was going to stay here, then she would accomplish something.

And civilizing Zafar would be no small accomplishment.

"So, do you have a…plan for how you want this to go?"

"I had thought that you might…give me tips?"

"Well, you can't go to a royal dinner wearing only pants."

He laughed, and she felt it all through her body. "Probably true."

"How long has it been since you had a Western-style dinner? At a tall table? And really with a salad fork?"

"A long time."

"Of course, when you entertain here, then it will be up to those visiting you to observe your customs."

"You truly are royally trained." He leaned back against the wall, his shoulders flexing, abs shifting. The man didn't have an ounce of spare flesh on his body.

"It didn't start with Tariq. My mother left when I was really small. And it was just me and my father. My father is a very important businessman. Oil tycoon, actually."

"Ah, and your connection to Tariq and Shakar begins to make sense."

Her face heated. She didn't like the implication. That it was all oil. She knew it was mostly oil, but there were feelings. There were. The fact that she was important on more than one level strengthened things, but it was more than that.

"Anyway, as I got older I used to help him coordinate dinners. Parties. I was hostess a lot of the time. It was hard for him to be a single dad, and he was as involved as he could be with me, and it was…it was nice to be able to help him that way. So you could say that hostessing is one of my talents. As is diplomacy. I went to the kinds of schools people think of as 'finishing schools,' but it's so much more than that. It's a very real education along with intense training for dealing with social situations. I'm versed in handling all kinds of scenarios. Any time you mix a lot of people, some of them competing for jobs or oil rights or money of any kind, things can be tense."

"I assume you have tricks for defusing those situations."

"The art of conversation. Or, more to the point, the art of bland inoffensive conversation. In your case, you'll be dealing with politicians of all different world views, and that will be…"

"A nest of vipers."

"Something like that."

She was starting to feel a little energized now. Starting to feel a renewed sense of purpose. This was giving her something to focus on. A plan, a goal. She liked feeling like she was being useful. Like she was accomplishing things.

This suddenly felt bigger than she was. Fixing a country, changing the shape of things for people. Making a positive impact. Zafar was going to make things better. Zafar wouldn't let the Bedouin people's daughters be taken from their homes to serve some sadistic ruler's fantasies.

And she could be a part of that new beginning. But not if she called Tariq. Not if she let fear push her into running.

No, she wasn't going to run.

She could do this. She might not ever claim credit, but she could start her role as Sheikha of Shakar by doing something valuable.

She trusted Zafar. The realization was a slightly shocking one, but it was the truth. She might not like it an overabundant amount, but she trusted the core of his character. And that was what counted.

"Breakfast in the courtyard tomorrow," she said, because she was sure someone could arrange it. "We'll talk silverware."

"I haven't had very much in the way of real conversation in the past fifteen years, and you want to talk silverware?"

"I told you, the art to getting along with people is bland conversation. How much more bland could it get?"

It turned out that nothing with Zafar could feel bland. Especially not since she was sitting with him in a garden that rivaled anything she'd ever seen. Lush green plants and shocking orange blossoms punctuated by dots of pink covered every inch of the wall that protected the palace from the rest of the world.

The combination of the thick stone wall, the fountains and the shade made the little alcove comfortable, even at midmorning. She had a feeling that by afternoon it would be nearly as unbearable as most other places in Al Sabah, but for now, it was downright pleasant.

"I ordered you an American breakfast," she said, putting her napkin in her lap and folding her hands over it. "Bacon and eggs."

"Do you think that many politicians will be eating bacon and eggs?"

"Fact of life, Zafar, everyone likes bacon. Turkey bacon, by the way, in case you have any dietary restrictions."

"I am not so devout," he said.

It didn't really surprise her. Zafar seemed to depend only on himself. Though, there were people here in the palace. People who had loyalty to him. People he seemed to care for in a strange way.

"It has made the paper," he said.

"What?"

"That I threatened Ambassador Rycroft. He said he saw me in person, and that I am clearly a wild man. That when you look in my eyes you see something barely more advanced than a beast. Of course the press was giddy with his description as they would so love to crucify me."

"I'm sorry."

"This means that my presentation is more important. That this project we are conducting is all the more important."

She nodded slowly. "I understand."

"I have spent too many years alone," he said, his voice rough.

"The men that are here," she said, picking up her fork, "how often did you travel with them?"

"Once a month we might patrol together, but many of them had home bases, while I felt the need to keep moving. To keep an eye on things."

"You said you didn't make a lot of conversation?"

"We didn't. We traveled together, did our best to right the wrongs my uncle was visiting on the desert people. Some of them were men, and the children of men cast out of the palace when my uncle took control. Others, Bedouins who suffered at the hand of the new regime. We didn't get involved in deep talks."

"Why is that?"

"Someone had to keep watch. And I was always happy

to let my men rest. Though we did spend time telling stories."

"Stories?"

"Morality tales, of one sort or another. A tradition in our culture. A truth wrapped in a tale."

She'd heard him do that. Weave reality into a story. Blanketing it so it was more comfortable to hear.

"So you were an army unto yourselves? Out there in the desert?"

"Nothing half so romantic. We were burdened with the need to protect because our people were under siege. It was all born of necessity. Of loss."

"If your people had any idea of what you'd done for them…they would embrace you as their ruler. I know they would."

"Perhaps. Or perhaps what happened in a desert out beyond the borders of the city will make no difference. Perhaps they will only remember what happened here."

"What happened here?"

Zafar gritted his teeth. He hated to speak of it. Of the day his parents died. The day he and his people lost everything.

He hated even more to speak of his role in it, but he didn't have a lot of other options. She had to understand.

She had to know why he was so despised.

"Things had been tense. There were rumors that the royal family might be the target of an attack. And routines were changed, security measures were taken. The sheikh and his wife were preparing to go into hiding until the threat had passed. But there was a breach in the security. And the time that the royal family was to leave the palace was given to their enemies. They never had a chance at escaping. What was meant to be a wholly secure operation, moving them until the threat was over, became the end."

"And how did you get the blame for this, Zafar? I don't understand."

"It was my fault," he said. "And I have spent every year, every day since then, fighting to atone for the destruction I brought on my own people. This is why the papers, why the people, are so anticipating my downfall. My exile was very much deserved. I was responsible for the death of my mother and father, the sheikh and sheikha. And the people of Al Sabah have long memories. They won't forget who they would rather have on the throne. And they won't forget why their most beloved rulers aren't with us any longer. And it's because of me."

CHAPTER SIX

ZAFAR COULD SEE the dawning horror in her eyes, and he was almost glad of it. Because they needed something to break this strange band of tension that was stretching between them, pulling them closer to each other, even as they tried to resist.

Even as he tried to resist. With everything he had in him.

But there was something so very fascinating about her. Something so tempting. But he knew what would happen if he touched her. War aside.

It would be like pouring water on the cracked desert earth. He would take everything she had, soak it in for himself, and at the end of the day, the ground on his soul would still be dry.

"You couldn't have done anything on purpose, Zafar."

"No," he said, his voice harsher than he intended. "I didn't do it on purpose, and in many ways that makes it much worse. I was a fool, manipulated into giving the truth because of trust. Because of love."

She blinked slowly a few times, a look of confusion on her face, as if the idea of him being in love, the whole concept, seemed foreign and unbelievable to her.

Reassuring. That he didn't in any way resemble the soft, stupid boy he'd been. Years in the desert had hardened him, and he was damned grateful for it.

"But if it was an accident..." she started.

"No. There is no excusing it." He didn't want to tell the story. Didn't want to speak of Fatin or the hold she'd had on him. About how, during a time of extreme turmoil for his country and his family, he'd only been able to think of one woman. Of how he'd wanted her.

He'd been able to spare no thought for anything else. For anyone else.

Thank God he'd cut that out of himself, that weak, sorry emotion. He'd sliced out his heart and left it to burn beneath the desert sun. Until he was impervious, until he was too hard and too weathered by the heat and wind to care about a damn thing.

Nothing but the cause. Nothing but the purpose.

And she had to realize that. She had to know. What manner of boy he'd been, what manner of man he'd become.

Why he'd had to bury that boy, deep, and destroy everything tender inside of him so that he would emerge better. So that he would never again cause such unthinking destruction.

"As with most tales, this one starts with a woman."

Ana's breath caught. She was instantly consumed with curiosity. About the woman. The one who had created emotion in Zafar. Emotion he seemed to be lacking now.

She noticed he liked to tell her things this way. As though they were nothing more than tales, and he was nothing more than the storyteller. Not a player in the piece.

"She was a servant in the palace. She had been for a long time. Beautiful, and smart. Ambitious. She didn't want to be a serving girl all of her life. She wanted more. And she was willing to do whatever needed to be done to get it. Including seducing the young prince of the royal family she served."

He looked detached, cold. Once again, this wasn't an

interaction, nor a heartfelt confession, it was a performance piece. A bit of the oral tradition the Al Sabahan people were famous for.

And yet the fact that it was personal, the fact that, though he was making the woman the star of the story, he was at the center of it, and he refused to tell it in that way, made it chilling. As cold as his eyes.

"She was his first woman. And that made him incredibly vulnerable to her. So when she asked what the new schedule was, when the sheikh and sheikha would be moved for their safety…he told her. Everything. Because in that moment, with his body sated from making love, and his heart full of hope for the future, their future, he would have given her anything she asked. And what she asked was such a small thing. Just little questions. With answers that had the power to shift the landscape of an entire country."

It was hard to latch on to the words. Hard to make sense of them. He was giving facts, honestly, but wrapped in a story, though she knew it was true. But he was holding back his emotion. Keeping it from his voice. Keeping it from her.

"Zafar…how did you…how did you survive that?"

"I wasn't the target. It was easy to get rid of me in a different way."

"I didn't mean physically."

"It was simple enough. I identified the problem, and I cut it out. Metaphorically. Were this a real tale, I would have cut my wicked heart out quite literally and left it to dry in the desert and gone on without it in my chest deceiving me. As it is, I put away feeling, emotion, and I focused on purpose. On reclaiming Al Sabah, not for me, but for my people."

"And the boy who gave it all for love?" she asked, looking at the hardened man in front of her and wondering, for just a moment, if it was even possible that the Zafar of the story and the Zafar standing in front of her had ever been one and the same.

"I left him out in the desert," Zafar said.

He'd been destroyed and remade out there. She could see that.

"Don't romanticize it," he said, his tone hard.

"What do you mean?"

"Don't lie to yourself. Don't try to make it seem like a misguided romantic gesture. It was nothing more than a sixteen-year-old boy using his balls as his brain. There is nothing romantic in that. A man in love is weak after an orgasm and she knew it. She exploited it. But there is no excusing it. She would have had no power had I been stronger. And though it's far too late to make it better, it could never happen again. Not to me. There is no allegiance I hold stronger than the allegiance I have to the people of Al Sabah. And there is nothing I would ever do to compromise it." His dark eyes glittered dangerously. "Nothing."

And she knew he meant that she would be caught up in that lack of compromise, too. That no matter what she wanted, no matter how long she was held at the palace, if it would compromise his vision for what constituted safety and success for his people, he would use her to that end.

It made her shiver inside. In that deep, endless place that Zafar's presence had created. Or perhaps, he hadn't created it; he'd just helped her discover its existence. Either way, it was disturbing, and taking up more of her than she wanted it to.

It was also far too strong for her liking.

If she wasn't careful, it might get bigger, take up more room inside. Obliterate her control. And she couldn't have that.

She had a mission. And it had nothing to do with heat and shaking and tightening stomachs.

She was going to help civilize the Sheikh of Al Sabah, and hopefully secure the future of two nations.

It really was nice to have a project. To be necessary. She knew what it was like to keep atoning.

She felt like she was still sweeping up the broken glass from something she'd destroyed years ago. And she would keep on going until she got every last shard.

CHAPTER SEVEN

ZAFAR HAD NEVER seen so much paperwork in his life. Laws, regulations, pages of tax code, various things to look at, read, sign and start over. Every time he put a dent in a stack of papers, the pile was refreshed with more.

The air was stale. Damned stale. He wasn't used to being indoors like this. Enclosed in stone, feet thick. It was like being buried above ground. Doomed to sign his name over and over for all eternity.

In short, he was in hell.

He stood and inhaled deeply. A rush of that stale, paper-laden air hit him hard, and his stomach pitched. He wasn't used to this. He craved heat and space. He closed his eyes, but rather than the vision of the desert he expected, he saw a pale blonde with full pink lips.

He opened his eyes and scooped up his pen, and the stack of papers he was currently working on, and walked out the door of his office, storming down the corridor. Perhaps he wouldn't use an office. Perhaps he would do all of his work outside.

As if you need to make yourself appear more unconventional. Or unhinged.

He continued down the corridor and found himself heading, not toward the courtyard, or toward the front entrance, but toward Ana's room.

Flames roared through his blood, and he couldn't credit

it. He'd gone for very long stretches at a time without female companionship. In truth, his sex life had been largely dormant. He had lovers he typically managed to see once or twice a year. But there had also been times when he'd gone more than a year without making a visit.

He was past the one-year mark now since the last time he'd had sex, if he wasn't mistaken. Which could explain why that pale little temptress had burrowed her way into his mind like she had.

Just a dry spell. Dryer than the damned desert.

Emotion he'd eliminated the need for. But not sex. Still, it was rare to crave it like this.

He pushed open the doors to her chamber, like they were the flaps on a tent, without knocking. He wasn't in the habit of observing those sorts of conventions.

"Talk to me," he said, walking across the room and sitting in one of the cream upholstered chairs, setting his paperwork on his knee.

Ana was standing there, frozen, pale eyes owlish, her curves hinted at by a thin gray T-shirt and low-riding shorts that revealed the full length of her ivory legs. He wondered who had thought to provide her with such clearly Western attire. But then, there was no reason for her not to dress in the way she found most comfortable. She was in hiding from the public, after all.

"What are you doing in here?" she asked.

"I cannot abide that office. It's far too small. Talk to me while I finish this."

"What do you want to talk about?"

"I don't know. Salad forks. I don't give a damn. Let's have a conversation. I will be expected to do that in my position, I imagine?"

"Why don't we talk about why you knock on a woman's bedroom door before you enter?"

"Boring. I don't want to talk about that."

"Well, I do, I only just put my top on. I was changing."

He looked up and their gazes clashed, heat arcing between them. His blood rushed south, racing to his member, hardening him, making him ready. In case. Just in case the heat wasn't one-sided.

It didn't matter. It couldn't happen.

Somehow, it only made her seem more tempting. Only made his blood run hotter.

"But I didn't see anything I shouldn't have, so it's moot. Now talk to me."

"It's nice weather we're having. Oh, wait, except it's not, because the weather is never nice here. It's hotter than the depths of hell, and it's so dry when I went to scratch an itch on my arm I bled. *I bled*, Zafar."

"Do you require lotion? I can have some sent."

"Yes. I do require lotion," she said, sniffing. "And some nail polish. And some makeup. I received a whole new wardrobe, but not that. A flatiron wouldn't go amiss, either. My hair is rebelling against the dry."

He lifted one shoulder. "If you wish."

"I'm not usually this precious. I promise. But I'm bored. I don't want to walk around outside because it's oppressive and I don't know Arabic well enough to read the books. I suppose internet access is out of the question?"

"You suppose correctly." He looked down at the papers on his lap. "If you're so bored, use this as a chance to begin your project. Teach me civilized conversation. Tell me about yourself. I told you about me."

She sighed and shook her head, shimmering golden hair falling over her shoulders. She truly was beautiful. He could see why the Sheikh of Shakar had been so eager to acquire her, and potential oil transactions were not the only reason. Clearly.

Tariq probably thought himself to be the luckiest man

on earth. A marriage that would strengthen his country and wealth…and a wife who possessed such poise and beauty.

Truly, Al Sabah would suffer by comparison. He would never be able to find her match.

"Me? Boring. I'm from West Texas, though for most of my life I've only spent school holidays there. My father is an oil tycoon. He has a knack for finding black gold. He's mainly made his finds on private land and made both him and the landowners very wealthy—"

"I didn't ask about your father. I asked about you."

She blinked a couple of times, as though she'd been hit over the head. "Oh. I guess…people are usually very interested in what he does."

"And you spend a lot of time organizing his events and so on."

She nodded. "Yes."

"Well, let's assume for a moment that I don't give a rat's ass about oil or money. Because I don't. And let's also assume that I feel the same about power and status."

"Okay," she said, trying to suppress a smile now, the corners of her lips tugging upward slightly. She was amused and a little shocked. And he found that he liked it. Liked that he'd made her feel something almost positive.

"Now, *habibti*, tell me about you."

Because he found he wanted to know. Suddenly he was hungry for information, for every detail about her. About this woman who was so contained under pressure, who appeared soft and vulnerable, but who possessed a core that was a pillar of stone, holding her up unfailingly no matter how the sands shifted beneath her.

"Um…I went to a girl's school in Connecticut. It was very strict, but I enjoyed it. All of our focus was on education, not on boys. I came home in the summer and around holidays—"

"To help with your father's events, I would imagine."

She bristled a bit at that. "Yes."

"And where was your mother?"

She looked up, out the window. "She left. When I was thirteen."

"Where did she go?"

"I don't know. I mean…she was in Manhattan for a while. And then she was in Spain. But I don't really know where she is now. And I don't really care."

"You are angry at her."

She bit her lip, as though she was trying to hold back more words. Words she didn't think she should speak, for some reason or another. "Yeah. Of course I am. She just left."

"And without her…he had you."

"Yes. When did you get insightful?"

"I have had too much time alone with my thoughts in the past decade or so. Too much thinking isn't always good. But it does produce some insight, whether you want it or not."

"I see. And did you have any great epiphanies about yourself?" She crossed her arms beneath her breasts, and his eyes were drawn down to them. Just perfect, enough to fill his palm. He could imagine it easily, her plump, soft flesh in his hands, her nipples hard against his skin.

"Just the one," he said, his voice rough.

"And it was?"

"That I was weak." His current train of thought mocked the implication that his weakness was in the past. "And that it could not be allowed to continue."

"Is that really it?"

"That I would be better dead than as I was," he said. "Because then I could do no more damage at least. But if I lived, I could perhaps fix what I had broken. So I lived."

"I can't say I ever thought I would be better off dead, but I know what it feels like to need to fix the broken things."

"Ah, *habibti*, I know you do. But at least you weren't behind the destruction."

She blinked and shook her head. "Does it matter in the end, Zafar, who caused it? Or how big of a thing it was? Broken is broken. Someone gets the blame. Someone has to try and hold life together after."

"So, that is what you are," he said. "The glue."

"I guess so. I hope so."

"And now?"

"I'll help you hold this together, too. Whatever you need."

"Why are you so willing to help now? You sound almost happy to be a part of my civilization."

"I am. It's my…project now, and I can tell you this with total honesty—if I say I'm going to do something, I'm going to do it, and I'll do it right."

"Being right is important to you."

"The most important."

Ana was a little embarrassed by her honesty, but really, why not? He'd told her everything. Had confessed to a youthful indiscretion that had caused the deaths of his parents, for heaven's sake. Why not tell him this. She'd never told anyone, not in so many words. How she had to be good. How she had to make the right choice. How everything felt like it was resting on her all the time. How she had to make herself needed so that the last remaining people in her life didn't decide she was too much trouble.

Didn't walk away because of her mistakes.

"See, I don't think being right or good is the most important thing," he said. Zafar looked down at the paper in his lap, taking a pen in hand and holding it poised above the signature line. He signed it, then moved it to the floor, holding his pen above the bottom line of the sheet that had been below it.

"You don't?"

"No. The important thing is how it all ends. It doesn't matter how you got there."

"This from the man who rescued women from ending up in his uncle's harem?"

"This from a man who bought a kidnapped woman from a band of thieves in the middle of the desert and is holding her captive in his palace until he is certain his country is stabilized," he said, looking up at her, his dark eyes intent on hers.

Her cheeks heated. Her heart pounded hard. Anger. She was angry. That was all, because she really didn't like remembering that she was at such a big disadvantage here. She wasn't used to it. She was used to being in charge. To making things happen.

She didn't like acknowledging that Zafar held the power here. That he held the keys to her very pretty prison cell. And that he walked into it whenever he liked.

"You need to shave," she said. Because she was going to start making some rules. Because she was going to take control of her project. And if she was going to stay here, she didn't need to make it easy or fun for him.

"I need to shave?"

"Yes. You look like you just crawled out from under a sand dune, which you did." He didn't really. He looked dangerous. Wicked and sexy and a whole lot of things she didn't want to admit. "You need some polish, which is what you want me to give you, right? A polish?"

He arched one dark brow. "That is a bit more suggestive than you might have meant."

Her face warmed. She wasn't entirely sure what he was getting at. What could she possibly polish that would… Her cheeks lit on fire. "I didn't mean it that way. Stop being such a man. Must you make everything…sexual?"

"It is something men have a tendency to do."

"Yeah, well, don't."

"Why does it bother you? Because you fear I might make an advance on you?"

She shook her head. "No. I know you wouldn't." It would undermine all of his other actions. And he had a young woman right here in the palace who clearly had a crush on him. Outside of that…she imagined there were a lot of women willing to submit to the desires of the sheikh.

Oh…wow. That sentence made her feel warm all over.

"Ah," he said, his voice deep, knowing. "You fear it because you enjoy it. Either because you find it entertaining, and know you shouldn't, or because you are…fascinated by the way it makes you feel, and you really know that should not be allowed."

"Not fascinated, as you put it. Not even amused."

"I don't believe you."

"And so what if you don't? What if I was? Would it make a difference?"

She held her breath during the ensuing silence, unwilling, unable to do anything to shatter the tension that was filling the space between them.

"None at all," he said, his voice hard.

"I didn't think so. Not to me, either. We're both bound by the same thing, Zafar. The need to do right. The need to fix. Now…how about the shaving?"

He rubbed his hand over his chin, the whiskers whispering beneath his touch. "I shall order a razor."

"You're going to do it here?"

"Yes. I had thought I might seeing as you are a large part of my civilization."

"All right. Order the supplies."

Ana leaned against the sink in the bathroom as Zafar looked down at the bowl of hot lather, the brush and the straight razor that had been provided by one of his serving girls.

A tremor ran through her body when she thought of the blade touching his skin. His hands, so large and masculine, didn't look geared toward fine work like drawing a blade over his skin without causing serious damage.

"Hold this," he said, handing her the end of a leather strap. She complied and he gripped the other end, bracing the back of the blade on the surface and dragging it down the length of the belt. Then he turned it and did the same, drawing it back up. He repeated the motion, again and again, her stomach tightening with each motion.

Then he handed the razor to her. "I think it's best if you oversee the project."

"Me?"

"Yes. I am yours to civilize, and this was your idea. Complete your project."

She felt like he was challenging her. Probably because he was. And she wasn't about to back down. Not now.

"Pretty gutsy of you. Handing me a blade and asking me to put it against your skin."

"You say that as though I think you could ever take advantage of me physically."

"I have a weapon."

He wrapped his hand around her arm, pressing his thumb to the pulse in her wrist. She knew he felt it quicken, knew he could feel just how delicate her bones were beneath his hand. He was very strong, and in that moment, she was very conscious of the fact that, if he had a mind to, he could break her using only that one hand.

She might be holding a weapon, but he was one.

"Indeed you do," he said, smiling, a wicked gleam in his eye. "Frightening." It was obvious he didn't mean it.

He released her and stepped back, gripping the bottom of his shirt and tugging it over his head, pulling the breath from her lungs right along with it. He cast the linen tunic to the floor and braced himself on the sink, his hands gripping the edge tightly. She couldn't help but look at him, at the movement of his abs with each breath he took, at the dark hair that did nothing to conceal his muscles but screamed at her, aggressively, insistently, that he was a man.

Much more man than she was used to.

She swallowed hard. "Right. Great."

"I suggest you gather your courage. The last thing I need is an unsteady blade."

"I don't use a straight razor but I shave my legs every day." She crossed her arms, deciding today, in this moment, she would lay diplomacy aside and go for bold. She'd been bold once. A child who ran instead of walked. Who laughed loud and often. Who spoke her mind. Until all of that brashness, all of that activity, had driven her mother away.

Until she feared it would drive her father away, too. Or the friends she'd made in school. Or Tariq.

But none of them were here now. She and Zafar were stuck with each other. She was going for broke. "I shave my bikini line. That's delicate work. I think I can handle this."

Something dark flared in his eyes, something hot and intense that she'd never, ever seen directed at her before. Not by anyone. Not by Tariq.

And she craved it. She had craved it for a long, long time, and she hadn't known it until this moment. Until the excitement and heat of it washed over her skin, sinking down through her, into her veins, pooling in her stomach.

Her breasts felt heavy, her nipples sensitive. She was suddenly aware that she could feel her nipples. So aware of parts of herself that she'd never been aware of before. He was magic. Except that sounded too light or impossible. He was something else altogether. Something dark and rich and indulgent, creating a desire in her that she'd never felt before.

"That is all very interesting," he said finally, his tone explicit, even though his words were benign.

"Yes. Well." And after she'd just scolded him for innuendo, here she was talking about her bikini line and pondering her nipples. "Is this hot?" she asked, pointing to the small marble bowl that was full of white foam.

"It doesn't matter to me."

"It does to me," she said. "Open pores would be nice. I don't really want to scrape your skin off."

He shrugged. "You can't hurt me, *habibti*."

"Because you're immortal?" she asked, picking up a black-handled brush with soft bristles.

"Because I have felt all the types of pain there are. There is no novelty there, nothing new. It all just slides off now."

"You're way too tall. I need you to sit."

And he did, on the tiny, feminine vanity stool that was there for her benefit. It was his own fault for insisting they use her bathroom.

It was made for a woman. This entire chamber was clearly made for a woman. Though, oddly, being in the middle of all this softness only made Zafar sexier. Yes, he was sexy, she would just admit it.

Because here he seemed rougher. Even more of a man, if that were possible.

And it appealed to her. To this new, wild piece of her that was moving into prominence.

She took a white cloth that was in a bowl of warm water and pressed it over his neck, his face, letting it sit for a moment while she took the brush and dipped it in the shaving cream, swirling in the thick foam.

"Tilt your head back." And he did. A little thrill raced through her at the sight of Zafar obeying her command.

She removed the towel, brushing it over his skin before setting it back on the edge of the sink. Then she bent in

front of him, picking up the brush and applying the cream
to his skin with circular motions. She could feel the roughness of the hair catching beneath the brush, could hear
nothing but the sound of their breathing and the lather
being worked over his face.

Her own breathing was getting heavier. Raspier. It was
certainly a lot harder to accomplish the closer she got to
him.

"Okay," she said. "Hold still because I don't want to be
responsible for the assassination of a world leader."

He obeyed again, his dark eyes trained on her as she
started to work the razor over his skin. She had a knot in
her throat, in her stomach. Because it was tense work. Because she was so close to him.

She took her other hand and gripped his chin, holding
him firmly and angling his head to the right so that she
could get a better look at his face, so that she could skim
the razor over the square line of his jaw with ease.

She dictated his movements, and he obeyed. It was an
interesting thing, holding a blade against her captor's skin.
And yet, that wasn't her dominant thought. It was about
how near he was. How good he smelled. Like spices today.
Like soap and, now, shaving cream.

"Hold really still," she said, when she got to the line
between his nose and upper lip.

He put his hand on her lower back, just before the metal
touched his skin. "Be careful," she said. "Don't surprise
me."

"I'm bracing myself," he said, his eyes locked with hers.

She should tell him to remove his hand. But she didn't.
It was warm and heavy on her body, and it reminded her
of that first night in the tent. When she'd let go of all her
tension and slept, rather than standing vigil. Rather than
fearing for her life. When, for the first time in…maybe
ever, she'd released every worry and simply drifted into

deep, heavy sleep, his protective hold on her, making her feel safe.

But this wasn't a protective hold. And it didn't feel safe. Not in the least.

But she didn't stop him.

She touched the steel to his flesh and breathed out as she moved, leaving his skin smooth. Taking away years with each stroke. It was like uncovering something he left buried, pieces of him revealed before her.

She couldn't fully focus on it, or enjoy it, because his touch was sending waves of sensation through her that were impossible to ignore and that took up far more of her brain power than she cared to admit.

When she ran the blade over his neck, his Adam's apple, a shiver of that same disquiet she'd felt when he'd first pulled out the razor went through her.

"This seems very dangerous," she whispered, her face so close to him that her lips nearly brushed his neck.

"Perhaps a bit," he said, his hand sliding to her hip, his fingers digging into her, and she wondered if they were meaning the same sort of danger.

Then she had to wonder which kind of danger she'd really been referring to.

"Quite a show of trust," she said. "For a man who, I imagine, doesn't trust very many people."

She looked up at his eyes and was surprised to see confusion there. "It is true," he said.

"You trust me, don't you?"

"I have no real choice," he said. "You have the power to upend my rule. To start a war between two nations. And at the moment—" he angled his head, tilting it back so that the edge of the blade pressed harder into his skin, so very near his throat "—you have the power to end me if you choose." For a brief, heart-stopping moment she almost thought he was requesting it. As though he wanted her to do it.

Instead, she just continued her work, trying to steady the tremble in her hand, more determined than when she'd started that she wouldn't so much as graze his skin. Wouldn't spill a drop of blood.

"There," she said, her voice a whisper. She wasn't capable of more. "Finished."

She stepped back, away from him, moving away from his touch. Then she took the towel and wiped off the excess shaving cream, leaving him sitting before her, an entirely different man.

She could see him now. See that he was a man in his early thirties, handsome beyond reason. She'd known he was arresting, that he had a mouth made for sins she could scarcely imagine, but she'd had no idea he was this…beautiful.

Because this was beauty. His jaw was square, his chin strong, lips incredibly formed. The loss of dark hair on his face made his brows more prominent, made his eyes that much more magnetic.

With shorter hair, he would look even better. With nothing to distract from that perfect face.

"You are staring," he said, standing, forcing her to look back down at his bare chest. She needed to look somewhere more innocuous. Somewhere that wouldn't make her feel tense and fluttery and…sweaty.

But there was no safe place to look, except at the wall behind him. Because everywhere, absolutely everywhere, he was a woman's deepest, darkest fantasy. The kind that came out in the middle of the night when she lay in bed, restless, aching and unsatisfied. The kind that she knew she shouldn't have, shouldn't give in to.

But did. Because she didn't possess enough strength to do anything else.

"I'm just surprised at what I uncovered," she said. Best to be honest, because she didn't have the brainpower to come up with a lie.

He laughed. "Expecting hideous scars, were you? Those are just in here." He pounded on his bare chest.

"I didn't know what to expect." She swallowed. "I do think you should cut your hair, and you should definitely enlist someone other than me to do it."

"Why is that?"

"I'll answer why to both possible questions. Because you don't need to hide behind all the hair. You'll shock people more if you step out completely clean, I think. Defy expectations and exceed them—that's what you want, isn't it? And secondly, because the only way I could cut your hair is if we took the fruit bowl in my bedroom and emptied it, then turned it upside down on your head. I don't think that's the look we want."

He laughed and it made her warm up inside. "I suppose not. And I see your point about…out-polishing their expectations."

"It would be good for you," she said. "Think about it… you show up at the party in a dark suit, tailored to fit, and your hair cut short, clean shaven. You won't look like a man who's just stepped out of exile, but a man who was born to his position. Which, you are."

He shook his head slowly. "I am glad I didn't walk a straight line from the cradle to the throne. I strongly regret what happened. The loss of my parents. But without it…I would have been a weak, spoiled and selfish ruler. I fear I would have been no better than my uncle. At least out in the desert I learned self-denial. At least I learned about what mattered. It is the one good thing to result from it all. I will be better for Al Sabah because of it. Sadly, Al Sabah is starting from a place of weakness. Because of my own weakness."

"You've transcended that weakness," she said. "You've spent the past fifteen years doing it. So show them, Zafar, show them your strength. Give them a reason to stand behind you."

CHAPTER EIGHT

ZAFAR LOOKED IN the mirror, which was something he didn't particularly like to do. It was a difficult task over the past few years, as he, in many ways, hated the man he saw. Plus, it wasn't like he carried a compact in his pocket. He saw no point in owning a mirror out in the desert.

But he was looking now. He'd had a haircut, and he had shaved himself in the few days since the shave Ana had given him.

He looked very different than he'd thought he did. He'd seen himself as a boy. Since then he'd always had a beard and long hair, and he'd looked at himself infrequently.

Seeing himself without anything covering his face, his hair short, was more shocking than he'd thought it might be. He was a stranger to himself, this, admittedly, more civilized version of the man he was looking back at him from the mirror.

His appearance had never mattered to him. Every day he rode through the desert, the safety and well-being of the people there his job. His duty. If he had word his uncle's men were around then he was there with his men, preventing any injustice that might happen, by any means necessary, and then melting back into the desert as though they had never been there.

As far as Zafar knew, his uncle had never known it was him. His uncle hadn't known of his continued existence.

He was sure Farooq imagined that he'd gone back to the dust, another victim of the unforgiving desert. And that had suited him well. The Bedouins were loyal to him, above all else. And the few times he'd tangled with soldiers from the palace…

They had left no men to return with a tale.

He looked at his reflection again, caught sight of the ruthless glint in his eye. The pride. The lack of remorse. Ah, there he was. This was the man he knew.

He pushed off from the sink and turned to walk out of his chamber and into the hall. He would find Ana. He needed to see if his new appearance met with her approval.

His gut tightened at the thought of her. He'd avoided her over the past few days, and it had been easy to do so. There was a lot of work to be done, more papers to sign, people to start meeting with, scheduling to sort out. Media to speak to.

For a moment, his hand burned as he thought of how he'd touched her while she'd shaved his face. She had curves, soft and womanly. The epitome of feminine appeal. Her face had been so close to his and it had taken every bit of his self-control not to lean in and claim her mouth.

But then, he very well might have found himself with a blade pressed to his throat in earnest.

He went to her room, but she wasn't there.

For some reason, the discovery made his chest feel tight. He walked quickly through the corridor and to the double doors that led to the courtyard.

And there she was, a shimmer of gold in the sunlight, sitting on the edge of a fountain.

"Ana."

She turned and her eyes widened, her lips rounding and parting. She'd looked at him like that after he'd shaved. A look of shocked wonder. Like someone who had been knocked over the head.

It was quite endearing in its way.

For his part, were he not well-practiced in hiding his responses, he was sure he would be wearing a similar expression. Seeing her out in the sun, in a white dress that left her legs and shoulders bare, pale hair shimmering in the light, was like a punch in the gut.

Heat pooled down low, desire grabbing him by the throat and shaking him hard. In that moment, he suddenly wanted so badly to touch her skin, to see if it was as soft as he imagined, that he would have gladly sold his soul, traversed the path into hell and delivered it to the devil by hand, just for a touch. A taste.

And it would cost his damned soul, no mistaking that.

But then, as it was damned already, did it really matter?

Yes. It did. Because Al Sabah mattered. His people mattered. He was beyond the point of redemption. He wasn't seeking absolution, because there was none to be had. But he would see his people served well. That was what he intended. To lead. To lead as a servant.

Anything else was beneath him. Any chance for more gone years ago.

It didn't matter how beautiful she looked with the sun shining on her, with her hair spilling over her shoulders like a river of liquid gold. It didn't matter that her breasts were made to fit in his hands, and he was certain they were.

A man only had so much emotional currency, and his had been spent the day of his parents' deaths. He'd forfeited it. To better serve. To better make amends.

And now he simply had nothing. So he would have to look, only. Look and burn.

"You look…"

"Civilized?"

"Um…I don't know if that's the right word. You are…" She bit her lip, and he envied her that freedom. He would love to bite that lip. "Look, this whole experience is all a bit, out of time for me. I'm used to having to be appropriate and well-behaved, to…contribute and be useful. But right now I'm just going to be honest. You're a very handsome man." Her cheeks turned pink.

"I'm not sure anyone has ever said that to me," he said.

"That surprises me."

"It has been a very long time since I was in a relationship where words like that were used. It has been…it's been longer than I can remember since I told a woman she was beautiful. You are beautiful," he said.

"Me?"

"Yes, you." It was a mistake to tell her that. A mistake to speak the words, and yet, he found he couldn't hold them back.

"Now, there's something I don't hear very often."

"Now I have to question the sanity of every male you've had contact with in the past five years."

"Thank you," she said. "But I've been engaged to Tariq for four years and as a result I haven't dated. And we've mostly dated remotely so…"

"And he has not told you how beautiful you are when he's holding you in bed?" he asked, knowing he shouldn't ask, because images of her in bed, naked and rumpled, made him crave violence against the man who had just had her. And even more, it made him crave her touch.

"I…we haven't…it's been a very traditional courtship. And by traditional, I mean the tradition of a hundred years ago, not the tradition of now." Her cheeks were even darker now, embarrassment obvious.

"What a fool," he said.

"What?"

"Tariq is a fool. If you were mine I would have staked a claim on you the moment I had you within reach."

She blinked rapidly. "I…our relationship isn't like that."

"And yet he loves you?"

"He cares for me."

"And you love him?"

"Waiting doesn't mean I don't love him. Or that he doesn't love me. In fact, I think it shows a great deal of respect."

"Perhaps. But if you were mine, I would rather show you passion."

"But I'm not."

It took him a moment to realize how close they had gotten to each other, that he was now standing near enough to her that if he reached his hand out, he could cup her cheek, feel all that soft skin beneath his rough, calloused palm. A gift far too fine for his damaged skin. For his damaged heart.

"No," he said, "and you should be grateful for that fact. Your fiancé sounds as though he's a better man than I."

"I'm sure he is," she said. She raised her eyes, and they met his. "But I...I don't feel..." She raised her hand, and it was her who rested her hand on his cheek. "What is this?"

"You're touching my face," he said, trying to sound normal. Trying not to sound out of breath.

"You know what I mean, I know you do. And I know... I know you know the answer."

He did. Chemistry. Sexual attraction. Lust. Desire. There were so many names for the feeling that made his stomach tight and his body hard. But it wasn't something he wanted to expose her to. It wasn't anything he could expose her to.

She put her other hand on his face, aquamarine eyes intent on his. "I don't even like you," she said. "I think I might respect you in a vague sort of way, but I think you're hard. And scary. And I know I don't have a hope in the world of ever relating to you. So, why do I feel like there's a magnet drawing us together?"

"Is it just since I shaved? Perhaps it's that you think I am…handsome, as you said."

She shook her head. "It started before that."

"Perhaps you should discontinue your honesty," he said, his voice rough. "It will not lead us anywhere good."

"I know," she said. "I know. But…can I try this? Please? Can I just…" She closed her eyes then, blocking her emotions from view. And then she leaned in, pressing her lips to his.

It was a soft touch. But it was like touching a live, naked wire to sensitive flesh. Quick, nothing more than brief contact, but it burned everywhere. Everything.

She drew back, her breath catching, her eyes wide-open again now. And he knew she'd felt it too, just like he had. Like an electric shock.

"Does it answer your question?" he asked.

She nodded.

"And I was right. Wasn't I? It is best not to be so honest from here on out, I think."

Ana felt like she'd been singed. Her heart was pounding in her chest and she was shaking inside. Everywhere. She had no idea why she'd just done that. Why she'd touched him. Why she'd kissed him.

Only he'd walked out of the palace, looking like a fantasy she'd never known she'd had, and for a moment the entire world had shrunk down to him, her, and the way he made her feel. The things he made her want.

And she'd needed to know. Was it all adrenaline and fear? Confused by the fact that he was an appealing, powerful man? Or was it attraction. Deep, lusting attraction that wasn't like anything she'd ever felt before.

The moment their lips had touched she'd had her answer. She didn't like her answer.

She'd kissed Tariq a few times. And before that, she'd kissed three or four boys at inter-school mixers. Light kissing, with a little tongue. Some of the boys had given more tongue than she'd liked.

But this had left them all so far in the dust it almost didn't seem like it could be considered the same activity. It was so dissimilar to every other kiss she'd had, she wondered if it was something different. Something more. Or if those first kisses had been failures. But they hadn't seemed like it at the time.

She'd liked kissing Tariq. Had thought dreamy thoughts about what it would be like to kiss him more. To do more than kiss. She'd been looking forward to being his wife in every way.

And then there was Zafar. He had walked into her life and swept her up in his whirlwind, leaving so many things devastated in his wake.

"Just tell me one thing and then we'll suspend honesty on the subject," she said, fighting the urge to reach up and touch her lips. To see if they felt hot.

"I will decide if I'll tell you after you ask the question, *habibti*."

"Okay." Normally she would be so embarrassed. Normally, she would never have kissed a man like that, and normally she would never ask the question she was about to. But normally, she lived life to keep everything around her smooth. She lived life in a calm and orderly fashion. She never ruffled feathers or made things awkward.

At least, that was what she'd trained herself to do after an act of clumsiness had resulted in her mother telling her all of her faults. All of the little ways she ruined the other woman's life. And then in her mother leaving. Because she couldn't stand to live with such a child anymore.

But in the past two weeks she'd left home to see her fiancé, the man she would marry, taking a step toward becoming sheikha of a new country, to becoming a wife. Then she'd been kidnapped. Then she'd been ransomed by Zafar and taken back to the palace and given the job of civilizing a man she was starting to think was incapable of being civilized. So she felt like she was entitled to be different.

She was starting to feel different. More in touch with the girl she'd been before pain had forced her to coat herself in a protective shell. To live her life insulated, quiet and never making waves.

Now she didn't mind if she made waves. Not here with Zafar. Here she felt bold. A little reckless. In touch with her body in a way she'd never been before.

"Is it always like that?"

"What?" he asked.

"Kissing. Does it always feel like that? And when I ask this question I'm assuming that the kiss made you feel the way it made me feel. I'm assuming it made you feel like you'd been lit on fire inside and like you wanted more. So much more it might not ever be enough. If it did…is it always like that?"

"I should not answer the question."

"Please answer."

He leaned in, resting his thumb on her bottom lip. She darted her tongue out, instinct driving her now, not thought, and tasted the salt of his skin. Heat flared in his dark eyes.

"No," he said, the word sounding like it had been pulled from him.

"No, you won't answer, or no, it's not normally like that?"

"It's never like this," he said. "I do not know how the brush of your lips against mine can make me *want* like this. Like the basest sexual act never has. But it doesn't matter."

She nodded slowly. "Yes. It matters."

"Does it change anything?"

"No."

And it didn't. But in some ways it was gratifying to know that she shared what was probably a normal level of chemistry with Tariq. That this thing with Zafar wasn't normal. That it wasn't something you were supposed to feel, that it wasn't something everyone had, that it was something she was somehow missing with the man she was going to marry.

That would have been a harder truth.

Maybe.

It wasn't actually all that comforting to know that she was experiencing some sort of intense, once-in-a-lifetime type attraction to a man she had nothing in common with. A man she could never, ever touch again.

Not if she valued her sanity. Not if she valued her engagement.

And she did. She valued both quite a bit.

"But I wanted to know because…because if it's something you feel with everyone, but I somehow don't feel it with Tariq…well, I needed to know that. But this is better."

"Is it?"

"Yes."

"I find it near the point of unendurable, and I have endured a lot. Dehydration. Starvation. All things you can forget if you go deep enough inside yourself. But this… with this, it comes from deep inside of me and I'm not certain how I'm supposed to escape it."

Ana swallowed hard, her throat suddenly dry, and she couldn't even blame the desert heat.

She looked down. "We just ignore it. There's no point to it anyway."

"None at all."

"So, in the spirit of ignoring this, you do look very civilized, but we are going to have to work on your manners."

"My manners?" he asked, his brow arched.

"Yes. What sort of dinner are you having at your big event?"

"Western-style dining."

"I thought as much, with all the ambassadors coming from Europe. How long has it been since you used a fork?"

"Certainly since I lived here at the palace. I did have some...etiquette lessons naturally, but it has been a long time since I've been expected to use any of it."

"You had to learn a whole new culture, didn't you?" she asked, realizing that royalty didn't act the same as the masses. And the Bedouin culture was different to the people in the city.

He nodded. "Yes. But I found acceptance there. And purpose. It was a place to rest and to find reprieve from the effort of existence. On your own, in the desert, survival is nothing short of a twenty-four-hour struggle. There is no end. There is no real sleep."

"I had a taste of that when I was out there. With them."

"I know you did. I wish I could have spared you that."

She shrugged. "I don't know. I wasn't hurt. Not really. Scared, but not hurt. I was lucky."

"You were unfortunate enough to get caught in the crossfire. I don't think I consider it lucky."

Except it was strange. What had happened before the kidnapping suddenly seemed the hazy and distant thing. Her whole life seemed hazy and distant. There was something so harsh and real about the light here, so revealing. It made it impossible to focus too much on the past. Or the future.

The present was far too bright.

"Well, as you said, this is pretty plush for a jail cell."

"You aren't a prisoner," he said.

"Except I can't leave."

"There is that."

Silence stretched between them.

"Dinner," she said. "Tonight."

"I shall make an effort to dress for it," he said.

"Great." She looked back at the fountain, the sunlight sparking off the water. She looked back at him and tried to breathe. It wasn't easy. "Pro-tip. The salad fork is on the left. Outside."

CHAPTER NINE

ANA FELT SELF-CONSCIOUS and a little silly. She had dressed up. Zafar had said he would dress for dinner, and because of that, she'd felt like she should, too.

So she was walking down the empty corridors of the palace in gold heels, provided by Zafar's very efficient dresser, and in a red dress that came up to her knees and draped over her shoulder like a Grecian-style gown, chiffon flowing over her curves as she walked.

She had her hair swept up into a French twist, her lips painted to match the dress. And she had to wonder why she was doing it. Why she was bothering.

Because the simple fact was, she was attracted to him. In spite of what she said about it not mattering. It was still there. And it was unnerving.

You can't do anything about it. You don't like him. And it would be wrong.

Yes. It would go against everything her father had been trying to build up. She had a flash, suddenly, of what Zafar had said when she'd told him about her father. That he wanted to know about her, not about her father.

But, her father aside, she had her commitment to Tariq. And she loved Tariq. Didn't she?

It was hard to picture him now. He was fuzzy, like there were heat waves standing in the way of her memories of him. And that was just wrong. It shouldn't be so easy to forget. Zafar's face shouldn't be so prominent in front of her mind's eye.

And she really shouldn't have put on red lipstick for the man. But since she'd complained about her lack of frills, more had been provided, and she hadn't been able to resist.

She sucked in a breath and turned the corner into the dining room. And was shocked to find it transformed. There was a formal, Western-style dining table with chairs all around it, and delicate white china place settings. It was something she would have organized for her father. Elegant and restrained, and odd in this setting because it was only for her and Zafar when it could have easily been a dinner for twenty-five.

And Zafar sat at the head of the table. He stole her breath. Her lungs contracted, the air rushing from them, and she couldn't breathe, couldn't think. She could only look.

He was sitting there in a black jacket, a black tie and a black shirt. The picture of masculine grace. The picture of civility.

Such a lie.

Because when she looked closer, at his face, the truth was plain. He was a predator, leashed and collared for the moment, by expectation, by duty. But it was only the leash keeping him from pouncing.

Were it not for the restraint of duty, he would be wholly unpredictable. Wholly frightening. A beast uncaged.

He stood, and she felt light-headed. His physique was outlined to perfection in the suit, exquisitely so. He was broad shouldered, broad chested, his waist and hips narrow. Impossibly hot.

She'd never seen such a good-looking man before. Ever. Not in the movies, not in magazines, just ever. And she knew that beneath that oh-so-sedate black jacket and shirt were muscles that would melt a lesser woman from the inside out.

Though, at the moment she herself felt a little melty, in spite of the fact that she was engaged. In spite of the fact that she knew she wanted nothing to do with him. Her fingers itched to put her hand on the knot at he base of his throat and loosen his tie.

Why would she want to ruffle him when he'd just now gotten all together? It was ridiculous.

"Good evening," he said. "I trust you found your afternoon restful?"

Restful? She'd kissed the man and spent the entire afternoon burning. "Quite," she said.

He moved away from his spot at the table and went to the chair that was positioned to the right of his own. He curled his fingers over the back of it, then pulled it out. "Have a seat."

She moved toward the chair, never taking her eyes off his face. She sat and he returned to his own seat.

"And how was your afternoon?" she asked.

"It was very good. A suit was delivered and I had it fitted to me. That was an experience I've not had for a long time."

"I imagine not."

She imagined tailored clothing was a luxury he'd been without since he'd been cast out of the palace. "Suspending with civil, bland conversation for a moment."

"You felt the need to notify me?"

"Just so you would know this isn't the kind of thing you'll talk about at your presentation."

He nodded. "All right."

"Are you ever angry?"

"Always, but about what specifically?"

"This." She indicated the suit. "This should have been yours. Always. You should have always had custom clothes and a position at the head of the table in the palace. You should have always been here, and not living out in the dirt in a tent. Doesn't it make you angry that you had it stolen from you?"

And she realized in that moment that part of the reason she was asking was because she was angry about everything she should have had.

About everything that had been taken from her because of the selfishness of others. Because of her mother. Because her mother had made her hate the girl she'd been. Had made her fold inward, smooth every rough edge. So that she would never again be in the way. Never be impulsive. Never truly be herself.

Why was she thinking about that? She'd never thought of it that way before, and now here she was having some kind of epiphany in front of an empty dinner plate with her captor to her right, looking at her like she'd lost her mind.

"I deserved to lose it," he said. "I've never been angry on my own behalf."

Neither had she. Until now.

"I'm just saying…you expect something from life. You're born into it, and it seems like you have some guarantee based on those beginning circumstances. Like… you're born into a certain family and you think…and you think you're going to have a certain future and then… you don't."

"Are we still talking about me?" he asked.

"Maybe. I don't know." She took a deep breath. "What's on the menu for the evening?" *Something bland, I hope.*

Any more excited and she was going to start saying and doing even dumber things. As if that were possible. What was it about this man? This place? It changed her. Made her say things, want things, feel things.

Maybe it was being kidnapped. She'd been freaking kidnapped, by a band of desert marauders, and she'd survived it. It made her feel stronger somehow. Made her feel like she'd found a hidden well of resilience she hadn't even known about.

But along with that, was the desire for more. Because she'd found more in herself. Because she knew there was more out there.

It was a dangerous desire. One that was coming too late. And one that really shouldn't be acted on. After all, she was under duress. And stuff.

But it was hard. So hard to ignore when everything in her felt like it was broken apart and shifted around. Like gigantic tectonic plates had shifted inside of her, creating an earthquake that wreaked havoc on her soul.

Dramatic, but there it was.

"What did you expect?" Zafar asked.

"Me? From life?"

"Yes."

"I didn't expect my mother to leave, or the way it would make me feel. Or for my father to need so much. I didn't expect for...I didn't expect for Tariq to be introduced, and for that union to be so important to...to..."

"But you love him, don't you?"

"I...yes." But for some reason the answer didn't seem as true this time. Not as true as it had seemed nearly two weeks ago when she'd been snatched out of a desert encampment and taken prisoner.

It went along with her sudden epiphany about her life growing up. With the change inside of her. What would it be like to make noise again? To stop walking so softly.

"And yet you characterize him as an unwelcome surprise?"

"Unexpected. Let's leave it at that. I just...you know, I was thirteen when my mother left. I thought I would be able to talk to her about boys. I thought that I would date. I thought I could be a kid. But...but my being a kid...that was what drove her away." She still remembered that moment, her mother, holding the broken doll and screaming at her about her clumsiness. Her childishness. "And so...I had to take care of my father and...I couldn't be another burden on his life. I had to go away to school because he didn't have a lot of time for me. I had to leave my home. And at school...they expected me to...be quiet. Be invisible. Then when I was home I had to be a hostess, as good as my mother would have been, even though I was only a child."

"Your father didn't bear his loss well."

She shook her head. "No. She was always fragile, and temperamental, but beautiful, a wonderful hostess. She liked having eyes on her, liked planning parties and organizing their social life. And she made vows to him. Of course he expected her to be there. Of course he wasn't equipped to deal with her leaving."

"And it was up to you to hold it all together?"

It was more than that. Deeper than that. But she didn't want to confess it. "Someone has to do the right thing, Zafar."

Something changed in his eyes, suddenly darker, hollower. "Yes, it's true. Someone must do the right thing even when they don't want to. Even when emotion asks you to do something differently. I never managed it. For my part, I cannot resent my lot in life because I was the cause of so much of it. Not like you. Your life has been upended through no fault of your own. And here I have only served to do more."

No fault? Maybe. Maybe not.

"Guilt, Sheikh?" she asked, her stomach tightening. Because she'd seen him look blank, she'd heard him profess guilt in a matter-of-fact manner. But she'd never heard it in his voice.

She heard it now.

"A useless emotion," he said, his voice blank now. "It fixes nothing."

"But you feel it."

"Another useless emotion to add to the day," he said, adjusting the fork on the table. "Salad fork," he said, lifting it. "Do I have that right?"

"Yes," she said, looking down at her plate. "Is dinner soon?"

As if on cue, the serving staff entered with silver trays, laying them on the table before them and uncovering them. There was rice and lamb, an Arabic feast on their Western table settings.

Like a melding of cultures. Except she felt like there was a wall between them. One that she wanted to breach now, and for the life of her she couldn't figure out why. Because she should want the wall. She should want the distance.

She was here to civilize him. Not to let him effect a change in her.

She'd spent her whole life striving to do right. To contribute rather than take. To be useful rather than a burden.

More than that, she just believed in right. In good. In doing good and being right. Because it was the best thing. It was the thing that kept the world from folding in.

It was who she had to be.

"It looks wonderful."

"Salt?" he asked.

"Oh, no, I couldn't."

"Blandness must be preserved," he said.

"At all costs. That's safe conversation."

"Ever the hostess."

"Yes indeed, but then, aren't I here to teach you?"

"You are. So I will leave it up to you to decide, then. Is it considered safe conversation to tell your hostess that she is beautiful to the point of distraction?"

"A bit too much like adding salt," she said, her cheeks heating.

"Then I shall refrain from telling you that I think your skin is like alabaster, though I think it's true. And even if there was no reason for me to abstain from complimenting you, I should never use those particular words. Because I think lines like that only seem romantic to a sixteen-year-old. Though, I think in truth I haven't made any attempts at being romantic since I was sixteen." He looked at her, his dark eyes blazing. "But perhaps it is for the best I stick to compliments of that nature. Because if I complimented you as a man…well, that would, I fear, over-salt things quite a bit."

"There's a very real possibility of that." Her pulse was pounding hard at the base of her throat, and she was sure that he could see it, almost certain that, in the silence of the room he could even hear it.

"Then I will say nothing. In the interest of safe conversation."

They'd passed safe conversation a few minutes ago. Maybe a few hours ago. And she wasn't sure what she could do to get things back on the right footing. Wasn't sure what she could do to forget the way his lips had felt beneath hers. Wasn't sure she could forget the rush of pure, unadulterated heat that had burst through her, like nothing she'd ever felt before. Like nothing she'd ever known was possible.

"I think that's for the best," she said. Then something in her rebelled, pushed her, prodded her. The deep, inner part of her, the Ana that had been repressed for so many years. "And I will say nothing about how that suit is cut so that you could almost be wearing nothing. Or maybe you'd be less indecent if you were wearing nothing. As it is, it just teases me."

"Now that, I fear, is not bland conversation in the least."

"I'm sorry. I don't know what came over me." She looked down at her plate again, then back up at him. "It won't happen again."

"I find myself disappointed by that."

"Then you'll just have to be disappointed." She sniffed and picked up her salad fork. "There is no salad."

"An oversight."

"I don't believe that," she said.

"Eat your rice with it."

She laughed. "I can't. It would be wrong."

"That will be my goal," he said, unapologetically taking a bit of rice with the aforementioned fork. "To uncivilize you a bit. A favor, as you're doing one for me."

"I'm afraid violations of table manners just can't come into it," she said, sniffing and picking up her entrée fork.

"Then perhaps we will have to think of other violations?"

She nearly choked. "Um...I think, as kind as the offer is, you have to be the focus for now."

"I don't know, in terms of needing to be uncivilized... you're about as far away from it as I am to being ready to walk into a room full of dignitaries."

"Then we'll fix that. You, I mean, not me. I don't have any wild Spring Break events coming up so it doesn't seem like I'll be needing any help with the...letting loose."

He breathed out heavily, dark eyes bleak. "And how do you propose to fix me, *habibti*?"

"You don't happen to know how to dance, do you?"

"I doubt I will be dancing at this event," he said.

"But you will eventually," she said, "and it's my job to make sure that you have adequate education in all matters of civility."

Zafar eyed the petite blonde in front of him. She was wearing casual linen pants and a loose tunic top, an adaptation of what he often wore around the palace. Though he had shown up for their dancing lesson in his suit. He felt strange about that decision now.

He had imagined she might revisit the red dress from the night before, but she had not.

"You dressed up," she said.

"It does no good for me to learn to dance if I can't manage to do it in a suit."

"I suppose that's true."

"Though I still question the necessity."

"You'll take a wife one day, won't you?"

He tried to imagine it. He had lovers, he had women that shared his bed for a couple of hours in an evening. Women he shared his body with. But that wasn't a wife. It wasn't sharing his life.

And he seriously doubted he had it in him to open himself up that much. To share all of himself. And he had to wonder what sort of life it would be for a wife. Being here in this castle, wandering around alone, going to sleep alone.

He would not share a bed with a woman, not after he slept. Because that was when the darkness crept in, unfiltered. In sleep, he had no purpose but to dream. And so he had no defense against the insidious, grasping claws of memory, guilt and unending shame.

Things he shut out in the day. Things he lived forever in the dark. His own private hell. Endless blackness. Weeping, wailing, suffering. Always.

He didn't know what he did during those dreams. If all of the screaming was in his head, or if he let it out. None of his men would have ever dared say. The desert kept secrets well.

But here? Yes, here he might truly find out the depth of the damage done. And he could very well not be able to hide it from his people.

If he let it, the enormity of everything would crash in on him. Breach the walls that he'd built up so strong, and swallow him whole.

"Yes," he said. "I will have to take a wife."

"Then you should learn how to dance. So that when you see her…across the crowded ballroom, and your eyes meet, and you make your way to her…you have something better to do than talk about the weather."

"I thought I wanted bland."

"Not with someone you're trying to know."

"Who says I need to know a wife? I simply need to marry her."

"Oh…Zafar. I only have a week left to civilize you?"

"Only a week until my unveiling. You could stay after. You might very well have to. I had thirty days, if you recall."

"I recall," she said. "Now, give me your hand."

He extended his hand to her and she wrapped her slender fingers around it, drawing him into her body. "Hand on my waist," she said, reaching down and grasping him with her other hand, putting his palm against her lower back. "And this one out."

"Music?" he asked.

"We'll count. A waltz is a three-count dance."

"A waltz? What the hell is this? A Jane Austen fantasy?"

"You know Jane Austen?"

"I have been out in the desert for fifteen years. I may have missed popular culture, but not classics."

"And you even consider her works to be classics?"

"I am a barbarian, but I'm not entirely without culture." He pulled her more tightly against him. "And anyway, one has to amuse themselves somehow." He paused, looking down at his feet. "Books were a luxury not often affordable. I came upon one, a gift from a merchant I aided. *Pride and Prejudice* in English. It is the only book I owned."

"I never...I never considered that. Not having access to books."

He shrugged. "Elizabeth Bennet is nice company. She has a sharp wit. Reminds me a bit of you."

"Oh, Zafar, you should have no trouble finding a wife."

"Although, I'm not exactly Mr. Darcy."

"Not so much."

"One, two, three," she began, her voice in staccato rhythm. "Follow my lead, one, two, three."

"I thought men were meant to lead."

"Not when they don't know how to dance. You can lead when you get this down. One, two, three."

He followed her steps, but everything in him was focused on where his hand rested, just on the rounded curve of her hip, on the brush of her breasts against his chest.

"One two three," she continued, but he could hardly hear. His eyes were focused on her lips, on the movement they made when she said the words. Numbers, an endless repetition. Something that shouldn't make a man feel anything, much less a fire in his blood that might reduce him to ash on the spot.

Blazing, hotter than the desert sun. He'd thought he'd withstood the most destructive heat in existence. In the wilderness. In his nightmares.

But this was a different kind of heat altogether. One that burned but didn't consume. Endlessly going on and on. Just when he thought the peak had been reached, it only went up higher.

Hotter.

What magic did this woman possess? Living out as he did, he could not discount the presence of the supernatural, and part of him wondered if she had some sort of power. Something to snare him.

Like a Jinn, made of smokeless, scorching fire. Whispering to his soul and telling him to commit sins he knew well he could not.

And when he looked in her eyes, he saw nothing but clear blue. It made him wonder if the desire for sin came, not from her, but from the depths of his own soul. It shouldn't be able to speak to him. It should have been choked out, dried and left to rot on the sand, along with his heart.

Both his heart and soul were so deceitfully wicked. That was why he tried to shut them down. To keep them from having a say in his actions.

When a man didn't have a trustworthy conscience he had to learn his purpose in his head and stick to it.

No matter how soft a woman felt beneath his hand. No matter how enticing the brush of her breasts, the promise of pleasure on her lips.

"Tell me something bland," he whispered, trying to ignore the burn beneath his skin. Trying to ignore the rush of blood to his groin. The ache that was building there.

"I'm counting. Isn't that bland?"

He looked at her pale pink lips. "It is not."

"I don't know how I could be more boring." She kept moving him to soundless music that must be playing in her mind, never losing the beat.

"It is your mouth," he said. "I find it distracting."

"That isn't my intent."

"Intent doesn't matter. It's the result. And the result is that I find myself unable to look away. And when I look at your lips, all I can think of is how it felt for them to touch mine."

"I'm engaged," she said, her tone firm. "Engaged and in love and…"

He pressed his lips against hers and the dancing stopped. She froze beneath his mouth, her body rigid for a second, and then it softened. Her fingers went to the lapels of his suit jacket, curling in tightly as she rose up on her tiptoes, deepening the kiss.

If there had been fire before, this was the introduction of oil. A burst of flame that threatened to destroy everything in its wake.

Her tongue slid against his, and he was pulled into the darkness. There was nothing else, nothing but the slick friction, nothing but her soft, perfect lips.

Until her, it had been a long time since he'd been kissed. Longer still since a kiss had been simply a kiss. And that simplicity gave it the power to be so much more.

He wrapped his arms more tightly around her and pulled her flush against his body, bringing those full, gorgeous breasts against his chest as he'd fantasized about doing for…had there ever been a time when he hadn't? Had there truly been a moment when he hadn't wanted her?

When he'd seen her as nothing more than a pale, fragile creature diminishing beneath the Al Sabahan sun? How had he ever seen her that way? In this woman lay the power to bring kingdoms crashing down. To bring a sheikh to his knees.

He wrenched his mouth from hers and kissed the curve of her neck, his teeth grazing the delicate skin at her throat. He pressed his thumb to the hollow there, felt her pulse pounding wildly. Felt each raw catch of breath.

He growled, his response feral, beyond thought or reason. Quite beyond civility.

She moved her hands to his shoulders, her fingers digging into his skin through the layers of his coat and dress shirt. Not enough. It would never be enough. He pulled away for a moment, shrugging his coat off and letting it fall to the floor.

Her fingers were fumbling with the knot of his tie. Of all the times, why the hell had he chosen to wear a suit now? A linen tunic was easily cast aside, robes quickly dispensed with. This Western style of dress gave no concession to lust-tinged urgency.

He struggled with the tie, and the collar of his shirt, tearing something, the tie or his collar, he wasn't sure. He didn't care. He was a sheikh. More clothes could be bought. Passion like this…it could only be taken in the moment.

"Oh…Zafar."

That, his name, seemed to suddenly knock her back to reality and she pulled away from him, struggling in his embrace. "Stop," she said, "stop."

He released his hold on her immediately, his hands at his side, his heart thundering so hard he feared it would simply stop before the next beat.

"What?" he asked, knowing he sounded angry, shocked. But he had felt, for a blissful moment in her arms, as if the blistered, hardened shell that covered him had been rolled back and he'd been exposed, new and tender, but feeling. And it had been incredible.

It had been beyond anything he'd ever before experienced, even with Fatin, who he'd believed he loved, who— damn his foolish, romantic soul—he *had* loved.

Ana's kiss made him feel like a new man.

Ana's kiss was more than he deserved.

And then the horror of it dawned on him, as the blood receded, as it went back to his brain, he realized what he had done.

Once is carelessness, twice is the measure of a man.

Or rather the foolishness of a man's measure. His body betraying him yet again. His cock controlling him.

He straightened. "Of course we have to stop."

"I'm engaged to Tariq."

An animal in him raged, wounded and seeking to lash out. "I don't give a damn about your engagement!" he roared. "The fate of a nation rests on me. Whether or not you're faithful to your fiancé is none of my concern. But war is. And I would never compromise the lives of my people, the future of my country to spread your legs. You are not so valuable as that."

His head pounding, heart threatening to burst through his chest, he turned and walked away, leaving her standing there, staring after him.

He had hurt her. He didn't care.

It was better he hurt her now. Better he hurt her this way.

Images flashed before his mind, images that were curled and burned around the edges, tinged in red. Blood soaked and inserted so deep into his mind it could never be removed.

It was this palace. These walls. That woman.

He wanted to vomit. He stopped walking and pressed his head to the wall, the cold stone cooling his blood. He stood for a moment, breathing through the nausea, through the pain that seemed to be everywhere. His mind, his treacherous member and his heart, as events from the past wove their way into the present and tangled themselves into an indecipherable mass in his mind's eye.

Violence was the only thing that stood out clearly. The reminder of why he must resist her. Of what he must spare her and all of his people from.

He pulled himself away from the wall and headed toward the gym. Simply walking away wouldn't be enough. There had to be a consequence. His body had betrayed him. And he would have to mete out punishment.

That was how she found him, two hours later. In the gym, soaked in sweat, knuckles raw, split and bleeding from punching the bag repeatedly.

"What are you doing?" she asked, standing there, feeling numb.

She was still dizzy and hot and ashamed from that kiss,

and after sulking in her room for a while she'd decided she had to go and find him and…something. Explain herself. Scream at him. Tell him he didn't know her life and he couldn't judge her.

And then she'd walked into his gym and seen him like this. Like a man possessed.

"Zafar," she said, "what are you doing?"

He looked at her this time, eyes black, soulless. He turned away, rolled his shoulders forward, sweat rolling down his back, running over sharp, defined muscles, down to the dip at his spine, just before the curve of his butt, barely covered by his descending suit pants.

He punched the bag again, a spray of pink sweat spreading through the air on contact.

"Stop!" she said, the shout torn from deep inside of her. She didn't care if she was loud. She didn't care if she was a nuisance. She didn't care if she made him angry or made herself seem less useful, or more of a burden.

She shouted it, let it fill the silence of the space.

It seemed to jolt him out of whatever world he was lost in. "What do you want?"

"Maybe you should tape your knuckles before you do that."

He looked down at his hands and lifted one shoulder. "Why?"

"So you don't turn your fists into hamburger."

"Doesn't matter."

"What do you mean it doesn't matter? What's wrong with you?"

"I deserve it," he spat.

"Why? For kissing me?"

"For endangering my entire country, yet again, because I can't seem to think with my brain." The implication was crude, and to Ana, it felt like a slap in the face.

"It only endangers things if I tell. I won't."

"It doesn't change my actions, you telling or not. It doesn't change the fact that *I* haven't."

"Were you kissing me because you love me?"

Those dark eyes swept her up and down. "No."

She nodded slowly. "I think you've changed. Granted, I didn't know the boy you used to be, but the man standing in front of me would never sacrifice anything for love. I doubt he could even feel it."

"I thank you."

"It wasn't a compliment."

"It can be nothing else to me. I have a country to defend, to take into the modern era, and I can't waste surplus energy on abstract emotions that don't matter."

"How can love not matter?"

"Why would it?"

"Because what drives you if not love? Don't you love your people?"

"I am loyal to them. I can hardly love them."

"Love is the fuel that keeps loyalty burning," she said, not sure where she'd found the strength to argue with the man standing in front of her. Because this wasn't her civilized dinner companion, or her dance partner. This was a wholly different beast. A man with scars on his skin and his soul, both cracked and bleeding. A man who radiated barely contained rage and violence.

"Is that right? Is that what keeps your engagement to your precious Tariq so strong? Loyalty fueled by love."

"No," she said, the realization creeping over her slowly. "That's not it. It's…my dad. I…I have to do this, Zafar, because *he* loves me. Because when everything in his life crumbled, when everything in my life crumbled, we were all each other had, and I feel like if I don't do this, I run the risk of losing the one person who was always there for me. The person who gave so much for my happiness."

"What did he give you, Ana? What did your precious

father ever give to you? You said yourself, you were the one who organized his life. You were the one who held it together. He sent you to school, used you as a party planner when you were home."

"He didn't leave me!" she shouted. "And you wouldn't think that would be too spectacular for a parent, but my mother *did*. So something must be difficult about me. Something must make people want to be away from me. But he stuck it out. He stayed. He gave me a home, and a place to come back to. I owe him for that."

"And you don't want to lose him."

"No. I don't. Does that make me sad and pathetic? If so then fine. But I've proven that I'm easy to walk away from, so I think I have just cause to feel paranoid."

"You are not easy to walk away from. Even a man with ice in his chest can see that."

"You walked away, too. So I think basically it's all a bunch of crap."

"I saved you. I ransomed you."

"So now you want a medal for not leaving me out in the desert with a bunch of criminals?"

"I spent the last cent I had on you. I thought it might mean something. That's all. Of course I wouldn't have left you there. I have many faults, and I am heartless, make no mistake, but I also know what is right. And *right* is not leaving an innocent out there like that."

She shook her head. "And when there's no emotion behind that kind of sentiment, it means very little. Hard to have my heart warmed when I know that moment was as fraught for you as the moment you have to choose what color underwear to put on in the morning."

He advanced on her, and she fought the urge to shrink back. She never considered herself brave. She'd never considered herself outspoken, or a fighter, but Zafar made her feel just strong enough to take on the world, somehow. Even when he was the main part of the world she was taking on.

He made her feel loud.

"Intent is irrelevant, as is emotion. Action is all that matters. Result, is all that matters. I poured my heart out to the woman I loved, because of love, and that love didn't stop her from relaying that information to the enemies of my family. It didn't stop them from brutally killing my mother and father. In front of me."

That stopped her short, cold dread making her fingers tingle. "Zafar..."

"Intentions mean nothing," he ground out. "Not when everyone is dead and you're sent out to the desert to rot. Tell me then, what did love mean? What did it fuel?"

"Zafar..."

"You can think what you want, what you *need*. But love is a trap, Ana. A lie. It is being used, in this case, to keep you in line. To manipulate you as it was used to manipulate me. That's the purpose of love."

"No. I can't believe that."

"Why? Because if you did then you would have no reason to do what you're told?"

"Because I would have nothing!" she exploded, her hands trembling, her stomach pitching. "You are the most horrible, horrible man. Stay here and pound the skin off your hands. I don't give a damn."

He advanced on her then, reaching around her waist and tugging her hard up against his body. He lowered his head, his nose nearly touching hers. "No, you couldn't. Because if you believed me...there would be nothing to hold you back, and then you might have to do something out of the box, something that takes you beyond your safe little world."

He dipped his head and took her mouth, hard and swift, his lips nearly bruising hers.

When he pulled away, she simply stared at him. She wouldn't back down. She wouldn't look away. "I have been kidnapped, then bought, dragged through this godforsaken desert back to your godforsaken castle. I have been held here against my will. I have overseen your personal hygiene and attempted to teach you to waltz. You have no right to call my world little. You have no right to imply that I am not brave. No right to imply that your words could crumble my life. I'm stronger than that. I'm better than that."

She tugged herself free from his grasp and spun on her heel, turning to walk out of the room.

"A big speech, *habibti*. And yet, you are still doing everything you're supposed to be doing. You are so well-trained."

She gritted her teeth and kept walking, trying to ignore the echo of truth in the words that settled in her bones.

CHAPTER TEN

THEY SPENT THE next several days avoiding each other. Zafar knew she was avoiding him because every so often he would be walking down a corridor and he could hear footsteps, or see a brief flash of gold as she disappeared quickly back around a corner.

It was his own fault. He had failed thoroughly in the assignment of acting civilized. Kissing her, yelling at her and then kissing her again.

But she made him feel that way. Wild, reckless and a bit unpredictable. He didn't like any of it.

But the event was tonight. His debut, for lack of a better word, and he wasn't feeling confident. Put him on the back of the horse, in the middle of the desert. Let him fight with his bare hands, to the death, any man who dared threaten his people, and he had no fear.

A ballroom and cocktail shrimp were another matter entirely.

And thanks to that article in the paper, everyone here was watching. Waiting to see if he was a madman. Or a man at all.

He supposed he had no choice but to show them.

He rolled his shoulders forward, already bound up in his tailored suit shirt and jacket. And there were ghosts here. Everywhere. He couldn't sleep at all or their icy fingers invaded his dreams.

He was starting to feel a little crazy, which was what he'd feared would become of him from spending so much time alone in the desert.

Ironic that it was more pronounced now that he was back here. Surrounded by an ever-growing staff, by civilization, by modern life, which should make things easier. Instead he saw shadows everywhere. Claws pulling him down into the abyss every time he closed his eyes. Forcing him to fight against sleep.

But he had no time to deal with it. And no interest in taking pills. They would only drag him under further. God knew if he would ever come back out of something like that.

He laughed, the sound flat and bitter in the empty corridor. He was grim today. Or perhaps he was every day.

Damn, but he was coming apart. He craved space and dry air. Not these obsidian walls that felt more like a tomb than a castle.

And then he saw her, out the window, in the courtyard, her hair like a golden flame, and he could breathe again.

He walked through the hall to the doors as quickly as possible, his heart pounding hard. He needed air. He needed to see her.

"Ana," he said, striding out into the heat. She turned, the sun catching the side of her face, illuminating clear blue eyes, and he could swear his heart started over. As though every day since he was born it had been going, steadily, enduring the beatings life had thrown his way. Now suddenly, it was back at one. New. Untarnished.

The feeling only lasted a moment. Still, the exhilaration of it lingered.

"Ana," he said again. "If you could stop being angry with me for a moment, I would appreciate it. I have a big event for myself personally and my country tonight, and I have no time for you to persist in your tantrum."

Her eyes widened. "In my tantrum? I know you didn't just say that."

"I did," he said. "And I meant it. The fate of a nation is at stake. I doubt a snit is worth the fate of a nation."

"A snit? You undermined my entire belief system and told me I was stupid and imprisoned by my notion of love."

"I didn't say you were stupid."

"Only that my worldview was."

"I didn't come here to fight."

"Oh no? Why are you here?"

"Because this damned thing starts in a little over three hours, I have additional staff infesting my castle and I have to put in an appearance that is both polished and civil and I thought you might…be available to speak to me for a moment."

"About?"

"Tell me that I can do this," he said. He hated displaying this level of weakness. This level of need. That he had to use her as an anchor for his sanity. To remind him he was a man, and that somewhere in his past he had been a man who understood these types of things. A man who could walk into a room full of people and command it, command them.

He didn't know why he thought he could get all of that from her. Except he wasn't getting it from the palace. The palace was splintering him, his mind, his thoughts. And the nights were getting so bad.

She somehow made it all seem better. She made it all seem clear. Her grace and poise made him feel like he could absorb some of it himself. Like it existed in the world and all he had to do was reach out and take it.

When he was left to himself, to his own devices, he couldn't find it.

"You need a pep talk?" she asked.

"I didn't say that."

"You sort of did."

"So, what if I do?"

"I didn't think you needed anyone. Fierce sand pirate that you are."

He frowned. "Are you joking?"

"Yes. Humor. I've even made time for it in my unexciting life. You should try it sometime."

"I've never had much time for joking. I've been too busy…"

"Surviving. Making amends. Wreaking havoc on your horrible uncle's men. I know. But now you're here. And you're going to have to play the part of suave, capable ruler. Check in your pockets for loose charisma if you need to."

He felt a laugh rise in his throat, escape his lips. "This is why I needed to see you," he said.

"Why?" she asked.

"Because you make things feel…not as heavy. You make my chest feel lighter. Breathing is a bit easier."

"You've been having trouble breathing?" she asked, the look in her eyes intensely sad.

"It's this place."

"Can you tell me? Everything?"

"I wouldn't," he said.

"Why?"

"I would hate to make your chest heavy, too."

Ana blinked, her eyes stinging. And she couldn't blame it on the sun. Something in her felt like it was being twisted, tied up in knots. Like he was holding on to vital pieces of her and manipulating them somehow.

She swallowed, then nodded. "I know. It's okay. I'm just glad I made you able to breathe. Zafar, you can do this."

"And you can't be there."

"I know."

"But I will remember this."

"Our conversation?"

"How it made me feel."

She took a deep breath. "Why are you being so nice to me? A few days ago you kissed me and then you freaked out at me and…and I don't get where we stand."

"Something about being near you…your civilization tactics have worked, clearly, and I feel more connected with that, with the more polished side of myself when I'm with you," he said, his voice rough, dark eyes compelling. "And beyond that…I want you. But there is nothing that can be done about that. I can do nothing to compromise the relations Al Sabah has with Shakar. And I can offer you nothing but an isolated life here in this glorified graveyard. I would never ask it of you. Which means the only thing that can come from my wanting you is sex. And that isn't sufficient, either."

"I know," she said. But it didn't stop her from feeling the same way. From wanting him. Even while she was still mad at him for the crap that he'd pulled the other day.

But the truth was, he was right. She'd been thinking about it, and nothing else, ever since their confrontation in the gym. And he was right.

She was afraid. Afraid of losing her father's love. His approval. And she did so much to make sure she never did. To make herself important to him so that he couldn't just leave her, too. To be quiet, to be good so that at the very least, if she wasn't important, she wasn't in the way.

And the reason things had felt so different since she'd come to Al Sabah was simple. There were no shackles here. There was no one looking at her with disapproval or expectation. She had to make her own decisions to survive, to keep sane, and there was no one to guide those decisions.

It made her see things a little bit differently. It made her see herself differently.

It made her see herself. Not as other people saw her,

but just through her own eyes. And it was different than she'd imagined. She looked at herself and saw the Stepford Daughter. Someone who was doing just as she was told so that she wouldn't make waves.

Someone who was earning favor with good deeds. And she wasn't even certain her father had ever asked for those things from her. But she'd been so afraid. After her mother left she'd wondered what she'd done to make it happen. Had been consumed with ensuring she never had to endure another abandonment like that.

And it had all made sense. Doing right kept things together, doing wrong, like her mother, made it fall apart.

She hadn't even realized how much of that reasoning was borne of fear. The fear that saying no to one of her father's requests would make him leave her. That she would be left with no one.

It made her think of Tariq. It made her question her feelings for him. Made her wonder if she was just agreeing to marry him, if she only thought she loved him, because it was the course that would make the least waves.

Because what she felt for Zafar was like nothing else ever. And no, she was sure she didn't love Tariq. Under the circumstances, that was impossible. But shouldn't a bit of the lust and need spill over to a future spouse? Shouldn't some of the heat and flame she felt for Zafar be there for the man she loved? Instead, all she felt for Tariq was a drive to cement their union. Almost like he was the finish line of her good deeds.

The thought made her feel…it made her feel frightened. And more uncertain than she'd ever felt in her life.

Like a butterfly breaking out of a cocoon. But her wings felt wrinkled and wet, and she just wanted to climb back inside and curl up. Go back to sleep. Back to feeling like security was all she needed, rather than feeling curiosity about the size of the world. About how high she could fly.

Except now it was too late to stuff herself back in the cocoon. But she wasn't ready for more yet, either.

"You'll do fine tonight, Zafar," she said. "And I really hope people realize how lucky they are to have you. I hope they feel everything you've given for them."

"What if they only remember what I took?"

And she realized she didn't have an answer for him. She was just a scared girl who had no idea what she was doing with her life, no idea what she wanted. And she was trying to tell a man who had witnessed unspeakable tragedy, who had lived his life in exile, who now had to rule a country, what to do. Trying to offer reassurance in a situation that very few people on the entire planet would ever have to face. If there was even anyone else dealing with it.

Zafar was alone. In his duty. And she couldn't walk with him. Couldn't hold his hand. Couldn't lead him in the waltz or remind him to smile.

She ached to do those things. To be there to help him. Not because it was the right thing, but because for some reason she wanted to stand beside this man while he tried to fix the broken things in his country.

"Just..." She cleared her throat. "Just make sure you use the right fork. All sins can be forgiven in light of good table manners."

"Then it is a good thing I had an excellent teacher."

If the palace empty made Zafar feel like he was enclosed in a crypt, full of people it felt like a crowded crypt, and that was even worse.

Leaders from around the world were in attendance. And some of Al Sabah's wealthiest citizens.

Tariq was not in attendance thanks to the damaged relationship between Al Sabah and Shakar. But in truth, Zafar wasn't in any way sad about it. If Ana's fiancé were present, he would feel obligated to send her back with him and damn appearances.

But he wasn't. Which meant Zafar could keep her, if only for a little while longer. Just until he had a chance to think of a solution.

Yes, because you've been working on that so diligently since you brought her here.

In truth, he knew he had not. Because he liked having her around. And if the sins of his past didn't prove what a bastard he was, then surely that did.

He affected a false smile and directed it at the very lovely ambassador from Sweden, who was currently giving him a winning smile of her own, trying to entice him to come and talk to her, he was certain.

She was lovely. Pale, with the same kind of Nordic beauty that Ana possessed. And yet, on her it was a bit too stark, unwelcoming. Looking at Ana was like stepping into winter. Crisp and clear and bright.

The ambassador started to move toward him, and he started looking for exits. Everyone wanted to talk to him. For hours now, he had been making conversation. Likely more conversation than he'd ever made in his life, and it had all occurred on one night.

He looked around the glittering ballroom, scanning the surrounding for an excuse to sidestep the woman making her way to him. He looked up, into the shadowy balconies that were set into the wall of the ballroom, and he saw a flash of red that sent his pulse into overdrive.

Ana wouldn't show up, would she? She had no reason to. She had every reason to hate him, considering the way he'd treated her a few days earlier. So then, perhaps that would be incentive for her to come, to see him make a fool of himself in front of dignitaries and kings.

He looked harder into the shadows, but didn't see any more movement. No more red.

He started moving toward the back door of the room, not caring how it looked. Not caring that he was surely ignoring people who wanted his attention. He was a sheikh now, after all, and it would stand to reason that he would have important business to do.

A brief flash of memory filtered through his mind.

When you see her...across the crowded ballroom...and you make your way to her...you have something better to do than talk about the weather.

It certainly wasn't the weather on his mind. He looked around him, took a sharp breath and continued on.

No one needed to know he was chasing after a woman. No one needed to know that he was following his weakness yet again.

There would be hell to pay for this, later. In nightmares. In physical pain, probably meted out in the gym. But right at the moment it seemed worth it. It seemed necessary.

He walked through the double doors and into the corridor, passing the security he hired for the event without making eye contact, as he went to the curved staircase that led up to the recessed balconies.

He put his hand on the railing, his fingers sliding over smooth, white stone as he made his way upstairs. He listened as intently as he could, keeping his footsteps silent. Wondering if he might hear the whisper of her gown's fabric. Hear her breathe.

He heard footsteps, and then, a soft, warm body collided with his with a muffled "Mmph."

He reflexively grabbed the person by the arms and held them out, steady, so he could get a look. "Ana," he said.

"Guilty."

"You aren't supposed to be here," he said.

"I know, but I had to make sure you were doing okay."

"And what did you observe?"

She lifted her chin. "You're the best looking man in the room."

"That, my dear, could be construed as non-bland conversation."

"I know. I don't…I don't think I care."

"Ana, you don't know what you're inviting."

"I probably do. I think…Zafar…I've been thinking. But I don't want to talk just now." And then she was leaning into him, soft lips pressing against his. His body was on fire in an instant, all caution, all common sense gone as her tongue traced the seam of his mouth gently.

He opened to her, and let her explore, let her take.

Because he was powerless to do anything else.

"Do you have any idea what you're doing?" he whispered.

"No," she said.

Ana had to admit it, because it was the truth. She didn't know what she was doing. She'd never kissed a man quite so passionately. She'd never wanted a man with quite so much ferocity.

She'd known she couldn't show her face at the party. She wasn't supposed to be here. No one could ever know she was here.

But she hadn't been able to resist. She'd put on the red dress she'd worn to dinner. And eventually she'd gotten up the courage to slip up to the balcony to catch a glimpse of him.

No one would recognize her, even if they saw her. Not from that distance. At least, that had been her reasoning.

Now there was no reasoning at all. She hadn't planned this. She hadn't expected it. She had no idea what it would mean for her future, or why she was taking such a chance. She only knew that she couldn't seem to stop herself.

That she didn't want to stop.

That for the first time in longer than she could remember she wasn't getting tripped up pondering the whys and why nots of every action she performed. That she wasn't worrying about what other people would think. Or what they might wish she would do differently.

How could she worry about it when nothing had ever felt so right? When the press of his mouth against hers seemed essential?

And then she found herself backed against the hard stone wall, the cool rock at her back, the heat and hardness of Zafar in front of her. She wrapped her arms around his neck, clung to him, poured everything she had into the kiss.

Desperation. Passion. Confusion. Anger.

She felt all of it, swirling inside of her, creating a perfect storm of emotion that seemed to push her harder, faster.

She was so consumed with it, with him, that she hardly realized her fingers had gone to the knot of his tie. That she was loosening it, tugging it from around his neck. That she was working the buttons on his shirt as quickly as possible.

She didn't realize it until her hand came up against hot, bare skin, rough chest hair that tickled her fingertips as she swept them beneath his collar so that she could get closer to him.

He kissed her hard, pressing his body to hers. And she could feel the hard ridge of his arousal against her thigh, evidence of how much he wanted her. That she wasn't feeling this alone.

And she wanted to weep with the triumph.

Because someone felt passion for her. Because even if Zafar only wanted sex, and her body, she was certain it was more need than anyone else had truly felt for her in years, if ever.

Her father wanted her to help him maintain the status quo. To help him shore up his profits. Tariq wanted her for a revenue increase to his country.

No one wanted *her*. And no one was honest about it.

Except that wasn't true now. Zafar wanted her. And if there was one thing she knew, even with her near nonexistent experience with men, it was that erections didn't lie. It was blunt, brutal honesty at its most basic and she reveled in it.

She arched against him, pressing her aching breasts to his chest, her heart thundering so loud and hard she was certain he could hear it, certain he could feel it.

He abandoned her mouth and kissed the side of her neck, her collarbone. The curve of her breast revealed by her dress.

"This is a beautiful dress," he said. "But it doesn't give me enough of you."

He reached behind her and tugged at the zipper tab, pulling it down and loosening the dress so that it hung off her curves. Then he pushed against the single strap that held it up and it fell to the floor, leaving her standing there in a darkened stairwell in nothing but a black strapless bra and matching panties.

If she'd been thinking clearly, she probably would have protested, or expressed some form of outrage. But she wasn't. So she didn't.

He put his hands on her waist, ran his fingertips over the line of her spine. The action, so simple, so seemingly sedate, sent a riot of need through her that made her breasts ache, made her slick between her thighs.

She'd never known what it was to want a man. Not like this.

He pressed a kiss to the valley between her breasts, then traced a line there with the tip of his tongue. And she shivered.

She laced her fingers in his hair, wanting to hold him there forever, wanting to tighten her hold and tug him back up to her lips so she could kiss him again.

She just wanted. With everything in her, with her entire being. And damn anyone else's opinion. Damn the consequences. Damn quietness.

He raised his head and kissed her again, and she made quick work of the rest of the buttons on his shirt. She pressed her palms flat against his hard, muscular chest, sliding her hands downward, to his stomach.

She'd never seen a man who looked like him. He'd completely shocked her the first time she'd seen him without a shirt. Bronzed and chiseled and so sexy it nearly hurt.

She'd never noticed how sexy men were because she'd never let herself see. Because she'd been so committed to an ideal she'd shut that part of herself off and channeled controlled bits of it to the "appropriate" place.

This was like a dam burst, and there was nothing appropriate about where her desire was being channeled. And she didn't care. Not in the least.

All that mattered was how amazing he felt. How right it felt to have his lips against hers. How she felt like she would die if she didn't have more of him.

All of him.

"I want you," she said, the words torn from deep inside of her, from a place she hadn't known existed. One filled with passion, with desire that stood apart from expectation and judgment. A place that was all hers.

And, in this moment, Zafar's.

He put his hands on her lower back, pushed his finger down beneath the waistband of her sheer black panties, the reached in farther, cupping her.

The intimate contact shocked her a little bit, but not enough to make her stop. And then he dipped between her thighs, his fingers skimming her slick folds and she jumped, arching into him.

"Shh," he said, kissing her, cutting off the strangled cry she hadn't realized had been on her lips. "It's okay. Do you like it?" He stroked her slowly and her whole body shook, internal muscles she'd been unaware of until that moment contracting tight.

"Yes," she whispered, letting her head fall back. He kissed her jaw, her neck, and pushed a finger into her, slowly. Her breath caught and she held on to his shoulders.

"Still good?" he asked, pressing deeper, moving one finger farther forward to her clitoris as he stroked in and out of her gently with another.

"Yes." She closed her eyes and leaned into him, widening her stance so he had easier access to her body.

She shuddered as he continued to subject her to sensual torture with his hands, his lips hot on her neck, his tongue sliding over her tender skin.

Everything in her went tight, so tight she could scarcely breathe. She thought she would break. And just when she thought she couldn't endure anymore, his final stroke over the sensitized bundle of nerves made everything in her release.

It was like chains that had been holding her, for months, years, all of her life, had suddenly let go. And she was falling, weightless, pleasure coursing through her body. And there was nothing, no thought, no worry, no fear of judgment, or anything else.

Nothing but the white-hot pleasure that burned on and on, leaving her scorched, but unharmed. Leaving her new.

Like a phoenix from the ashes.

And for one whole minute, as she rested against his chest, her breathing returning to normal, she felt stronger, more sure, than she ever had before.

But the minute passed too soon.

And then she realized she was in a stairwell in nothing but her underwear, and she'd just let the man who was holding her captive, the man who was not her fiancé, bring her to orgasm with his hands.

There weren't enough swearwords. There really weren't. So she went through them all in her head. Twice.

And then she said one of them, the worst one she could think of, out loud because why not? Only Zafar was here. And he had just seen the most shameful, embarrassing moment of her life. She didn't have to worry too much about manners in this case. Especially not when he was holding her half-naked body against his.

But he was the one who drew away suddenly, his dark eyes haunted, his hands shaking as he pushed them through his hair. He was pale, a sheen of sweat on his gray-tinged forehead.

"I...I am sorry. Forgive me." And she was pretty sure he wasn't talking to her. "Forgive me," he said again, buttoning up his shirt as he walked down the stairs, away from her, leaving her standing there staring after him, her body buzzing, her head pounding. Her heart aching.

What had she done?

She dropped down to her knees, her legs too weak to hold her up.

"What did you do?" she said out loud.

She shifted so that she was sitting, her back to the wall, and she picked up her dress from the ground, sliding it onto her lap, holding it up over her breasts. A tear slid down her cheek. She hadn't even felt tears building, but they were here, and they were falling, faster than she could wipe them away.

If her father knew, if Tariq knew, they would hate her.

And everything would be for nothing. Her whole life, all that quiet, would be for nothing.

She scrunched her face up, lights filtering in from the ballroom below splintering and turning into glittering stars, fractured by her tears.

What had just happened with Zafar had been the single most beautiful moment in her life. In his arms she'd felt alive. She'd felt more like Ana. The Ana who was waking up from hibernation. The Ana she might have been if life really did come with a guarantee.

If she'd been free to grow up without all the baggage. Without all the fear and anxiety that one wrong move would see her abandoned by both parents.

But the beauty of the moment withered and died quickly. And it left behind the reality. She had betrayed the man she'd promised to marry. She'd done what she wanted to do, instead of doing what was right.

And she feared that, just like her mother's priceless porcelain doll, everything was too broken to be put back together.

That she had, once again, cut the tether that held the people she loved in her life.

It couldn't happen again. She could never speak of it. She couldn't even remember it. She would weather the rest of her captivity, and then she would go back to Shakar. Back to Tariq and her father.

They would never see how badly broken she was inside. And everything could go on as it was supposed to.

There was no other option.

CHAPTER ELEVEN

"We have to leave."

Zafar's voice pierced her sleep-fogged brain. She looked out the window and saw that it was still gray out. Ana rolled over in bed, put her hands over her face. "Right now?"

"Yes," he bit out. "Now."

"What about liaising and being diplomatic?" Cold dread washed over her and she sat upright. "Unless you talked to Tariq."

"No," he bit out, "I didn't. But I have been awake all night and I have decided that you failed in your task."

"I...failed." The words sent a cold stone of dread sinking down into the bottom of her stomach. So strange, because it shouldn't matter if Zafar thought she'd failed at something. But failing, being wrong, being worthless, was such an ingrained fear that no matter who spoke, the words had the power to wound her. "Why? What did they say about you? What did they say about the ball?"

"Oh," he bit out, "they loved me. They've called Rycroft a flaming idiot and said that he was slandering me in his article. Suave, they said, and handsome. But, Ana, I am not civilized, no matter what they say. And that was your job. To civilize me. And you did not. Why else would I be keeping a woman locked in my palace, keeping her from her father, her fiancé, giving no notice that she wasn't dead, rather than sending her straight back to her home, regardless of the fallout? There is no honor in that. No civility."

"Zafar…you did what you had to do."

"Stop it," he growled. "Stop trying to placate me. Stop trying to smooth things over. Some things cannot be fixed. Some things are not in your power to repair." He paced at the foot of her bed, frightening and mystifying in his anger. "Do not absolve me. It is a heresy. You don't know the sins you're trying to forgive."

"Fine. Stay in your self-imposed hell then, Zafar Nejem. I don't care. But make good on your word and take me back home. You can castigate yourself for all your wrongdoing on the way."

She flung off the covers and got out of bed, realizing she had nothing to pack. That nothing here was hers. That she would leave everything, including Zafar, behind and there would be no evidence that she was ever here. No evidence he had ever been part of her life.

That he'd been the first man to kiss her passionately. The first man to touch her intimately. The first man to give her an orgasm.

The first man to make her wonder if there was more to life than she was allowing herself to live. The first man to make her want to stand out in the open and scream at the sky so people would know she was there. So she would stop just blending in.

And she would just leave it. Leave him. It would be nothing more than a blip on the radar of her life. A couple weeks out of time, with nothing more than the life she'd led at home with her father coming before, and nothing but her marriage to Tariq after.

All the anger drained out of her, leaving her lips feeling cold. Leaving her feeling dizzy.

"That is the question. Commercial flights to Shakar

were barred during my uncle's rule. If I fly you there, we may create more of a spectacle than we would like."

"Take me back the way we came in," she said. She pictured it then, the journey to the palace on the back of his horse, the wind, harsh and arid and clean in her face.

"On a horse?"

She nodded. "Yes. No one will have to know. Leave me where I was taken. I'll lie about what happened."

"It's not so simple, and you know that. Were it that simple we could have done that from the beginning."

"I know. But…I'll lie to buy you time. Or I'll tell Tariq how you saved my life, but I'll make sure that I express nothing but deep gratitude to you and to the people of Al Sabah. I won't let there be a war."

She didn't know where the strength was coming from. She'd always liked to fix things. Had always tried to take a chance at reclaiming her life. At fixing what she'd broken.

So odd how, in all ways, she saw Zafar in herself. Guilt, blame and shame, a constant companion, and the need to try and remake everything, make it new again, fix the damage caused by their actions, an ever-present drive and burden.

But this was different. This was true conviction. A vow she was making to him that she would keep no matter what.

"Trust me," she said. "I'll fix it."

"Why do you want to do it this way?"

"Because…because I need to finish my adventure before I stop having them. Especially sad since this was my first one."

"Is that what this has been for you, *habibti*?" he asked. "An adventure?"

She shook her head, her throat tightening. "No. It's been more than that, but I'm not sure what to say. I don't even know what I feel."

He let out a heavy breath, then straightened, every inch the commanding king. "Dress yourself. Pack adequate clothing for three to five days of travel. The desert is unpredictable and often there are obstacles that prevent things from going as quickly as we might like."

"Sandstorms."

"Yes. But you will be with me. I will not let any harm come to you." She felt like he was talking about more than just the desert. Like more than just physical harm. "I promise you that."

"I believe you."

"I will gather tents and food. It will not be as rough of a journey as it was coming here."

"And will you bring servants?"

Their eyes locked, tension crackling between them, and the despair she'd felt last night in the stairwell was burned away by the heat that ignited in her veins. "No," he said. "It is best not to involve any more people than necessary."

She nodded, feeling like a hand was tightening around her throat. "No, that wouldn't do."

"Not at all."

"I'll get ready, then."

"I will wait out in the courtyard. No one can see us leave. There is still extra staff here. People who are not mine."

"I understand."

He nodded once and turned and walked out of the room, leaving her standing there, feeling like, yet again, her life had been turned completely upside down.

Strange how she was coming to expect it. How it seemed to jar something loose in her. How she sort of enjoyed it.

Well, it was coming to an end now. Because she was going back to Shakar. Back to Tariq.

She sucked in a shaking breath and started looking for a bag to pack her clothes in.

* * *

"Ready?" Zafar looked down from his position on his horse, his face mostly covered by his headdress.

She nodded her pale head. She looked…different. There was a quiet strength to her posture, her hair drawn back into a tight bun. He had always seen her as extremely self-possessed, the exception being the brief emotional meltdown she'd had when he'd first rescued her from her kidnappers.

But now she was somewhere beyond self-possessed. She had a core of steel, and he could see it. Could see that she wouldn't be bending. But he didn't know what she'd set her will to. And that was the part that concerned him most.

Aside from what being alone with her might do. Aside from what his own intentions might actually be. God have mercy on his tattered soul.

Last night he had been inexcusable with her. And no mater the outcome, he had to return her to her fiancé. To her father.

He had been wrong to keep her.

And he had been more than wrong to touch her. In that moment, when he'd pressed her against the wall and kissed her, when he'd put his hand between her thighs and felt all of her heat about his fingertips…he'd been conscious of the gates of hell opening up behind him, the flames licking his back, demons threatening to pull him in.

But not before they'd spurred him to commit the deadliest sin possible. A fitting end to his life. Except it wouldn't really be the end. He couldn't even count on being dragged into the comparable bliss of hell.

He would have to stay in this life and deal with consequences. Yet again.

Consequences he'd earned with his libido, with his disgusting lack of control. Control he'd thought he'd found out in the desert, deprived of every good thing. But back here, back where he'd started, he seemed to lose all the strength the desert had infused in him.

This, then, would be the test.

He reached down. "Need help?"

She shook her head and approached the horse, putting her small bag of clothes into the saddlebag with his other supplies before pulling herself up behind him onto the horse, wrapping one arm around his waist, her thighs bracketing his, her tempting heat against his back.

Soon the desert sun would block that. Would make it impossible to distinguish her body from the arid air.

He took the head scarf from his lap and handed it back to her. "Take this, *habibti*. You need protection from the sun."

She said nothing, but she took it from him, and the movements behind him seemed to indicate that she was following orders.

She wrapped her arm back around his waist, leaning forward, her chin digging into his back. The contact, and the pain, soothed him.

"Let's go," she said.

His agreement came in the form of spurring his horse on and heading toward the back gate of the palace. Out into the desert.

Here, he would find his salvation or his damnation.

And he wasn't entirely sure which one he was hoping for.

He didn't push his horse the way he had that first day they'd met. Instead, they rode at a more decent pace, and they arrived at the oasis just as the sun was becoming too punishing for her to endure.

"We'll stop here," he said, indicating the outcrop of rocks. "There is water just behind the rocks. I'll set up the tent there. Under the trees."

He got off the horse, and she dismounted too, pausing to stroke the beast's nose. "He needs a name, Zafar."

Zafar turned and looked at her, brow raised. "Why?"

"Calling him *horse* is stupid. I don't call you Grumpy Man, do I?" Approaching the subject of the horse's name was easier than confronting what had passed between them last night.

Thinking about the horse's name was easier, too. Which was why she'd spent the silent ride to the oasis pondering that instead of how being in his arms had felt. Of how hard and muscular he was, and about just how much she'd enjoyed contact with that hard muscular body last night.

Yes, thinking of a name for the Horse was much safer.

"I was thinking Apollo," she said, following Zafar to the oasis, where he was headed, bundled-up tent in hand.

"Why?"

"It's transcendent. Godlike."

"He is neither."

"Excuse me. Are you maligning the noble steed carrying us through the desert on its back?"

"I'm hardly maligning him. I just don't think it's a good name for him."

"You've had him for how long?"

He tossed her a quick glance before setting the tent down by the water and continuing on in his labor. "Nine years."

She shook her head. "And you haven't named him. Any name is better than Horse."

"Not Apollo."

"Achilles. Archimedes. Aristotle?"

"Why Greek and why all with *A?*"

"He seems Greek. And also I'm moving alphabetically."

"He is an Arabian horse. He should have an Arabic name."

"All right, name away."

"Sawdaa. Means black."

She crossed her arms beneath her breasts and didn't bother to keep herself from looking at his backside while he worked on the tent. "Original."

"Better then *Horse,* yes?" he asked, finishing with the tent's frame.

"Barely."

"All right then, what would you call him? Not the name of a Greek god, demigod or philosopher, please."

"Since you said *please.* How about Sadiqi. Friend."

"I know what it means."

"Well, he's your friend."

"He's my horse."

"You love nothing, Zafar? Nothing at all? Are you so determined to keep it that way that you can't even name your horse?"

He straightened and shot her a dark glare. "You know nothing about what I've been through. Telling you...it doesn't make it real for you. You don't know what I had to do to survive. To move forward. To make myself a valuable person."

"I admit," she said, walking down to where he stood and taking a position beneath the shade of a palm, "my life story has less blood spilled than yours. But I know what it's like to try to change yourself so you can have some value. I know what it is to break everything."

She closed her eyes and leaned her head back against the tree as she let her least favorite memory wash over her. "I ran through my mother's sitting room. She had her own sitting room, a parlor for entertaining her friends. And she kept her collection of antique dolls in there. She loved them." She swallowed. "I was always loud. Brash. And I moved too quickly. So one day I ran through her sitting room and I knocked against the doll cabinet."

She could still remember the little sandy-haired doll

tipping off the shelf, landing wedged between the locked cabinet door and the shelf. And she'd prayed so hard that it wasn't broken.

Her mother had come running in and opened the cabinet, and pulled out the now-hollow-faced doll, the porcelain reduced to dust on the bottom on the ground.

"I broke it," she said, trying so hard not to picture the look on her mother's face. Trying and failing. "My mother said…she said I was making her crazy. That I was always ruining things. That I'd ruined everything. Ruined things she'd loved." She swallowed the lump that was building in her throat. "I don't think I was one of the things she loved anymore."

Ana breathed in deep. "She left the next day. I'm twenty-two years old, and I know my mother didn't leave me because of a broken doll. I know there were other things. I know she probably had some problems. But then…then all I could think was…if I were more careful. If I had taken more care to listen to her, to move slower. Maybe be quieter and more poised. More helpful….if I had been those things she wouldn't have left. And if I wasn't careful…maybe my father would leave, too. After all, I ruin everything."

Her voice choked off. She hated this. Hated that she was doing this now, with him. But this was the truth of it. The truth of her life, that she hid behind fake smiles and feeling polished and pulled together.

She'd pulled her hair into a bun and learned how to say yes to everything, to be efficient, to do what was expected of her.

"You do not ruin everything," he said, his voice rough. Then he swore, vilely, harshly. On her behalf. It made her stomach tighten.

"Zafar…"

He crossed to where she was standing, every inch the desert marauder he'd been when she'd first met him, only a small wedge of his face visible, the rest concealed by his headdress.

He tugged the bottom of it down. And she saw the difference from the first day she'd met him. His clean-shaven jaw. She'd done that. She'd changed him, at least on the outside.

It made her feel strange. Powerful.

"You did not make her leave," he said. "My mother was taken from me by death. No force in heaven or hell could have removed her from me, no matter my behavior, had she been given a choice. And it is not because I was a better son than you were daughter. I was dissolute. Lazy. Obsessed with women, sex. And yet she loved me, because of *her* heart, not because of mine. Your mother's rejection... it was not because of you. It was her heart, *habibti*. It was her heart that was damaged, not yours."

"You say that but...you claim you don't even have a heart. How do you know all this?"

"Because," he said, his voice hoarse, "these past years my emotions have been dried out, unused. Dead. If anything on earth would make me wish to have them back... Ana, it's you."

A tear rolled down her cheek and she didn't bother to wipe it away. She had always tried to be who she thought she had to be. Had always tried so hard to be perfect.

But with Zafar, something in her was unleashed. The wild child she'd been born as, maybe. The girl who'd run through the halls of her family home, who'd liked to laugh and be silly. Who hadn't trembled at the thought of having a grade point average that dipped below perfect. Who hadn't been consumed with making sure she improved every situation, rather than being a bother.

She'd constructed a shield for herself. So perfect and shiny. And she wanted it gone now. She didn't want to be the person she'd built herself to be. She wanted to be the person she was born to be.

She remembered her despair last night after their near-lovemaking session in the stairwell. It hadn't been because she was sorry. It had been because she was afraid. Afraid of wanting something for her, something that her father wouldn't want for her.

And Tariq…clearly she had to examine her options there. She did not love him. She'd never been more certain of that. She'd wanted to marry him just to please her father; she'd just been too stubborn to acknowledge it.

Right now, she knew what she wanted.

"Zafar," she said, her voice a near whisper. She cleared her throat. She wasn't going to ask for this with any shame, any embarrassment. "I want you to unmake me. Out here. Just like it happened for you. I don't want to be who I was. I don't want to be weak. I don't want to be quiet. I don't want to live for anyone else. I just want…Zafar, I want. For me. Please…"

"You want to be…unmade?" he asked, his voice rough.

"That's what you told me the desert did for you. That it took the boy you were and made you the man you were. That you had to unmake yourself so you could reemerge the man you needed to be. I need that."

She pushed away from the tree and closed the distance between them. "I have spent so much of my life walking on tiptoes. Trying to be the person I thought I needed to be in order to be bearable. But it's not bearable to me anymore. I don't like me. I am trained to do as I'm told, and that day in the gym…you were right about me, Zafar—I dare not step out of line because I'm afraid if I do my father, or my friends, or the teachers I had who were more like mentors, that they would decide I wasn't worth the trouble. So I made myself indispensable to them. Want to plan a party? I'll help. Need me to marry a sheikh so you can secure easy access to oil? I can do that, too. I'll even do my best to love him. So…no one could get rid of me because I made everything easy for them."

"Except me," he said. "You don't make my life easier. You make it a damn sight harder."

"I'm glad," she said. "I'm…I'm so glad. And I know you want to get rid of me, but honestly, I can't blame you."

"Circumstances being what they are," he said, his voice rough.

"Yes. Naturally."

"How would I go about unmaking you, *habibti*?" he asked, his tone lowering, dark eyes intense on hers. She looked away, her breath coming in short, uneven bursts. "Ana," he said, his voice surprisingly soft. She looked back at him.

Then she turned away, running to the edge of the water. And tilted her head back, the sun scorching her face. She opened her mouth and took a breath, air burning all the way down.

And then she screamed. Her voice echoing all around them. Her. Ana. She was here. She wanted to be heard. She wanted to make a sound. Make an impact that was bigger than the dreams of other people. Have a life that meant more than serving the desires of other people.

Then she turned, shaking, her throat raw, and walked back toward Zafar, his expression looking as though it was carved out of stone.

"I don't want to be quiet," she said.

"And so you are not."

She shook her head. "No. I'm not. And I want…I want more than that even." She met his eyes, dark and intense. "Make love with me."

"Ana…I can offer you nothing. Nothing beyond a physical encounter. Is that really what you want?"

"Yes."

She debated whether or not to tell him she was a virgin. And decided against it. Because, given her very obviously inexperienced kissing technique, he'd probably guessed. And she didn't want to bring it up and make things any more awkward than they were.

"Why would you want me?" he asked. "I am a great sinner. Responsible for the near fall of a nation. Plus, I have not treated you admirably."

On that, she would give him total honesty. He was giving her honesty, the look in his dark eyes haunted. He needed to know why she would choose him, and she had so many reasons.

"Because, before you…I can't remember the last time I felt this way. Not just the desire, the sense of wildness. That's what it is, Zafar. I've felt from the moment I first met you that you'd opened up this part of me I'd tried to choke out. A part I'd thought just didn't exist anymore. But I was wrong. It's the part of myself I closed off. Because I was afraid of being rejected. But I wasn't afraid with you. Mainly because I wanted you to let me go." She laughed. "I didn't have to please you and I just pleased myself and I found this part of me I'd buried. A part of myself I'm so glad to have back."

She put her hand on his cheek. "And as for the desire… I've never known anything like this. I don't want to go my whole life without exploring it."

"Attraction is easy enough to come by. You will find it, maybe with Tariq."

"Not like this," she said. "Tell me honestly, and then I'll leave it alone. Has another woman made you feel the way that I do? You told me this wasn't normal. That this was stronger than most lust. It must be, because I spent most of high school being a paragon, focusing on school and things that made me…useful. And then even more in college because of Tariq, because of that alliance. Even my

major, International Studies…it was all for the future with
him. To be useful in that future and that meant forsaking
anything else. But I can't ignore this, and that right there,
that says something. But if it's not the same for you, then
tell me. And maybe I can let it go."

He looked away. "I have never felt this before."

"Then take me," she said. "Have me. Give us both this
gift."

"I cannot," he said, the denial dragged from him.
"Whether you like the idea of it or not, according to custom, you belong to the Sheikh of Shakar, and my taking you is grounds for war. I have caused a war because
I couldn't resist a woman. I caused death and destruction
because of my lust."

"But I don't want to manipulate you. I just want you,"
she said. "I have belonged to other people for a long time.
Tonight…I don't want to be Tariq's property. And I don't
want to be yours. I want to be mine. And I know what I
want."

He growled and dipped his head, kissing her hard and
deep, swiftly, pulling away from her abruptly. "Be sure," he
said. "Be very sure, because I can't stop myself. I am shaking, down to my bones, Ana. For you. Because of you."

Her heart tightened, ached. "I'm sure," she whispered,
kissing him. "I'm sure."

"I am so glad I don't have to make conversation about
salad forks now. Because all of those times, what I wanted
to say was that you were beautiful. That I wanted you to
the point of distraction. That your body is enough to make
grown men drop to their knees and give thanks to God
that they were born men. I wanted to tell you that your red
dress should be illegal. That taking it off you was one of
the single greatest privileges I'd ever been given. But of
course I could not, because I was relegated to the bland.
But not now."

"No. Not now. Now I just want you. All of you."

"You don't know what you're asking for," he said, tracing a line over her cheekbone with his fingertip, down to her lips.

"Then show me."

"Ana…"

"Zafar, what do you see when you look at me?"

"Beauty," he said, without hesitating.

"Anything more?"

She looked in his eyes, and she realized she didn't need more. He was here, putting everything on the line for her, betraying himself for the passion that had ignited between them.

There was heat and sand and Zafar.

Everything else burned away.

"There is so much more," he said, his lips on her neck, her collarbone, his hands tugging at the hem of her shirt, drawing it up over her head. "So much," he said, pressing a kiss to the curve of her beast, just above the line of her bra.

"Show me," she said, lacing her fingers in his hair, fighting the release of the sob that was building in her chest, pressure so intense she was afraid she might burst.

He stepped away from her and turned, his back to her, his eyes on the water in front of them. And then he reached in front of his body and started working the tie on his robes, divesting himself of the layers, placing them on the sandy ground, until he was completely naked.

Her breath caught, choked her. She'd never seen a more beautiful sight than the view of him, lit by the sun, his shoulders broad and powerful, the muscles in his back sharply defined, his waist trim, dimples just above his truly glorious butt, round and muscular and just everything she thought a man's backside should be.

And when he turned, she was certain her heart stopped. He was really, well and truly beyond her experience. She'd never seen a naked man in person. She'd seen limited pictures of the male member. But hadn't seen much in the way of erect men. Unwanted spam emails, the contents of which she always closed her eyes against and deleted as quickly as possible, hardly counted.

A textbook drawing outlining the different parts of male anatomy also didn't count.

He was much larger than she'd imagined he might be, but she wasn't worried. She knew that generous size was supposed to be a good thing. So she was fairly certain that, first time, mandatory pain notwithstanding, his proportions were an asset to her.

He made his way back to her and took her hand, leading her to where he'd left his robes laid out on the sand.

He pulled her down to the soft ground with him and pulled her into his strong arms, stroking her hair as he kissed her, as he held her up against the hard, bare length of his body.

She wrapped her arms around his neck, tangled her legs, still clad in jeans, with his. He put his hand on her back, spread his fingers wide over her skin before grasping the clasp of her bra and releasing it, pulling the undergarment off and tossing it aside.

He continued to kiss her, not giving her a moment to be concerned about her nudity as his hands skimmed over her curves, sending delicious sensation all through her body. She already knew how good Zafar could make her feel, with just ten minutes and one hand he'd rocked her world completely. Now, with him pressed to her, his hands roaming her entire body, no scratchy lace between her chest and his, no chance of anyone discovering him, she had a feeling he might truly demolish her world and build a whole new one.

And she didn't mind.

He gripped her hips and pushed her onto her back, settling between her legs, his erection pressed hard and firm into the cradle of her body, still covered by her jeans.

He kissed her deep, his hands bracketing her face then roaming down to cup her breasts, tease her nipples, drawing a hoarse cry from deep within her.

He moved his hand down between her thighs then, stroking her through the denim. She arched against him, needing more. Needing everything.

He undid the snap on her jeans and reached inside, his fingers brushing over the thin fabric of her panties, the touch enticing, the lace's sheer veil adding something to the feeling, making her more sensitive somehow.

Then he reached beneath the web of lace, his fingers touching her damp heat. "Oh, yes," she breathed, resting her head on his shoulder, her fingers curling into his skin, her nails likely digging into his flesh, but she didn't care.

She had to hold on to him, had to keep herself anchored to the ground somehow.

He pushed her pants and underwear down her hips, and she helped, pushing the bundle of fabric off to the side with her foot, then returned to the very important task of kissing him. Everywhere. His lips, his neck, his chest and back to his gorgeous, perfect mouth. She thought of all the years he'd gone without being touched.

Oh, yeah, she knew he'd had lovers. Mistresses. Bed partners. But they hadn't touched him like this. They hadn't wanted to just have his skin against theirs to feel close. Hadn't wanted to touch him because not touching him was as unthinkable as not breathing.

She knew it. She just did.

She could feel herself getting close to the edge again, his hands in between her thighs, stroking and teasing as he'd done that night at the palace.

"Not like that," she said, kissing his neck. "You. Inside me."

"Not yet," he said. "Not yet."

He lowered his head and kissed her between her breasts, before shifting and taking one nipple deep into his mouth, sucking, sliding his tongue over the tightened bud.

Then he worked his way down her body, his lips and tongue creating an erotic path that she was so glad he'd decided to forge.

Then his broad shoulders were spreading her thighs, his breath hot against her sex. And he leaned in, his tongue stroking long and wet over her clitoris. She arched against him, her hands going to his head reflexively. To pull him away, to hold him there, she wasn't sure. But instead of doing anything, she just laced her fingers through his hair and let the dark pull of pleasure drag her under.

Her orgasm swept over her like a wave, crashing through her, robbing her of breath, leaving her spent and shaking in the aftermath. Gasping for air.

And then he was claiming her mouth again, hard and deep, while the head of his penis met the entrance to her body, her slickness easing the way for him as he pushed inside of her.

It was tight, and painful at first. No sharp horrible pain, which some of her friends had professed to experience. But it was still more something to be endured than something she was enjoying. It was so foreign, being filled by another person, being so close to him.

She looked up into his eyes, just as he thrust fully into her, and a sharp cry escaped her lips.

"Are you okay?" he asked, concern written on his face.

"Yes," she said, feeling so full she might burst. "Yes. I'm so much more than okay."

"I didn't know," he said, his voice choked.

"I know. I'm sorry."

"I'm not." He put his hand on her thigh, lifted it so that

her leg was draped over his hip, seating him deeper inside of her. "I'm not."

Then he lowered his head and started moving inside of her, his thrusts steady, measured, and the more he moved, the less it hurt, the more pain gave way to pleasure, discomfort to dissolving and making way for a deep, soul-rending sensation that was building low in her body, in her chest, spreading through her, taking her over.

She wrapped her arms tightly around his neck, beginning to find her own rhythm, moving her hips back against his, bringing her clitoris into contact with his body, like striking a match every time he pushed back inside of her, sending a streak of heat through her veins.

"Zafar," she said, her climax rising inside of her, everything in her tightening to an unbearable degree, preparing for the release she knew would come. A release she wasn't sure she could withstand.

"I'm here," he said, his words labored. "I'm here for you, Ana."

Her name. Not an endearment. *Her* name.

His pace increased, his movements becoming erratic, hard and intense. She cried out her pleasure, ripples of it working its way through her body endlessly.

Then, too soon, far too soon, he withdrew from her, still over her, his hand on his shaft, stroking himself twice until he found his own release, spilling himself before lowering himself to kiss her lips again.

"Ana," he said, breathing hard. "I…"

"Later," she said. "There will time for yelling at me later. I'm so tired now."

"We need to get in the tent." He stroked her cheek with his thumb. "You'll burn out here."

"I can't move."

He hauled himself into a sitting position and scooped her up against his chest, standing, and walking her into the small structure, bigger by quite a bit than the one they'd traveled in at first. "Wait here," he said.

She stood in the center of the bare, clean tent, feeling dizzy. Shocked. Wonderful.

He returned a second later with a large bedroll under his arm. He spread it out on the floor of the tent. "Sleep now," he said. "We'll talk later."

"Will you sleep, too?" she asked.

He shook his head, his dark eyes unreadable. "I don't sleep with anyone."

CHAPTER TWELVE

ANA FELT LIKE she'd been wounded. "Not even with me? Not even…after that?"

"I can't," he said, turned and walked out of the tent, closing the flap behind him.

She lay down on the mattress, her knees curled up to her chest. She had just given everything for this man. Her virginity. Her future.

Because she loved him, she realized that now.

That was why she just wanted to touch him. It was why she wanted him to hold her.

Of all the stupid things.

Loving Zafar wouldn't make her father happy. It would make Tariq very unhappy. Hell, Zafar would probably be pissed, too.

A slow smile spread over her face. She didn't care. She just loved him. It didn't matter if it would make anyone else's life easier. It didn't matter if it made other people unhappy.

She wasn't sacrificing her life to make other people happy. She wasn't marrying a man who didn't inspire her passions. She wasn't marrying a man she didn't love just to make her father love her more. Just to find a piece of security.

She was Analise Christensen. And there had been a

time when she'd had fun. When she'd run instead of walking. When she'd lived loudly.

But she'd let life blow out her spark.

And Zafar had helped her find it again. So this was all his fault, really, and if he didn't like it, he was going to have to deal with it.

Her smile broadened. Two or three weeks ago, she would never have done this. Wouldn't ever have stepped so far off the path she'd been assigned to.

But now she was off that path. Pushing her way through the forest, through the trees and bushes, finding her own way. Terrifying. Liberating.

She rolled into a sitting position and pushed up off the mattress, suddenly not so tired anymore. She was completely naked, but she didn't much care.

She pushed open the tent flap and saw Zafar leading the newly named Sadiqi down to the water.

He was dressed now, but not in his robes. In thin pants and a tunic top, his hair ruffled, standing on end. Because of her.

"You can't just walk away."

Zafar looked up from where he stood at the edge of the lake, his heart lodging in his throat, all of his blood rushing back to his groin as he looked at Ana, standing in the sun, pale and pink and completely naked.

Her blond hair tumbled over her shoulders, her breasts highlighted by the late-afternoon light. So round and soft. Utter perfection in his hands. In his mouth. Against his chest while he was inside of her, chasing ecstasy.

But she'd been a virgin, and he'd made a very grave error. Even without that little revelation, it had been a grave error. But now he knew there would be no hiding their affair.

"I think it's pretty rude to do all that to a woman and then walk away," she said.

"Ruder still would have been staying and doing it again," he said, his throat tight.

"I don't think I'd mind that."

"Perhaps not."

"But you don't want to come back in there with me?"

"This cannot be… Ana, you were a virgin and you are not now. I imagine Tariq will notice."

"First of all, you can't undo what's been done. Second… I'm not going to marry Tariq."

He felt like he'd been punched in the chest. "Why?"

"Because I don't want to. Because I was only doing it to appease my father. I thought it was love, but honestly, if you put your mind to it I think you can manufacture love quite simply. That's all it was. I was told marrying him would be good for our family, and so I set my mind to loving him so that I could please my father. And…and I thought, if I had a husband who was a sheikh, who was bound by this kind of duty…no matter what happened he would never cast me out. A royal couple stays together, if for no other reason than the media. And that's pathetic, and sad, but I didn't know how else to keep someone with me, Zafar. But now…now I don't care. I just don't. I'm the one that has to live my life. I think…I think I started feeling this way when my friends and I went on the desert tour. I wanted to experience a taste of freedom, of something a bit wild. Something not strictly sanctioned, and so I arranged that. But it was more than that. I just think I wanted something more. Then I was kidnapped, and then there was you. And now here we are. And I feel different. I feel like this was the journey I had to take."

"I'm glad that my personal hell was a step along the way of your journey," he bit out.

"That's not what I meant."

"It's what you said."

"You…Zafar, you were unexpected. Unwanted." A

tear slid down her cheek, her face crumpling. And he just wanted to pull her into his arms and tell her everything would be okay. But he couldn't promise that. He could promise her nothing. "But you are absolutely the most important thing…I could never have found this, I could never have found me, without you. I would have made vows to a man that I had no business making them to. I would have…I would have ruined my life and never fully realized it. Like suddenly the fog cleared and now I see everything, where before I could barely see past my nose. And I didn't even know how far life went, how broad the scope. I would never have known."

Zafar left Sadiqi standing at the river's edge. The horse wouldn't wander off. He never had. He truly was a faithful friend, regardless of what he'd said earlier.

He was glad she'd talked him into giving him a name. What was she doing to him?

"I must take you back still. You know that, right?"

"I do."

"I need to see you returned safely, and from there whatever you choose to tell your father and Tariq, whatever decisions you make, are yours."

"It's hot."

"I know. That's why we stopped."

"Will you come into the tent and lie down with me?"

Such a sweet, open request and he felt unable to refuse it. The truth was, he wanted nothing more than to pull her into his arms, her sweet softness against him, his face buried in her hair, inhaling her scent, a hand cupping her breast. He wanted it so much it made him ache.

But it wasn't her status as another man's fiancé, which she claimed she no longer was, that made it an impossibility.

It was him.

He couldn't sleep with her. For fear the darkness would

swallow them both. That he would lash out against her in the night. He couldn't ask her to stay with him because he would use her as a dying man used an oasis. He would quench his thirst with her body, her soul, and give nothing back.

He would be able to give her nothing. He would be worth nothing.

He had to keep his eyes on his people. He had to focus on his kingdom. Wishing he could love a woman, aching over a woman, was that same old weakness, and he simply couldn't allow it.

Yet he wanted to. So much it was a physical need that tore through him, leaving emotions he'd thought long dead in tatters.

"For now," he said. "While we travel...I will have you in my bed."

She nodded. "Yes."

He would endure days of not sleeping just for that privilege, for this little moment out of time where he would be Zafar as he was meant to be. So that he too could be unmade, here with her, and simply be the man he might have been.

A man whose past wasn't stained with blood. Whose future wasn't filled with endless, rigid responsibility.

Just a man who wanted a woman. He looked into Ana's clear blue eyes. Yes, just for these few days. It would be enough.

It would have to be.

He watched her walk around the tent from his position on the mattress. She'd never dressed after the first time they'd made love. She reminded him of Eve, walking around naked and unashamed. As though she was comfortable just as she was made. As though she had sprung from creation, formed...not just for him.

For herself.

She was so fierce. Glorious in her nakedness.

He was undone.

"Come here," he said.

She smiled at him and it hit him hard. There was such warmth in her expression, such desire. She looked at him and saw the man he might have been, and that was a gift he treasured. Something he wanted never to destroy. But if he stayed with her, he would.

She would see.

"Zafar?" She got down on her knees in front of him and bent to kiss him, her hair sliding forward, creating a glossy curtain around them. "You look too serious," she said, kissing him again.

He put his hand on her back, lowered it, cupping her backside. "It is nothing," he said, looking at her clear blue eyes, like the sun-washed Al Sabahan sky. Only there was caring there. Forgiveness. And he deserved none of it. She was too much beauty, too much strength.

"Let me help you forget."

He wrapped his arms around her and kissed her deeper, pulling her down so that he was on his back and she was over him. He wanted her, no matter what it meant for him. No matter if it meant all the honor and purpose he purported to have wasn't nearly as strong as the weakness of his body. No matter if it reached in and undid the years of exile.

Almost especially because it reached in and undid the years of exile.

He was parched, so thirsty for touch, for connection, for her, that there was no way he could deny it. A man who would drink poisoned water in the middle of the desert just for that moment of satisfaction.

Though Ana wasn't the poison. It was all in him.

He shut that thought out, turned his focus away from

the flames of hell, still licking at his ankles, as they had been for the past fifteen years, and focused on the heat of her lips, of her bare body against his.

He pushed all thoughts and recriminations away so he could listen to the sound of her palms sliding over his chest, her breathing increasingly labored as she became more aroused, the breathy sounds of pleasure that came from pale lush lips.

He kissed her neck and she moaned, low and long. "Ever so much more enticing than a one, two, three count," he said, remembering the day she'd tried to teach him to waltz. "Though I found that quite distracting, as well."

"Did you?" she asked, her voice choked.

"Yes." He pushed into a sitting position, her legs wrapped around his back, her breasts at just the right height for him to taste her. And he did. He traced the tightened, sugar-pink buds with his tongue, relishing her sweetness. Sucking her deep into his mouth. She arched against him, her hands in his hair, tugging, the slight pain the only thing keeping him anchored to earth.

He lifted his head and looked up at her face, flushed with desire, her eyes focused on him. "I liked you giving me instruction."

"Really?"

"Yes, I think you should do it now."

"What?"

"Count, *habibti.*"

She huffed out a laugh, then lifted a trembling hand to trace the line of his lips. "My pleasure, I suppose."

"Ours," he said. "Are you ready for me?"

"Always."

She drew up slightly, onto her knees, and he positioned himself at the slick entrance of her body, gritting his teeth as she lowered herself onto him, as he sank deep within her body. He could drown in this, in the pleasure, white-hot, so much so it was nearly painful.

She raised herself up, hands gripping his shoulders, fingernails digging into his skin. "One," she said, "two," back down, "three."

He held tightly to her, his hands on her hips, letting her lead, for the moment, holding her steady.

"One, two, three." She repeated the numbers with the motions, her voice a bit more strangled each time, her nails biting harder into his skin. "One, two… Ohhh."

He chuckled. "Do you think I'm qualified enough to lead this dance?" He kissed the top of her shoulder.

"You were right," she said, panting. "I need to be un-civilized. And right now, I don't need you to act polished. I just need you."

It was all the permission he needed. He growled and gripped her waist hard, reversing positions so she was on her back and he was over her. She arched, pressing her breasts to his chest. "Yes, Zafar. Please."

She didn't have to ask twice.

He put his hand beneath her, on her butt, lifting her up into his thrusts as he pushed them both toward plea-sure. There was nothing quiet or civil about their joining. His skin burned where her nails met his flesh, his heart pounding so hard he thought it might bruise his body in-side, leaving a dark stain over his chest.

She draped her legs over his calves, locking him to her, holding him. He increased the pace, and she went with him, matching his every thrust, his every groan of pleasure.

And when he felt himself being tugged downward, his orgasm gripping him and taking him down beneath the waves, he felt her go with him. And they clung together, riding out the storm in each other's arms.

The desert was still there, dry and harsh around them,

and they were insulated from it, refreshed, renewed. Lost in another world, another space and time, where there was nothing but this.

Nothing but Zafar. Nothing but Ana.

He held her afterward, his arms locked tight around her, breathing an impossibility. He was still lost to the world, to reality, floating underwater with Ana. He rested his head on her chest, between her breasts, listening to her heartbeat. So alive. So soft and warm and perfect.

If only this was all there was. If only he had been created this second, born from the sand. If only he didn't have all those years, all those sins, all that blood in his past.

But in this moment, it didn't matter. Nothing mattered but this.

Nothing mattered but Ana.

Zafar smelled sulfur. As he always did when hell found him on earth. Fire and gun smoke. And screaming. And pain. So much pain.

And his mother's face. Her eyes. So scared. Wounded.

Then they met his. And he wanted to scream that he was sorry. That it was his fault. He wanted to fall down on his knees and take the beatings. But his enemies seemed to have no interest in hurting him. Not physically.

They just wanted him to watch. Wanted him to see what his confessions to Fatin had enabled them, empowered them to do. How the foolish prince of Al Sabah had given power over to another nation.

His hands were chained, his legs chained, his mouth gagged. The confession pushed at his throat, made him feel like his chest would explode. He wanted to scream and he couldn't.

Instead, tears streamed down his face, the only release his enemies had allowed him.

As he watched his mother die. In pain. In fear. As his

father watched, part of the older man's torture. And then met the same fate.

Zafar was back there, his cheeks wet, waiting to be killed.

Praying he would be killed.

And then he woke up.

He was gasping for breath in the dark, a feral shout leaving his throat scraped raw, his skin slick with sweat, his face damp with tears.

He was poised, ready to fight, ready to kill. To destroy those who had hurt his family, who had killed them. And he realized he held his enemy in his hand, fingers curled tightly around his neck.

Zafar reached for his knife, which he always kept near his bed, and discovered it wasn't there. And he was naked, no weapon in the folds of his robes. Nothing to use against the people who had killed his parents.

Who had left him here to deal with the pain by himself.

But his thumb was pressed against his enemy's throat, and one push would end it all.

"I will kill you with my bare hands, then," he growled, looking down for the first time, trying to focus on his enemy's face. All he saw was a pale shadow, glistening eyes in the darkness.

Slowly everything cleared, and he realized where he was. Who it was in his tent.

Damn him to hell. He had fallen asleep. With Ana.

"Ana." He released his hold on her immediately and she fell back. He wanted to go to her, to comfort her, to touch her. But he had no right to touch her. Not after he'd put his hands on her like that.

He was still breathing hard, each breath a near sob, sweat coating his skin. He shivered as the heat in him died out, gave way to a chill that permeated his entire being. "Ana, I'm sorry. I'm sorry. I would not hurt you. I would not."

She stood, slowly, her whole frame trembling. And he looked away.

He didn't want to see her eyes. He didn't want to see her now that she'd truly seen him. Now that she'd seen everything ugly and destroyed inside of him.

Now that she'd nearly been cut on the jagged edges of his soul.

"I know," she said, her voice shaking.

He collected himself enough to find his bag, and pulled out a battery-powered lantern, lighting it so that he could see.

And then he wished he hadn't. There was a tear glittering on her cheek, sliding down to her chin. And she didn't wipe it away.

"Ana," he said, the pain wrenching his soul so deep he thought he would break. "This is why I don't sleep with anyone. This is why…"

"What do you see?" she asked.

He shook his head. "No…Ana…do not ask for that. Do not try and help me when I have…"

"How can you live with it inside of you?" She approached him and extended her hand, as though she meant to touch him.

He jerked back, unable to take the balm of her touch. Undeserving of it.

"I have to," he said. "It was my fault. It was my…it is my burden, one I earned."

"Tell me."

"No." He shook his head. "No. I have done enough damage to you." He raised the light and saw a slash of red on her neck. "Oh, Ana, I have done enough damage to you," he said again, his voice rough.

"Zafar, let me have this. Let me help you."

He shook his head, turning away and forking his fingers through his hair. "You know it already. I told Fatin where my parents would be that day. When they were moving to an alternate location for safety. Because she asked and I thought nothing of it. It was all very Samson and Delilah. If only I had been betraying myself alone. But it was them, too. We were all captured. Held in the throne room of the palace." He started shaking while he spoke of it, but now that he'd started, he couldn't stop, he had to finish. "We were bound. I was in chains. They were not just content to kill my parents. They had to torture them. My mother first, so my father and I could see. Then my father, for me to watch. To watch the strongest man I had ever known be reduced to nothing. A demonstration of power and evil I had never before fathomed."

He drew in a breath. "My hands were bound. My feet. My mouth gagged. I wanted to tell them it was my fault. I wanted to beg them to kill me. I could say nothing. I could only…I could only cry like an infant, desperate for his mother to hold him. Knowing it would never happen again. And that it was my own fault. You see, Ana, I thought I was a man, but I realized in that moment I was nothing more than a foolish child whose stupidity had torn away everything important in his life."

He swallowed. "And they didn't kill me. They left me and I prayed for death, lying on the floor of the throne room with my parents' bodies. I prayed for death." He closed his eyes. "I didn't receive it. My uncle found me in the morning. Our army defeated theirs in the end. But it was too late to save my parents."

He looked down at his hands. "And he asked me how it had happened, so I confessed. And he sent me away. I am under no illusions here. It suited my uncle to tell me those things. He was not the one who had led the rebellion that killed my parents, but he was just the sort of man to seize the chance to have power if there was an easy way to grasp it. He told me there were bound to be rumors and I would be better off if I wasn't in the city. That I had to leave the palace. That I would never make a king of Al Sabah. And I believed him. So I ran. Out into the desert until my lungs burned. Until I lay in the sand and waited to die there. But again, I was denied."

"The Bedouins found you."

"Yes, it was the beginning of my allegiance to them. Because I realized that while death was certainly the kinder option for me, it would do no good for anyone else. Especially when it became clear the manner of man my uncle was. Power hungry, with much more love for himself than for the people of my country. But I was a disgraced boy, and he was a man with an army, so my battles had to be waged another way."

Ana couldn't breathe. Zafar had woken her from her sleep with a guttural scream and then his hand had wrapped around her throat. It had been terrifying. Confusing. She'd frozen, searching his face in the dark. And she'd realized that he wasn't there, tears on his cheeks, his eyes unseeing.

She'd been afraid to move. Afraid to make a sound. She knew what sort of man he was, how strong, how able to end her with the press of his thumb.

Now, hearing his story, she understood what demons tormented him. What haunted him in his sleep.

She pushed her fear aside. Pushed everything aside and focused on him. On his pain. His need. She crossed to him and wrapped her arms around his neck. He stood stiff, but she didn't care. She stroked the back of his neck. Held him like he was a child, because it had been too long since someone had soothed him that way.

"Zafar, it's not your fault."

"It is," he said, his voice tortured.

"No. It's not. Zafar, I would tell you anything now because I trust you, and if you betrayed that trust and went and caused harm with it, whose fault would it be?"

"Ana…"

"No. Zafar, if a child breaks a doll and their mother leaves, whose fault is it?"

"Ana, please don't do this."

"Whose fault is it?"

"Never yours, Ana. Never yours."

"And yet it was yours?"

"I didn't break a doll. I broke the whole country. I broke my life. My parents' lives. I might as well have landed the killing blow myself."

"No." Her heart broke for him, his pain living in her, roaring in her chest. "Zafar, you can't think that. You have to…you have to stop blaming yourself or you'll never be free of it."

"You're wrong, Ana. I have to realize my own fault so that it never happens again…even knowing it… Have I not made the same mistake? I was too weak to resist you."

"This is different."

"Is it?"

"I love you," she said.

"She said she loved me."

Anger, passion, desperation, mixed together in her chest, combusted, exploded. "I'm *not her*," she screamed, so easy for her to do now. To make a sound. To demand she be heard. "I gave you my body, my soul. I gave you who I am, and there is no one else on earth who has that. I love you."

He shook his head. "No. You don't love me. You love who you think I could be, maybe, but you're wrong."

"About loving you?"

"About who I could be. I am broken, Ana, so deep it won't ever be fixed."

"Love goes deep, Zafar. Let it in. Let it heal you."

"That's not how it works."

"Enough water can quench even the most cracked earth. An oasis like this can be here, even in the middle of the desert. You don't know how much love I have to pour out. Don't tell me what it can and can't do."

"It is a drop of water in an entire desert, *habibti*," he said. "It will never be enough."

A tear slid down her cheek. "You think so? I thought you knew me, but now I doubt it."

"It is you who doesn't know me."

"And you think my feelings don't matter? You think me naive? Zafar, I just saw your worst." She took a step toward him, wrapped her hand around his and placed it at the base of her neck. "I know what manner of man you are, Sheikh Zafar Nejem, and I'm standing here offering you everything."

He lowered his hand, his fingers trembling. "Then you are naive and a fool."

"And you...do you feel anything for me?"

"I am the desert. I have nothing to give. I'll only take."

"Don't give me your mystic storytelling metaphors. Give me words. Tell me you don't love me," she said, her lips cold.

"I do not love you. I love nothing, *habibti,* not even myself. I just want to ensure my people get returned to them what I stole. That is all I am. I will never be a husband to you. Never a father for your children."

"But you said you would marry."

"Someone else. Not you."

She felt it like a blow. "Then what was this? This compromising everything so we could sleep together? So you could get off? That's just...stupid."

"Lust and heat. Both addle a man's brain."

"What if I'm pregnant? You weren't...careful last time."

He nodded once. "I will offer whatever support you need. But it would be better if I wasn't involved in any way beyond the monetary. Let us pray that there is no child."

He was gone, her Zafar, the man she had made love to for hours today. The man who had made her reach down deep and find her own strength. The warrior had returned—the fierce, frightening man he'd been the first moment she'd met him and he'd paid for her with a bag of silver.

Strange how he had purchased her with the last of his coins, and yet, in the end, she felt she'd paid the highest price.

"Take me back," she said.

"Now?"

She nodded. "Yes. I've had enough sleep."

"As have I," he said. "Dress. We will be ready to leave in a few moments."

Zafar left the tent, his clothes still outside by the water. And Ana stood there, her heart falling to pieces inside of her. It wasn't fair. She should have known better than to believe there was a future with him. Going into it, she hadn't even wanted one, and yet her feelings had grown.

And in that moment when he'd been his darkest, she'd realized the truth. That seeing him as he was, seeing all of the brokenness, she only loved him more. Knowing what he'd been through, knowing the man he was in spite of it, because of it, she wanted to be with him.

He was strong. He was brave. He was hurting.

But he didn't want her love. He didn't want her.

She dressed quickly, putting on new clothes, not the clothes she'd been wearing before they'd made love the first time. Her hands were shaking, her stomach sick.

She would leave Al Sabah. And she couldn't bring Zafar, the man, with her. But she would bring Al Sabah and Zafar with her. He was in her, his effect on her blended in with the marrow of her bones, strengthening her, reminding her of who she could be.

He couldn't ever take that from her. In spite of all the pain she was in now, at least he couldn't take her newfound strength, her resolve to find her own place in life, her own happiness.

She would leave here stronger for having known him. And with a broken heart for having lost him.

She was fatigued and windburned by the time they reached the border that stretched between Shakar and Al Sabah. They had ridden for hours without stopping, time melting into a continuous stretch that she could only measure in painful, tearing heartbeats.

"I will have you call your father now," he said. "And I will wait with you until he is here."

"But you…"

"I won't be seen.".

This man who thought he had no heart.

"Good. I don't want you to be injured." It was too late for her heart, but even so, she didn't want him to get hurt.

She dialed her father's number with shaking fingers.

When he answered, it was like a dam inside of her burst. "Dad," she said, her throat tightening, a flood of tears pouring from her eyes.

"Ana?" her father sounded desperate.

"Yes."

"We were searching," he said. "Please know that we were. But we didn't want the media in on it. We couldn't risk making your captors nervous. Where are you? Do they still have you?"

"No," she said, looking at Zafar, his eyes blank. "No. I'm free." The word held so many layers, so much meaning. And all because of the man standing before her.

"How?"

She knew she couldn't say. Knew she could never say. "I was ransomed by a stranger. I'm near the encampment where I was taken. Can you please come and get me?"

Zafar handed her a paper with the GPS coordinates on it, silent, watchful. Ana read them off for her father.

"I need to go," she said.

"Ana...wait."

She hung up. She knew Zafar wouldn't speak to her while she waited. But she wasn't going to spend her last moments with Zafar talking to someone else, no matter how much she missed her father.

She would miss Zafar so much more.

They were in a vast area, only an outcropping of jagged rocks there to provide shade. And it was almost like seeking shelter in a clay oven, the rocks absorbing the heat and radiating it outward.

Still, Zafar stood by them, watching, and she stood with him, a small space between them, both of them looking in the direction her father and Tariq would be coming from. They didn't speak; they didn't touch.

But she drank him in. She would have to fill herself now, because after this she wouldn't see him again. Her life an endless, vast desert without him.

"Only a minute now," he said, finally.

She turned to him. "Look at me."

He obeyed, and she let the image of his face burn into her. The hard planes and angles, his golden skin and dark eyes. Those eyes, which held so much pain, so much passion.

"I need to memorize you," she said.

"I have already done so," he said.

Her heart squeezed tight. "I wish you the best," she said. "I'll be back in America. If you're ever curious."

He closed his eyes for a moment, as though blocking out an onslaught of pain. "I will forget that information. I can't know. Then I might search for you. And it would be a disservice to you."

She heard the sound of helicopter rotors in the distance. "Go," she said, feeling panicked. They couldn't find him. They could never know.

He nodded once and went back to Sadiqi, covering his face and head again, and riding off toward another rock formation. And then she didn't see him anymore, as though he'd melted into the sand.

Ana saw the helicopter now, drawing closer. Her salvation. Her family.

And yet, for the first time she felt undeniably homesick. And when she thought of home, it wasn't the old mansion in Texas, it wasn't the boarding school in Connecticut where she'd spent much of her teenage years. It wasn't even the palace in Al Sabah.

It was in Zafar's arms.

And it hit her then that she would never be home again.

Ana dropped to her knees as the helicopter descended to earth, and wept.

Zafar rode until his lungs burned, until his eyes were blinded by sharp, stinging sand. He suspected the sand wasn't entirely responsible for the stinging in his eyes.

Leaving Ana was like leaving behind part of himself.

Parts of the heart he'd imagined he'd cut out. But no, it was there. It was beating. Beating for her. And it was why he had to leave.

How could he consign her to a life with him? A life with a man so filled with darkness? A man who might wrap his hands around her throat in the night, thinking her an imaginary enemy?

He couldn't do that to her. He couldn't love her right.

He did love her. In a broken, selfish way. He would bring her back to his palace and keep her for himself. Keep her in his bed. Watch her stomach grow round when she was pregnant with his child.

She could even be pregnant with his child now. But he thought of his hands, covered in innocent blood and the blood of the guilty, cradling a child, and he ached inside. How could he be a father? How could he ever be a man worthy of Ana?

He looked into the distance, into the sun.

He would be a man worthy of his people. And he would hope that someday she would read about him, about Al Sabah, and she would have something to be proud of him for.

If that was all he could ever have, then he would take it.

He didn't deserve for her to love him, but he would try to earn it. He would try to be a man worthy of Ana's love.

It was the very best he could have. Somehow it still left him feeling cold inside.

That night, he lay down without a tent, his eyes fixed on the inky black sky. His thoughts on Ana. His heart beating with love for her.

And when he slept, there were no nightmares.

CHAPTER THIRTEEN

ANA SAT ON the edge of the bed. The room was large, light and airy. A room fit for a princess. Kind of Tariq, since last week she'd told him, officially, that she wouldn't become his sheikha.

He'd insisted that she stay until she'd had a full recovery. Whatever that meant.

There would never be a full recovery. Not from this.

Heartbreak wasn't fatal. It was worse. It hurt all the time. And she had a feeling it wouldn't just heal. Not when she was so changed from her time with Zafar. Not when her strength had been unveiled by him.

She would be marrying Tariq in the next year if not for Zafar. And it would be the wrong decision. She would be making choices to please everyone else still. And now... now she couldn't. She knew her father wasn't happy about the dissolution of her engagement to Tariq, and how could he be? It was costing him millions in profits.

But he was staying here in Shakar with her. And he'd never expressed his disappointment to her. She just knew it was there. But he hadn't left. He hadn't disowned her. He'd even told her he loved her several times.

She looked out the window, at the gardens. At the beauty. She didn't regret that this wouldn't be her home. She felt nothing for Tariq now. Nothing except for a kind of…affection. Because she did know him, and she did like him. But she didn't love him.

That had been underlined by the fact that when she'd seen him, her thoughts had stayed firmly occupied with Zafar. That she'd never once wavered on her decision to break off the engagement. Not even when she was afraid of how her father would react.

A clear head, time and distance had also made her sure of two other things: She wasn't pregnant with Zafar's baby. And she wanted to be with him more than anything.

She let out a long slow breath and closed her eyes, picturing his face. So precious. So perfect. She missed him, and every second of missing him was a slow and painful hit on her heart. Each beat another punch against the bruise.

There was a knock on her door and she stood, taking a deep breath. "Yes?"

Tariq walked in, tall, broad and handsome as ever. And her heart did nothing. "Good afternoon, *habibti.*"

"Please don't call me that," she said.

He frowned. "I know things aren't that way between us now. But I confess I keep hoping you might change your mind."

"Do you love me?"

"No." His answer was instant, void of venom or emotion.

"Then I won't."

"And I won't lie to change your mind, on that you have my word."

"Thank you." She looked away from Tariq, out the window and past the gardens this time, toward Al Sabah. "Tariq, you've been good to my family."

"There is no honor in forcing a woman to marry you," he said. "And no honor in treating you poorly for making the decision."

"You are a good man."

"It has been said, though I'm not certain I have reaped any particular reward for it."

"You could still make deals with my father."

He nodded slowly. "I intend to. It is wise, whether or not you're my wife."

"Have you spoken to him yet?" For a moment she was afraid her father already knew. That he was already aware of the fact that he would have no bad consequences for her breaking the engagement, and that was why he'd been so quick to forgive her for it.

"No," Tariq said. "I will, over dinner today."

She let out a breath. "I'm so pleased to hear it." And then she had a thought, one that might fix things. It might not fix them either, because in the end, Zafar was still the one who had to make the final decision. But she could take care of everything on her end.

"Tariq, our marriage was supposed to ensure loyalty and fair treatment. And I would like for us to strike a deal together, separate from the deal you're making with him."

"What would that be?"

"Swear to me that you will be loyal to my family. That we have your protection. Always."

He regarded her closely, his dark eyes unreadable. "I swear it."

"No matter what. If, of course, we don't mount an attack against Shakar."

He arched a brow. "If you do not mount an attack against Shakar?"

"Covering the bases."

He looked at the wall behind her. "Especially for the indignity you suffered, I shall swear it. On my life, your family, however large it becomes in the future, has my protection. You have my word, and I am a man of my word. But if you would like it in writing…you may have that, too."

"I would," she said, her heart lifting, tears stinging her eyes. "I would like that very much. And the use of a helicopter. For my indignity."

"For your indignity," he said slowly.

Her throat tightened, her hands shaking. "Appreciated."

Zafar woke every night, but not to visions of death and violence.

To the illusion of soft skin, soft sighs of pleasure. To the impression of Ana in his arms and in his bed.

But she was never there.

He closed his eyes against a wave of pain. It was a particularly bad one. Waves like that crashed over him a few times a day, in contrast to the low-level ache that hummed in the background constantly.

He moved to the window of the throne room, the damned mausoleum. The scene of the most horrendous moment of his life. But fifteen years on, and that pain was finally fading. Because of the emotions he'd let in.

There was no longer room for anguish, anger and pain to be the star of his heart. Not when he'd started loving Ana.

Except he'd sent her away. But what other choice did he have?

"Sheikh." One of his men strode into the throne room, his expression fierce. "There is someone here to see you."

"May I ask who?"

"Of course. It is the woman. The woman who came here with you the first day."

He shook his head. "No. It cannot be."

"But it is. I would not mistake her. Ever. I have never seen a woman so pale."

"It cannot be a hallucination, because you wouldn't hallucinate on my behalf, would you?" he asked, feeling stunned.

"Sheikh, do I send her away?"

"No. No, send her to me." Zafar's heart was pounding, and as his man left the room, he thought of every possible scenario that might bring her here. To warn him of war, to share her engagement. To throw herself into his arms.

Considering his treatment of her, the last was the least likely.

It was only a moment, one that felt like an eternity, and she walked into the throne room, blond hair in a bun, her curves showcased by a knee-length dress that was sophisticated and sexy as hell.

"Zafar," she said, her expression neutral. "I came to deliver something to you."

"What is it?"

"An agreement. From the Sheikh of Shakar."

"I see." He wondered if that meant her engagement to Tariq remained intact. For all that he imagined she would be better off with the other man, the thought made him see red. Made him feel like his world was falling down around him.

She held out a sheet of paper, folded in half. "Read it."

He took it from her and unfolded it. "This is…a pledge from the Sheikh of Shakar. To protect your family, as it is now and as it grows. Always. Why show this to me?"

"Because I think I found a solution to your problem. But you have to hear me out. I'm not offering you this to fix your problems. I'm offering it to fix mine. This isn't to make you love me."

"What do you mean, *habibti*?"

She smiled. "I like it when you call me that."

"Explain," he said, his heart pounding.

"Become my family. Marry me. You will not have to worry about war breaking out over it. This—" she pointed to the paper "—protects you. It protects me. It protects Al Sabah. But only if you marry me."

"Are you proposing to me, Ana?"

"Yes," she said, her voice choked. "Yes. And do you know why?"

"Why?" he asked, his voice rough.

"Because. More than a week away from you, and you're all I can think about. Because, in spite of everything you said to me, I still love you. Because you helped me find my strength. Because you are a horrible dancer. Because you don't respect the salad fork, and God knows there has been far too much respecting of salad forks in my life. You made me want more, Zafar. You make me want to do more, feel more, be more."

"Ana," he said. "I...I want so badly to accept, not just the treaty offer, but your hand. Your love. But I'm so scarred inside. Why would you want me? You are everything beautiful and life giving. You talk about what I've done for you, but do you have any idea of what you've done for me?"

"No," she whispered.

"I have felt, for so many years, that death would have been the sweeter option for me. That I should have died that day. That the gates of hell were open and ready to pull me in. But you closed them. *You* did. When I sleep at night...I see your face and not that day. For years I didn't sleep right, Ana, and it was worse when I came here. But today I stood in this room and I saw your face instead of the images of that day."

"What changed?" she asked. "Because that last night... it wasn't me you were dreaming about."

"I let myself love you. And when I let that in, I couldn't be filled with anger and hopelessness anymore. I could no longer wish for death with even the smallest part of myself. You filled too much of me. You filled this place with new memories. And you've made me want again. I've been so afraid of wanting, because I was so sure I was as weak as I had ever been and that if I wanted...I would crumble. I would destroy everything again. But I can't call loving you a weakness, because I have never felt stronger. My heart, my soul...I no longer feel I've left them in the desert. I feel like they're in me, where they belong."

"Zafar...if I ever had a doubt that you were the man for me, I don't now. Because we healed each other. You were the man I needed. It was your brokenness that helped me see my own, that helped me find my strength."

"And it was your strength that lifted me out of the pit."

"Then stop talking crazy about why we can't be together."

"You could have a better man than I am."

"I don't want a better man. I want you."

He laughed. "Thank you."

"You know what I mean. I want to stand by you and help you fulfill your purpose here. I want Al Sabah to be my purpose, too. Your home is my home. Because it's where you are."

"And my heart is yours," he said, his voice rough. "It is damaged. I foolishly gave it to someone once before and saw my whole world crash down. I removed it from myself so I would never make the mistake again. Left it neglected and dying. And you revived it. Revived me. If you would take it, knowing all of that, then I would be the most blessed man in all the world."

"I will," she said. "Gladly."

"Know this, Ana, my love, you will never have to be anyone but yourself with me. You will never have to quiet yourself. Whether we decide to be civilized for a ball or uncivilized in our bedroom, it will be fine, because I only want you. I don't want you to simply please me or make me comfortable. I don't want you to slot meekly into my life. I want you to challenge me, tell me when I'm wrong. Butt heads with me. I want you to be fire and strength. To be who you are."

She closed her eyes and tilted her head back, a smile curving her lips. "Those are the most wonderful words I've ever heard. And you are the first person to ever say them."

"I will never stop telling you," he said. "Every day I'll tell you how much I appreciate you."

"I love you," she said. "I love you. I love you. One. Two. Three."

"Perfect." He pulled her into his arms and kissed her, pouring all of his love into the kiss, all of his passion. "Oh, Ana," he said, kissing her brow, her cheek, the corner of her mouth. "Do you remember that day I took you from the kidnappers?"

"No," she said, smiling. "Forgot. Not a big deal. Of course I do."

He swung her up into his arms and pulled her against his chest, taking them down the corridor that led to his bedchamber.

"I told you," he said, pushing open the door. "I was your salvation."

"You did."

He crossed the room and laid her on the bed, pulling his shirt over his head and joining her. "I was wrong, Ana."

She cupped his cheek with her hand, blue eyes looking into his. "Were you?"

"Yes, my love." He bent and kissed her, a kiss full of promises he would keep for the rest of their lives. "You were mine."

* * * * *

Too angry to stop and clear her vision, she would have walked straight into a wall if someone hadn't reached out and grabbed her by her upper arms.

With a soft gasp Aspen looked up, about to thank whoever had saved her. But the words never came and her quick smile froze on her face as she found herself staring into the hard eyes of a man she had thought she would never see in the flesh again.

The air between them split apart and reformed, vibrating with emotion, as Cruz Rodriguez stared down at her with such cold detachment she nearly shivered.

Eight years dissolved into dust. Guilt, shame, and a host of other emotions all sparked for dominance inside her.

'I…' Aspen blinked, her mind scrambling for poise…words…*something*.

'Hello, Aspen. Nice to see you again.'

From as far back as she can remember **Michelle Conder** dreamed of being a writer. She penned the first chapter of a romance novel just out of high school, but it took much study, many (varied) jobs, one ultra-understanding husband and three very patient children before she finally sat down to turn that dream into a reality.

Michelle lives in Australia, and when she isn't busy plotting loves to read, ride horses, travel and practise yoga.

Recent titles by the same author:

DUTY AT WHAT COST?
LIVING THE CHARADE
HIS LAST CHANCE AT REDEMPTION
GIRL BEHIND THE SCANDALOUS REPUTATION

THE MOST EXPENSIVE LIE OF ALL

BY
MICHELLE CONDER

Published in Great Britain 2014
by Mills & Boon, an imprint of Harlequin (UK) Limited,
Eton House, 18-24 Paradise Road, Richmond, Surrey, TW9 1SR

© 2014 Michelle Conder

ISBN: 978 0 263 91108 4

Harlequin (UK) Limited's policy is to use papers that are natural, renewable and recyclable products and made from wood grown in sustainable forests. The logging and manufacturing processes conform to the legal environmental regulations of the country of origin.

Printed and bound in Spain
by Blackprint CPI, Barcelona

THE MOST
EXPENSIVE LIE
OF ALL

This book is dedicated to Amber and Corin for opening up the world of polo for me and doing it with such warmth and generosity. You guys are great.

To a formidable squash champ, Juan Marcos, who promptly responded to my queries about his game.

And also to my lifelong friend Pam Austin, who wrote down every memory she ever had of her visits to Mexico—which could have been a novel in itself.

Thank you!

CHAPTER ONE

'Eight-three. my serve.'

Cruz Rodriguez Sanchez, self-made billionaire and one of the most formidable sportsmen ever to grace the polo field, let his squash racquet drop to his side and stared at his opponent incredulously. 'Rubbish! That was a let. And it's eight-three *my* way.'

'No way, *compadre*! That was my point.'

Cruz eyeballed his brother as Ricardo prepared to serve. They might only be playing a friendly game of squash but 'friendly' was a relative term between competing brothers. 'Cheats always get their just desserts, you know,' Cruz drawled, moving to the opposite square.

Ricardo grinned. 'You can't win every time, *mi amigo*.'

Maybe not, Cruz thought, but he couldn't remember the last time he'd lost. Oh, yeah, actually he could—because his lawyer was in the process of righting that particular wrong while he blew off steam with his brother at their regular catch-up session.

Feeling pumped, he correctly anticipated Ricardo's attempted 'kill shot' and slashed back a return that his brother had no chance of reaching. Not that he didn't try. His running shoes squeaked across the resin-coated floor as he lunged for the ball and missed.

'*Chingada madre!*'

'Now, now,' Cruz mocked. 'That would be nine-three. My serve.'

'That's just showing off,' Ricardo grumbled, picking himself up and swiping at the sweat on his brow with his sweatband.

Cruz shook his head. 'You know what they say? If you can't stand the heat…'

'Too much talking, *la figura*.'

'Good to see you know your place.' He flashed his brother a lazy smile as he prepared to serve. '*El pequeño*.'

Ricardo rolled his eyes, flipped him the bird and bunkered down, determination etched all over his face. But Cruz was in his zone, and when Ricardo flicked his wrist and sent the ball barrelling on a collision course with Cruz's right cheekbone he adjusted his body with graceful agility and sent the ball ricocheting around the court.

Not bothering to pick himself up off the floor this time, Ricardo lay there, mentally tracking the trajectory of the ball, and shook his head. 'That's just unfair. Squash isn't even your game.'

'True.'

Polo had been his game. Years ago.

Wiping sweat from his face, Cruz reached into his gym bag and tossed his brother a bottle of water. Ricardo sat on his haunches and guzzled it.

'You know I let you win these little contests between us because you're unbearable to be around when you lose,' he advised.

Cruz grinned down at him. He couldn't dispute him. It was a celebrated fact that professional sportsmen were very poor losers, and while he hadn't played professional polo for eight years he'd never lost his competitive edge.

On top of that he was in an exceptionally good mood, which made beating him almost impossible. Remembering the reason for that, he pulled his cell phone from his kitbag to see if the text he was waiting for had come through, frowning slightly when he saw it hadn't.

'Why are you checking that thing so much?' Ricardo queried. 'Don't tell me some *chica* is finally playing hard to get?'

'You wish,' Cruz murmured. 'But, no, it's just a business deal.'

'Ah, don't sweat it. One day you'll meet the *chica* of your dreams.'

Cruz threw him a banal look. 'Unlike you, I'm not looking for the woman of my dreams.'

'Then you'll probably meet her first,' Ricardo lamented.

Cruz laughed. 'Don't hold your breath,' he replied. 'You might meet an early grave.' He tossed the ball in the air and sent it spinning around the court, his concentration a little spoiled by Ricardo's untimely premonition.

Because there *was* a woman. A woman who had been occupying his thoughts just a little too often lately. A woman he hadn't seen for a long time and hoped to keep it that way. Of course he knew why she was jumping into his head at the most inopportune times of late, but after eight years of systematically forcing her out of it that didn't make it any more tolerable.

Not that he allowed himself to get bent out of shape about it. He'd learned early on that the things you were most attached to had the power to cause you the most pain, and since then he'd lived his life very much like a high-rolling gambler—easy come, easy go.

Nothing stuck to him and he stuck to nothing in return—which had, much to everyone's surprise, made him a phenomenally wealthy man.

An 'uneducated maverick', they'd called him. One who had swapped the polo field for the boardroom and invested in deals and stock market bonds more learned businessmen had shied away from. But then Cruz had been trading in the tumultuous early days of the global financial crisis and he'd already lost the one thing he had cared about the most. Defying expectations and market trends seemed inconsequential after that.

What had really fascinated him in the early days was how people had been so ready to write him off because of his Latino blood and his lack of a formal education. What they hadn't realised was that the game of polo had perfectly set him up to achieve in the business world. Killer instincts combined with a tireless work ethic and the ability to think on his feet were all attributes to make you succeed in polo and in business, and Cruz had them in spades. What he didn't have right now—what he *wanted*—was a text from his lawyer advising him that he was the proud owner of one of East Hampton's most prestigious horse studs: Ocean Haven Farm.

Resisting another urge to check his phone, he prowled around the squash court, using the bottom of his sweat-soaked T-shirt to swipe at the perspiration dripping down his face.

'Nice abs,' a feline voice quipped appreciatively through the glass window overlooking the court.

Ah, there she was now.

Lauren Burnside, one of the Boston lawyers he sometimes used for deals he didn't want made public knowledge before the fact, her hip cocked, her expression a smooth combination of professional savvy and sexual knowhow.

'I always thought you were packing a punch beneath all those business suits, Señor Rodriguez. Now I know you are.'

'Lauren.' Cruz let his T-shirt drop and waited for her hot eyes to trail back up to his. She was curvy, elegant and sophisticated, and he had nearly slept with her about a year ago but had baulked at the last minute. He still couldn't figure out why. 'Long way to come to make a house call, counsellor. A text would have sufficed.'

'Not quite. We have a hitch.' She smiled nonchalantly. 'And since I was in California, just a hop, skip and a jump away from Acapulco, I thought I'd deliver the news *mano-a-mano*.' She smiled. 'So to speak.'

Cruz scowled, for once completely unmoved by the flick of her tongue across her glossy mouth.

He knew women found him attractive. He was tall, fit, with straight teeth and nose, a full head of black hair, and he was moneyed-up and uninterested in love. It appeared to be the perfect combination. '*Untameable*,' as one date had purred. He'd smiled, told her he planned to stay that way and she'd come on even stronger. Women, in his experience, were rarely satisfied and usually out for what they could get. If they had money they wanted love. If they had love they wanted money. If they had twenty pairs of shoes they wanted twenty-one. It was tedious in the extreme.

So he ignored his lawyer's honey trap and kept his mind sharp. 'That's not what I want to hear on a deal that was meant to be completed two hours ago, Ms Burnside.' He kept his voice carefully blank, even though his heart rate had sped up faster than during the whole squash game.

'Let me come down.'

For all the provocation behind those words Cruz could tell she had picked up his *not interested* vibe and was smart enough to let it drop.

'She your latest?'

'No.'

Cruz's curt response raised his brother's eyebrows.

'She wants to be.'

Cruz folded his arms as Lauren pushed open the clear door and stepped onto the court, her power suit doing little to disguise the killer body beneath. She inhaled deeply, the smell of male sweat clearly pleasing to her senses.

'You boys have been playing hard,' she murmured provocatively, looking at them from beneath dark lashes.

Okay, so maybe she wasn't that smart. 'What's the hitch?' Cruz prompted.

She raised a well-tended brow at his curtness. 'You don't want to go somewhere more private?'

'This is Ricardo, my brother, and vice-president of Rodriguez Polo Club. I repeat: what's the hitch?'

Lauren's forehead remained wrinkle-free in the face of his growing agitation and he didn't know if that was due to nerves of steel or Botox. Maybe both.

'The hitch,' she said calmly, 'is the granddaughter. Aspen Carmichael.'

Cruz felt his shoulders bunch at the unexpectedness of hearing the name of the female he was doing his best to forget. The last time he'd laid eyes on her she'd been seventeen, dressed in nothing but a nightie and putting on an act worthy of Marilyn Monroe.

The little scheme she and her preppy fiancé had concocted had done Cruz out of a fortune in money and, more importantly, lost him the respect of his family and peers.

Aspen Carmichael had bested him once before and he'd walked away. He'd be damned if he walked away again.

'How?'

'She wants to keep Ocean Haven for herself and her uncle has magnanimously agreed to sell it to her at a reduced cost. The information has only just come to light, but apparently if she can raise the money in the next five days the property is hers.'

Cruz stilled. 'How much of a reduced cost?'

When Lauren named a figure half that which he had offered he cursed loudly. 'Joe Carmichael is not the sharpest tool in the shed, but why the hell would he do that?'

'Family, darling.' Lauren shrugged. 'Don't you know that blood is thicker than water?'

Yes, he did, but what he also knew was that everyone was ultimately out for themselves and if you let your guard down you'd be left with nothing more than egg on your face.

He ran a hand through his damp hair and sweat drops sprayed around his head.

Lauren jumped back as if he'd nearly drenched her designer suit in sulphuric acid and threw an embarrassed glance towards Ricardo, who was busy surveying her charms.

Cruz snapped his attention away from both of them and concentrated on the blank wall covered in streaks of rubber from years of use.

Eight years ago Ocean Haven had been his home. For eleven years he had lived above the main stable and worked diligently with the horses—first as a groom, then as head trainer and finally as manager and captain of Charles Carmichael's star polo team. He'd been lifted from poverty and obscurity in a two-dog town because of his horsemanship by the wealthy American who had spotted him on the *hacienda* where Cruz had been working at the time.

Cruz gritted his teeth.

He'd been thirteen and trying to keep his family from going under after the sudden and pointless death of his father.

Charles Carmichael, he'd later learned, had ambitious plans to one day build a polo 'dream team' to rival all others, and he'd seen in Cruz his future protégé. His mother had seen in him an unmanageable boy she could use to keep the rest of his siblings together. She'd said sending him off with the American would be the best for him. What she'd meant was that it would be the best for all of them, because Old Man Carmichael was paying her a small fortune to take him. Cruz had known it at the time—and hated it—but because he'd loved his family more than anything he'd acquiesced.

And, hell, in the end his mother had been right. By the age of seventeen Cruz had become the youngest player ever to achieve a ten handicap—the highest ranking any player could achieve and one that only a handful ever did. By the age of twenty he'd been touted as possibly the best polo player who had ever lived.

By twenty-three the dream was over and he'd become the joke of the very society who had kissed his backside more times than he cared to remember.

All thanks to the devious Aspen Carmichael. The devious and extraordinarily beautiful Aspen Carmichael. And what shocked Cruz the most was that he hadn't expected it of her. She'd blindsided him and that had made him feel even more foolish.

She had come to Ocean Haven as a lonely, sweet-natured ten-year-old who had just lost her mother in a horrible accident some had whispered was suicide. He'd hardly seen her during those years. His summers had been spent playing polo in England and she had attended some posh boarding school the rest of the year. To him she'd always been a gawky kid with wild blonde hair that looked as if it could use a good pair of scissors. Then one year he'd injured his shoulder and had to spend the summer—her summer break—at Ocean Haven, and *bam!* She had been about sixteen and she had turned into an absolute stunner.

All the boys had noticed and wanted her attention.

So had Cruz, but he hadn't done anything about it. Okay, maybe he'd thought about it a number of times, especially when she had thrown him those hot little glances from beneath those long eyelashes when she assumed he wasn't looking, and, okay, possibly he could remember one or two dreams that she had starred in, but he never would have touched her if she hadn't come on to him first. She'd been too young, too beautiful, too *pure*.

He found himself running his tongue along the edge of

his mouth and the taste of her exploded inside his head. She sure as hell hadn't been pure *that* night.

Gritting his teeth, he shoved her out of his mind. Memory could be as fickle as a woman's nature and his aviator glasses were definitely not rose coloured where she was concerned.

'You okay, *hermano*?'

Cruz swung around and stared at Ricardo without really seeing him. He liked to think he was a fair man who played by the rules. A forgive-and-forget kind of man. He'd stayed away from Ocean Haven and anything related to it after Charles Carmichael had given him the boot. Now his property had come up for sale and objectively speaking it was a prime piece of real estate. The fact that he'd have to raze it to the ground to build a hotel on it was just par for the course.

Of course his kid brother wouldn't understand that, and he wasn't in the mood to explain it. He'd left Mexico when Ricardo had been young. Ricardo had cried. Cruz had not. Surprisingly, after he'd returned home with his tail between his legs eight years ago, he and his brother had picked up from where they'd left off, their bond intact. It was the only bond that was.

'I'm fine.' He swung his gaze to Lauren. 'And I'm not concerned about Aspen Carmichael. Old man Carmichael died owing more money than he had, thanks to the GFC, so there's no way she can have that sort of cash lying around.'

'No, she doesn't,' Lauren agreed. 'She's borrowing it.'

Cruz stilled. Now, that was just plain stupid. He knew Ocean Haven agisted horses and raised good-quality polo ponies, but no way would either of those bring in the type of money they were talking about.

'She'll never get it.'

Lauren looked as if she knew better. 'My sources tell me she's actually pretty close.'

Cruz ignored Ricardo's interested gaze and kept his face visibly relaxed. 'How close?'

'Two-thirds close.'

'Twenty million! Who would be stupid enough to lend her twenty million US dollars in this economic climate?' And, more importantly, what was she using for collateral?

Lauren raised her eyebrows at his uncharacteristic outburst, but wisely stayed silent.

'Hell!' The burst of adrenaline he used to feel when he mounted one of his ponies before a major event winged through his blood. How on earth had she managed to raise that much money and what could he do about it?

'Do you want me to start negotiating with her?' Lauren queried.

'No.' He turned his ordinarily agile mind to come up with a solution, but all it produced was an image of a radiant teenager decked out in figure-hugging jodhpurs and a fitted shirt leaning against a white fencepost, laughing and chatting while the sun turned her wheat-blonde curls to gold. His jaw clenched and his body hardened. Great. A hard-on in gym shorts. 'You focus on Joe Carmichael and any other offers lurking in the wings,' he instructed his lawyer. 'I'll handle Aspen Carmichael.'

'Of course,' Lauren concurred with a brief smile.

'In the meantime find out who Aspen is borrowing from and what exactly she's offering as collateral—' although as to that he had his ideas '—and meet me in my Acapulco office in an hour.'

Ricardo waited until Lauren had disappeared before tossing the rubber ball into the air. 'You didn't tell me you were buying the Carmichael place.'

'Why would I? It's just business.'

Ricardo's eyebrows lifted. 'And *handling* the lovely Aspen Carmichael will be part of that business?'

People said Cruz had a certain look that he got just before a major event which told his opponents they might as well pack up and go home. He gave it to his brother now. 'This is not your concern.'

His brother, unfortunately, was one of the few people who ignored it.

'Maybe not, but you once swore you'd never set foot on Ocean Haven again. So, what gives?'

What gave, Cruz thought, was that old Charlie had kicked the bucket and his son, Aspen's uncle, Joseph Carmichael, couldn't afford to run the estate and keep his English bride in diamonds and champagne so was moving to England. Cruz had assumed Aspen would be going with them—to sponge off him now that her grandfather was out of the picture.

It seemed he had assumed wrong.

But he had no intention of talking about his plans with his overly sentimental brother, who would no doubt assume there was more to it than a simple opportunity to make a lot of money. 'I don't have time to talk about it now,' he said, making a split-second decision. 'I need to organise the jet.'

'You're flying to East Hampton?'

'And if I am?' Cruz growled.

Ricardo held his hands up as if he was placating an angry bear. 'Miama's surprise birthday party is tomorrow.'

Cruz strode towards the changing rooms, his mind already in Hampton—or more specifically in Ocean Haven. 'Don't count on me being there.'

'Given your track record, the only person who still has enough hope to do that is Miama herself.'

Cruz stopped. Ricardo's blunt words stabbed him in the heart. His family still meant everything to him, and he'd help any of them out in a heartbeat, but things just weren't the same any more. With the exception of Ricardo, none of his family knew how to treat him, and his mother constantly threw him guilty looks that were a persistent reminder of the darker days of his youth after he'd gone to the farm.

Charles Carmichael had been a difficult man with a formidable temper who'd liked to get his own way, and Cruz had never been one to back down from a fight until *that* night. No, it had not been an easy transition for a proud thirteen-year-old to make, and if there was one thing Cruz hated more than the capricious nature of the human race it was dwelling on the past.

He glanced back at Ricardo. 'You're going to be stubborn about this, aren't you?'

Ricardo laughed. 'You've cornered the market in stubborn, *mi amigo*. I'm just persistent.'

'Persistently painful. You know, bro, you don't need a wife. You *are* a wife.'

Aspen decided that she had a new-found respect for telemarketers. It wasn't easy being told no time after time and then picking yourself up and continuing on. But like anyone trying to make a living she had to toughen up and stay positive. Stay on track. Especially when she was so close to achieving her goal. To choke now or, worse, give up, would mean failing in her attempt to keep her beloved home and that was inconceivable.

Smiling up at the beef of a man in front of her as if she didn't have a head full of doubts and fears, Aspen surreptitiously pulled at the waist of the silk dress she'd worn to impress the polo patrons attending the midweek chukkas they held at Ocean Haven throughout the summer months.

In the searing sunshine the dress had taken on the texture of a wet dishrag and it did little to improve her mood as she listened to Billy Smyth the Third, son of one of her late grandfather's arch enemies, wax lyrical about the game of polo he had—thankfully—just won.

'Oh, yes,' she murmured. 'I heard it was the goal of

the afternoon.' Fed to him, she had no doubt, by his well-paid polo star, who knew very well which side his bread was buttered on.

Billy Smyth was a rich waste of space who sponged off his father's cardboard packaging empire and loved every minute of it—not unlike many others in their circle. Her ex-husband still continued unashamedly to live off his own family's wealth, but thankfully he'd been out of her life for a long time, and she wasn't going to ruin an already difficult day by thinking about him as well.

Instead she concentrated on the wealthy man in front of her, with his polished boots and his pot belly propped over the top of his starchy white polo jeans. Years ago she had tried to like Billy, but he was very much a part of the 'women should keep silent and look beautiful' brigade, and the fact that she was pandering to his unhealthy ego at all was testament to just how desperate she had become.

When he'd asked her to meet him after the game she had jumped at the chance, knowing she'd dance on the sun in a bear suit if it would mean he'd lend her the last ten million she needed to keep Ocean Haven. Though by the gleam in his eyes he'd probably want her naked—and she wasn't so desperate that she'd actually hawk herself.

Yet.

Ever, she amended.

So she continued to smile and present her plan to turn 'The Farm', as Ocean Haven was lovingly referred to, into a viable commercial entity that any savvy businessman would feel remiss for not investing in. So far two of her grandfather's old friends had come on board, but she was fast feeling as if she was running out of options to find the rest. Ten million was small change to Billy and, she thought, ignoring the way his eyes made her skin crawl as if she was covered in live ants, he seemed genuinely interested.

'Your grandpop would be rolling in his grave at the thought of the Smyths investing in The Farm,' he announced.

True—but only because her grandfather had been an unforgiving, hard-headed traditionalist. 'He's not here anymore.' Aspen reminded him. 'And without the money Uncle Joe is going to sell to the highest bidder.'

Billy cocked his head and considered his way slowly down to her feet and just as slowly back up. 'Word is he already has a winner.'

Aspen took a minute to relax her shoulders, telling herself that Billy really didn't mean to be offensive. 'Yes. Some super-rich consortium that will no doubt want to put a hotel on it. But I'm determined to keep The Farm in the family. I'm sure you understand how important that is, being such a devoted family man yourself.'

A slow smile crept over Billy's face and Aspen inwardly groaned. She was trying too hard and they both knew it.

'Yes, indeed I do.'

Billy leered. His smile grew wider. And when he rocked back on his heels Aspen sent up a silent prayer to save her from having to deal with arrogant men ever again.

Because that was exactly why she was in this situation in the first place. Her grandfather had believed in three things: testosterone, power, and tradition. In other words men should inherit the earth while women should be grateful that they had. And he had used his fearsome iron will to control everyone who dared to disagree with him.

When her mother had died suddenly just before Aspen's tenth birthday and—surprise surprise—her errant father couldn't be located, Aspen had been sent to live with her grandfather and her uncle. Her grandmother had passed away a long time before. Aspen had liked Uncle Joe immediately, but he'd never been much of an advocate for her during her grandfather's attempts to turn her into the perfect debutante.

So far she had been at the mercy of her controlling grandfather, then her controlling ex, and now her misguided, henpecked uncle.

'I'm sorry Aspen,' her Uncle Joe had said when she'd managed to pin him down in the library a month ago. 'Father left the property in my hands to do with as I saw fit.'

'Yes, but he wouldn't have expected you to *sell it*,' Aspen had beseeched him.

'He shouldn't have expected Joe to sort out the mess of his finances either,' Joe's determined wife Tammy had whined.

'He wasn't well these last few years.' Aspen had appealed to her aunt, but, knowing that wouldn't do any good, had turned back to her uncle. 'Don't sell Ocean Haven, Uncle Joe. Please. It's been in our family for one hundred and fifty years. Your blood is in this land.'

Her mother's heart was here in this land.

But her uncle had shaken his head. 'I'm sorry, Aspen, I need the money. But unlike Father I'm not a greedy man. If you can raise the price I need in time for my Russian investment, with a little left over for the house Tammy wants in Knightsbridge, then you can have Ocean Haven and all the problems that go with it.'

'*What?*'

'*What?*'

Aspen and her Aunt Tammy had cried in unison.

'Joseph Carmichael, that is preposterous,' Tammy had said.

But for once Uncle Joe had stood up to his wife. 'I'd always planned to provide for Aspen, so this is a way to do it. But I think you're crazy for wanting to keep this place.' He'd shaken his head at her.

Aspen had been so happy she had all but floated out of

the room. Then reality at what exactly her uncle had offered had set in and she'd got the shakes. It was an enormous amount of money to pay back but she *knew* if she got the chance she could do it.

The horn signifying the end of the last chukka blew and Aspen pushed aside her fear that maybe she *was* just a little crazy.

'Listen, Billy, it's a great deal,' she snapped, forgetting all about the proper manners her grandfather had drummed into her as a child, and also forgetting that Billy was probably her last great hope of controlling her own future. 'Take it or leave it.'

Oh, yes and losing that firecracker temper of yours is sure to sway him, she berated herself.

A tiny dust cloud rose between them as Billy made a figure eight with his boots in the dirt. 'The thing is, Aspen, we're busy enough over at Oaks Place, and even though you've done a good job of hiding it The Farm needs a lot of work.'

'It needs some,' Aspen agreed with forced calm, thinking she hadn't done a good job at all if he'd seen through her patchwork maintenance attempts. 'But I've factored all that into the plan.' *Sort of.*

'I just think I need a bit more of a persuasive argument if I'm to take this to my daddy,' he suggested, a certain look crossing his pampered face.

'Like…?' A tight band had formed around Aspen's chest because, really, it was hard to miss what he meant.

'Well, hell, Aspen, you're not that naïve. You *have* been married.'

Yes, unfortunately she had. But all that had done was make her determined that she would never be at any man's mercy again. Which was exactly where arrogant, controlling men like this one wanted their women to be. 'For just you, Billy?' she simpered. 'Or for your daddy as well?'

It took Mr Cocksure a second or two to realise she was yanking his chain and when he did his big head reared back and his eyes narrowed. 'I ain't no pimp, lady.'

'No,' she said calmly, flicking her riot of honey-coloured spiral curls back over her shoulder. 'What you are is a dirty, rotten rat and I can see why Grandpa Charles said your kind were just slime.' *Who gave a damn about proper manners anyway?*

Instead of getting angry Billy threw back his head and hooted with laughter. 'You know. I can't believe the rumours that you're a cold one in the sack. Not with all that fire shooting out of those pretty green eyes of yours.' He reached out and ran a finger down the side of her cheek and grinned when she raised her hand to rub at it. 'Let me know when you change your mind. I like a woman with attitude.'

Before she could open her mouth to tell him she'd mention that to his wife he sauntered off, leaving her spitting mad. She watched him pick up a glass of champagne from a table before joining a group of sweaty riders and willed someone to grab it and throw it all over him.

Of course no one did. Fate wasn't that kind.

Turning away in disgust, she cursed under her breath when a gust of hot wind whipped her hair across her face. Too angry to stop and clear her vision, she would have walked straight into a wall if it hadn't reached out and grabbed her by her upper arms.

With a soft gasp she looked up, about to thank whoever had saved her. But the words never came and the quick smile froze on her face as she found herself staring into the hard eyes of a man she had thought she would never see in the flesh again.

The air between them split apart and reformed, vibrating with emotion as Cruz Rodriquez stared down at her with such cold detachment she nearly shivered.

Eight years dissolved into dust. Guilt, shame and a host of other emotions all sparked for dominance inside her.

'I…' Aspen blinked, her mind scrambling for poise… words…*something*.

'Hello, Aspen. Nice to see you again.'

Aspen blinked at the incongruity of those words. He might as well have said *Off with her head*.

'I…'

CHAPTER TWO

CRUZ STARED DOWN at the slender woman whose smooth arms he held and wished he hadn't left his sunglasses in the car. At seventeen Aspen Carmichael had been full of sexual promise. Eight years later, with her golden mane flowing down past her shoulders and the top button of her dress artfully popped open to reveal the upper swell of her creamy assets, she had well and truly delivered. And he was finding it hard not to take her all in at once.

'You…?' he prompted casually, dropping his hands and raising his eyes from her cleavage.

She glanced down and quickly closed the top of her dress. Clearly only men offering part of their vast fortunes were allowed to view the merchandise. The realisation of his earlier assumption as to what she might be using as leverage to raise her cash was for some reason profoundly disappointing.

'I…' She shook her head as if to clear it. 'What are you doing here?'

'Old Charlie would roll over in his grave if he heard you greeting a polo patron like that,' Cruz drawled. *Even one he didn't think would ever be good enough for his perfect little granddaughter,* he added silently.

Cruz's velveteen voice, with no hint at all of his Mexican heritage, scraped over Aspen's already raw nerves and she didn't manage to contain the shiver this time.

She couldn't tell his frame of mind but she knew hers and it was definitely disturbed. 'My grandfather probably feels like he's on a spit roast at the moment.' She smiled, trying for light amusement to ease the tension that lay as thick as the issues of the past between them.

'Are you implying he's in hell, Aspen?'

He probably was, Aspen thought, but that wasn't what she'd meant. 'No. I just…you're right.' She shook her head, wondering what had happened to her manners. Her composure. Her *brain*. 'That was a terrible greeting. Shall we start again?'

Without waiting for him to reply she stuck out her hand, ignoring the racing memories causing her heart to beat double time.

'Hello, Cruz, welcome back to Ocean Haven. You're looking well.' Which was a half-truth if ever she'd uttered one.

The man didn't look well. He looked superb.

His thick black hair that sat just fashionably shy of his expensive suit jacket and his piercing black eyes and square-cut jaw were even more beautiful than she remembered. He'd always had a strong, angular face and powerful body, but eight years had done him a load of favours in the looks department, settling a handsome maturity over the youthful virility he'd always worn like a cloak.

The apology she'd never got to voice for her part in the acrimonious accusations that had no doubt contributed to him leaving Ocean Haven eight years ago hovered behind her closed lips, but it seemed awkward to just blurt it out.

How could she tell him that a couple of months after that night she had written him a letter explaining everything but hadn't had the wherewithal to send it without feeling a deep sense of shame at her ineptitude? It was little comfort knowing she'd been distracted by her grandfather's stroke at the time, because she knew her behaviour that night had probably brought that on too. After he had recovered sending Cruz a letter had seemed like too little too late, and she'd pushed out of her mind the man who had fascinated her during most of her teenage years.

And maybe he was here now to let bygones be bygones. She didn't know, but why pre-empt anything with her own guilt-riddled memories?

Because it would make you feel better, that's why.

'As are you.'

As she was what? Oh, looking well. 'Thank you.' She ran a nervous hand down the side of her dress and then pretended she was flicking off horse dust. 'So…ah…are you here for the polo? The last chukka just finished, but—'

'I'm not here for the polo.'

Aspen hated the anxious feeling that had settled over her and raised her chin. 'Well, there's champagne in the central marquee. Just tell Judy that I sent—'

'I'm not here for the champagne either.'

Even more perturbed by the way he regarded her with such cool detachment she felt as if she was frying under the blasted summer sun. 'Well, it would be great if you could tell me what you *are* here for because I have a few more people to schmooze before they leave. You know how these things go.'

He looked at her as if he was seeing right inside her. As if he knew all her secrets. As if he could see how desperately uncomfortable she was. *Impossible*, she thought, telling herself to get a grip.

Cruz could almost see the sweat breaking out over Aspen's body and noted the way her cat-green eyes wouldn't quite meet his. He didn't know if that was because he was keeping her from an assignation with Billy Smyth, or someone else, or because she could feel the chemistry that lay between them like a grenade with the pin pulled.

Whatever it was, she wasn't leaving his side until he

had won over her confidence and figured out a way to handle the situation.

His brother's silky question about 'handling the lovely Aspen Carmichael' came into his head. He knew what Ricardo had meant and looking at Aspen now, in her svelte designer dress and 'come take me' heels, her wild hair curling down around her shoulders as if she'd just rolled out of her latest lover's bed, he had no doubt many men had 'handled' her that way before. But not him. Never him.

So far he'd drawn a blank as to how to contain her money-grabbing endeavours without alerting her to his own interest in Ocean Haven. Until he did he'd just have to rein himself in and keep his eyes away from her sexy mouth.

'I'm here to buy a horse, Aspen. What else?'

'A horse?'

Aspen blinked. That was the last thing she had expected him to say, though what she *had* expected she couldn't say.

'You do have one for sale, don't you?' he continued silkily.

Aspen cleared her throat. 'Gypsy Blue. She's a thoroughbred. Ex-racing stock and she's gorgeous.'

'I have no doubt.'

Aspen frowned at his tone, wondering why he seemed so tense. Not that he *looked* tense. In his bespoke suit with his hands in his pockets, his hair casually ruffled by the warm breeze, he looked like a man who didn't have a care in the world. But the vibe she was picking up from him was making her feel edgy—and surely that wasn't just because of her sense of guilt.

'Are you hoping the horse will materialise in front of us, Aspen, or are you going to take me to see her?'

'I...' Aspen felt stupid, and not a little perturbed to be standing there trying not to look at his chiselled mouth. Which was nearly impossible when the memory of the kiss they had shared on that awful night was swirling inside her head. 'Of course.' She glanced around, hoping to see Donny, but knew that was cowardly. It was really *her* responsibility to show him the mare, not her chief groom's.

'She played earlier today, so she should be in the south stables.' It was just rotten luck that she happened to be in the building where she had kissed Cruz on that fateful night. 'Hey, why don't I take you past the east paddock?' she said, using anything as a possible distraction. 'Trigger is out there, and I know he'd remember you and—'

'I'm not here on a social visit, Aspen.'

And don't mistake it for one, his tone implied.

No polo, no champagne, no socialising. Got it.

Still, she hesitated at his sharp tone. Then decided to let it drop and listened to the sound of their feet crunching the gravel as they walked away from the busy sounds of horse-owners loading tired horses into their respective trucks. It was all very normal and busy at the end of the afternoon's practice, and yet Aspen felt as if she was wading through quicksand with Cruz beside her.

She cast a curious glance at him and wondered if he felt the same way. Or maybe he didn't feel anything at all and just wanted to do his business and head out like everyone else. In a way she hoped that was the case, because the shock of seeing him again had worn off and his tension was raising her stress levels to dangerous proportions.

But then he had a reason for being tense, she reminded herself, and her skin flushed hotly as the weight of the past bore down on her. Years ago she had promised herself that she would never let pride interfere with the decisions she made in her life, but in avoiding the elephant walking alongside them wasn't that exactly what she was doing now?

Taking a deep breath, she stopped just short of the stable

doors and turned to Cruz, determined to rectify the situation as best she could *before* they made it inside.

Shading her eyes with one hand, she looked up into his face. Had he always been this tall? This broad? This good-looking?

'Cruz, listen. This feels really awkward, but you took me by surprise before when I ran into you—*literally.*' She released a shaky breath. 'I want you to know that I feel terrible about the way you left The Farm all those years ago, and I'm truly sorry for the role I played in that.'

'Are you?' he asked coolly.

'Yes, of course. I never meant for you to get into trouble.'

Cruz didn't move a muscle.

'I didn't!' Aspen felt her temper flare at his dubious look, hating how defensive she sounded.

She'd gone down to the stables that night because Chad—now thankfully her ex—had stayed for dinner so he could present his idea to her grandfather that he would marry her as soon as she turned eighteen. Aspen remembered how overwhelmed she had felt when neither man would consider her desire to study before she even thought about the prospect of marriage.

She'd known it was what her grandfather wanted, and at the time pleasing him had been more important than pleasing herself. So she'd done what she'd always done when she was stressed and gone down to be with the horses and to reconnect with her mother in her special place in the main stable.

Gone to try and make sense of her feelings.

Of course in hindsight letting her frustration get to her and kicking the side of the stable wall in steel-capped boots hadn't been all that clever, because it had brought Cruz down from his apartment over the garage to investigate.

She remembered that he had looked gorgeous and lean

and bad in dirty jeans and a half-buttoned shirt, as if he had just climbed out of bed.

'What's got you in a snit, *chiquita*?' he'd said, the intensity of his heavy-lidded gaze in the dim light belying the relaxed humour in his voice.

'Wouldn't you like to know?' she'd thrown back at him challengingly.

Inwardly grimacing, she remembered how she had flicked her hair back over her shoulder in an unconscious gesture to get his full attention. She hadn't known what she was inviting—not really—but she hadn't wanted him to go. For some reason she had remembered the time she had come across him kissing a girlfriend in the outer barn, and the soft, pleasure-filled moans the girl had made had filled her ears that night.

Acting purely on instinct she had wandered from horse stall to horse stall, eventually coming to a stop directly in front of him. The warm glow of his torch had seemed to make the world contract, so that it had felt as if they were the only two people in it. Aspen was pretty sure she'd reached for him first, but seconds later she had been bent over his arm and he had been kissing her.

Her first kiss.

She felt her breathing grow shallow at the memory.

Something had fired in her system that night—desperation, lust, need—whatever it had been she'd never felt anything like it before or since.

Looking back, it was obvious that a feeling of entrapment—a feeling of having no say over her future—had driven her into the stables that night, but it had been Cruz's sheer animal magnetism that had driven her into his arms.

Not that she really wanted to admit any of that to him right now. Not when he looked so…*bored.*

'This is old news, Aspen, and I'm not in the mood to reminisce.'

'That's your prerogative. But I want you to know that I told my grandfather the next day that he'd got it wrong.'

'Really?'

'Yes, really.' But her grandfather had cut her off with a look of disgust she hadn't wanted to face. She looked up at Cruz now, more sorry than she could say. 'I'm—'

'Truly sorry? So you said. Have you become prone to repeating yourself?'

Aspen blinked up at him. Was it her imagination or did he hate her? 'No, but I don't think you believe me,' she said carefully.

'Does it matter if I do?'

'Well, we used to be friends.'

'We were never *friends*, Aspen. But I was glad to see your little indiscretion didn't stop Anderson from marrying you.'

Aspen moistened her parched lips. 'Grandfather thought it best if I didn't tell him.'

Cruz barked out a laugh. 'Well, now I almost feel sorry for the fool. If he'd known what a disloyal little cheat you were from the start he might have saved himself the heartache at the end.'

Oh, yes, he hated her all right. 'Look, I'm sorry I brought it up. I just wanted to clear the air between us.'

'There's nothing to clear as far as I'm concerned.'

Aspen studied him warily. He wasn't moving but she felt as if she was being circled by a predator. A very angry predator. She didn't believe that he was at all okay with what had transpired between them but who was she to push it?

'I made a mistake, but as you said you're not here to reminisce.' And nor was she. Particularly not about a time in her life she would much rather forget had ever happened.

She turned sharply towards the stables and kept up a brisk pace until she reached the doors, only starting to feel herself relax as she entered the cooler interior, her high heels clicking loudly on the bluestone floor. Her nose was filled with the sweet scent of horse and hay.

Cruz followed and Aspen glanced around at the worn tack hanging from metal bars and the various frayed blankets and dirty buckets that waited for Donny and her to come and finish them off for the day. The high beams of the hayloft needed a fresh coat of paint, and if you looked closely there were tiny pinpricks of sunlight streaming in through the tin roof where there shouldn't be. She hoped Cruz didn't look up.

A pigeon created dust motes as it swooped past them and interested horses poked their noses over the stall doors. A couple whinnied when they recognised her.

Aspen automatically reached into her pocket for a treat, forgetting that she wasn't in her normal jeans and shirt. Instead she brushed one of the horses' noses. 'Sorry, hon. I don't have anything. I'll bring you something later.'

Cruz stopped beside her but he didn't try to stroke the horse as she remembered he might once have done.

'This is Cougar. Named because he has the heart of a mountain lion, although he can be a bit sulky when he gets pushed around out on the field. Can't you, big guy?' She gave him an affectionate pat before moving to the next stall. 'This one is Delta. She's—'

'Just show me the horse you're selling, Aspen.'

Aspen read the flash of annoyance in his gaze—and something else she couldn't place. But his annoyance fed hers and once again she stalked away from him and stopped at Gypsy Blue's stall. If she'd been able to afford it she would have kept her beloved mare, and that only increased her aggravation.

'Here she is,' she rapped out. 'Her sire was Blue Rise, her dam Lady Belington. You might remember she won the Kentucky Derby twice running a few years back.' She sucked in a breath, trying not to babble as she had done over her apology before. If Cruz was happy with the way things were between them then so was she. 'I have someone else interested, so if you want her you'll have to decide quickly.'

Quite a backpedal, Cruz thought. From uncomfortable, apologetic innocent to stiff Upper East Side princess. He wondered what other roles she had up her sleeve and then cut the thought in half before it could fully form. Because he already knew, didn't he? Cheating temptress being one of them. Not that she was married now. Or engaged as far as he knew.

'I've made you angry,' he said, backpedalling himself.

This wasn't at all the way he needed her to be if he was going to get information out of her. It was just this damned place. It felt as if it was full of ghosts, with memories around every corner that he had no wish to revisit. He'd closed the door on that part of his life the minute he'd carried his duffel bag off the property. On foot. Taking nothing from Old Man Carmichael except the clothes on his back and the money he'd already earned.

Of its own accord his gaze shifted to the other end of the long walkway to the place where Aspen had approached him that night, wearing a cotton nightie she must have known was see-through in the glow of his torch. He hadn't been wearing much either, having only thrown on a pair of jeans and a shirt he hadn't even bothered to button properly when he'd heard something banging on the wall and gone to investigate.

He'd presumed it was one of the horses and had been absolutely thunderstruck to find Aspen in that nightie and a pair of riding boots. She'd looked hotter than Hades and when she'd strolled past the stalls, lightly trailing her slender fingers along the wood, he couldn't have moved if someone had planted a bomb under him.

It had all been a ploy. He knew that now. He'd kissed her because he'd been a man overcome with lust. She'd kissed him because she'd been setting him up. It had been like a bad rendition of Samson and Delilah and she'd deserved an acting award for wardrobe choice alone.

His muscles grew taut as he remembered how he had held himself in check. How he hadn't wanted to overwhelm her with the desperate hunger that had surged through him and urged him to pull her down onto the hay and rip the flimsy nightie from her body. How he hadn't wanted to take her *innocence*. What a joke. She'd played him like a finely tuned instrument and, like a fool, he'd let her.

'Like I said before.' She cleared her throat. 'This feels a little awkward.'

She must have noticed the direction of his gaze because her voice sounded breathless; almost as if her memories of that night mirrored his own. Of course he knew better now.

About to placate her by pretending he had forgotten all about it, he found the words dying in his throat as she raised both hands and twisted her flyaway curls into a rope and let it drop down her back. The middle button on her dress strained and he found himself willing it to pop open.

Surprised to find his libido running away without his consent, he quickly ducked inside the stall and feigned avid interest in a horse he had no wish to buy.

He went through the motions, though, studying the lines of the mare's back, running his hands over her glossy coat, stroking down over her foreleg and checking the straightness of her pasterns. Fortunately he was on autopilot, because his undisciplined mind was comparing the shapeliness of the thoroughbred with Aspen's lissom figure and imagining how she would feel under his rough hands.

Silky, smooth, and oh, so soft.

Memories of the little sounds she'd made as he'd lost

himself in her eight years ago exploded through his system and turned his breathing rough.

'She's an exceptional polo pony. Really relaxed on the field and fast as a whip.'

Aspen's commentary dragged his mind back to his game plan and he kept on stroking the horse as he spoke. 'Why are you selling her?'

'We run a horse stud, not a bed and breakfast,' she said with mock sternness, her eyes tinged with dark humour as she repeated one of Charles Carmichael's favourite sayings.

'Or an old persons' home.' He joined in with Charles's second favourite saying before he could stop himself.

'No.' Her small smile was tinged with emotion.

Her reaction surprised him.

'You miss him?'

She shifted and leant her elbows on the door. 'I really don't know.' Her eyes trailed over the horse. 'He had moments of such kindness, and he gave me a home when Mum died, but he was impossible to be around if he didn't get his own way.'

'He certainly had high hopes of you marrying well and providing blue stock heirs for Ocean Haven.' And he'd made it more than clear to him after Aspen had returned to the house that night that Cruz wouldn't be the one to provide them under any circumstances.

'Yes.'

Her troubled eyes briefly met his and for a moment he wanted to shake her for not being a different kind of woman. A more sincere and genuine woman.

'So what do you think?'

It took him a minute to realise she was talking about the mare and not herself. 'She's perfect. I'll take her.'

'Oh.' She gave a self-conscious laugh. 'You don't want to ride her first?'

Oh, yes, he certainly did want to do that!

'No.'

'Well, I did tell you to be quick. I'll have Donny run the paperwork.'

'Send it to my lawyer.' Cruz rubbed the mare's nose and let her nudge him. 'I hear Joe is planning to sell the farm.'

She grimaced. 'Good news travels fast.'

'Polo's a small community.'

'Too small sometimes.' She gestured towards the mare. 'She'll ruin your nice suit if you let her do that.'

'I have others.'

So nice not to have to worry about money, Aspen thought, a touch enviously. After the abject poverty she and her mother had lived in after her father's desertion, the wealth of Ocean Haven had been staggering. It was something she'd never take for granted again.

'Where are you planning to go once it's sold?'

'It's not going to be sold,' she said with a touch of asperity, stepping back as Cruz joined her outside the stall. 'At least not to someone else.'

He raised an eyebrow. 'You're going to buy it?'

'Yes.' She had always been a believer in the power of positive thinking, and she had never needed that more than she did now.

Gypsy Blue whickered and stuck her head over the door and Aspen realised her water trough was nearly empty. Unhooking it, she walked the short distance to a tap and filled it.

'Let me do that.'

Cruz took the bucket from her before she could stop him and stepped inside the stall. Aspen grabbed the feed bucket Donny had left outside and followed him in and hooked it into placc.

'It's a big property to run by yourself,' he said.

'For a girl?' she replied curtly.

'I didn't say that.'

'Sorry. I'm a bit touchy because so many people have implied more than once that I won't be able to do it. It's like they think I'm completely incompetent, and that really gets my—' She gave a small laugh realising she was about to unload her biggest gripe onto him and he was virtually a stranger to her now. Why would he even care? 'The fact is…' She looked at him carefully.

He had money. She'd heard of his business acumen. Of the companies he bought and sold. Of his innovative and brilliant new polo-inspired hotel in Mexico. He was the epitome of a man at the top of his game. Right now, as he leant his wide shoulders against the stall door and blocked out all sources of light from behind, he also looked the epitome of adult male perfection.

'But the fact is…?' he prompted.

Aspen's eyes darted to his as she registered the subtle amusement lacing his voice. Did he know what she had just been thinking? 'Sorry, I was just…' *Just a bit distracted by your incredible face? Your powerful body? Way to go, Aspen. Really. Super effort.* 'The fact is—' she squared her shoulders '—I need ten million dollars to keep it.'

She forced a bright smile onto her face.

'You're not looking for an investment opportunity, are you?'

CHAPTER THREE

SHE COULDN'T BELIEVE she'd actually voiced the question that had just formed in her mind but she knew that she had when Cruz's dark gaze sharpened on hers. But frankly, with only five days left to raise the rest of the money and Billy Smyth firmly out of the picture, she really was that desperate.

'Give you ten million dollars? That's a big ask.'

Her heart thumped loudly in her chest and her mouth felt dust dry. 'Lend,' she corrected. 'But you know what they say…' She stopped as he straightened to his full height and she lost her train of thought.

He shoved both hands into his pockets. '*They* say a lot of things, Aspen. What is it exactly you're referring to?'

'If you don't ask you never know,' she said, moistening her lips. 'And I'm desperate.'

Cruz's eyes glittered as he looked down at her. 'A good negotiator never shows that particular hand. It puts their opponent in the dominant position.'

Heat bloomed anew on her face as his tone seemed to take on a sensual edge. 'I don't see you as my opponent, Cruz.'

'Then you're a fool,' he returned, almost too mildly.

Aspen felt her hopes shrivel to nothing. What had she been thinking, approaching a business situation like that? Where was her professionalism? Her polish?

But maybe she'd known he'd never agree to it. Not with the way he obviously felt about her.

'What would I get out of it, anyway?'

The unexpected question surprised her and once again her eyes darted to his. Had she been wrong in thinking he wouldn't be interested? 'A lot, actually. I've drawn up a business plan.'

'Really?'

She didn't like his sceptical tone but decided to ignore it. 'Yes. It outlines the horses due to foal, and how much we expect to make from each one, and our plans to purchase a top-of-the-line stallion to keep improving the breed. We also have a couple of wonderful horses we're about to start training—and I don't know if you've heard of our riding school, but I teach adults and children, and— well… There's more, but if you're truly interested we can run through the logistics of it all later.' Out of breath, she stopped, and then added, 'It has merit. I promise.'

'If it has so much merit why haven't any of the financial institutions bankrolled you?'

'Because I'm young—that is usually the first excuse. But really I think it's because unbeknownst to any of us Grandfather hadn't been running his business properly the last few years and—' Realising that yet again she was about to divulge every one of her issues, she stopped. 'The banks just don't believe I have enough experience to pull it off.'

'Perhaps you should have thought about furthering your education instead of marrying to secure your future.'

Aspen nearly gasped at his snide tone of voice. 'I didn't marry to secure anything,' she said sharply. Except perhaps her grandfather's love and affection. Something that had always been in short supply.

Upset with herself for even being in this position, and with him for his nasty comment, Aspen thought about telling him that she was one semester out from completing a degree in veterinary science—and that she'd achieved that while working full-time running Ocean Haven. But she knew that in her current state she would no doubt come across as defensive or whiney, and that only made her angry.

'If you have such a low opinion of me why pretend any interest in my plans for The Farm?' she demanded hotly, slapping her hands either side of her waist. 'Are you planning to steal our ideas?'

That got an abrupt bark of laughter from him that did nothing to improve her temper. 'I don't need to steal your ideas, *gatita*. I have plenty of my own.'

'Then why get my hopes up like that?'

'Is that what I did?'

Aspen stared him down. 'You know that's exactly what you did.'

He stepped closer to her. 'But maybe I *am* interested.'

His tone sent a splinter of unease down her spine but she was too annoyed to pay attention to it. 'Don't patronise me, Cruz. I have five days before The Farm will be sold to some big-shot investment consortium. I don't have time to bandy around with this.'

'Ocean Haven really means that much to you?'

'Yes, it does.'

'I suppose it *is* the easiest option for a woman in your position,' he conceded, with such arrogance that Aspen nearly choked.

Easy? Easy! He clearly had no idea how hard she worked on the property—tending horses, mending fences, keeping the books—nor how important Ocean Haven was to her. How it was the one link she had left with her mother. How it was the one place that had made her feel happy and secure after she'd been orphaned. After her marriage had fallen apart.

She was incredibly proud of her work and her future plans to open up a school camp for kids who'd had a tough start in life. Horses had a way of grounding troubled adolescents and she wanted to provide a place they could come to and feel safe. Just as she had. And she hated that Cruz was judging her—*mocking her*—like every other obnoxious male she had ever come across. That she hadn't expected it from him only made her feel worse.

Hopping mad, she had a mind to order him off her property, but she couldn't quite kill off this avenue of hope just yet. He was supposed to be a savvy businessman after all, and she had a good plan. Well, she hoped she did. 'Ocean Haven has been in my family for centuries,' she began, striving for calm.

'I think the violinist has packed up for the day…'

Aspen blinked. 'God, you're cold. I don't remember that about you.'

'Don't you, *gatita*? Tell me…'

His voice dropped an octave and her heartbeat faltered. 'What *do* you remember?'

Aspen's gaze fell to his mouth. 'I remember that you were…' *Tall. That your hair glints almost blue-black in the sun. That your face looks like it belongs in a magazine. That your mouth is firm and yet soft.* She forced her eyes to meet his and ignored the fact that her face felt as if it was on fire. 'Good with the horses.' She swallowed. 'That you were smart, and that you used to keep to yourself a lot. But I remember when you laughed.' *It used to make me smile.* 'It sounded happy. And I remember that when you were mad at something not even my grandfather was brave enough to face you. I rem—'

'Enough.' He sliced his hand through the air with sharp finality. 'There's only one thing I want to know right now,' he said softly.

If she remembered his kisses? Yes—yes, she did. Sometimes even when she didn't want to. 'What?' she asked, hating the breathless quality of her voice.

'Just how desperate *are* you?'

His dark voice was so dangerously male it sent her brain into overdrive. 'What kind of a question is that?' She shook her head, trying to ward off the jittery feelings he so effortlessly conjured up inside her.

He reached forward and captured a strand of her hair between his fingertips, his eyes burning into hers. 'If I were to lend you this money I'd want more than a share in the profits.'

Aspen felt her chest rising and falling too quickly and hoped to hell he wasn't going to suggest the very thing Billy Smyth had done not an hour earlier.

Reaching up, she tugged her hair out of his hold. 'Such as…?'

His eyes looked black as pitch as they pinned her like a dart on a wall. 'Oh, save us both the Victorian naïveté. You're no retiring virgin after the life you lived with Chad Anderson—and before that, even. You're a sensual woman who no doubt looks very good gracing a man's bed.' He paused, his gaze caressing her face. 'If the terms were right I might want you to grace mine.'

Was he kidding?

Aspen felt her mouth drop open before she could stop it. Rage welled up inside her like a living beast. Rage at the injustice of her grandfather's will, rage at the way men viewed her as little more than a sexual object, rage at her mother's death and her father's abandonment.

Maybe Cruz had a reason for being upset with her after she had failed to correct her grandfather's assumption that they were sleeping together years ago, but that didn't give him the right to treat her like a—like a whore.

'Get out of my way,' she ordered.

His eyes lingered on her tight lips. 'Make sure you don't

burn your bridges unnecessarily, Aspen. Pride can be a nasty thing when it's used rashly.'

She knew all about pride going before a fall. 'It's not rash pride making me reject your offer, Cruz. It's simple self-respect.'

'Whatever you want to call it, I'm offering you a straightforward business deal. You have something I've decided I want. I have something you need. Why complicate it?'

'Because it's disgusting.'

'What an interesting way to put it,' he sneered. 'Tell me, Aspen, would it have been less *disgusting* if I'd first said that you were beautiful before taking you to bed? If I'd first invited you out for a drink? Taken you to dinner, perhaps?' He took a step towards her and lowered his voice. 'If I had gone down that path would you have said yes?' His lips twisted with mocking superiority. 'If I had romanced you, Aspen, I could have had you naked and beneath me in a matter of hours and saved myself a hell of a lot of money.'

Aspen threw him a withering look, ignoring the sudden mental picture of them both naked and tangled together. 'You can save yourself a hell of a lot of money *and* skin right now and get off my property,' she said tightly.

His nostrils flared as he breathed deeply and she suddenly realised how close he was, how far she had to tilt her head back to look up at him. 'And for your information,' she began, wanting to stamp all over his supersized ego, 'I would *never* have said yes to you.'

'Really?'

He stepped even closer and Aspen felt the harsh bite of wood at her back. Caged, she could only stare as Cruz lifted one of her spiral curls again; this time carrying it to his nose. Her hands rose to shove him back but he didn't budge, and almost immediately her senses tuned in to the warm packed muscle beneath the thin cotton of his shirt, to the fast beat of his heart that seemed to mirror her own racing pulse.

A flash of memory took her back eight years to the feel of his mouth on hers. The feel of his tongue rubbing hers. The feel of his hands spanning her waist. Heat pooled inside her and made her breasts heavy, her legs unsteady. She remembered that after they'd been caught she had been so shocked by her physical reaction to him and so scared of her grandfather's wrath she'd fallen utterly silent—ashamed of herself for considering one man's marriage proposal while losing herself in the arms of another. Cruz hadn't raised one word of denial the whole time and she still wondered why.

Not that she had time to consider that now… He leant forward as if her staying hands were nothing more than crepe paper. His breath brushed her ear.

'Let me tell you what I remember, *gatita*. I remember the way your curvy backside filled out those tight jodhpurs. I remember the purple bikini top you used to wear riding your horse along the beach. And I remember the way you used to watch me. A bit like the way you were watching me stroke the mare before.' His hand tightened in her hair. 'You were thinking about how it would feel if I put my hands on you again, weren't you? How it would feel if I kissed you?'

Aspen made a half coughing noise in instant denial and tried to catch her breath. There was no way he could have known she'd been thinking exactly that.

'Have you turned into a dreamer, Cruz?' she mocked with false bravado, frightened beyond belief at how vulnerable she suddenly felt. 'Because really a dream would be the only place I would ever want something like that from you.'

Dreamer?

Cruz felt his jaw knot at her insolent tone. How dared she accuse him of being a dreamer when *she* was clearly the dreamer here if she thought she could buy and hold onto the rundown estate Ocean Haven had become?

Memories of the past swirled around him and bit deep. Memories of how she had felt in his arms. How she had tasted. Memories of how she had stood there, all dazed innocence, and listened to her grandfather rail at him. He'd been accused of ruining her that night but it was her—her and that slimy fiancé of hers, Chad Anderson—who had tried to ruin him. She and her lover who had set him up for a fall to clear the way for Chad to take over as captain of Charles Carmichael's dream team.

There'd been no other explanation for it, and he'd always wondered how far she would have taken things if her grandfather had turned up five minutes later. Because that was all it would have taken for him to twist her nightie up past her hips and thrust deep into her velveteen warmth.

His eyes took her in now. Her defiant expression and flushed face. Her rapidly beating pulse and her moist lips where her pink tongue had just lashed them. Her hands were burning a hole in his shirt and he was already as hard as stone—and, by God, he'd had enough of her holier-than-thou attitude.

'You would have loved it.' Cruz twisted her hair into a knot at the back of her head and pulled her roughly up against him. '*Will* love it,' he promised thickly, wrapping his other arm around her waist and staunching her shocked cry with his mouth.

Her lips immediately clamped together and she pushed against him, but that only brought her body more fully up against his as her hands slipped over his shoulders. She stilled, as if the added contact affected her as much as it affected him, and with a deep groan he ran his tongue across the seam of her lips. He felt a shiver run through her and then she shoved harder to dislodge him. He told himself he wasn't doing his plan any favours by forcing himself on her, but the plan paled into insignificance when compared to the feel of her warm and wriggling in his arms. He wanted her to surrender to him. To admit that the chemistry that had exploded through him like a haze of bloodlust as soon as he had seen her again wasn't just one-sided.

But some inner instinct warned him that this wasn't the way to get her to acquiesce, and years of experience in gentling horses rushed through him. He marshalled some of that strength and patience now and gentled her. Sucking at her lips, nipping, soothing her with his tongue. She made a tiny whimper in the back of her throat and he felt a sense of primal victory as she tentatively opened her mouth under his, aligning her body so that her soft curves were no longer resisting his hardness but melting against him until he could feel every sweet, feminine inch of her.

With a low growl of approval he gentled his hold on her and angled her head so that he could take her mouth more fully. When her lips opened wider and her arms urged him closer he couldn't stop himself from plundering her, couldn't resist drawing her tongue out so that she could taste him in return.

An unexpected sense of completeness settled over him—a sense of finding something he'd been searching for his whole life—and he didn't want the kiss to end. He didn't want this maddening arousal to end.

If he'd had any idea that it would be like this again he wasn't sure that he would have started it. But now that he had he didn't want to stop. *Ever.* She tasted so sweet. So silky. So *good*.

He made a sound low in his throat when she circled her pelvis against his in an age-old request and he couldn't think after that. Could only grab her hips and smooth his hands over her firm backside to mould her against him.

'Yes,' he whispered roughly against her mouth. 'Kiss me, *chiquita*. Give me everything.'

And she did. Without reservation. Her mouth devouring his as if she too had dreamed of this over and over and over. As if she too couldn't live without—

'Ow!'

Her sharp cry of pain echoed his deeper one as something pushed the back of his head and bumped his forehead into hers. He pulled back and glared over his shoulder to where the horse he had just agreed to purchase snorted in disgust.

Aspen blinked dazedly, rubbing at her head. Then the stunned look on her face cleared and he knew their impromptu little make out session had well and truly finished.

'You bastard.'

She raised her arm and slapped his face. The sound echoed in the cavernous stall and he worked his jaw as heat bloomed where her palm had connected.

About to tell her that she had a good arm, he was shocked to see that she had turned white and looked as if she might pass out.

'Aspen?'

She looked at him as if *he* had hit *her*. 'Now look what you made me do!' she cried.

Well, wasn't that typical of her—to blame him?

'I didn't *make* you do anything. You hit me. And if I'm not mistaken all because you enjoyed my kisses just a little too much.'

'Oh!'

She pushed against him with all her might and he was only too glad to step away from her.

'I've already turned down one slimy rat today and now I'm turning down another.' Her glare alone could have buried him. 'Now, get off my property before I have every man available throw you off.'

'I'm flattered you think it would take that many.'

'Oh, I bet you are.' Every inch of her trembled with feminine outrage. 'But I'm not prepared to take chances with a bully like you.'

'I didn't bully you, *chiquita*. You were asking for it.'

'Don't call me that.'

Cruz rubbed his jaw and scowled. 'What?'

'You know what.'

His brain must still have been on a go-slow because he couldn't recall what he'd called her. The thought irked him enough that he said, 'Maybe you should think about the way you act and dress if you don't want men thinking you're free and easy in bed.'

'Oh, my God. Are you serious?'

'Silky dresses that outline every curve, killer heels and just-out-of-bed hair all tell a man what's what.'

Fascinated, he watched her pull herself up to her full five feet and four inches—six in the heels.

'Any man who judges me on the way I look isn't worth a dime. You and Billy—'

Cruz raised his hand, cutting short her dramatic tirade. 'I am not like him,' he snarled.

'Keep telling yourself that, Cruz.' She tossed her head at him. 'It might help you sleep better at night.'

'I sleep just fine,' he grated. 'But if you should decide to change your high and mighty little mind about my offer I'll be staying at the Boston International until tomorrow morning.'

'Don't hold your breath.' She reefed open the stall door and stomped past him. 'I'd have to be crazy to accept an offer like that.'

Cruz ran a shaky hand through his hair and listened to the staccato sound of her high heels hammering her ire against the stone floor.

Her words, 'don't hold your breath' rang out in his head. Hadn't he told his brother the same thing a few hours ago? *Hell*. If he had, he couldn't remember why.

CHAPTER FOUR

'DAMMIT.' ASPEN CURSED as her hair caught around the button she had just wrenched open on the front of her dress. 'Stupid, idiotic hair.'

She yanked at it and winced when she heard the telltale crackle that indicated that she'd left a chunk behind. Then the pain set in and she rubbed her scalp.

God, she was angry. Furious. She pulled at the rest of her buttons and stopped when she caught sight of herself in the free-standing mirror that stood in the corner of her bedroom. Slowly she walked towards it.

An ordinary female figure stared back. An ordinary female figure with a flushed face and a wild mane of horrible hair. And tender lips. She put her fingers to them. They *looked* the same as they always did, but they *felt* softer. Swollen. And there was a slight graze on her chin where Cruz's stubble had scraped her skin.

Her pelvis clenched at the remembered pleasure of his mouth on hers. He hadn't even kissed her like that eight years ago. Then he'd been softer, almost tender. Today he'd kissed her as if he hadn't been able to help himself. As if he'd wanted to devour her. And never before had she kissed someone like that in return. Thank God Gypsy Blue had tried to knock some sense into them.

She had no idea why she'd acted like that with a man who had insulted her so badly. Maybe it was the fact that seeing him again had knocked her sideways. Somehow he had dazzled her the way he'd used to dazzle the women at polo matches. He was so attractive the crowds had always doubled when he had played, because all the wives and girlfriends had insisted that they simply *loved* polo and had to spend the *whole* day watching it. Really, they'd just mooned over him when he'd been on the field and drunk champagne and chatted the rest of the time. He'd dazzled her friends too.

Unconsciously she licked her tender lips and felt his imprint on them. Really she felt his imprint everywhere—and especially in the space between her thighs.

Heaven help her! She would have had sex with him. Had inadvertently *wanted* to have sex with him. The realisation of that alone was enough to shock her. She hated sex!

So why was she currently reliving Cruz's wicked kisses over and over like a hopeless teenager? He hadn't kissed her out of any real passion—he'd kissed her to make a point and to put her in her place and by God she had let him! Putting up a token resistance like the Victorian virgin he had accused her of acting like and then melting all over him like hot syrup.

She scratched the hair at her temples and made her curls frizz. Grabbing the offending matter, she quickly braided it, pulled on her jeans and shirt and stomped down to the stables.

Donny raised a startled eyebrow as she muttered a few terse words in his direction and started work at the other end. The rhythmical physical labour of putting away tack and shifting hay, of bantering with the horses and going through the motions of bedding them down for the night, was doing nothing to eradicate the feeling of all that hard male muscle pressed up against her.

'Make sure you don't burn your bridges unnecessarily, Aspen. Pride can be a nasty thing when it's used rashly.'

Pride? What pride. She had none. Well, she'd had enough to say no to both him and Billy Smyth.

'Oh, Billy Smyth! There's no way I would have slept with him even if he wasn't married,' she told Delta as she brushed her down vigorously.

But you would have with Cruz Rodriguez. Even without the money.

'I would not,' she promised Delta, knowing that if she had sex again with any man it would be too soon.

She stopped and leant her forehead against the mare. She breathed in her comforting scent and stared out over the stall door, looking up when something—a rat, maybe—disturbed a sleeping pigeon.

Her eye was immediately drawn to a rusty horseshoe lodged firmly between two supporting beams. Her mother had told her the story about how it had got there when she was little and it was the first thing Aspen had looked for when she had come to Ocean Haven, missing her mother desperately. Since then, whenever she was in a tricky situation she came out here and sought her mother's advice.

'And, boy, do I need it right now,' she muttered.

Delta nudged her side, as if to tell her to get on with it.

'Yes, I know.' She patted her neck. 'I'm thinking.'

Thinking about how much this place meant to her. Thinking about the dreams she had that would never materialise if she lost it. And she would lose it. To some faceless consortium in five days. Her stomach felt as if it had a rock in it.

Cruz's offer crept back into her mind for the thousandth time. He was right; it was pride making her say no.

So what if she said yes?

No, she couldn't. Cruz was big and overpowering and arrogant. Exactly the type of man she'd vowed to keep well away from.

But you're not marrying him.

No, but she would have to sleep with him. Which was just as unpalatable.

Sighing, she contemplated the peeling paint on the stall door. Her mother's face swam into her mind. Her tired smile. The day she had died she had been so exhausted after working two jobs and caring for Aspen, who had been sick at the time, that she'd simply forgotten that cars drove on the left-hand side of the road in England and she'd stepped out onto a busy road. It had been horrific. Devastating.

Aspen felt a pang of remorse and a deep longing. She had to keep Ocean Haven if only to preserve her mother's memory.

Feeling weighted down by memories, she continued brushing Delta. She had eked out a life here. She felt whole here. Protected. And, dammit, if she could keep it she would. She hadn't worked this hard to lose everything now.

Rash pride.

Rash pride had stopped her grandfather and her mother from reaching out to each other and maybe changing their lives for the better. Rash pride had made her grandfather refuse to listen to her own concerns about Chad after she had mentioned her doubts to him right before the wedding.

Rash pride wasn't going to get in the way of her life decisions any more. If Cruz Rodriguez wanted her body he could damned well have it. She didn't care. She hadn't cared about that side of things for years. And, anyway, once he found out what a dud she was in bed he'd change his mind pretty quickly.

Familiar fingers of distaste crawled up her spine as she recalled her wedding night before she could prevent herself doing it. She swallowed. What surprised her most was that being in Cruz's arms had been nothing like being in Chad's. But then Chad had often been drunk during their brief marriage and the alcohol had changed him. After that first night Aspen had frozen so much on the rare occasions he had approached her that he'd sought solace elsewhere. And made sure she knew about it. Always being deeply apologetic the following day when the alcoholic haze had retreated.

She'd stayed with him for six months and tried to be a better wife, but then he'd unfairly accused her of sleeping with his patron. It had been the final straw and she'd fled to Ocean Haven and never looked back.

She shivered.

'If you should happen to change your high and mighty little mind I'll be staying at the Boston International until tomorrow morning.'

Had she changed her mind?

There was no doubt that Cruz hated her after what had happened eight years ago, but he must also want her to make such an extreme offer. Could she put her concerns aside and sleep with him? She already knew she responded differently with him, felt differently with him, but what if she froze at the last minute as she had with Chad? What if he laughed at her when he learned about her embarrassing problem?

Rash pride, Aspen...

She groaned. To find out was to experiment, and to experiment meant opening herself up to knowing once and for all that *she* had been the problem in the bedroom and not Chad—as she sometimes liked to pretend when she was feeling particularly low.

'Coward,' she said softly.

Delta whickered.

'Oh, not you, beauty.' Aspen fished inside her pocket for a sugar cube. 'You're brave and courageous and would probably not bat an eyelid if I told you that Ranger's Apprentice had paid money to mount you if it meant saving The Farm.'

Aspen unwound Delta's tail from the tight bundle it had been wrapped in for the polo and wondered what would become of her beloved horses if she had to leave. Wondered if they'd be well cared for.

She felt she should warn the unsuspecting mare. 'If I keep The Farm I probably will be putting you in with him next season. I hope you don't mind. He's quite handsome.'

Not that looks had anything to do with the price of eggs.

She sighed as Donny stopped by Delta's stall and said that his lot were all set for the night and he would help out with some of the others if Aspen needed it.

At the rate she was going Aspen would need an army to get the horses done before the week was out.

She smiled at him. He had worked on the farm for six years now and she'd be lost without him. 'You're a gem, but I'm good. You go home to Glenda and the kids.'

'You're sure?' He shifted his gum around in his mouth. 'You seem a little wound up.'

Oh, she was. Ten million dollars wound up.

'Donny, what would you do if everything you loved was being threatened?' she asked suddenly.

He stuck a finger through his belt buckle and considered his shoes. 'You mean like Glenda and Sasha and Lela? Like my home?'

'Yeah,' Aspen said softly. 'Like your home.'

Donny nodded. 'I'd fight if I could.'

Aspen smiled. 'That's what I thought.'

Donny turned to go and then looked back over his shoulder. 'You sure you're all right, boss?'

'Fine. See you Monday.'

Cruz was going crazy. When a man let his ego get in the way of common sense that was the only conclusion to make. And the only one that made sense.

What other explanation could there possibly be when

he had just offered a woman he didn't even like ten million dollars to sleep with him?

And what would he have done if she'd said yes? Because he'd had no intention of going through with it. The very idea was ludicrous. He'd never paid for sex in his life.

So he wanted her? Big deal. It was because she was even more alluring than he remembered. And more stuck-up. Her hair was longer too, her cheekbones more defined, her breasts fuller, her mouth— He laughed. What was he doing? A full inventory? Why? There were plenty of women in his sea. Plenty more beautiful than this one when it came down to it.

And, yes, he liked to pit himself against an opponent for the sheer thrill of it, but making that offer to Aspen Carmichael had felt a bit like riding a nag into the middle of a forty-goal polo game without a bridle or a saddle and telling his opponents to have at him.

He certainly hadn't come anywhere close to finding a way to ensure that she wouldn't be able to raise the money to buy Ocean Haven herself—which had been his original goal.

Cruz poked at the half-eaten steak sandwich on his plate and stuffed an overcooked chip into his mouth. All he'd done instead was lump himself in with the likes of Billy Smyth and he was nothing like his lot.

No, you're worse, his conscience happily informed him. *You'd like to screw her* and *steal her family home out from under her as well.*

Yeah, whatever.

Unused to having a back and forth commentary inside his head about a woman—or about his decisions—he shoved himself to his feet and headed outside to see if the answer to his problem was written in the stars.

Of course it wasn't, but he stood there and let the warm evening air wash over him until memories of the past sailed in on the scent of jasmine and lilac. The sickening ball that had settled in his gut as he'd driven through the stone archway to Ocean Haven returned full force.

Focusing on something else, he listened to the distant murmurs of the light-hearted partying he could hear coming up off the darkened beach. Probably teenagers enjoying yet another stunning summer evening. Light flickered and wisps of smoke trailed in the moonlight. He imagined that many of them would be pairing off before long and snuggling down beside a campfire.

Unbidden, his mind conjured up an image of Aspen flirting with Billy Smyth earlier that day. He'd watched them for a couple of minutes before approaching her, not really wanting anyone to recognise him and start fawning all over him.

Aspen had used all her feminine wiles so the unhappily married Billy would notice her, but it hadn't been until she had let him run his finger down the side of her face and held his cheek afterwards, as if preserving his touch, that real bitterness and anger had rolled through Cruz like an incoming thunderstorm. Would she have let Smyth kiss her and shove her up against the wall of the stable as she had done with him earlier? Had she *planned* to later on?

'Damn her anyway.' He slammed the palm of his hand against the bronze railing and told himself to forget about her. Forget about the way she had caught fire in his arms once again. Forget about the way he had done the same in hers. Unfortunately his body was more than happy to relive it, and he was once again uncomfortably hard as he headed inside and downed the rest of his tequila.

As far as Cruz was concerned the Aspen Carmichaels of the world deserved everything they got. So why was he hanging around his hotel room feeling like the worst kind of male alive?

No reason.

No reason at all.

The hotel phone rang and he crossed to the hall table and picked it up, almost disappointed to find that the number on the display was a local one. Because he knew who it was even before he answered it. And now was the time to tell her that he had no intention of giving her the money in exchange for her delectable body. No intention at all.

But he didn't say that. Instead he threw his conscience to the wind and said, 'I'll pick you up at seven in the morning.'

There was enough of a silence on the other end of the line for him to wonder if he hadn't been mistaken, but then Aspen's husky tones sounded in his ear.

'Why?'

'Because I'm flying back to Mexico first thing in the morning.'

She cleared her throat. 'I can wait until you're next in Boston.'

She might be able to. He couldn't.

'You need that money by Monday, don't you?'

Again there was a pause long enough to fill the Grand Canyon. He waited for her to tell him to go to hell.

'Yes,' she said as if she was grinding nails.

'I'll see you tomorrow, then.'

He hung up before she could say anything else and stood staring at the telephone. He didn't know what shocked him more: the fact that he hadn't rescinded his ludicrous offer or the fact that he had made it in the first place. What didn't shock him was the fact that she had accepted.

He waited for a sense of satisfaction to kick in because he had finally come up with a way to stop her going after anyone else for the money. Instead he felt a sense of impending doom. Like a man who had bitten off more than he could chew. Because he had no intention of lending her the money and he didn't like what that said about him.

Maybe that he needed more tequila.

'Just have a shower, *imbecil,* and get some sleep,' he told himself.

Come Saturday The Rodriquez Polo Club would run the biggest polo tournament in Mexico for the second year and he had a Chinese delegation coming over to view the proceedings. They had some notion that he could form a partnership with them to introduce polo into China via a specialised hotel in Beijing. So he had to be on site for the next three days and be at his charming best.

'Better get rid of the *chica,* then,' he told his reflection grimly as he stripped off and stepped into the shower. Because watching Aspen flick her hair and flirt with everything in pants was not, he already knew, conducive to putting him in a good mood.

Ah, hell, maybe he should just forget the whole thing. Forget buying Ocean Haven. Yes, it was an exceptional piece of land, with those rolling hills and the bluff that looked out over the North Atlantic Ocean. But there were plenty of beautiful spots in the world. What did he really want it for anyway?

He squirted shampoo over his head and rubbed vigorously.

The fact was eight years ago Aspen Carmichael had set him up so that her over-indulged fiancé could take his place on the dream team without batting a pretty eyelash. She'd walked up to him and shyly put her arms around his neck and, like a fool who had fantasised about her for too long, he'd lost control. He would have done anything for her back then because, if he was honest, he'd liked her a little bit himself. Liked her a lot, in fact, and he hated knowing that she'd so easily fooled him.

But not this time. This time he would be the one holding all the cards. He relaxed for the first time that night. And why not? Why not take what she had offered him eight years ago? She was older now, and obviously still prepared to use her delectable body to get what she wanted. *So, okay—game on, Ms Carmichael. Game on.*

And if a small voice in his head said that he was wrong about her—well, he couldn't see how.

So what that she had loved the horses and been kind to everyone she came into contact with? So what if her apology earlier had seemed genuine? She knew how to play the game, that was all *that* said about her, but in the end she'd used him for her own ends just like everyone else in his life had done.

So, no, he didn't owe Aspen-damned-Carmichael any-damned-thing. And if this was fate's way of evening the score between them then, hell, who was he to argue?

CHAPTER FIVE

ASPEN WAS PACKED and ready by six the following morning. She'd told Mrs Randall, their long-time housekeeper, that she was going to Mexico to look over Cruz's horses for future growth opportunities. It was the best explanation she could come up with at short notice, especially when Mrs Randall had looked so pleased at the mention of Cruz's name.

'He missed his family terribly, that boy. Of course he was too proud to show it, but I suppose that was why he left so suddenly when he was a young man. He wanted to get back to them.'

Aspen would have liked to believe that homesickness had contributed to Cruz leaving The Farm eight years ago, but she suspected it was more because she had put him in an untenable situation.

Guilt ate at her, and all the confusing emotions she'd experienced at that time came rushing back. Her desperate need for approval from her grandfather, her fear of the future, her confusing feelings for Chad and the amazing pull she'd always felt towards Cruz.

Fortunately Mrs Randall was doing her Thursday morning market shopping when Cruz drove up in a mean black sports car, because Aspen was sure her confused state would have been on display for the wily older woman to see and that would have only added to her anxiety. Especially when she had decided that the best way to approach the situation was to be optimistic and positive. Treat it as the business transaction it was.

Shielded by the velvet drapes in the living room, she watched as Cruz climbed out of the car and literally prowled towards the front steps of the house, breathtakingly handsome in worn jeans that clung to his muscular thighs and a fitted latte-coloured T-shirt that set off his olive skin tone and black hair to perfection.

Not wanting him to think she was nervous at the prospect of seeing him, Aspen waited a few minutes after he'd pressed the bell before opening the door; glad that just last week she had given the front door a fresh lick of white paint and cleaned down the stone façade of the portico with an industrial hose.

'Good morning.' She hoped he hadn't heard her voice quaver and told herself that if she was really going to go through with this she needed to do better than she was now. 'Did you want coffee or tea?'

His gaze swept over her face and lingered on her chin, and when he unconsciously rubbed his jaw she knew he had noticed the mark—*his* mark—that she had made a futile effort to cover with concealer. Involuntarily her own eyes dropped to his mouth and heat coursed through her; she was mortified and embarrassed when his lips tightened with dismissal and he turned abruptly to scan the rest of the hallway.

'No. My plane's on standby. Let's go.'

Great. She wasn't even going to have the benefit of other commuters to ease the journey.

Turning to pick up her keys from the hallway table, she spotted the document she had spent half the night drafting. She couldn't believe she'd forgotten it. But then rational thinking and Cruz Rodriguez didn't seem to go together for her very well.

'I'd like you to sign this first.'

He looked at it dubiously. 'What is it?'

It was a document stipulating a condition she hoped he'd agree to and also preventing him from reneging on their deal if he found himself dissatisfied with the outcome of their temporary liaison. Which he undoubtedly would. But since this was a business arrangement Aspen wanted to make sure that when their physical relationship failed he was still bound to invest in Ocean Haven.

'Read it. I think it's clear enough.'

He took it from her and the paper snapped in the quiet room. The antique grandfather clock gauged time like a marksman.

It wasn't long before he glanced back at her, and Aspen swallowed as he laughed out loud.

Her mouth tightened as she waited for him to collect himself. She'd had an idea that he might have some objections to her demands but she hadn't expected that he find them comical.

'Once?' His eyes were full of amusement. 'Are you're kidding me?'

She wasn't. *Once*, she was sure, was going to be more than enough for both of them.

'No.'

When he looked as if he might start laughing again Aspen felt her nerves give way to temper.

'I don't see what's so funny?'

'That's because you're not paying the money.'

He circled behind her as if she was some slave girl on an auction block and he was checking her over.

She swung around to face him. 'If you read the whole document it says that I'm planning to pay you back the money anyway, so technically it's free.'

'With what?'

He unnerved her by circling her again, but this time she stood stock-still. 'I don't know what you mean.'

'What are you intending to pay me back with?' he murmured from behind her.

'The profits from The Farm.'

He scoffed, facing her. 'This place will be lucky to break even in a booming market.'

His eyes held hers and the chemistry that was as strong as carbon links every time they got within two feet of each other flared hotly. Aspen took a careful breath in. He was pure Alpha male right now, and his self-satisfied smile let her know that *he* knew the effect he was having on her.

Not that it would help either one of them in the long run. But she had to concentrate. If she didn't there was a chance she'd end up with nothing. Less than nothing. Because she'd lose the only tie she had left to her mother.

'That's your opinion. It's not mine.'

He studied her and she didn't know how she managed not to squirm under that penetrating gaze.

'It would want to be a damned good once, *gatita*.'

Aspen raised her chin. It was going to be horrible.

'It's a good deal.' She repeated what she'd said to Billy Smyth and so many others before him. 'Take it or leave it.'

He regarded her steadily, his eyes hooded. 'I tell you what. You make it one night and I'll agree.'

One night?

'As in the *whole* night?'

His slow smile sent a burst of electrical activity straight to her core. 'What a good idea, *gatita*. Yes, the whole night.'

Bastard.

'What *is* that you're calling me?' she fumed.

His smile was full of sex. '*Kitten.* You remind me of a spitting kitten who needs to be stroked.'

'Fine.' Aspen picked up the pen but didn't see a thing in front of her.

'Wait. Before you make your changes I want to know what this is.' Cruz stabbed his finger at her second point—the one that said he had to pay no matter what happened or didn't happen between them. 'Is this your way of telling me you're going to welsh on me?'

She frowned. 'Welsh on you?'

'Renege. Back out. Break your word.'

'I know what it means,' she snapped, wondering if he wasn't having a go at her character. 'And rest assured I am fully prepared to uphold my end of the bargain. I just want to make sure you do as well.'

Her throat bobbed as he continued to watch her and Cruz wondered if she had guessed that he was stringing her along.

Once!

He nearly laughed again. But he had to hand it to her. The document she had crafted was legally sound and would probably hold up well enough in a court of law.

Something about the way she stood before him, all innocently defiant, like a lamb to the slaughter, snagged on his conscience like an annoying burr in a sock, which you'd thought you'd removed only to have it poke at you again.

He couldn't do it. He couldn't let her go into this blind. 'There's something you should know.'

Her eyes turned wary. 'Like what?'

'I own Trimex Holdings.'

Aspen frowned. 'If that's supposed to mean something to me it doesn't.'

'Trimex Holdings is currently the highest bidder for Ocean Haven.'

He watched a myriad of emotions flit across her expressive face as the information set in. Shock. Disbelief. Anger. Uncertainty.

'So…' She frowned harder. 'This isn't real?'

How much he wanted her? Unfortunately, yes.

He tried not to let his gaze drop once again to the spot on her chin. He'd obviously grazed her with his stubble the day before and, although he'd hate to think that he'd hurt her, there was a part of him that was pretty pleased to see her wearing his mark. The moronic part.

Oh, yeah, it was real enough. But he knew that wasn't what she was referring to.

'My offer?'

'Yes.'

'It's real.'

'That doesn't make sense. Why would you lend me money to buy a property you are trying to buy for yourself?'

'Because I believe I'll win.' And he had just decided to instruct Lauren to keep upping his offer until it was so ludicrously tempting Joe Carmichael would see stars.

Aspen shook her head. 'You won't. Joe is very loyal to me.'

All families were loyal until money was involved. 'Care to back yourself?'

She looked at him as one might a maggot on a pork chop. 'I never realised how absolutely ruthless you are.'

'I'm absolutely successful. For a reason.'

She shook her head. 'You're not going to be this time. But can I trust you?'

The fact that she questioned his integrity annoyed him. 'I didn't have to tell you this, did I?'

'Fine,' she snapped, pacing away from him to the other side of the neat sitting room. She glared at him. Shook her head. Then paced back. Picked up the pen. 'It's not like I have a better option right now.'

Her fingers shook ever so slightly as she put pen to paper and something squeezed inside his chest.

'I'll do it.'

Impatient for this to be finalised, he grabbed the pen and replaced 'once' with 'one night'. Then he scrawled the date and his signature on the bottom of the page.

His gaze drifted down over her neat summer tunic which showed the delicate hollows either side of her collarbones and hinted at her firm breasts before it skimmed the tops of her feminine thighs. She'd been soft and firm pressed up against him yesterday. Svelte, he decided, glancing at her fitted jeans and ankle boots.

His body reacted predictably and he told himself it was past time to stop looking at her.

The flight from East Hampton to Acapulco took five hours. It might as well have been five days. Cruz had barely uttered a word to her since leaving The Farm—not much more than 'This way', 'Mind your step' and 'Buckle up; we're about to take off'. And Aspen was glad. She didn't think she'd be able to hold a decent conversation with the man right now. He wasn't a rat, she decided. He was a shark. A great white that hunted and killed without compunction.

And she was playing the game of her life against him.

Thank heavens she had her uncle on her side. But could she trust Cruz to give her the money? He'd looked startled and not a little angry when she had questioned his integrity. Yes, she was pretty sure she could trust him. His pride alone would mean that he upheld his end of the deal.

The deal. She had just made a bargain to sleep with the devil. She shuddered, glancing across the aisle to where Cruz was seated in a matching plush leather chair and buried in paperwork. It was beyond her comprehension that she should still want him. Which was scary in itself when she considered that she didn't even like sex. And, yes, she'd enjoyed kissing him, but that wasn't sex. She knew if they'd been anywhere near a bed she would have clammed up.

Urgh… She hated the thought of embarrassing herself in front of him. He was so confident. So *arrogant*. She hated that he just had to look at her and she had to concentrate extra hard to think logically. His touching her made her want to do stupid things. Things she couldn't trust.

And she particularly hated the thought of being vulnerable to him. Especially now. Now when he had made it clear that he'd win anyway. That she was doing this for nothing. It just made her more determined that he wouldn't.

Aspen pulled out her textbook. Questioning whether she had done the right thing in coming with him wouldn't change anything now. She'd signed the document she herself had drafted and she'd assured him that she wouldn't 'welsh' on him.

It would mean that her beloved home was hers. It would mean she would have the chance to put all the naysayers who didn't believe that a girl on her own could run a property the size of Ocean Haven in their places. And it would mean that for the first time in her life she would be free and clear of a dominating man controlling her future. That alone would be worth a little embarrassment with the Latin bad boy she had once fantasised about.

It was a thought that wasn't easy to hold onto when the plane landed on a private airstrip and a blast of hot, humid air swept across her face.

Cruz's long, loose-limbed strides ate up the tarmac as if the humid air hadn't just hit him like a furnace. He stopped by a waiting four-by-four and Aspen kept her eyes anywhere but on him as she climbed inside, doing her best to ease the kinks out of shoulders aching with tension.

Still, she noticed when he put on a pair of aviator sunglasses and clasped another man's hands in a display of macho camaraderie before taking the keys from him.

He was just so self-assured, she thought enviously, and she hated him. Hated him and everything he represented. Yesterday she'd been willing to greet him as a friend, had felt sorry for the part she had played in his leaving The Farm. Now she wished her grandfather had horsewhipped him. It was the least he deserved.

But did he?

Just because he wanted to buy her farm it didn't make him a bad guy, did it? No, not necessarily bad—but ruthless. And arrogant. And so handsome it hurt to look at him.

'You know I hate you, don't you?' she said without thinking.

Not bothering to look at her, he paused infinitesimally, his hands on the key in the ignition.

'Probably,' he said, with so little concern it made her teeth grind together.

He turned the key and the car purred to life. Then his eyes drifted lazily over her from head to toe and she felt her heart-rate kick up. He was studying her again. Looking at her as if he was imagining what she looked like without her clothes on.

'But it won't make a difference.'

His lack of empathy, or any real emotion, drove her wild. 'To what?'

'To this.'

Quick as a flash he reached for her, grabbed the back of her neck before she'd realised his intention and hauled her mouth across to his. Aspen stiffened, determined to resist the force of his hungry assault. And she did. For a moment. A brief moment before her senses took over and shut down her brain. A brief moment before his mouth softened. A brief moment before he pulled back and looked at her with lazy amusement. As if he was already the victor.

'He won't sell to you,' she blazed at him.

His smile kicked up one corner of his mouth. 'He'll sell to me.'

Aspen cut her gaze from his. She hated his insolent confidence because she wished she had just a smidgeon of it herself. 'How long till we get there?' she griped.

He laughed softly. 'So eager, *gatita*?'

'Yes,' she fumed. 'Eager to get out of your horrible company. In fact I don't know why we didn't just do this on the plane. Or at The Farm, come to think of it.'

His head tilted as he regarded her. 'Maybe I want to woo you.'

Aspen blew out a breath. 'I wonder what your mother would have to say about your behaviour?'

'Damn.' Cruz forked a hand through his hair, his lazy amusement at her expense turning to disgust.

He cursed again and gunned the engine.

'Problem?' she asked, hoping beyond hope that there was one.

'You could say that.' His words came out as a snarl.

She waited for him to elaborate and sighed when he didn't. This situation was impossible. There was no way she would be able to relax with this man enough to have sex with him. Which was fine, she thought. It would serve him right, all things considered.

Switching her mind off, she turned her attention outside the window. From the air Mexico was an amazing contrast of stark brown mountains and stretches of dried-up desert against the brilliant blue of the Pacific Ocean. On the ground the theme continued, with pockets of abject beauty mixed with states of disrepair. A bit like her own mind, she mused in a moment of black humour.

But gradually, as Cruz drove them through small towns and along broken cobblestoned streets alive with pedestrians and tourists fortified against the amazing heat with wide-brimmed hats, Aspen felt herself start to relax.

She snuck a glance at Cruz's beautiful profile. His expression was so serious he looked as if he belonged on a penny. The silence stretched out like the bitumen in front of them and finally Aspen couldn't take it any longer. 'So you went back to Mexico after you left The Farm?'

He cut her a brief glance. 'You want the low-down on my life story, *gatita*?'

No, she wanted to know if it would take a silver bullet to end his life, or whether an ordinary one would do the trick.

One night, Aspen.

'I was making polite conversation.'

'Choose another topic.'

Okay.

'Why do you want my farm?'

'It's a great location for a hotel. Why else?'

Aspen glared at him. 'You're going to tear it down, aren't you?' Tear down the only home she'd ever loved. Tear down the stables.

'Perhaps.'

'You can't do that.'

'Actually, I can.'

'Why? Revenge?'

She saw a muscle tick in his jaw. 'Not revenge. Money.'

Aspen blew out a breath, more determined than ever that he shouldn't get his hands on her property. 'How much further is it to the hotel?' she asked completely exasperated.

Cruz smiled. 'You sound like you're not expecting to enjoy yourself, *gatita*.'

She didn't answer, and she felt his curious gaze on her as she stared sightlessly out of the window.

'It will be a while,' he said abruptly. 'We have a small detour to make.'

Aspen glanced back at his austere expression. 'What sort of detour?'

'I have to stop at my mother's house.'

'Your mother's house?' She frowned. 'Why would you take me to meet your mother?'

'Believe me, I'm not happy about it either,' he said. 'Unfortunately my brother has arranged her surprise birthday party for today and I promised I'd show up.'

'Your mother's…' She cleared her throat as if she had something stuck in it. 'You could have warned me.'

'I just did.'

She blew out a frustrated breath.

'Don't make a big deal out of it,' he cautioned. 'I'm not.'

'Well, that's obvious. But how can I not? What will she think of me?'

'That you're my latest mistress. What else?'

Cruz saw a flash of hurt cross her face and hated how she made him feel subtly guilty about the situation between them. He had nothing to feel guilty about. She had asked him for money, he had laid down his terms, and she'd accepted. And now that she knew he was in direct competition with her his conscience was clear. Or should have been. Still, it picked at him that he might be making a decision he would later regret. His body said the opposite and he ran his eyes over her feminine, but demure outfit. All that wild hair caught back in a low ponytail just begging to be set free.

'I don't have anything for her,' she said in a small voice.

Cruz forced himself to concentrate on a particularly dilapidated section of road before he had an accident. 'I've got it covered.'

She fell blessedly silent after that as he navigated through the centre of town and he was just exhaling when she spoke again.

'What did you get her?'

'Excuse me?'

'Your present. I would know what it was if I was really your mistress.'

'You *are* my mistress,' he reminded her. 'For one night anyway.'

If possible even more colour drained from her face, and it irritated him to think that she saw sleeping with him as such a chore. By the time he was finished with her she would be screaming with pleasure and begging for more than one night.

'Money,' he said, pulling his thoughts out of his pants.

'Sorry?'

'I'm giving her money.'

'Oh.'

Her nose twitched as if she'd just smelt something foul.

'What's wrong with that?' he snapped.

'Nothing.'

Her tone implied *everything*.

'Money makes the world go round, *gatita*,' he grated.

'Actually, I think the saying is that love makes the world go round.'

'Love couldn't make a tennis ball go round,' he said, knowing from her tight expression that she didn't approve or agree. Well, he didn't give a damn. *She* hadn't been given up as a child. 'Look, my mother sold me to your grandfather when I was thirteen. I think I know what she likes.'

Aspen looked aghast. 'I had heard that rumour but I never actually believed it.'

'Believe it,' he said, hating the note of bitterness that tinged his words.

'I'm sure she didn't *want* to send you away.'

Cruz didn't say anything. She sighed and eventually said, 'I know how you feel.'

'How could you possibly know how I feel?' he mocked.

'You grew up on a hundred-acre property and went to a private school.'

'I wasn't born into that, Cruz. My father left my mother when I was three and she struggled for years to keep our heads above water while she was alive. What I was getting at was that my grandfather paid my father to stay away.'

Cruz frowned. He'd assumed her mother had lived off some sort of trust fund and her father had died. 'Your father was a ski instructor, wasn't he?'

'Yes.'

'Probably better that you didn't have anything to do with him.'

'Because of his profession?'

'No, because he accepted being paid off. A parent should never give up a child, no matter what.'

'I'm sorry that happened to you,' she said quietly.

Cruz didn't want her compassion. Especially not when he understood why his mother had done it. Hell, wasn't that one of the reasons he worked so hard? So that if he did ever marry no wife of his would ever have to face the same decision?

He shrugged it off, as he always did. 'I had a lot of opportunities from it. And worse things happen to kids than that.'

'True, but when a child feels abandoned it's—'

He cut off her sympathetic response. 'You move on and you don't look back.'

Aspen registered the pain in his voice, the deep hurt he must have felt. She experienced a strange desire to make him feel better—and then reminded herself that he was a wealthy man who was determined to steal her home away from her and was so arrogant he was lending her money to challenge him.

'I'd like to stop for flowers,' she said stiffly.

Cruz turned down a side street and cursed when the

traffic came to a standstill along a busy ocean-facing bou-
levard, completely oblivious to the cosmopolitan coastline
that sparkled in the sun.

'What?'

'I'd like to stop for flowers.'

'What for?'

She looked pained—and stiff. 'Your mother's birthday,
for one, and the fact that I'm visiting someone's home and
don't have a gift.'

'I told you I have it covered.'

'And given your attitude to money I'm sure it's very
generous, but I would prefer to give something more personal.'

Cruz ground his teeth together, praying for patience.

Five minutes later he swung the big car onto the side of
the road in front of a group of shops. When she made to
get out of the car, he stopped her. 'I'll get them. You wait
here and keep the door locked.'

'But they're supposed to be from me.'

'Believe me, my mother will know who they're from.'
The last time he'd given her flowers he'd picked wild dahl-
ias by the side of the road when he'd been about twelve.

Not long after that Aspen was relieved when Cruz pulled
into the circular driveway of a large *hacienda,* with fat
terracotta pots either side of a wide entrance filled with
colourful blooms.

She stepped out of the car before Cruz reached her side
and saw his scowl grow fiercer as he unloaded a box of
brightly wrapped presents from the back.

'You told me you were giving your mother money,' she
said, confused.

'I am. These are for my nieces and nephews.'

That surprised her, and she wondered if maybe he had
a heart beating somewhere inside his body after all. The

thought lasted for as long as it took for his eager nieces and nephews to descend on him in a wild flurry.

It was as if Santa had arrived and, like that mythical person, Cruz was treated with deference and a little trepidation. As if he wasn't quite real. Aspen saw genuine affection for him on the faces of his family, but it was clear when no one touched or hugged him that all was not quite right between them.

For his part, Cruz didn't seem to notice. His cool gaze was completely tuned in to the delighted squeals of his six nieces and nephews as they unearthed remote-controlled cars, sporting equipment and several dolls. That was when Aspen realised that the gifts were either an ice-breaker or possibly a replacement for any real affection between them.

'This is Aspen,' he said once the furore had died down. 'Aspen, this is my family.'

Succinct, she thought as each one of his family members warily introduced themselves, clearly unsure how to take her. Deciding to ignore the way that made her feel and make the best of the situation, she smiled at them as if there was nothing amiss about her being by Cruz's side.

'These are from both of us,' she said, handing Cruz's mother the elaborate posy he had purchased and watching as her gentle face lit up with pleasure. She must once have been a great beauty, Aspen thought, but time and life had wearied her, lining her face and sprinkling her thick dark hair with silvery streaks. She gazed up at her son with open adoration and Aspen could have kicked Cruz when he barely mustered a stiff smile in return.

An awkward silence fell over his sisters until his brother, Ricardo, took charge and led them all out to the rear patio, where the scent of a heavenly barbecue filled the air.

Cruz's youngest sister, Gabriella, who looked to be about nineteen, hooked her arm through Aspen's and took it upon herself to introduce her two brothers-in-law, who each had a pair of tongs in one hand and a beer in the other.

Gabriella pointed out the small vineyard her mother still tended, and the lush veggie patch in raised wooden boxes. Three well-fed dogs lazed beneath the shade of a lemon-coloured magnolia tree and the view of the ocean from the house was truly spectacular.

'Cruz has never brought a girlfriend here before,' Gabriella whispered.

Aspen smiled enigmatically. She knew the label hadn't come from Cruz but she wasn't about to correct his sister and embarrass them both. And, anyway, 'girlfriend' sounded much better than mistress to her ears, even if it did mean that she had terrible taste in men.

Returning to the patio, she found Cruz sprawled in a deckchair at the head of the large outdoor table, with his sisters and his mother crowded around him like celebrity minders who were worried about losing their jobs. One after the other they asked if he was okay or if he needed anything with embarrassing regularity, offering him food and drink like the Wise Men bestowing gifts on the baby Jesus.

The two brothers-in-law had cleverly retreated to tend the state-of-the-art barbecue, and Aspen tried her best to appreciate the amazing view of grapevines tripping down the hillside towards the azure sea below.

The conversation was like listening to an uninterested child practising the violin: one minute flowing and easy, the next halting and grating. Nobody seemed to know which topic of conversation to stick to.

Even worse, Cruz's mother kept throwing guilty glances his way, while treating him like a king. Cruz either didn't notice, or pretended that he didn't, conversing mainly with his brother about work issues.

It made her think about what Mrs Randall had said the day before. *He missed his family terribly, that boy.*

Ironically, Cruz didn't look as if he had missed them at all, and yet Aspen sensed from his intermittent glances along the table that Mrs Randall had been right.

What had it been like for him? she wondered. On The Farm, all alone and cut off from his family? And how did one reconnect after that?

Bizarrely, she started to feel sorry for him, and found herself wanting to break through the solid barrier he seemed to have erected around himself.

Thankfully one of the older boys brought out the new basketball Cruz had bought and called for everyone to play Four Square. Gabriella jumped up and mercifully asked Aspen to join in. It was the only time Cruz wasn't asked if he wanted to partake.

One of the children quickly drew out four squares and Aspen patiently waited for a cherubic-looking boy with a mop of curly black hair to explain the rules while his ten-year-old sister tapped her foot impatiently and said, 'We know…we *know*.'

Before long there was a mixed line of adults and kids and Aspen found she was enjoying herself for the first time that day, laughing with the children and jockeying for position as king of the game.

When one of the older children tried a shifty manoeuvre the ball went spinning off towards the stone table. Cruz deftly caught it and threw it back to Aspen.

Some devil on Aspen's shoulder made her toss the ball straight back at him. 'Come and play.'

'No, thanks.'

'He never plays games when he comes,' Gabriella whispered.

Aspen gave her a half-smile, knowing exactly how it felt to hanker after the affection of someone who wouldn't give it. She remembered that her grandfather and her uncle had been far too serious to play games with her and she'd very quickly learned not to ask.

Sensing that Cruz was far too serious as well, and that if he just lightened up a little everyone else could start to as well, she bounced the ball back in his direction.

'Are you afraid you'll lose?' she challenged lightly.

He stood up from the table and placed his beer bottle down with deliberate restraint.

Every member of his family seemed to hold their collective breath—even the two men tending the sizzling barbecue—waiting to see what he would do. If a tree had fallen in Africa they would have heard it.

Aspen saw the moment Cruz became conscious of the same thing and the smile on her lips died as he stared at her with a dangerous glint in his eyes. He came towards her slowly, like a hungry panther, his black hair glinting in the sunlight just as she remembered.

A shiver of awareness skittered over her skin. Her mind told her to run, but her body was on another frequency because it remained rooted to the spot.

Towering over her, Cruz took her hand and carefully placed the ball in it, as if he was handing back a newborn baby—or a bomb about to go off. He leant closer, and Aspen forgot about their audience as his gaze shifted to her mouth.

'I said no.'

When his gaze lifted to hers there was an implicit warning for her to behave deep within his cold regard. Then without a word he spun on his heels and stalked towards the garden.

Aspen released a shaky breath and heard Gabriella do the same.

'Doesn't he scare you when he frowns at you like that?'

His sister was right. His anger should have scared her. Terrified her, in fact. Her grandfather had wielded his temper like a weapon and when Chad had been drunk he had been volatile and moody. But Cruz didn't scare her in that way. Other ways, yes. Like the way he made her feel shivery and out of control of her senses. As if when he touched her he consumed her, controlled her.

That scared her.

Pushing her troubled thoughts aside, she sought to reassure Gabriella. 'No, he doesn't scare me that way. I think his bark—or his look—is more ferocious than his bite.'

The sound of the back door opening drew Aspen's gaze from Cruz's retreating figure and she watched Ricardo back out of the doorway, an elaborate birthday cake resplendent with pink icing and brightly coloured flowers held gingerly in his arms.

'Where's Cruz?' he asked, casting a quick glance at the now vacant chair.

There was a bit of low murmuring that Aspen understood, despite not speaking Spanish, and she felt a guilty flush highlight her cheekbones. It was her fault that Cruz had stalked off.

'I'll go and get him.'

Ricardo looked as if he was about to argue with her but then changed his mind. 'Thank you.'

Following the path Cruz had taken, she found him out by the small vineyard, his head bent towards a leafy vine laden with bunches of purple grapes. The bright sun darkened his olive skin as he stood there, which was extremely unfair, Aspen thought, when her skin was more likely to turn pink and blister.

A bee buzzed lazily past her face and she stepped out of its way.

Cruz must have heard the sound of her steps on the dirt

but he gave no indication of it, putting his hands in his pockets and staring out across the ocean like a god from the days of old. Strong. Formidable. *Impenetrable*.

'I was hoping for a moment's peace,' he said without turning around, his deep voice a master of creation.

'They're about to serve the birthday cake,' Aspen informed him softly.

'So they sent you to find me?'

'No.' She stood beside him and watched tiny waves break further out to sea. 'I volunteered.'

He made a noise that seemed to say she was an idiot. And she was—because she had an overpowering urge to reach out to him.

'They don't know how to treat you, you know.' She glanced up at him, no longer able to ignore what had been going on since they arrived. 'Your mother seems to be suffering. From guilt? Remorse? It's not clear, but it *is* clear that she loves you. They all do.'

Cruz tensed and dug his hands further into his pockets. Aspen had inadvertently picked a scab off an old wound. He knew his mother felt guilty. He'd told her she shouldn't but it hadn't worked. He had no idea what to do about that and it made being around his family almost impossible, because he knew that without him around they would be up singing and dancing and having a great time.

'Don't start talking about what you can't possibly understand,' he grated harshly.

'I understand that you're upset…maybe a little angry about what happened to you,' she offered gently.

He swung around to face her. 'I'm not angry about that. When my father died it was my job as the eldest boy to take care of my family while the girls ran the house. It's what we did. Rallied around each other and banded together.'

'Oh, dear, that must have made it even harder for you to leave them.'

Cruz scowled down at her. 'It's not like I had a say in it. Old Man Carmichael offered my mother money and she preferred to send me away than to let me provide for the family my way.'

'Which was…?'

Mostly he'd worked at a nearby *hacienda* and tended rich people's gardens. Sometimes he'd done odd jobs for the men his father had become involved with, but he hadn't been stupid enough to do anything illegal. Anything criminal.

'Boring stuff.'

'And your mother didn't work herself?'

'She cleaned houses when she could, but I have one brother and four sisters. All were under ten at the time. My father's family were what you would politely term dysfunctional, and my mother had been an only child to elderly parents. If I hadn't stepped up, nobody else would have.'

'I'm sorry, Cruz. That's a lot for a child to have heaped on his shoulders. You must have really struggled.' She grimaced. 'I guess that's why they treat you like you're a king now.'

He looked at her sharply. 'They don't treat me like a king. They act like it didn't happen. They tiptoe around me as if I'm about to go off at them.'

She paused and Cruz caught the concern in her gaze. Something tightened in his chest. What was he doing, spilling his childhood stories to this woman? A person he didn't even *like*.

As if sensing his volatile thoughts she murmured half to herself and he had to strain to capture the words. '…not real.'

'Excuse me?' He glanced at her sharply. 'Are you saying my feelings for my family are not real?'

'Of course not. Though it might help them relax a bit if you scowled a little less.' She shot him a half-smile. 'I can see that you love your family. Which is strangely reassuring though I don't know why. But there's no hugging. No touching.' Her pause was laden with unwanted empathy. 'Truthfully, you remind me of my grandfather. He found it tough to let anyone get close to him as well.'

His eyes narrowed. Nobody in his family talked about the past—not even Ricardo. Cruz had come back from Ocean Haven eight years ago angry—yes, by God, *angry*—and he'd stayed that way. And he liked it. Anger drove him and defined him. Made him hungry and kept him on his guard.

He looked at Aspen. Unfortunately for her he was *really* angry now. 'I don't remember reading anywhere in that makeshift document of yours that pop psychology was part of our deal.'

Her eyes flashed up at him. 'I was only trying to help. Though I don't know why,' she muttered, half under her breath, inflaming his anger even more.

'Helping wasn't part of it either. There's only one thing I want from you. Conversation before or after is not only superfluous, it's irrelevant.'

She gave him that hurt look again, before masking it with cool hauteur, and he felt his teeth grind together.

Dammit, why couldn't he look at her without feeling so…so *much*?

All the time.

Lust, anger, disappointment, hunger. A deep hunger for more—and not just of that sweet body which had haunted more dreams than he cared to remember.

He reminded himself of the type of woman she was. The type who would use that body to further her own interests.

She'd used it to good effect to deceive him years ago and hadn't cared a damn for his feelings. That was real. That was who she was. And once he'd had her in his bed, had slaked his lust for her—*used* her in return—then she'd be out of his life and his head.

Hell, he couldn't wait.

CHAPTER SIX

IT WAS EARLY evening by the time Cruz turned onto the long stretch of driveway that led to the Rodriquez Polo Club. A hotel, Aspen had heard it said, that was a hotel to end all hotels.

She didn't care. She was too keyed-up to be impressed. And, anyway, it was just a hotel.

Only it wasn't *just* anything. It was magnificent.

A palatial honey-coloured building that looked about ten storeys high, it curved like a giant horseshoe around a network of manicured gardens with a central fountain that resembled an inverted chandelier.

As soon as their SUV stopped a uniformed concierge jumped to attention and treated Cruz with the deference one usually expected only around royalty.

Expensively clad men and women wandered languidly in and out of the glassed entrance as if all their cares in the world had disappeared and Aspen glanced down at her old top and jeans. Despite the fact that her grandfather had once been seriously wealthy, Ocean Haven hadn't done well for so long that Aspen couldn't remember the last personal item she'd bought other than deodorant. Now she felt like Cinderella *before* the makeover, and it only seemed to widen the gulf between her and the brooding man beside her.

'Well, I can see why it's rated as seven stars and I

haven't even seen inside yet,' she said with reluctant admiration. 'And, oh…wow…' she added softly. A row of bronzed life-sized horses that looked as if they were racing each other in a shallow pool with shots of water trickling around them glowed under strategically placed lights, adding both pizazz and majesty to the entrance. 'There's so much to see. I almost don't want to go inside.'

'Unfortunately we're not allowed to serve meals on the kerb so you'll have to.'

Aspen switched her gaze to Cruz at his unexpected humour and her pulse skittered. He was just so handsome and charismatic. What would it feel like, she wondered, to be with him at the hotel because she *wanted* to be there and he *wanted* her to be there with him?

The unexpected thought had her nearly stumbling over her own feet.

Why was she even thinking like that?

The last thing she needed was to become involved with a man again. And Cruz had told her in no uncertain terms that he expected sex and nothing else. No need to pretty it up with unwanted emotion.

How had she convinced herself that she'd be able to do this? Not only because of her own inherent dislike of sex but because it was so cold. What would happen once they got upstairs? Did they go straight to the bedroom? Undress? Would he undress her? No. Probably not.

Fortunately she didn't have much time to contemplate the sick feeling in the pit of her stomach as the doorman swept open the chrome and glass doors and inclined his head as Cruz strode inside. Aspen scurried to keep up and couldn't help but notice the lingering attention Cruz garnered with effortless ease.

Another deferential staff member in a severely cut suit descended on him and Aspen left them to stroll towards a circular platform with a large wood carving of a polo player on horseback.

'Aspen?'

Having finished up with his employee, Cruz waited impatiently for her to come to him but Aspen couldn't help returning her gaze to the intricate carving.

'Did you do this?'

He looked startled. 'Why would you think that?'

'I just saw some smaller versions in your mother's house and they reminded me of the wood carvings you used to do in your spare time. Were they yours?'

He paused and Aspen felt a little foolish.

'I haven't done one of those in years.'

It was the most he'd said to her since leaving his mother's and her curiosity got the better of her. 'You don't play polo any more either. Why is that?'

For a minute she didn't think he had heard her.

'Other things to do.'

'Do you miss it?' she asked, imagining that he couldn't not, considering how good he was.

'Mind your step when you come down,' he said, turning away from her.

Right. That would be the end of yet another conversation, she thought, wondering why she'd even bothered to try and engage him. Her natural curiosity and desire to help others was clearly wasted on this man.

She thought back to his angry response to her gentle prodding at his mother's house and shook her head at her own gumption. What did she really know, anyway? Her own relationship history wasn't exactly the healthiest on the planet.

Following Cruz to the bank of elevators, she decided to keep her mouth shut. It was hard enough contemplating what she was about to do without adding to it by trying to come up with superfluous conversation.

When the lift opened directly into Cruz's private suite Aspen gasped at the opulence of the living area, but Cruz ignored it all, striding into the room and throwing his wallet and keys onto a large mahogany table with an elaborate floral arrangement in the centre. With barely a pause he pushed open a set of concertina glass doors that led to a long balcony. Beyond the doors Aspen could just make out a jewel-green polo field.

Stepping closer, she saw that beyond the field there was an enormous stone stable with an orange tiled roof and beyond that white-fenced paddocks holding, she knew, some of the finest polo ponies in the world.

'Wow....' She breathed hot evening air that carried the scent of freshly mown grass and the lemony scent of magnolia with it. 'Is that a swimming pool out there to the right?'

'Yes.' Cruz had his hands wedged firmly in his pockets as he stood behind her. 'It's a saltwater pool the horses use to cool off in.'

'Lucky horses.'

'If you take ten steps to your left and look around the corner you'll see a pool and spa *you* can use.'

Happy to move out of his commanding orbit, Aspen followed his directions.

'Oh...' She stared at a sapphire-blue lap pool which had a large spa at the end of it. The pool was shielded on one side by a thick hedge and from above by a strategically placed cloth sail that would block both the sun and any paparazzi snooping around. 'You don't do things by halves, do you?'

'Mexico is a hot place.'

Then why did she feel so cold?

Shivering, she glanced back at him, her attention caught by piercing black eyes and the dark stubble that highlighted his square jaw. Those broad shoulders...

She shivered again, and tossed her head to cover her reaction. 'Time to get this party started, I'd say.'

'Party?' He raised a cool eyebrow at her. 'In the pool?'

Aspen cast a quick glance at the inviting water, alarmed as an image of both of them naked and entwined popped into her head. It was so clear she could almost see them there—his larger, tanned body holding her up, the silky feel of the water lapping at her skin as it rippled with their movements, her arms curved over his smooth shoulders as she steadied herself, his hands stroking her heavy breasts....

She felt her face flame. She had the romantic—the *fantasy*—version of sex in her mind. The real version, she knew from experience, could never live up to it.

'Of course not.'

'Have you ever made love in the water, Aspen?'

Had he moved closer to her? She glanced at him with alarm but he hadn't moved. Or hadn't appeared to.

She inhaled and steeled her spine. 'The pool doesn't appeal to me.'

'Pity. It's a nice night for it.'

Aspen didn't want to complicate this. A bed was more than adequate for what was about to happen between them. And she could close her eyes more easily in a bed.

'A bed is fine.'

She wondered if Cruz would put a towel down, the way Chad had done.

A muscle ticked in Cruz's jaw and he stared at her as if trying to discern all her deepest thoughts. Then he turned abruptly away. 'Actually, I find I don't enjoy making love on an empty stomach.'

'This has nothing to do with love,' Aspen reminded him assertively.

Halfway to returning indoors, Cruz stopped and his

black eyes smouldered. 'When I touch your body, Aspen, you'll think it does.'

Oh, how arrogant was *that*? If only he knew that all his Latin charm was wasted on her.

Aspen hurled mental daggers at his broad back and wondered why he didn't want to get this over with as soon as possible. By all accounts he seemed to want her—but then so had Chad in the beginning. Oh, this was beyond awful. She hated second-guessing Cruz's desire. Hated hoping that with him it would be different. She knew better than to count on hope. It hadn't brought her mother or her father back into her life. It hadn't made her grandfather love her for herself in the end.

This time when she looked around the vast living area she noticed a bottle of champagne in a silver ice bucket on the main dining table. Maybe that was what she should do. Get drunk.

As if reading her mind, Cruz tightened his mouth. 'Come—I'll show you to your room.'

Aspen felt her heart bump inside her chest. *He's just showing you the room, you fool, not asking you to use it.*

Yet.

Standing back to let her pass, Cruz indicated towards a closed door. 'The bathroom, which should be stocked with everything you'll need, is through there.'

Aspen nodded, feeling completely overwhelmed.

When it became obvious she wasn't going to say anything Cruz turned to go. 'I'll leave you to freshen up.'

She noticed a book on the bedside table. 'This is your room,' she blurted out.

'You were expecting someone else's?'

'No. I…' She spared him a tart look. 'I thought you might like your own space.'

'I like my bed warm more.'

Right.

'Dinner should be served in twenty minutes.'

After he closed the door behind him Aspen sagged against the silk-covered king bed and wondered how long it would be before he realised she was a dud.

Feeling completely despondent, she picked up the novel beside the bed and noticed it was one of her favourites. Surprised, she flicked through it. Could he really be reading it or was it just for show? Just to impress the plethora of mistresses who wandered in and out of his life?

An hour later she was wound so tight all she could do was pick at the delicious Mexican dinner that for once didn't include *tacos* and *enchiladas*.

'Something wrong?'

Her eyes slid across Cruz's powerful forearms, exposed by his rolled shirtsleeves.

Was he serious? She was about to embarrass herself with a man who didn't even like her in order to save her home. Of *course* there was something wrong.

'Of course not,' she replied, feigning relaxed confidence.

He frowned down at her plate. 'Is it the *birria*? If it's too hot for you I can order something else.'

Oh, he'd meant the food. 'No, no, the food's lovely.'

He put down his fork and brought his wine glass to his lips. Now, *there* was relaxed confidence, she thought a little resentfully.

'Then why is most of it still on your plate?'

He licked a drop of red wine from his lower lip and Aspen couldn't look away. Remembered pleasure at the way his mouth had taken hers in the most wonderful kiss vied with sheer terror for supremacy. Unfortunately sheer terror was winning out, because he looked like a man who would expect everything and the kitchen sink as well.

'I…um…I ate a lot at the party.'

'No, you didn't. You barely touched a thing.'

'I'm not a big eater at the best of times.'

'And these are far from the best of times—is that it, Aspen?'

It was more of a statement than a question and Aspen wondered if perhaps he felt the same way. 'You could say that,' she said carefully.

'Is that because you're still in love with Anderson?'

'Sorry?' She knew her mouth was hanging open and she snapped it closed. '*No*. No, that was a disaster from the start.'

'So you're not still pining for him?'

'No.'

His eyes narrowed thoughtfully. 'Why was it a disaster?'

Had she really just told him being married to Chad had been a disaster? 'Don't ask.'

'I just did.'

'Yes, well, I'd rather not talk about it, if it's all the same to you.'

He sat staring at her and Aspen wished she knew what to say next. His unexpected question about Chad had completely derailed her.

'Come here.'

The soft command made her senses leap and she felt her breath quicken with rising panic. He was trying to control her, and she knew she couldn't let him do that.

She tossed her hair back behind one shoulder. 'You come here.'

Despite the fact that he hadn't moved she could sense the tightly coiled tension within him. It radiated outward across the table and stole the breath from her lungs. And for all her dismissive tone she still felt like a puppet on his string—despite her resolve not to be.

He watched her with heavy-lidded eyes and she was

totally unprepared for the scrape of his chair on the terra-cotta tiles as he stood up.

Aspen's heart jumped as if she'd been startled out of a trance.

Determined to remain neutral—outwardly at least—she didn't move. Couldn't, if the truth be told. Her limbs were completely paralysed—by his laconic sensuality as much as her own blinding insecurities.

'You have amazing hair.'

She snatched in a quick breath to feed her starving lungs. She could feel the heat emanating from his strong thighs beside her shoulders and even though he hadn't touched her she started to tremble. Her only saving grace was that he couldn't possibly be aware of her inner turmoil, and she stared straight ahead as she felt him roll a strand of her hair between his fingers as if it were the finest silk.

She couldn't do this. Already she was freezing up, and to put herself at another man's mercy was truly frightening.

Chad's roughness crowded her mind and permeated her soul, and it was as if Cruz ceased to exist in that moment.

'Dammit, Aspen. What is wrong with you?'

Cruz's dark, annoyed voice only added fuel to the raging fire of Aspen's insecurities. Panic enveloped her and galvanised her into action.

Gouging the floor tiles with her chair, she forced it back and moved in the opposite direction from the one Cruz was in. Unfortunately that only brought her to the balustrade. She gripped the iron railing, enjoying the coolness of the metal against her overheated palms, and pretended rapt attention in the glowing lights that outlined the low boards around the darkened polo field.

'What bothers you the most about this?' he grated. 'The money aspect or the fact that it's me you'll be sleeping with?'

Aspen knew he stood close behind her—every fibre of

her being felt as if it was attuned to every fibre of his—but she didn't turn around. Honestly, she should have known that when it came to the crunch she would fall at the first hurdle. But of course she needed to do this—her mind was so fogged that she couldn't comprehend any other way to save her farm.

'It's not the money.' She tilted her gaze to take in the starry sky. She was planning to pay him back every cent he loaned her, plus interest, so she'd reconciled that in her mind before he'd even picked her up. No, it was… 'It's—'

'Me?' The single word sounded like a pistol-shot.

Interesting, she thought, holding a conversation with someone you couldn't see. It made her other senses come alive. Her sense of hearing that was so in love with the deep timbre of his voice, the feel of the heat of his body that seemed to reach out like a beckoning light, his smell… Unconsciously she rubbed at the railing and felt the smooth texture of the iron beneath her sensitive fingertips.

'It's more the fact that you don't like me,' she said on a rush.

She hadn't realised how true that was until the words left her mouth. A beat passed and then she felt his hands on her shoulders, gently turning her. Embarrassed by the admission, she forced herself to meet his gaze. Because she knew she was right.

He stared at her, not saying anything, his large hands burning into the tops of her shoulders, his thumbs almost absently caressing her collarbones. It was hard to read his expression with only a candle flickering on the table and a crescent moon ducking behind darkened clouds. It was even harder when he lowered his gaze to his hands, his inky lashes shielding them.

He gently slid those large hands up her neck to the line of her jaw, setting off a whole host of sensations in their wake. Aspen stiffened as she felt the pad of one of his thumbs slowly graze her closed mouth. His eyes locked on her lips as he pressed into the soft flesh, making them feel gloriously sensitised.

They were both utterly still. The only movement came from his thumb as it swept back and forth, back and forth, across her hyper-sensitive flesh. Back and forth until her lips started to buzz and gave beneath the persuasive pressure, allowing him to reach the moisture within. Aspen trembled as he spread her own wetness along her bottom lip and then opened her lips wider, until he was touching her teeth. He traced their shape just as thoroughly, only they weren't as malleable as her lips and stayed firmly closed.

She should have known that he wouldn't stop there. Unfairly he was bringing his fingers into play, to knead the side of her neck, pressing firmly into her nape. On a rush of heat her senses were overloaded and her teeth parted, giving him greater liberties.

Only he didn't immediately take them, and without even realising it Aspen tilted her head, seeking to capture his thumb between her teeth, silently inviting him inside. Still he hung back, and with a small sound in the back of her throat she couldn't stop her mouth from closing around his thumb and sucking on his flesh, couldn't stop her tongue from wrapping itself around it as she sought to taste him.

Cruz didn't know if he'd ever experienced anything as erotic as Aspen drawing his thumb into her wide mouth, her cheeks hollowing as she sucked firmly and then softening as she used her tongue to drive him wild. With every stroke his erection jerked painfully behind his zipper and, unable to hold back any longer, he pulled his thumb from her mouth and replaced it with his own.

She immediately latched onto his mouth as if she was just as desperate as he was, and he backed her against the cast iron balustrading and didn't stop until he was hard up against her.

Incapable of thought, he let his instincts take over and hooked one of her legs up over his hip so he could settle into the cradle of her thighs, all the time ravaging her mouth until she fed him more of those hot little moans.

The deep neckline of her otherwise demure dress, which had tantalised him all night, was no barrier to his wandering hands and he deftly moved the soft jersey aside and cupped her, squeezing her full breasts together. He strummed his thumbs over her lace-covered nipples and felt exalted when she arched into him, moaning more keenly as he slowly increased the pressure.

He groaned, licked his way to her ear, bit it, and then trailed tiny kisses down over her neck, sucking on her soft skin. She smelled like flowers and tasted like honey and he knew he'd never experienced anything so sweet. So heady.

Her leg shifted higher as she sought a deeper contact, and her fingers dug into his shoulders as if she was trying to hold herself upright.

'Cruz, please....'

Needing no further invitation, he pushed her bra aside and leant back so that he could look at her.

'Perfect. You fit perfectly into my hands.'

He moulded her fullness, watching her beautiful raspberry-coloured nipples tighten even more as they anticipated his mouth on them. His body throbbed as it anticipated the same thing, and he tested the weight of each breast before drawing his thumb and fingertips together until he held just the tips of each nipple between his fingers, his touch too light to fully satisfy.

She cried out and arched impossibly higher, as if in pain, and he bent his head and gave her what he knew she needed, soldering his lips to one peak and pulling her turgid flesh deeply into his mouth while rubbing firmly over the other.

'Cruz! Oh, my God!'

She buried her hands in his hair and clung—and thank goodness she did. The taste of her made his knees feel weak and his hunger to be buried deep inside her impossibly urgent.

Wrapping one arm around her waist, he lifted her and ground his hardness against her core, his self-control shredded by her wild response. 'I want you, Aspen.' He smoothed his hand down the silky skin of her thigh and rode her skirt all the way up. 'Tell me you want me, *mi gatita*. Tell me this has nothing to do with money.'

He registered the rigidity in her body at the same time as his rough words reverberated inside his head, and both acted like a bucket of cold water on his libido.

What was he saying? More importantly, what was he *asking*?

'I...'

She looked up at him, flushed with passion. Dazed. Beautiful. The breeze whispered over her hair.

'I'm sorry,' she whispered breathlessly.

Sorry?

So was he.

The last time he had wanted something this badly he had lost everything. And he couldn't take her like this.

Couldn't take her because he was paying her.

Once again the image of a lustful Billy Smyth with his hand stroking her face clouded his vision. Up to yesterday Cruz would have said that he wasn't a violent man, but just the thought of her sleeping with anyone else curdled his blood. If he hadn't offered her this deal where else might she be tonight—and who with?

The question just added ice to the bucket and he unwound her arms from around his neck.

'Cruz...?'

Was he crazy? He had a hot woman in his arms so why was he hesitating? He couldn't explain it; he just knew it didn't feel right.

His hard-on pressed insistently against his fly, as if to say it had felt very right ten seconds ago, and he stepped away from her so he wouldn't be tempted to pull her back into his arms.

Something of his inner turmoil must have shown on his face, because she blanched and he thought she might throw up.

'Steady.'

He went to grab her but she pulled back sharply and quickly righted her dress as best she could before wrapping her arms around herself.

'I can't believe it. I've ruined it,' she muttered, more to herself than him.

On one level he registered the comment as strange, but part of him had already agreed with her—because, yes, she *had* ruined it. She was ruining everything.

His desire to buy Ocean Haven.

His peace of mind.

'That sounds like revenge,' she'd said earlier.

'Go to bed, Aspen,' he said wearily, upset with himself and his unwelcome conscience.

Her eyes were uncertain pools of dark green when she looked at him. 'But what about—?'

'I'm not in the mood.'

He turned sharply and tracked back into the penthouse before he threw his aggravating conscience over the balcony and did what his body was all but demanding he do.

Aspen stood on the balcony, the night air cooling her overheated skin as the realisation that he was rejecting her sank in. She swallowed heavily, her mind spinning back to those last few moments. She felt like an inept fool as memories of Chad's hurtful rejection of her years ago tumbled into her mind like an avalanche. His repulsed expression when he'd told her to go out and buy a bottle of lube.

At the time she'd been so naïve about sex she hadn't even known what he was talking about. So he'd clarified. *'Lubrication. You're too dry. It's off-putting.'*

Completely mortified, she'd searched the internet and learned that some women suffered dryness due to low oestrogen levels. She hadn't investigated any further. She'd shame-facedly done what he'd asked, but they'd never got round to using it. He hadn't wanted to touch her after that.

And no matter how many times she told herself that Chad's harsh words were more to do with his own inadequacies in the bedroom than hers it didn't matter. She didn't believe it. Not entirely. There was always a niggle that he was right.

Don't go there, she warned herself, only half aware that she had pressed her hand to her stomach. *Chad's long gone and you* knew *this was going to happen with Cruz so, okay, deal with it. And quickly. Then you can go home to Ocean Haven and be safe again.*

Fortifying her resolve, she moved inside and found Cruz pouring a drink, his back to her.

'You still have to lend me the money,' she said, glad that her voice sounded so strong.

Cruz felt his shoulders tense and turned slowly to face her.

She was a cool one, all right. Haughty. Dismissive. *Way too good for him.*

Slowly he folded himself into one of the deep-seated sofas. 'No, I don't,' he said, wanting to annoy her.

'Yes, you do. You signed—'

'I know what I signed.' He swirled his drink and ice clinked in the glass as he watched her. Her eyes were cool to the point of being detached. Damn her. That was usually *his* stock in trade.

'Then you know that if it turns out you don't want...' She stopped whatever it was she was about to say and raised her chin. 'I trusted you.'

He ignored the way those words twisted his gut. Her soft declaration was making his conscience spike again. 'The agreement didn't stipulate which night.' He waited for his words to sink in and it didn't take long. 'Consider yourself off the hook for tonight. As I told you, I'm not in the mood.'

She frowned. 'When *will* you be in the mood?'

Right now, as it happens.

'I don't know,' he said roughly, annoyed with his inability to control his physical response to her.

Of course that answer wasn't good enough for her.

'And if *I'm* not in the mood when you decide you are?'

This wasn't going to work. If he stayed here he'd damned well finish what he had started outside.

He sprang to his feet and those green eyes widened warily. And well they might. He stalked towards her and wrapped one hand around that glorious mane of hair. He tilted her face up so that she was forced to meet his steely gaze, unsure if he was angry with her or himself or just in general.

'When I decide to take you, Aspen, rest assured you'll be in the mood.'

Then he kissed her. Long and deep and hard.

Aspen held the back of her hand against her throbbing mouth as Cruz marched out through the main door to the lift.

And good riddance, she wanted to call out to his arrogant back. Except she didn't. She felt too shattered. Lack of sleep last night, the roller coaster of a day today. It all crashed in on her.

Not wanting to wait around in case he suddenly reappeared, she fled to the bedroom, hoping sleep would transport her back to East Hampton. Literally.

Only it wasn't her room she was in, and she quickly snatched her things together and headed to one of the spare bedrooms.

Ha—she would show him who wasn't 'in the mood'.

She let out a low groan as those words he had flung at her came rushing back. The embarrassing thing was she couldn't have been more in the mood if he had lit scented candles and told her he loved her.

And he had seemed to be totally in the mood.

When she found herself trying to analyse the exact moment it had all gone wrong she pulled herself up. That was a one-way street to anxiety and sleeplessness and she wouldn't go there again. Not for any man.

By the time Cruz let himself back into the penthouse his frame of mind had not improved. He'd gone down to the stables—something he'd always done when he felt troubled—but it hadn't made him feel any better.

In fact it had made him feel worse, because now that Aspen had walked back into his life—or rather he had walked back into hers—he couldn't get her out of his head.

Worse, he couldn't get the game he was playing with her out of his head. He'd had a lot of time to think about things since he'd picked her up, and although he'd like to be able to say that it had started out as an underhand way of getting what he wanted the truth was it hadn't even been that logical. He'd taken one look at her and wanted her. Then he'd made the mistake of touching her. Kissing her. He'd never felt so out of control. Something he hadn't anticipated at all.

He'd convinced himself that he could sleep with her for one night and send her home.

So much for that.

The reality was that right now he wanted her in his bed—and not because he was paying her a pit full of money but because she wanted to be there. And didn't that make his head spin? The last time he'd wanted something from a Carmichael he'd been kicked in the teeth, and he was about as likely to let that happen again as the sun rising in the west.

He thought about her comment about his family treating him like a king. He'd been so caught up in his own sense of betrayal and, yes, his anger at missing out on *knowing* them that he hadn't considered his own involvement in continuing that state of affairs. Now he saw it through Aspen's eyes and it made him want to cringe. Yes, he held himself back. But distance made things easier to manage.

But she had understood that as well, hadn't she? *'That's a lot for a child to have heaped on his shoulders. You must have really struggled.'*

Yes, it had been a lot. Particularly when Charles Carmichael had been such an exacting and forbidding taskmaster. Maybe others understood what he had gone through but no one had dared say it to his face.

And her suggestion that he could scowl a little less...?

He scowled now. Maybe he should just go and find her, have sex with her and be done with her. But something about that snagged in his unconscious. Something wasn't right about her hot and cold responses but he couldn't put his finger on what it was.

'I can't believe it. I've ruined it.'

Why would she have said that? If anything he'd ruined it by stopping. But she hadn't questioned that, had she? She'd had a look on her face that was one of resigned acceptance and moved on.

And hard on the heels of that thought was her comment about her marriage to Anderson being a disaster. He'd wanted to push her on that but had decided not to. Now he wished he had. There was something about the lack of defiance in her eyes when she had mentioned her ex that bothered him. Almost as if she'd been terribly hurt by the whole thing.

He frowned. The truth was he shouldn't give a damn about Aspen Carmichael, or her feelings, or her comments, and he didn't know why he did.

Throwing off his tangled thoughts, he tentatively pushed open his bedroom door and stopped short when he found the room empty. His wardrobe door lay open and a stream of feminine clothing crossed his room like a trail of breadcrumbs where she had obviously dropped them as she'd carried her things out.

Gingerly he picked them up and placed them on the corner chair. She'd no doubt be upset to realise she'd dropped them. Especially the silky peach-coloured panties. He rubbed the fabric between his thumb and forefinger and his body reacted like a devoted dog that had just seen its master return after a year-long absence.

'Not tonight, Josephine,' he muttered, heading for the shower.

A cold one.

Cruz rubbed his rough jaw and picked up his razor. Unbidden, Charles Carmichael's rangy features came to his mind. Initially he had admired his determination and objectivity. His loyalty. Only those traits hadn't stacked up in the end. The man had been ruthless more than determined, cold rather than objective, and his loyalty had been prejudiced towards his own kind.

Had *he* degenerated into that person? Had *he* become a hollow version of the man he'd thought he was? He stopped shaving and stared at the remaining cream on his face. Why did his life suddenly feel so empty? So superficial?

Hold on. His life wasn't empty or superficial. He barked out a short laugh. He had everything a man could want. Money. Power. Women. Respect.

His razor nicked the delicate skin just under his jaw.

Respect.

He didn't have everyone's respect. He didn't have Aspen's. And he didn't have his own right now, either.

He thought again about the night Aspen had set him up. He supposed he could have defended himself against Carmichael's prejudiced accusations and changed the course of his life, but something in Aspen's eyes that night had stayed him. Fear? Devastation? Embarrassment? He'd never asked. He'd just felt angry and bitter that she had stolen his future.

Only she hadn't, had she? He'd disowned it. He'd thrown it all in. Nobody made a fool of a Rodriguez—wasn't that what his *padre* would have said?

He took a deep steadying breath, flexed his shoulders and heard his neck crack back into place.

So, okay, in the morning he would tell Aspen to go home. He wouldn't sleep with her in exchange for the money. She could have it. But she still wasn't getting The Farm. He wanted it, and what he wanted he got.

End of story.

CHAPTER SEVEN

WHEN SHE WOKE the next morning and decided she really couldn't hang out in her room all day Aspen ventured out into the living area of Cruz's luxury penthouse and breathed a sigh of relief to find it empty. Empty bar the lingering traces of his mouth-watering aftershave, that was.

After making sure that he really had gone she sucked in a grateful breath, so on edge she nearly jumped out of her skin when the phone in her hand buzzed with an incoming text.

Make yourself comfortable and charge whatever you want to the room. We'll talk tonight.

'About a ticket home?' she mused aloud.

The disaster of the previous night winged into her thoughts like a homing pigeon.

In the back of her mind Aspen had imagined that they would try to have sex, she would freeze, Cruz might or might not laugh, and Aspen would return home. Then she would get on with her life and never think of him again.

Only nothing was normal with Cruz. Not her inability to hate him for his ruthlessness or her physical reaction to him. Because while she had been in his arms last night she had forgotten to be worried. She'd been unable to do anything but feel, and his touch had felt amazing. So amazing that she'd mistakenly believed it might work. That this time she would be okay. Then she'd panicked and he'd stopped. And she really didn't want to analyse why that was.

'Urgh.' She blew out a breath. 'You weren't going to replay that train wreck again, remember?'

Right.

Determinedly she dropped her phone into her handbag and poured herself a steaming cup of coffee from the silver tray set on the mahogany dining table.

There was an array of gleaming dome-covered plates, and as she lifted each one in turn she wondered if Cruz had ordered the entire menu for breakfast and then realised that he wasn't hungry. Her own stomach signalled that she was ravenous and Aspen placed scrambled eggs and bacon on a plate and tucked in.

Unsure what do with herself, she checked in with Donny and Mrs Randall and then decided to do some studying. She was doing a double load at university next semester, so she could qualify by the end of the year, and she needed to get her head around the coursework before assignments started rolling in.

But she couldn't concentrate.

A horse whinnied in the distance and another answered.

The call of the wild, she mused with a faint smile. She walked out onto the balcony and leant on the railing. The grooms in the distance were leading a group of horses through their morning exercises and the sight made her feel homesick.

It was probably a mistake to go looking for her, but after three hours locked in a business meeting with his executive team, who had flown in from all over the States for a strategy session, Cruz's brain was fried. Distracted by a curly-haired blonde. He told his team to take an early lunch, because he knew better than to push something when it wasn't working. Once he'd found Aspen and organised for her to return to Ocean Haven he'd be able to think again. Until then at least the members of his team could find something more productive to do than repeat every point back to him for the rest of the day.

But, annoyingly, Aspen wasn't anywhere he had expected her to be. Not in his penthouse, nor the hotel boutiques, not one of the five hotel restaurants, nor the day spa. When he described her to his staff they all looked at him as if he was describing some fantasy woman.

Yeah, your fantasy woman.

Feeling more and more agitated, he stopped by the concierge's desk in case she had taken a taxi into town on her own. It would be just like her to do something monumentally stupid and cause him even more problems. Of course the concierge on duty knew immediately who he was talking about and that just turned his mood blacker.

'The strawberry blonde babe with the pre-Raphaelite curls all the way down to her—?'

'Yes, that one,' Cruz snapped, realising that someone— him—had neglected to inform his staff that she was off-limits.

Oblivious to his mounting tension, the concierge continued blithely, 'She's in the stables. At least she was a couple of hours ago.'

And how, he wanted to ask the hapless youth, *do you know that?* His mind conjured up all sorts of clandestine meetings between her and his college-age employee.

Growling under his breath, Cruz stalked across the wide expanse of green lawn that had nothing on her eyes towards the main stable. He reminded himself that if he'd waited around for her to wake up he would now know where she was and what she was up to.

Survival tactics? his conscience proposed.

Busy, Cruz amended.

He heard the lovely sound of her laughter before he saw her, and then the sight of her long legs encased in snug jeans came into view. He couldn't see the rest of her; bent as she was over the stall door, but frankly he couldn't take his eyes off her wiggling hips and the mouthwatering curve of her backside.

Another giggle brought his eyes up and he had to clear his throat twice before she reared back and stood in front of him. Cruz glanced inside the stall in time to see one of his men stuffing his wallet into his back pocket, a guilty flush suffusing his neck.

Unused to such testy feelings of jealousy, and on the verge of grabbing his very married assistant trainer by the throat and hauling him off the premises, Cruz clenched his jaw. 'I believe your services are required elsewhere, Señor Martin.'

'Of course, sir.' His trainer swallowed hard as he opened the stall door and ducked around Aspen. 'Excuse me, *señorita.*'

'Oh, we were just—' Aspen stopped speaking as Luis turned worried eyes her way, and she glanced at Cruz to find his icy stare on the man. He might have been wearing another expensive suit, but he looked anything but civilised, she noted. In fact he looked breathtakingly *un*-civilised—as if he had a band of warriors waiting outside to raid the place.

Irritated both by his overbearing attitude and the way her heart did a little dance behind her breastbone at the sight of him, Aspen went on the attack. 'Don't tell me.' She arched a brow. 'You've suddenly decided you're in the mood?'

'No.'

His expression grew stormier and he stepped into her space until Aspen found herself inside the stall with the almost sleeping horse Luis had been tending to.

'What are you up to, Aspen?' he rasped harshly, blocking the doorway.

Wanting to put space between them, Aspen stepped lightly around the mare and picked up the discarded brush Luis had been using to groom her.

'I feel bad that Luis didn't get to finish in here because of our conversation so I thought I'd brush Bandit down for him.'

'I meant *with* him?'

She paused, not liking the tone of his voice. 'If you're implying what I think you are then, yes, I did offer to sleep with Luis—but unfortunately he only has a spare nine million lying around.' She shrugged as if to say, *What can you do?*

'Don't be smart.'

Aspen glared at him. 'Then don't be insulting.'

He looked at her as if he was contemplating throttling her, but even that wasn't enough to stop the thrilling buzz coursing through her body at his closeness.

Aspen shook her head as much at herself as him. 'You really have a low opinion of me, don't you, Cruz?'

'Look at it from my point of view.' He balled his hands on his hips. 'I come out here to find you giggling like a schoolgirl and one of my best trainers stuffing his wallet back into his pocket. What am I supposed to think?'

Aspen's gaze was icily steady on his. 'That he was showing me pictures of his children being dragged along by the family goat.'

A beat passed in which she wouldn't have been surprised if Cruz had turned and walked away as he had the night before. It seemed to be his *modus operandi* when confronted with anything remotely emotional. Only he didn't.

'I'm sorry,' he said abruptly, raking a hand through his hair. 'I might have overreacted.'

Aspen had never had a man apologise to her before and it completely took the wind out of her sails. 'Well, okay…'

For the first time in her dealings with him he looked a tad uncomfortable. 'I didn't come here to quarrel with you.'

'What *did* you come here for? If you're checking on Bandit's cankers I had a look at the affected hoof before and it's completely healed.'

Cruz frowned. 'That's for the vet to decide, not you.'

'The vet was busy and I know what I'm doing. I'm one semester away from becoming a fully qualified vet. Plus, I've treated a couple of our horses for the disease. So,' she couldn't resist adding, 'not just marrying to secure my future, then.'

A muscle ticked in his jaw. 'You enjoyed telling me that, didn't you?'

'It did feel rather good, yes.'

They stared at each other and then his mouth kicked up at the corners. 'I suppose you want another apology?'

What she wanted was for him to stop smiling and scowl again so she could catch her breath. 'Would it be too much to hope for, do you think?'

'Probably.'

Aspen couldn't hold back a grin and quickly ducked down to pick up Bandit's rear hoof and clean it.

'You've changed,' he said softly.

She looked up and he nodded to the tool in her hand.

'You used to be much more of a princess type.'

'Really?' Her green eyes sparkled with amusement. 'That's how you saw me?'

'That's how all the boys saw you.' He shrugged. 'We got your horse ready and you rode it and then we brushed it down at the end. Back then you wouldn't have even known how to use one of those.'

Aspen grimaced and went back to work on the horse. 'That was because my grandfather wouldn't let me work with the horses. He had very clear ideas on a woman's place in the world. It was why my mother left. She didn't really talk to me about him, but I remember overhearing her talking to a friend and saying that he didn't understand anyone else's opinion but his own.'

Satisfied that the horse's feet were clean, Aspen patted her rump and collected the wooden toolbox. 'You're done for the day, girl.'

She glanced up as Cruz continued to block the doorway. The sound of someone moving tack around further along the stable rattled between them.

'Why did you set me up that night?'

The suddenness of the question and the harshness of his tone jolted her.

'What are you talking about?' She couldn't think how she had set him up, but—

'Eight years ago. You and your *fiancé*.'

'Fiancé?'

She frowned and then realised that he was talking about the night her grandfather had found them. She had no idea what he meant by setting him up, but it shocked her that he thought she'd been engaged to Chad at the time. Then she recalled her grandfather's vitriolic outburst. Something she'd shoved into the deepest recess of her mind.

She grimaced as it all came rushing back. 'Chad and I weren't actually engaged that night,' she said slowly.

'Your grandfather certainly thought you were.'

'That's because I later learned that he had accepted Chad's proposal on my behalf.'

Cruz swore. 'You're saying he forced you to go along with it?'

Aspen hesitated. 'No. I could have turned him down.'

'But you didn't?'

'No, but I certainly didn't consider myself engaged when I walked into the stables and saw you there.'

'How about when you kissed me?'

Aspen shifted uncomfortably. 'No, not then either.'

'That still doesn't answer my question.'

Aspen couldn't remember his question, her mind so full of memories and guilt. 'What question?'

'Why you set me up.'

She shook her head. 'I don't really understand what you mean by that.'

Cruz took in her wary gaze, frustration and desire biting into him like an annoying insect. 'You're saying it was a coincidence that your grandfather just *happened* to come across us and then just *happened* to kick me off the property, thereby paving the way for Anderson to take over as captain of the dream team?'

Her eyes widened with what appeared to be genuine shock. 'I would never...' She blinked as if she was trying to clear her thoughts. 'Grandfather said it was your decision to leave Ocean Haven.'

Cruz scoffed at the absurdity of her statement. 'It was one of those "you can go under your own steam or mine" type of offers,' he said bitterly.

But he could admit to a little resentment, couldn't he? He'd given Charles Carmichael eleven years of abject devotion that had been repaid with anger and accusations and the revocation of every promise the old man had ever made him.

Memories he'd rather obliterate than verbalise turned his tone harsh. 'He accused me of *deflowering* his precious *engaged* granddaughter and you let him believe it.'

'I don't remember that,' she said softly. 'I told him afterwards that we hadn't been together.'

Cruz wasn't interested in another apology. 'So you said.'

'But you still don't believe me?'

'It's irrelevant.'

'I don't think it is. I can hear in your voice that it still pains you and I don't blame you. I should never have let him think what he did. Not even for a second.'

'What you can hear in my voice is not pain but absolute disgust.'

He stepped closer to her, noting how small and fragile she looked, her shoulders narrow, her limbs slender and fine. He knew the taste of her skin, as well as her scent.

'When it happened...' He forced himself to focus. '*Then* I was upset. Devastated, if you want to know the truth. I thought your grandfather and I were equals. I thought he respected me. Maybe even cared for me.' He snorted out a breath and thrust his hand through his hair. 'I thought wrong. Do you know what he told me?'

Cruz had no idea why he was telling her something so deeply private but somehow the words kept coming.

'He told me I wasn't good enough for his granddaughter. He didn't want your lily-white blood mixing with that of a second-class *Mexicano*.'

'But my blood isn't lily-white. My mother saw to that in a fit of rebellion. My grandfather could never get past her decision and because they were both stubborn neither one could offer the other an olive branch. My mother wanted to go home to The Farm *so* many times.'

Aspen swallowed past the lump in her throat.

'But my grandfather had kicked her out. It was the same with you. Two days after you left he had a stroke and I'm sure it was because he had lost you. Of course no one outside the family knew about it, but I knew it had to do with what happened and I felt terrible. Ashamed of myself. But I was scared, Cruz.'

She looked at him with remorseful eyes and no matter what he thought of her it was impossible to doubt her sincerity.

'You know my grandfather's temper. I didn't know what he'd do to me.'

'Nothing,' Cruz bit out. 'He was angry at me, not you. He thought the world of you.'

'As long as I did what he wanted.' She shivered. 'I was so frightened when I arrived at Ocean Haven. I'd heard about the place from my mother and I'd loved it from a small child. I'd never met my grandfather before and I was determined that he wouldn't hate me. And he didn't. But nor did he like me questioning him or going against his wishes. At first that was okay, because I was little, but as I got older it became harder to always be agreeable. That night...' She stopped and looked at him curiously. 'Why didn't you defend yourself against him? Why didn't you tell him that it was *me* who had kissed *you*?'

'It hadn't exactly been one-way.' He ran a hand through his hair. 'And you looked...frightened.'

Aspen gave him a small smile. 'I was that, all right. I'd never seen him in such a rage. I didn't know what to do and I froze. It's a horrible reaction I've never been able to shake when I'm truly petrified. That night, if he had found out that I instigated things with you after he'd told me I was expected to marry Chad, I thought...I thought...'

Cruz briefly closed his eyes. 'You thought he'd disown you like he had your mother.'

The truth of what had happened that night was like a slap in the face.

'It seems silly now, but...'

'It was like history repeating itself. Your mother with the ski instructor...you with the lowly polo player.'

'*I* didn't think that, but he was so angry.' She shuddered at the memory. 'And I never wanted to leave the one place my mother loved so much. She used to talk about it all the time. Do you know that skewed horseshoe wedged between two roof beams in the stable?'

Cruz knew it. Old Charlie had grumbled about it whenever he was in a bad mood.

'Apparently years ago Mum and Uncle Joe were playing hooky with a bunch of them and when she was losing she got in a terrible snit and aimed one at his head.' Aspen laughed softly, as if she were remembering her mother recounting the story. 'Unfortunately she was a terrible shot and released it too soon. It went shooting up towards the roof and somehow it got stuck. Which was lucky for my uncle because she obviously put her back into it.' She smiled. 'Every time I see it, it's as if she's still here with me.'

She looked at him.

'That night I was so angry with my grandfather for ignoring my wishes that I went to the stable to talk to her. When you showed up and you weren't dressed properly I... I can't explain it rationally.'

Her eyes flitted away and then she seemed to force them back to his.

'I had wanted to kiss you for so long and I wasn't thinking clearly. I know you don't want to hear this but I am sorry, Cruz. I should have stood up for you. But I was selfishly worried about myself and—'

Cruz cupped her face in his hands and kissed her. Lightly. 'It's okay. I remember his temper.'

Aspen gave him a wobbly smile. 'I think I inherited that from him.'

He shook his head, his thumbs stroking her cheekbones. 'You're not scary when you're angry. You're beautiful.'

She made a noise somewhere between a snort and a cough and he couldn't resist kissing her again, his lips lingering and sipping at hers.

This time the noise she made was one of pleasure, and Cruz slid his hand into her hair to hold her head steady, nudging the toolbox out of his way with his knee so that he could shift closer. She pressed into him and he wrapped his other hand around her waist, deepening the kiss. Slowly.

Deliberately drawing out the sweet anticipation of it for both of them.

Aspen's arms rose, linked around his neck and time passed. How much, he couldn't have said.

Slowly she drew back, lifting her long lashes to reveal eyes glazed with passion. 'Wow…' she whispered.

Wow was right.

She moistened her lower lip, her eyes flitting from his, and he frowned. He could have sworn he saw a touch of apprehension in them. He nipped at her lower lip, kissed her again.

With a thousand questions pounding through his head—not least why she seemed nervous when it came to intimacy—he reluctantly ended the searing kiss and leant his forehead against hers. Their breaths mingled, hot and heavy.

'I don't hate you, Aspen,' he said, answering her question of the previous night. Her bewitching green eyes returned to his and he found himself saying, 'I have a formal dinner at the hotel tonight. Come with me.'

Aspen felt dazzled. By the conversation. By his sweet, tender kisses. By the piercing ache in her pelvis that made a mockery of her previous experiences with Chad. 'I'd like that…'

And she did—right up until she found an emerald-green gown laid out on her bed next to black stiletto sandals still inside their box.

Standing stock-still in the centre of the spare room Aspen stared at the exquisite gown.

'Don't wear that. You look awful in it. Here. Put this on.'

Aspen shivered. Chad's voice was so clear in her head he might as well have been standing beside her.

Cruz wasn't Chad. She knew that. But somehow her stomach still felt cramped. Because the dress symbolised some sort of ownership. Some sort of control. And she knew she couldn't give him that—not over her.

It made her realise just what she'd been thinking when he had invited her to the dinner. She'd been thinking it was a date. That it was real.

But this wasn't real. She wouldn't even be here if it wasn't for the deal he had offered her. A deal she had accepted and still hadn't fulfilled. Which she needed to do to keep Ocean Haven. How had she forgotten that? How had she forgotten that he was trying to steal it away from her?

But she knew how. He'd kissed her so tenderly, so reverently, it had been as if eight years had fallen away between them. And she couldn't think like that. Because as much as she hated the coldness of the deal they had struck she also knew that she couldn't afford to feel anything. She couldn't afford to want anything from him other than money. That way was fraught with disaster. It would turn her from an independent woman in charge of her own destiny back into the people-pleaser she had tried to be for her grandfather. For Chad.

She stared at the dress. Cruz was an extraordinarily wealthy man who was used to getting what he wanted. For some reason he had decided that he wanted her. For a night. But that didn't mean she had to wear clothes he'd chosen as well.

Before she could think too much about it she strode out into the living room. The sun was hanging low in the sky and it illuminated his fit body as he stood in front of the window, talking into his cell phone.

As if sensing her presence he turned, scanned her face and the dress she was holding, and told whomever he was talking to that he had to go.

She held the dress out to him. 'I can't wear this.'

He frowned. 'It doesn't fit?'

'No. Yes. Actually, I don't know. I haven't tried it on.'

He smiled. 'Then what's the problem?'

'The problem is—' She dropped her hand and paced away from him. 'The problem is that I'm not a possession you can dress up whenever you like. The problem is I'm an independent woman who has some idea about how to dress herself and doesn't need to be told what to wear by some high-powered male who has to own everything.'

A heavy silence fell over the room as soon as her spiel had finished but somehow her words hung between them like a hideously long banner dragged through the sky by a biplane.

'I take it your grandfather didn't like your choice in outfits?' He dropped into a plush sofa. 'Or was it Anderson?'

For a minute his astute questions floored her. 'Chad has *nothing* to do with this,' she bit out.

His beautiful black eyes glittered with confidence and Aspen was suddenly embarrassed to realise that she had just exposed a part of herself she hadn't intended to.

'At some point we need to talk about him.'

Aspen felt her heart hammer inside her chest. 'We so do not.'

His eyes became hooded. 'We will, but not now. As to the other.' He waved his hand at the emerald silk crushed in her hand. 'It's just a dress, Aspen. I assume you didn't pack anything formal?'

'No.' Deciding to ignore her embarrassment, she forged on. 'But I can buy my own clothes if I need to.'

Clearly exasperated, he looked at her from under long thick lashes. 'Fine. I'll forward you the bill.'

Aspen could tell he had no intention of doing that. 'You may have bought a night with me, Cruz, but that doesn't mean you own me.'

'I don't want to own you.' He laid his arm along the back of the sofa. 'Wear it. Don't wear it. It's irrelevant to me.'

'What *is* relevant to you?' she asked, goaded by his

nonchalant attitude. 'Because it seems to me that you've cut yourself off from everything that could have meaning in your life other than work. Your family. Your polo playing—' Aspen stopped, breathlessly aware that he had risen during her tirade and that he was nowhere near as relaxed as he had appeared.

'The dress was a peace offering.' He grabbed his suit jacket from the back of the nearby chair. 'But you can bin it for all I care.'

Feeling all at sea as he stalked out of the penthouse, Aspen returned to her room and leant against the closed door.

A peace offering?

She felt stupid and knew that she had acted like a drama queen. And she knew why. She was tense. The thought of sex with Cruz was hanging over her head like a stalactite. And felt just as deadly.

Glancing at the bed, she ignored the tight feeling in her chest and tossed the dress onto it. Then she stripped off and scalded herself with a hot shower, all the while knowing that as she plucked and preened and soaped herself with the delicious vanilla-scented soap that she was doing so with Cruz in mind. Which made her feel worse. This wasn't a romance. It was a deal.

A deal that would end as soon as they'd slept together.

A deal that could still go wrong if her uncle decided that he needed the money Cruz was willing to part with to turn Ocean Haven into a horrible hotel.

Trying not to dwell on that, she rolled her eyes at herself when she realised she'd changed her hairstyle five times. She looked at the spiralling mess. All her fiddling had turned her hair to frizz. *Great*.

Salvaging it as best she could, she stomped back into the bedroom and spied the offending gown she had flung onto the bed. Even skewed it rippled, and dared any woman not to want to wear it.

And given the contents of her suitcase what choice did she really have? None. And she hated that because she'd had so little choice in what had happened to her growing up on Ocean Haven. After Chad she had vowed she'd never be beholden to anyone again—especially not a man. But one night with Cruz didn't make her beholden to him, did it?

Once he'd lent her the money and she'd paid him back, as she would the other investors, they would be back on an equal footing. She exhaled. One night, straight up, and then she was home free.

Why did that leave her feeling so empty?

She looked again at the dress. Grimaced. Trust him to have such superb taste.

CHAPTER EIGHT

'ARE YOU EVEN listening to what I'm saying?'

Cruz glanced at Ricardo, who was debriefing him on who was attending the formal dinner that night and how impressed the Chinese delegation were with the facilities. The Sunset Bar, where they had decided to catch up for a drink before the evening proceedings, was full to bursting with excited players and polo experts from all over the globe.

'Of course,' he lied. 'Go on.'

Ricardo frowned, but thankfully continued working his way through the list.

Cruz studied it also, but his mind was elsewhere. More specifically his mind was weighing up how he was going to steal The Farm out from under Aspen's gorgeous fingertips when he now knew the truth about that fateful night.

He took a healthy swig of his tequila. He'd been *so* sure she had done him wrong eight years ago he'd been blind to any other possibility. *Tainted*, he realised belatedly. Tainted by his own deep-seated feelings of inferiority and hurt pride.

Hell.

He couldn't escape the knowledge that seeing Aspen again had unearthed a wealth of bitterness he hadn't even realised he'd buried deep inside himself—resentments he'd let fester but that no longer seemed relevant.

What is *relevant to you?*

Hell, that woman had a way of working her way inside his head. But as much as he hated that he knew in good conscience he couldn't take Ocean Haven away from her. He'd never be able to face himself in the mirror again if he did. But what to do? Because if he also let her continue with her foolhardy plan to borrow thirty million dollars to keep it she'd be bankrupt within a year.

Of course that wasn't his problem. She was an adult and could take care of herself. But some of that old protectiveness he had always felt towards her was seeping back in and refused to go away. He wanted to fix everything for her, but she was so fiercely guarded, so intent on doing everything herself. It was madness. But so was the fact that he couldn't stop thinking about her. That he even *wanted* to fix things for her in the first place.

Realising that Ricardo was waiting for him to say something, Cruz nodded thoughtfully. 'Sam Harris is playing tomorrow. Got it.'

'Actually,' Ricardo said patiently, 'Sam Harris is sick. Tommy Hassenberger is taking his place.'

'Send Sam a bottle of tequila.'

'I already sent flowers.'

Cruz shook his head at his brother. 'And you think you need a *wife*?'

Normally his brother would have returned his light ribbing, but to Cruz's chagrin he didn't this time.

'What's up?' he said instead.

Cruz rubbed his jaw and realised he should have shaved again. 'Nothing.'

'You're a million miles away. It wouldn't have anything to do with Aspen Carmichael, would it?'

Bingo.

'If I say no, you'll assume I'm lying, and if I say yes, you'll want to know why.'

Ricardo shook his head and laughed. '*Dios mio*, you've got it bad.'

Cruz dismissed Ricardo's comment. He *wanted* her badly, yes, and he was happy to admit that, but he didn't *have* it bad in the way his brother was implying.

A hush fell over the bar at the same time as the skin on the back of his neck started to prickle. Then Ricardo let out a low whistle under his breath.

'*Mi, oh, mi....*'

Slowly Cruz turned his head to find Aspen framed in the open double glass doorway of the bar like something out of a 1950s Hollywood extravaganza, the silky green gown he'd bought her flowing around her slender figure like coloured water. His mouth went dry. The halterneck dress was deceptively simple at the front but so beautifully crafted it lovingly moulded to her shape exactly as it was supposed to. She'd pinned her hair up in a soft, timeless bun—which must mean she had a fair amount of skin showing, as he was pretty sure the dress dipped quite low at the back.

Okay, make that completely backless, he corrected, fighting a primitive urge to bundle her up in his arms and return her to his room. His bed.

She hadn't spotted him yet, and when a male voice called out her name Cruz watched her turn her head, the wispy tendrils of hair she had left to frame her face dancing golden beneath the halogen lighting. Her expression softened as she spied a few of his polo players lounging in the club chairs that circled a small wooden table.

She walked towards them and Cruz tried not to react, but it was impossible to stop his gut from tightening as the men watched her with unrestrained lust in their eyes.

She looked so delicate.

So sensual.

So *his*.

The need to stamp his ownership all over her took hold and he didn't bother to contain it. For right now, for tonight, she was his—and he didn't care who knew it. In fact, the more who did the better. It would save him from having to keep tabs on her during dinner, and the four European jocks already halfway to being tanked would, he knew, be the best candidates to spread the news.

As conversation once again resumed in the bar he ignored Ricardo's keen gaze and went to her.

She had her back to him and he felt her jump as his thigh lightly grazed her hip. She looked up and he bent his head, let his eyes linger on her mouth, gratified by her quick intake of breath.

If it were possible, the more time he spent with her the more time he *wanted* to spend with her. It was a sobering thought, if he'd been in the mood to care.

He cupped Aspen's elbow in his palm. 'Gentlemen, if you'll excuse us?'

Slowly each man registered Cruz's proprietorial manner, but only Tommy Hassenberger had the nerve to look disgruntled. 'Looks like I'm too late,' he complained.

'You were too late when you were born, Tommy,' one of his friends joked, making the others laugh.

Aspen grinned, said she'd catch up with them at the formal dinner, and then felt intoxicated as Cruz placed his hand on the small of her back to guide her from the room, the heat of his palm scorching her bare skin.

She hadn't known what to expect when she had entered the bar but she had decided to try and relax. To try and forget about their deal and her fears and just brave it out. Cruz had invited her to dinner—a formal event, not a date—and for all she knew that was a peace offering as well.

'You wore the dress,' he said, his gravelly voice stroking her already heightened senses.

'Yes. I couldn't not in the end. Thank you.'

'You look stunning in it.'

The look he gave her made her burn.

Aspen took in his superbly cut tuxedo. 'You look—' *Simply divine.* 'Nice too,' she croaked.

He gave her a small smile. 'Aspen, I need to tell you something.'

Cruz gazed down at the utterly stunning woman at his side and a ball of emotion rushed through him. Seeing her like this…having her beside him…all the animosity of the past fell away and he just wanted to take her upstairs and make love to her with a need that floored him.

'What is it?'

Aspen tilted her head and Cruz heard a roaring in his ears as their eyes connected. Reality seemed suspended and—

'Señor Rodriguez, sir, the first lot of guests are assembled in the Rosa Room.'

Cruz turned towards his head waiter. 'Thank you, Paco. I'll be along in a minute.'

'Certainly.'

The waiter inclined his head and left and Cruz lifted Aspen's fingers to his lips. He could see her pulse racing and his did the same.

'I wish I'd never planned this idiotic dinner.'

'It's not idiotic.' She smiled up at him, her eyes almost on a level with his chin because she was wearing the stilettos. 'It's to welcome honoured guests to your flagship hotel for tomorrow's tournament. It's important.'

Not half as important as what he wanted to be doing with her upstairs right now.

His nostrils flared as he fought to control the urge to drag her into the nearest darkened corner. On one level he thought he should be concerned about the intensity of his hunger for her, but on another he just couldn't bring himself to examine it. There was something about her that sent his baser instincts off the scale.

Nothing a night of straightforward, short-term hot sex wouldn't cure.

He smiled at the thought and, with the situation once again under his control, he tucked her elegant hand in the crook of his elbow and prayed for the evening formalities to fly by.

The dinner took all night. As it was supposed to.

The first course had been Mushroom-something. Aspen couldn't remember and Cruz, possibly noticing her picking at it dubiously, had swapped it for his goat's cheese soufflé. Then there'd been the main course. Beef or chicken. This time Aspen had swapped with him when she'd seen him eyeing her steak.

He'd smiled, grazed her chin with his knuckles and then resumed talking to two well-dressed Asian men, who'd nodded with polite restraint. Now and then he'd twined his fingers with hers when she'd left her hand on the tabletop while he talked, as if it was the most natural thing in the world for him to do. As if this really was a date.

Aspen had chatted to the wife of the Mayor, who was very down to earth and full of Latin passion, and their daughter who was studying to be a doctor. They'd swapped war stories of bad essay topics, boring lecturers and horror exams and then it had been time for dessert.

She was full. Even though she'd hardly eaten a thing.

Her dinner companions excused themselves, and Aspen was just contemplating whether she should move to the other side of the table to speak with an older woman who sat on her own when Cruz slid his fingers through hers again. His hand was so much bigger than hers, his skin tone darker, the hairs on the back of his wrists absurdly attractive.

He stroked his thumb over her palm and goosebumps raced themselves up her arm.

He glanced in her direction, brought her hand briefly to his lips and then answered one of the Asian men's questions.

The Mayor's daughter returned and Cruz dropped Aspen's hand as the girl produced a photo of her horse on her phone. Aspen made polite responses, all the time disturbingly aware of the man beside her.

Something had changed between them since she'd come downstairs. He was behaving as she imagined a man in love would behave. Little intimate glances, tucking her hair behind her ear, pouring her water, holding her hand…

Chad had seemed nice in the beginning too. Wooing her. Treating her lovingly. Somehow it had all come unstuck the year Cruz had left and her grandfather had been too sick to send the team to England. Chad had been unable to get a permanent ride that year and had started drinking more. By the time their wedding had rolled around she'd barely recognised him as the man who had courted her and treated her so deferentially. He'd moved back home when his father had threatened to halve his trust fund, and his father had used the opportunity to encourage Chad to get a real job. Aspen had tried to smooth things over but that had only seemed to make him resentful.

On their wedding night— No, she didn't want to remember that.

She glanced at Cruz to find him deep in conversation. Would he be rough? She swallowed, her gaze drawn to his hands, wrapped around a wine glass. He stroked the slender stem with the pad of his thumb. Aspen recalled how he had stroked her lips the same way and heat erupted low in her belly. For a man with such size and strength he had been gentle. Suddenly his thumb stopped moving and Aspen felt the air between them shift even before her eyes connected with his.

Her mouth dried and her heart thumped. Fear and desire commingled until she felt emotionally wrung out.

'Aspen?'

She glanced up but didn't really see him.

'Everything okay?'

Oh, God, that deep, sensual voice so close to her ear. She couldn't help it. She trembled. Then pulled herself together.

'Fine.' *Just me being a nincompoop.*

Nincompoop? Her mother had used that word when she'd been laughing at herself.

A wave of sadness overtook her and immediately made her think of Ocean Haven. Her horses. Her mother. Aspen had gained wealth by moving in with her grandfather but not love, and certainly not security.

Cruz moved his hand to the back of her chair. 'You look miles away.'

A wave of panic washed through her and she made the mistake of glancing up at him.

As soon as their eyes met his sharpened with concern. 'Hey, what's wrong?'

'Nothing.' She forced a smile. 'I just need to go to the bathroom.'

He scanned her face but thankfully didn't push her. 'Don't be long. We'll go when you get back.'

Oh, help.

She got up, stumbled and snagged the tablecloth with her leg. Cruz leaned over and held it while she straightened up. The deliciously sexy gown he had bought her swayed around her body and settled. She felt his eyes on her as she started to walk away, the dress floating around her legs as light as butterfly wings. Of course that was nothing compared to the butterflies using her belly as a trampoline.

Once in the bathroom she told herself to calm down and splashed cold water on her wrists, dabbed it on her cheeks. She checked her make-up, shocked to see her face so flushed. It was because every time he touched her she thought of sex.

A woman smiled at her in the mirror and Aspen dropped her gaze lest the woman accurately read her mind. Then she realised how rude that was and raised her eyes only to find the person had gone.

She let out a shaky laugh at her absurd behaviour. She felt like… She felt like… She frowned. She couldn't remember ever feeling this nervous.

Well, maybe she could. On her wedding day. She'd had a similar fluttering feeling in her stomach then that had turned out to be a bad omen.

She stared at herself. Fear knotted her insides. She couldn't do this. Her eyes looked like two huge dots in her face. She just couldn't do it. She was so anxious she'd probably throw up all over him.

An older woman entered the bathroom and Aspen pretended to be wiping her hands.

She'd have to tell Cruz.

Would it mean she'd still get the money if she backed out?

Oh, who cares about the money? This was no longer about the money. This was now about self-preservation. This was about going back to the wonderful, predictable life that she loved.

Yes, but there won't be that life if you don't go through with this.

She'd backed herself into a corner and the only way out was through Cruz. A man who, for all his surface arrogance, genuinely cared about his family and was smart. And also ruthless. He would chew her up and spit her out without a backward glance if she let him.

'Let's not forget why you're here, Aspen,' she told her reflection softly.

He was pitting himself against her for Ocean Haven. Her farm. She should hate him for that alone but she didn't, she realised. She didn't hate him at all. Because she had come to understand him a little better. Understand what he had thought of her. What had shaped him as a boy. What had shaped him as a man.

How did you hate someone you instinctively sensed was good underneath? And what did that even matter?

Shaking her head at her reflection, she refastened a few loosened strands of hair and wondered where all her positive self-talk had run off to.

Maybe down the toilet.

She smiled at her lame attempt at humour and nearly walked straight into Cruz where he leant against the wall opposite the ladies' room.

'You were taking so long I got worried. I was just about to go in but I didn't want to surprise you.'

'I would have been okay.' She let out a shaky breath. 'It's the old lady in the cubicle you might have had some trouble with.'

Cruz laughed and it broke the tension. He held out his hand. 'Shall we go?'

She looked at his perfect, handsome face. Then his hand, palm up. He was strong, maybe stronger than Chad, but he wasn't nasty. Even when he'd thought she had done him wrong he still hadn't picked on her the way Chad would have done. No, Cruz was arrogant and controlling, but he was honest and straight down the line. A straight arrow. Black and white. No shades of grey.

'Aspen?'

She saw hunger and desire in his eyes and it made her feel hot all over. Maybe she could do this. *Maybe.*

She glanced at his hand, wondered if she was as crazy as her uncle had suggested and placed hers in it.

He smiled.

She swallowed.

It wasn't until they were halfway across the foyer that she saw a familiar figure—a man—leaning against the reception desk. He had his back to her, so she couldn't see his face, but he was average height with blond hair and a slightly stocky bodybuilder's physique.

Chad?

Cruz pressed the lift button and Aspen's attention was momentarily snagged by their reflection in the gold-finished doors. They looked good together, she thought. He was tall and broad, and she looked feminine and almost otherworldly in the beautiful green dress.

His eyes met hers and she couldn't look away.

Then the lift doors opened. Aspen snuck another quick glance over her shoulder but the man she had spotted wasn't there. She let out a relieved breath. After their last acrimonious argument Chad had kept to his own part of the world and she to hers.

Still, she stabbed repeatedly at the penthouse button and only realised how questionable her behaviour looked when she noticed Cruz's bemused expression and realised he hadn't swiped his security tag across the electronic panel.

His eyebrows rose and Aspen's gaze dropped to the space between their feet, her heart beating too fast. Seeing the man who might or might not have been her ex-husband had been terrible timing. Just when she'd begun to think maybe her night with Cruz would be all right it was as if the powers that be had sent her a message to take care.

To remind her that being in a man's control was when a woman was at her most vulnerable.

As the lift ascended Cruz pushed away from the mirror-panelled wall and invaded her space, startling her out of her dark reverie when he placed his warm hands either side of her waist.

'Okay, talk to me. You're as nervous as a pony facing the bridle for the first time. The same as you were last night.'

Aspen gave a low laugh at his analogy and jumped when his thumbs stroked her hip bones through the dress. She couldn't tell him she thought she'd just seen Chad. That would raise a whole host of questions that she did not want to answer. And what if she was wrong? Then she'd just look stupid. Or paranoid.

'I'm fine.'

'You're shaking.'

Was she?

He gave her a look. 'Is it the deal? Because—'

'It's not the deal. Actually I'd forgotten all about that again.'

Her answer seemed to please him but she didn't have time to consider his satisfied—'Good.'—because the lift doors opened.

When he'd released her he placed his hand on the small of her back as he ushered her through to the living room. The housekeeper had been and the room was cast with shadows by the floor lamps that had been switched on for their convenience.

'Do you want a drink?'

'Yes, please.'

She'd said that too loudly and his eyes narrowed.

'Of…?'

Aspen forced a smile. 'Gin and tonic.' She winced. She hated gin and tonic.

She wandered over to the wall to study one of the paintings she'd admired the evening before but never taken the time to look at. An overhead light outlined it perfectly and she gasped.

'That's a Renoir.'

'I know.'

He was right behind her and she heard the tinkle of ice as he handed her the drink she didn't want.

'You're not having one?'

'No.' He perched on the arm of a nearby sofa, watching her. 'Something wrong with it?'

'What?'

He motioned patiently towards the highball in her hand. 'Your drink?'

'No. It's fine. At least, I'm sure it's fine.' It was all about maintaining control. If she did that she could get through this. 'Look, maybe we should just…start.'

'Start?'

Aspen could have kicked herself, and she moved towards a side table so she could let out a discreet breath and put the drink down. She knew he hadn't taken his eyes off her and she told herself that he wanted her. She'd felt how aroused he had been last night, and again in the stable that day. He had felt huge!

So why had he stopped? Was he struggling to maintain an erection with her as Chad had done? She shuddered. On those occasions Chad had been particularly vile.

Cruz tilted his head and looked as if he was about to say something, and then he changed his mind. Instead he uncurled his large frame and came towards her until he practically loomed over her. Then he reached for her hair.

She didn't mean to do it, of course, but she flinched and his hand stilled. 'I'm just going to take your hair down.'

She stared at his chest and tried to slow her heartbeat.

'Is that okay?'

She nodded, not trusting herself to speak.

'Turn around.'

It took all of her willpower to give him that modicum of control, but when she did turn around he stroked her shoulders.

'You have a beautiful back. Lean and supple. Strong.'

He kneaded the bunched muscles either side of her neck and her involuntary sigh of pleasure filled the quiet room.

'That feels so good. I know I must be really tight.'

Cruz groaned inwardly, knowing she hadn't meant that comment the way his depraved mind had interpreted it. Yes, she did feel tight. Too tight. Too nervous.

He wanted to ask her what was wrong, but she moaned softly and her head lolled on the graceful stem of her neck and the question died in his throat.

All through dinner he'd imagined doing this. Touching her, tasting her. He'd been harder than stone all night and he wasn't sure if he'd committed to five hotels in China or fifty. Nor did he care. Right now he'd put a hundred on Mars if someone asked him to.

Aspen moaned again and shifted beneath his pressing thumbs.

'Harder or softer?' he asked, the rough timbre of his voice reflecting his deep arousal.

He heard her breath catch, and then his did as well as her gorgeous bottom brushed his fly.

'Harder,' she whispered, and a shudder ripped through him.

The musky perfume of her skin was ambrosia to his senses and he trailed soft kisses across her shoulders. Her head fell forward and she braced her hands on the side table in front of her. Cruz registered her position on a purely primal level and knew all he'd have to do was lift that long silk skirt, tear whatever excuse for a pair of panties she was hiding underneath, bend her a little more forward and slide right into her—and he very nearly did.

But he wanted more of her taste in his mouth first, and with unsteady hands he gripped the side of her waist and trailed tiny moist kisses down the column of her spine until he reached the small of her back.

She undulated for him, arching backwards, and unable to hold himself back any longer he rose, spun her around to face him and slanted his mouth across hers. Not softly, as he had done earlier in the stables—he was too far gone for that—but hard, with barely leashed power and a deep driving hunger to be inside her.

She opened for him instantly, her fingers impatient as they delved into his hair to anchor him to her. That was okay with him. He barely noticed the bite of her short nails, concentrating instead on the throbbing sense of satisfaction as his tongue filled her mouth. He tasted coffee and cream and couldn't suppress a groan.

Somehow some of her earlier hesitation seeped into the minute part of his brain that still functioned on an intellectual level and he attempted to steady himself—before he just dragged her to the floor and had done with it.

Then her tongue stroked his and his mind gave out. Sensation hot and strong coursed through him, just as it had every other time he'd kissed her, and he couldn't help curving her closer so that they touched everywhere.

The silky fabric of her dress slid against his jacket in an erotic parody of skin on skin. Which was what he wanted. What he needed. And, keeping his mouth firmly on hers, he shucked out of it and then lashed at the buttons on his shirt.

She moaned, her warm hands pushing the fabric off his body as she shaped his arms and his shoulders before clinging once more around his neck.

Cruz reached behind her neck. His fingers felt clumsy in his desperation as he finally managed to undo the two pearl-like buttons that held the top of the dress together.

Aroused to an unbearable pitch, he smoothed a hand down to the small of her back, his lips cruising along her jawline until he could tug on the lobe of her ear. She was wearing tiny gold studs and he tongued one as he bit down gently on her flesh and brought his hands around to cradle both breasts in the palms of his hands. She trembled delightfully and her responsiveness rocked him to his core.

His thumb caught her nipple and she cried out, gripping him tighter. Cruz knew that neither of them was going to make it to the bedroom so he didn't even try. Instead he lifted her onto the side table and hoped it would hold.

It did, and he pulled back and looked down at her.

Her nipples pebbled enticingly beneath his lingering gaze and he plumped one breast up. 'You're so beautiful,' he breathed, taking the rosy tip into his mouth.

Arousal beat through his body, hot and insistent, and he urged her thighs wider so that he could settle his erection between her legs. Unfortunately the table wasn't high enough for him to take her on it and he knew he'd have to lift her onto him when the time came.

'Thank heavens you're wearing a dress,' he growled around her tight, wet nipple, his impatient hands delving beneath the reams of fabric to find her.

Moments later he felt her panic in the stiffening of her thighs and the press of her fingernails on his shoulders.

'Wait!'

His blurred mind tried to take in the change and he mentally pulled back.

'We might need some lubricant,' she blurted out against his neck.

Lubricant?

Cruz stilled, and was struck by how slight and vulnerable her body felt compared to his much larger frame curved over her. Instantly his libido cooled as he recalled those times she had flinched away from him when he'd reached for her. He frowned. Had she *never* experienced pleasure during sex?

He brought one hand up between them to cup her jaw and brought her eyes to his. 'Aspen, what's wrong?'

'I'm just…' She licked her lips, her mortified gaze flitting sideways. 'I don't have much natural lubrication. I should have told you earlier.'

Stunned, Cruz could only stare at her. He could tell she was serious but he had briefly felt her moist heat through her panties and knew she needed extra lubrication the way Ireland needed rain.

As if taking his prolonged silence as a rejection, she shoved his chest hard enough to dislodge him and desperately scooted off the table.

Only her stilettos must have come off when he'd lifted her because her feet tangled in the fabric of her dress and she pitched forward.

Cursing, Cruz grabbed hold of her before she fell. 'Aspen, wait.'

'No. Let me go.'

Ignoring her attempts to break free, he gently tugged her back into his embrace. She immediately buried her head against his neck and he brought one hand up to stroke her hair. His heart thundered in his chest as his dazed mind tried to process what was happening.

He waited until he felt her breathing start to even out and then he leaned back so he could look at her face.

'Who told you that you didn't have any natural lubrication?'

She groaned and burrowed even more fully against him.

Cruz cupped her nape soothingly. 'I know you're embarrassed. Was it Anderson?'

'It happens to some women.'

Cruz had no doubt she was correct, but he had already felt how damp she was through her lace panties and, whatever problems she had, he very much doubted this was one of them.

'I'm sure it does *chiquita*, but it hasn't happened to you.'

She pulled back. 'You're wrong. Chad and I... Can we not talk about this?'

He was going to kill the moron.

Cruz nudged her chin up until her baleful glare met his. He nearly smiled at her thorny gaze but this was too serious. 'Did he hurt you?'

She wet her lips, dropped her eyes.

'Aspen?'

'Oh, all right.' She sighed. 'On our wedding night Chad was... I was anxious. Chad had been drinking heavily and I knew I had made a mistake. Actually, I knew I'd made a mistake even before the wedding, but it became bigger than I was and I didn't know how to stop it. And Chad could be charming.' She gave an empty laugh. 'You might not know that, being a man, but my friends thought he was wonderful. But the alcohol changed him and that night...' She swallowed. 'That night...'

'He raped you,' he said flatly.

'No. It was my fault. I was nervous.'

Cruz barely held himself in check. 'Do *not* blame yourself.' He guided her eyes back up to look at him. 'He would have known that you were nervous.' He cursed under his breath. 'Hell, Aspen. You were all of eighteen.'

She gave him a wobbly smile and Cruz enfolded her in his arms. He held her until he felt her trembling subside.

'He didn't mean to, Cruz. It just wasn't easy.'

Uh-huh. When he did kill him he'd do it slowly.

'It's fine. I knew this would happen anyway. You can let me go.'

Let her go?

She tried to pull away, and when he looked at her she had that same resigned look on her face that she'd had the previous night.

'When I first arrived at Ocean Haven to work for your grandfather,' he began tentatively, 'I missed my family so much I cried myself to sleep every night for a month and I felt pathetic. You were right yesterday when you said it was a lot for a kid to take on. At the time, though, I thought I just needed to man up.'

'Oh, Cruz.'

Her hand curled around his forearm, and even though he knew he was sharing the memory with her to take her mind off her own past part of him still soaked up the comfort of her touch.

'I thought my mother was turning her back on me. That I was an embarrassment to the family.'

'No.' Aspen shook her head fiercely. 'I only met her yesterday but I *know* that can't be true.'

'Probably not. And what Anderson told you isn't true either.' When her eyes fell to the side Cruz tipped her chin up. 'Aspen, you're a beautiful, sensual woman and I want to prove that to you if you'll let me.'

She frowned. 'I don't see how.'

He cupped her face in his hands, halting her words. 'I want you, Aspen. I want to kiss you and touch you and make love to you until all you can think about is how good you feel. The question is, do *you* want that to happen?'

The question might also be what the hell was he talking about? It was one thing to make a woman feel good in bed. It was quite another to want to slay her demons for her.

Ignoring the fact that he had never donned the white knight suit before, and what that meant, Cruz waited for her answer.

And waited.

Finally, still clutching her dress to her chest, her eyes wide and luminous in the over-bright room, she nodded. 'I think so.'

'Then relax and let me take care of you. And, Aspen…?'
He waited for her to look at him from beneath the fringe of

her dark lashes. 'If you want me to stop at any time, then we'll stop. Understand?'

She paused and her green eyes opened a little wider. 'You'd really do that, wouldn't you?'

For a brief moment Cruz savoured all the ways he would break every bone in Chad Anderson's body, starting with his pompous head and working his way down.

'In a heartbeat, *mi chiquita*. No questions asked.'

CHAPTER NINE

ASPEN BREATHED IN Cruz's warm, musky scent as he carried her to his bedroom and told herself to relax. But it was impossible. She was too embarrassed. Her old panic had returned full force when she'd felt Cruz's warm hand slide between her thighs and now she clung to his neck like a spider monkey as he laid her on the bed.

'Aspen?'

The bedcover was cool at her back and his naked chest was hot at her front as he tried to prise her hands from around his neck. In her earlier fantasies about sex it was romantic and sensual. Dreamy and wonderful. Hot and desperate. This felt awkward and tense.

She didn't look at him as he turned onto his side, visualising how gauche she must appear, with her hair spread out around her and her body partially exposed, with the bodice of her dress undone and metres of silk twisted up around her waist. Keeping her eyes scrunched tight, she adjusted the skirt down her legs.

'Can you turn out the light?' She could feel it burning holes in her retinas even though her eyes were clamped shut.

'I will if it makes you more comfortable, but I won't be able to see you if I do that.'

'That would be the general idea.'

'Open your eyes, *gatita*.'

'Is it a prerequisite?'

His low chuckle had her squinting up at him. He looked lazy and indolent with his head propped in his hands, his gaze extremely male and hot as it met hers. Well, clearly only one of them was feeling awkward and tense.

'You're very comfortable with this, aren't you?'

'You will be too, very soon,' he promised. 'More than comfortable.'

He brought his hand up to her face and started drawing lazy patterns with his finger over her cheeks and nose and down the side of her neck to her collarbone. It wasn't easy for her to give him control, but Aspen lay as still as a stone, slowly recognising that her skin was tingling with a pleasant sensation and that goosebumps had risen up along her upper arms.

'How much pleasure have you actually had during sex, *mi chiquita*?'

She swallowed and would have turned from him then, but his magical finger edged along the loose side of her dress and feathered across her nipple. She sucked in a shallow breath, letting it out on a rush. 'Not much,' she answered honestly. *None* seemed too big an admission to make.

'Mmm...' Cruz ducked his head to her shoulder and trailed a line of kisses to the sensitive curve of her neck. 'Then we'll have to change all that. I am now taking it as my personal mission to teach you about pleasure.'

He shifted closer so that she could feel the heat of his body burn into the side of hers.

'Nothing but pleasure.'

He looked at her as if he wanted to devour her. As if he couldn't think of anything else but her. The thought frightened her, because her desire for him had grown exponentially over the course of a couple of days and she didn't know how that had happened.

He had invaded her thoughts and her dreams and seemed to make a mockery of her declaration that she would never again be at any man's mercy. Because here she was, lying nearly naked on his bed and feeling way out of her depth. And yet as scary as that thought was, as she looked at him like this, his face half in shadow from the bedside lamp, he looked amazing. His strong features and wide shoulders promised to fulfil all of her hidden desires and she felt utterly and completely safe with him, she realised with astonishment. Something she would have said she would never feel again in a man's arms.

Warmth returned deep inside her. Warmth and a sense of wonder that made her feel hot and restless. Her gaze fell to where her hands rested on his gorgeous chest and then she slowly returned her eyes to his. The look in his was both tender and hungry and it made her insides melt.

Reaching up, she stroked the sexy stubble already lining his jaw. 'Make love to me, Cruz. Please.'

As if he'd been waiting for her to say those exact words he took one of her hands and brought her palm to his lips. His answer, 'It will be my pleasure...' rumbled through his chest and arrowed straight into her heart.

His next kiss was hot and deep and sensation swamped her, sending sparks of excitement everywhere, cutting off her ability to think. Her inhibitions and worries seemed to be caught up with some primal desire and this time desire won out.

There was just no room to consider anything other than Cruz's big hands on her body, stroking her, adoring her. His whispered words of encouragement as he discarded her dress and moved her tiny thong down her thighs raised her level of anticipation to an unbearable pitch.

Within seconds she was naked beneath him and his mouth was tracking a path to her breast. Aspen held still, already anticipating the heady pleasure his mouth would bring. And she wasn't disappointed. Cruz drew the tight bud gently into his mouth, licked, circled, nipped and did things to her nipple that were surely illegal. Aspen felt dizzy and her hazy mind didn't even register when his hand slid over the outside of her thighs. Then every neuron in her brain tightened and focused as she felt his hand drift inwards.

'Still with me, *chiquita*?' he asked, blowing warm air across her moist breast.

'Yes, oh, yes.' She curled her hands around the defined muscles in his shoulders. 'But you're still partially dressed.'

'Not for long,' he assured her. 'But let's take care of something first.' He gently pressed her upper body back down on the bed. 'Lie back, *gatita*. This is all for you.'

Aspen complied, but she still tensed when his hand returned to her closed thighs. She half expected him to open them and maybe move over the top of her, to push himself inside her. What she didn't expect was that he would bend one of her knees up and start stroking her leg as one might a domestic cat. Or a startled horse.

And then she couldn't think at all, because he brought his mouth back to her breast and laved the tip with his tongue. She pressed closer, husky little sounds urging him on, and her lower body clenched unbearably with every tug of his lips on her nipple. Then his hand started circling higher on her leg. Slowly. So slowly it was sheer torture. She couldn't stop herself from restlessly trying to turn towards him. She needed weight, she realised, and pressure.

'Patience, *chiquita*,' he implored, his breathing heavy.

'I don't have any,' she groaned, and then gasped as his fingers lightly grazed over the curls between her legs before circling her belly and dipping down again, this time lingering a little longer and pressing a little lower.

Unbelievably Aspen shifted her legs a little wider of her

own accord and knew in that moment that she truly wanted this to happen. That she wanted more. That she wanted all of him. Inside her. Her fear of disappointing him, of failing, of him hurting her was completely eradicated as need spiralled through her and drove everything else out of her mind. If it didn't work out she no longer cared. She just needed *something*. Him!

She waited breathlessly as his finger ran along the seam between her legs again, only to exhale as it continued moving up to link with one of hers.

'Cruz, please...' She curled her free hand around his neck and dragged his mouth back to hers.

'You want me to touch you, *chiquita*?' he said against her lips.

'You know I do.' Then she had a horrid thought. 'Don't you want to?'

He stilled and held her gaze as he brought the hand he held down to the front of his pants. He was huge. That was Aspen's first thought. And her second was that she wanted to see him, touch him.

'Never doubt it,' he said fiercely. 'Never.'

His kiss was hard and hungry and then he wrenched his mouth from hers.

'But I'm trying to go slow. Make sure you're totally ready for me.' He took her hand in his again, linking his fingers over the back of hers. 'And I have something to show you.'

He laid her hand palm-down on her belly and then slowly guided her hand over her silky curls.

'Open your legs wider, *chiquita*,' he murmured beside her ear. 'No. More. Yes, like that...'

And then he directed her hand even lower until, with a gasp, Aspen felt herself as she never had before.

'Oh, my God—that feels...'

'Wet?'

Cruz ran the tip of his tongue around the whorl of her ear and she nearly came off the bed.

He pressed her hand downwards. 'Silky? Sexy?'

Yes!

Lost in a maelstrom of sensation, Aspen closed her eyes and let her feelings take over. She didn't know what to focus on as her fingers slipped over her body, making her want to press upwards.

'And now...' Cruz shifted until he lay on his stomach between her splayed legs, his olive skin dark against the cream bedcovers. 'Now I'm going to taste you.'

Aspen tried to close her legs in a hurry. 'Cruz, you can't.'

He looked up, the skin on his face tight as he held his hands still on her open thighs.

'Let me, Aspen. Remember? I promised you nothing but pleasure.'

Tensing just a little, she let him move her legs wider again and closed her eyes as he dipped down and opened her with his skilled tongue.

She'd heard of men doing this, of course. She had been to an all-girls school, and she knew that some girls liked it and some didn't. She had always put herself in the latter camp. Cruz's low groans of pleasure as he licked and lapped at her sensitive flesh shifted her firmly to the former.

She thought maybe he asked if she was okay, but by that stage he had brought his fingers into play and Aspen couldn't breathe, let alone answer. Her whole body was burning and intensely focused on something that seemed just out of reach. She writhed and twisted beneath him, delighting in the scrape of his stubble against her tender skin, not even registering that she was calling his name until he moved over her.

'It's okay, *chiquita*. Let go.'

Let go? Of what?

And then it happened. Somehow the gentle stroking of his fingers sped up and they moved in such a way that she felt something inside her shift. Within seconds her body had exploded into a thousand tiny pieces.

Distantly she was aware that he had moved down her body again, but she was in such a blissful state of completion she felt as if she was floating.

'Aspen, open your eyes.'

Were her eyes closed again?

Opening them, she saw Cruz watching her.

'How was that?'

She smiled. 'That was the most exquisitely pleasurable experience of my whole life.'

'And I'm just getting started,' he drawled arrogantly.

Aspen laughed, and then her breath caught as he rose over her with latent male grace; his powerful biceps bunched as he completely covered her and took her mouth with his again.

She felt the heavy weight of his erection against her stomach and unbelievably her lower body clenched, needing pressure again. She squirmed upwards, opening her legs automatically.

Groaning, Cruz rolled off her, yanked his pants off in a rustle of fabric and reached into the side drawer for a condom. She watched, completely motionless, as he tore the wrapper apart with his teeth and then held his hard length with one hand while he applied it.

'You keep looking at me like that, *mi gatita*, and I'll have no need for protection,' he husked, his gravelly voice rolling straight to her pelvis.

Aspen felt herself blush, but she didn't look away. He was too mesmerising. Too…

'Beautiful,' she said. 'You're beautiful.'

She ran her hand over his tanned back, briefly marvelling at the smooth heated texture of his skin and the way he trembled beneath her touch. Had *she* done that? Her eyes flew to his and she noticed the sheen of perspiration lining his forehead.

A smile of abject female joy slowly crossed her face. He saw it and groaned. Captured her mouth with his and pushed her onto her back, coming over the top of her in a position of pure male dominance. For once it didn't scare her. Because in that moment she felt a sense of feminine power she'd never known she had. And it was exhilarating. Drugging. *Freeing*.

'Hook your legs around my waist,' he instructed gruffly.

She did, and immediately felt the smooth rounded head of his penis at her entrance. Totally caught up in the wonder of it, she dug her hands into the small of his back as she pulled him closer.

He hesitated and for a moment her old fear returned, her nerves tightening in anticipation of possible pain, and then he nudged her so sweetly her breath rushed out on a sob. She clasped his head and brought his mouth down to hers, tears burning the backs of her eyes as he slowly eased inside her body.

She easily accommodated him at first, but then she did feel too full. Too stretched.

'Relax, *amada*,' he crooned against her lips. 'I've got you.'

He kissed her hungrily and withdrew almost all the way, before slowly pushing forward again, his tongue filling her mouth and mimicking his lower body's movements until Aspen felt as if she was melting into the bed.

He raised his face above hers and he looked intense. Focused. 'You feel amazing.'

He adjusted his weight and Aspen moaned, arching towards him.

'But you're so tight. I feel like I'm hurting you.'

'No.' She flexed her hips and rubbed against him, gasping as she felt him lodge deeper. 'It feels sensational. *You* feel sensational.'

Cruz groaned and seemed to praise God as he started moving inside her, his strokes smooth and slow before gradually picking up pace. Every time his big body pushed into hers Aspen clung harder to his damp shoulders, her body growing tighter and tighter until with a sudden pause she felt another rush of liquid heat, right before her body convulsed into a paroxysm of pleasure.

Dimly she was aware of Cruz still moving inside her, of her pleasure being completely controlled by the powerful movements of his. And it was endless as he drove into her, over and over and over, until with a pause of his own he tilted her bottom and surged into her with controlled power. Once, twice more, until she cried out and felt him rear his head back and fall over the edge with her.

Again time seemed endless as Aspen stared at the ceiling, slowly coming back into her body. She felt wonderful. Blissfully, sinfully wonderful. Her body was a sweaty, sensual mass of completion. Her hand lifted to Cruz's hair and she caressed the silky strands, enjoying his harsh breaths sawing in and out against her neck.

A smile curved her mouth as she recalled the moment Cruz had guided her hand between her legs so she could feel how wet she was. And she had been. Unbelievably wet—and soft. It had been like touching somebody else's body.

Unbidden, Chad's drunken taunts came to mind and she realised that it had been he who was unable to perform, not her. Deep down, and in moments of total confidence, she had told herself that exact thing, but believing it to be true was something else entirely. Especially when he was such a gregarious and charming person when he wasn't drinking. He was like a Jekyll and Hyde character, she realised, but after tonight what had happened in the bedroom with him would never haunt her again. She wouldn't let it.

Hours later Cruz woke and used the remote console beside his bed to open the curtains. The sky was pale blue outside so he knew it wasn't much after dawn.

Slightly disturbed by the whirring sound of the drapes, Aspen snuggled deeper beneath the covers he'd pulled over them both some time during the night.

Cruz's arm tightened around her shoulders. Last night had blown his mind. First finding out that Aspen had clearly had a poor excuse of a sex-life before him, and second, realising that *he* had had a poor excuse of a sex-life before her. Hell, he'd never come so hard or so often as he had last night, and he was half expecting to be rubbed raw.

He glanced at her delicate features softened by sleep. Her rosy cheeks and the dark sweep of her lashes. He grew hard just thinking about last night.

One night.

He frowned as their deal slid back into his mind like an insidious serpent. Her damned document. At the time one night had seemed like more than enough. He'd thought she was a vacuous princess type he had once lusted after and needed to get out of his system. He'd thought he'd take her to bed, slake his lust for her and move on.

Of course he'd still move on, but…

He thought about the hotel he'd planned to build on Ocean Haven. Last night he'd given up on that plan and, surprisingly, he didn't care. Aspen had been as much a victim of Charles Carmichael's warped ideas about what was right and wrong as he had been—maybe more so.

And the truth was he didn't need Ocean Haven and she did. Ergo, she should have it. Which seemed to be what her uncle thought as well, because he was still obstinately refusing Lauren's increasing offers on Cruz's behalf. He smiled. Stubborn old goat—he might not be as sanctimonious as his old man, but he'd inherited that attribute from him, all right.

And good for him—because as soon as Cruz got up he would tell Lauren to pull out of that particular race. Aspen had won and for once he didn't mind losing. One day he'd share that with Ricardo. Have a laugh. One day when he understood it better.

But for now he had to face facts.

Fact one: Aspen would want to return to Ocean Haven some time soon. Fact two: he was supposed to be flying to China to check out the site of the first of his—what was it?—fifty new hotels first thing tomorrow. Fact three…

Fact three was that he wanted neither of those things to happen. Fact four was that he didn't know why that was, and fact five was that she felt divine curled up against his side. Fact six was that he was definitely going crazy because he was yapping to himself again.

His throat felt as if he had a collar and tie around it.

Previously, making sure that he was rolling in money had been all that he could think about. He'd put his polo career on hold indefinitely to achieve it. After he'd left Ocean Haven he could have picked up any number of wealthy patrons who would have happily paid any fee to have him play for them, but he would still have been at their beck and call. Still disposable. Still an outsider in a world of rank and privilege. So he'd worked hard to change that. And, although many might say he had now achieved his goal, pride—or maybe that old sense of being vulnerable—drove him onwards.

But was it enough now? Hadn't he started to question how much satisfaction he actually derived from pushing himself so hard? Hadn't that old feeling of wanting a family started poking into his mind again? Wasn't that one of the reasons he'd tried not to visit his own family? And here was fact seven: he hated that feeling of being the one left out. Maybe Aspen was right about that. Maybe if he became more human around his family they might be the same with him.

Madre de Dio.

He was doing it again.

Cruz closed his eyes and let himself absorb the slender length of the woman who was pleasantly draped over his side like a human rug. Gently, so as not to disturb her, he stroked her hair. She shifted and the rustle of the sheets carried her scent to his nose. She smelled good. Superb.

His mind conjured up how she had looked last night, spread out beneath him while he made her come with his mouth. His body hardened and he had to bite back a groan. He wasn't sure he could do it again, and he was damned sure she was probably too sore, but his body had other ideas.

Trying to stanch the completely normal reaction of his body to the closeness of a naked woman, Cruz carefully extricated himself from under Aspen's warm body. Better he get up now, have a shower and start the day. It was going to be a busy one. First a round of meetings to finalise what he hadn't done yesterday, and then the polo matches would start just before lunch and run till the afternoon.

He would have made it too—except Aspen chose that moment to move again and attached herself to him like scaffolding on a building site. She moaned and smoothed her hand over his chest.

Cruz had closed his eyes, his senses completely focused on the southerly trajectory of her hand, when she suddenly snatched it back.

'I'm sorry. I...' She sat up and pushed the tangled mass of curls back from her face.

Fact eight: she looked adorable when she woke up. All

soft and pink, with her lips still swollen from where they
had ravaged each other.

Unable to help himself, he dropped his eyes to her chest
and she gave a small squeak, quickly dragging the sheet up
over her nakedness. But not before he'd had a good glimpse
of creamy breasts that wore grazes from his beard growth.

For some reason her obvious distress eradicated his own
desire to put as much distance between them as possible.
Which was surprising when he recalled how he had opened
up about his childhood last night. That alone should have
had him eating dust. But her loser ex had done her a disservice when it came to intimacy, and Cruz wasn't about
to make that worse because he had itchy feet.

'Good morning.'

She turned wild eyes up at him. Dampened her lips.
'Good morning.'

Silence lengthened between them and Cruz realised
he had no idea what to say. This was the equivalent of a
one-night stand and, while he'd never had what could be
considered a long-term relationship, he didn't indulge in
one-night stands either.

'This is—'

'Awkward?'

She let out a shaky breath. 'Yes, but last night was…'

'Wonderful.'

She pulled a pained face. 'You don't have to say that. I
mean yes, it was good, great for me but…oh, never mind.'

Cruz felt a well of rage at Anderson for hurting her. He
wanted to reassure her that he was actually being honest,
but he suspected she'd see his words as hollow.

'Spend the day,' he found himself saying instead.

'Why?' Her shocked eyes flew to his and he made sure
his own surprise at his invitation didn't show on his face.
But why shouldn't she spend the day? He had a first-rate

polo tournament starting in a few hours. She loved polo. She ran a horse stud.

'I thought you were busy today?' she said.

'I am.' Her reserved response had him putting the brakes on the surge of pleasure he'd experienced at the thought of her staying with him. 'But there's plenty for you to stay for. The polo, for one. It's going to be an incredible event.'

She gave him a wan smile that made his teeth want to grind together. 'I don't want to complicate things.'

Confused by his own reaction to her reticence, he took refuge in annoyance. 'And how is watching a polo tournament complicating things?'

'Our deal—'

'Forget the deal.' He got out of bed. 'Stay because you want to. Stay because the sun is shining and because there's going to be a world-class polo tournament here that's sold out to the general public. Stay because you work too hard and you need a break.'

'Well, when you put it like that...'

Torn between wanting to kiss her and sending her home, Cruz nearly rescinded his offer when the cell phone on his bedside table rang.

They both looked at it.

'What's your decision?'

She dampened her lips. 'Yes, okay, I'd like to watch the polo.'

Aspen stood on the penthouse balcony and stared out over the shiny green polo field. Horse floats, white marquees, riders, grooms, horse-owners and hotel employees scurried about as they readied themselves for the day ahead.

Yet despite the heady anticipation in the air that preceded a major event all Aspen could think about was what she was still doing here.

Replaying their awkward morning-after conversation in her head, she cringed. When Cruz had first asked her to stay Aspen had felt her heart jump in her chest at the thought of spending the day with him. Then he'd confirmed that he'd be busy and she'd felt like an idiot. Of course he was busy. He had invited her to watch the polo, not to spend the day with *him*.

When his phone had rung she had automatically said yes because he'd looked beautiful and sleep-tousled and she hadn't wanted to leave.

Now she didn't think she could leave fast enough.

Because last night had changed her. She felt it deep within her bones. Last night had been everything she'd ever dreamed making love could be, because Cruz had taken the time to make it that way for her and she could already feel herself wanting to make more out of it than it was. Wanting to make it special, somehow. But what woman *wouldn't* want to do that when she'd just been so completely loved by a man like Cruz Rodriguez?

No, not loved, she quickly amended. Pleasured.

God.

She buried her forehead against her arms, which were resting on the balustrading.

It was beyond clear that Cruz had asked her to stay out of politeness or—worse—pity. She, of course, had said yes out of desire. Desire to spend more time with him. Desire to experience his lovemaking again. Desire to re-experience the pleasure she felt sure only he could give her.

But he was as much of a Jekyll and Hyde character as Chad when it came down to it, because he had come to Ocean Haven specifically to try and take her farm.

She had forgotten that. *Again.*

Was she a glutton for punishment? Was she so used to having men control her that she'd gladly fall in with the plans of another self-interested, power-hungry male?

Because while Cruz might have shown her the best night of her life, it didn't change the reality of why she was even here.

'Forget the deal,' he'd all but snarled.

Last night she had. This morning it was impossible to do so in the cold light of day.

Or course last night she had been in the grip of a wonderful sense of feminine power with Cruz that could easily become addictive if she let it. A smile curved her lips, only to fade away just as quickly. Cruz had freed her from years of feeling as if there was something wrong with her and she'd be forever indebted to him for that. He was also trying to buy her home out from under her, and that was like a sore that wouldn't heal. If she stayed today it would be for the wrong reasons. It would be because she was hoping for more from him. Something she didn't want from any man. Did she?

Aspen groaned. How could she even think about staying longer under the shade of such conflicting emotions?

The simple answer was that she couldn't. And dwelling on it wasn't going to make it any different.

Decision made, she spun on her heel and went to pack her suitcase.

Cruz looked up, annoyed, as his PA opened the door to his meeting. It was taking him all that he had to concentrate as it was, without yet another irritating interruption.

'What is it, Maria?'

He frowned as he heard Aspen's hasty, 'It's okay…don't interrupt…' in the background.

Maria glanced over her shoulder. 'Ah, Señorita Carmichael wishes to speak with you.'

'Send her in.'

Aspen materialised in the doorway and Cruz saw her suitcase by the side of the door.

He frowned harder. 'What's going on?'

'I can see you're busy.' She threw a quick glance around the room at his executive team. 'It can wait.'

'No, it can't.' He pinned her with a hard look, unaccountably agitated as he registered her intention to leave him. 'Is something wrong?'

'No, no. I just came to say goodbye. I didn't want to leave without letting you know I was going.'

'I thought you had decided to stay?'

She swallowed. 'Our deal was concluded this morning and—'

Cruz swore. 'I thought I'd already told you to forget the deal. It's not relevant. I'm not going to buy Ocean Haven any more. It's yours free and clear.'

A myriad of emotions crossed her lovely face, not completely unlike the morning when he had first told her that he *was* going to challenge her for The Farm.

Disbelief, shock, wariness, a tentative joy…

Three days ago he wouldn't have conceived of giving up something he wanted as much as he had wanted Ocean Haven, but a lot had changed in three days. He'd found out the truth about the night he'd left The Farm and he'd made love to Aspen. Held her in his arms all night. Woken with her still in his arms in the morning. When he looked at her he felt things he'd never felt for any woman before her. Feelings he was still unable to categorize.

'Really?' She took a hesitant step towards him. 'You're serious? It's mine?'

'Yes,' he said gruffly, wondering why it was that he couldn't look at her without wanting to strip her clothes off.

'Oh, Cruz…'

She looked as if she might cry, and just when he was about to back away she gave a gurgle of laughter and rushed over to him, jumping up to wind her arms around his neck. Instinctively Cruz grasped the backs of her thighs, and it seemed completely natural to raise her legs and lock them around his hips.

In an instant the chemistry between them ignited and he filled his hands with her taut curves as he sought to steady them both.

'Thank you, thank you… This means so much to me. You have no idea.'

Before he could formulate a sane response she leant forward and kissed him, her silky tongue sneaking out to wrap around his. Cruz held in a groan and took charge of the kiss. This was what he'd wanted from the minute he'd woken up this morning.

Then he'd held himself back. Now, with her honeyed taste on his tongue, he didn't bother. Her mouth was the greatest aphrodisiac he'd ever known.

She moved her hips and Cruz pressed himself more snugly against the seam of her jeans. She murmured something and he almost ignored it, but the words 'We're not alone…' and 'Everyone is watching…' somehow permeated his addled brain.

He glanced around at his stunned executive team. She was right. Not one of them had looked away and he couldn't say he blamed them. He was just as shocked that he'd forgotten they were still in the room as they were at seeing him with a woman locked in his arms.

He released a careful breath.

'Excuse me, everyone. I'm going to have to adjourn this meeting. Again.'

He held Aspen as still as a statue until the door snicked closed. Then he devoured her, pulling at her clothes and unzipping his jeans. He shoved aside the laptop on the mahogany table and laid her down. Her shirt was open around her and her breasts were heaving against the delicate cups of her plain white bra. She looked wild and wanton, her hair spilling out of the French braid she had secured it in.

His hands skimmed her, claimed her, and she arched up off the table towards him.

'That door isn't locked,' she got out between gasps of pleasure.

'No one will come through it unless they want to start looking for a new job.'

'This is…'

'Madness?' His hands felt clumsy as he yanked her jeans down her legs. 'You need to start wearing skirts more,' he complained.

She let out a husky laugh, and then her breath hitched as he ripped her panties aside and parted her legs. She was already slick and ready and he growled his appreciation.

'I've never wanted a woman as much as I want you.'

He ducked his head down and bathed her silky wetness with his tongue. Her legs fell further apart and he saw her watching him as he licked and sucked on her sweetness. The picture of his dark head nestled between her creamy thighs nearly unmanned him, and when he felt her inner walls start to tremble with her imminent release he rose up and pulled her towards the edge of the table.

'Not without me, *mi gatita*. I want to feel you come around me.'

Quickly applying a condom, Cruz hooked her legs over his forearms and drove into her. Her gasp was raw and shocked and, given everything she had revealed to him last night, he tried to check himself.

'No, don't stop. Please.'

Her hands clutched his forearms, urging him closer, and Cruz closed his eyes and pumped himself into her, grazing her clitoris with his thumb to maximise her pleasure. She came hard and fast at exactly the moment he did. Pleasure turned him inside out. The world might have ended at that moment and he wouldn't have had a clue.

CHAPTER TEN

'You do miss it.'

'What?'

'Playing polo.'

'What makes you say that?'

'Oh, I don't know.' Aspen smiled up at Cruz. 'The wistful look on your face right now, perhaps.'

They were leaning on the fence post of one of the stable yards, watching the grooms and riders put the finishing touches to their horses before the main tournament got under way.

'I'm assessing the state of the horses.'

Aspen cocked her head and studied his profile, shadowed from the sun by a baseball cap. His hair curled sexily at the sides. 'Why did you give it up?'

He turned his head, his black eyes piercing. 'Money.'

'Ah. I'm sensing there's a theme here.' She laughed.

'No theme,' Cruz growled without heat. 'I didn't have much when I left Ocean Haven and I knew that polo wasn't going to give me what I needed.'

Aspen nodded. 'Money gives you the security that Ocean Haven gives me, but it's our loss. Watching you play polo was like watching poetry in motion.'

He looked at her strangely and then gave her a small smile. 'Those days are long gone now. And, while I did miss it, my life is full enough as it is. By the way…' His tone turned serious. 'Anderson is here. He was injured last month in Argentina so he wasn't expected to turn up. I told him to keep away from you.'

Aspen reeled. So it *had* been Chad she had glimpsed last night in the hotel foyer. She sucked in a deep breath and let it out slowly. She hadn't seen him in years, and while she really didn't want to she didn't want Cruz feeling as if he had to defend her just because she had unexpectedly opened up to him.

'You don't have to fight my battles for me, Cruz.'

He shook his head as if he knew better and tapped the tip of her nose affectionately. 'Somebody has to.' He took off his cap and fitted it to her head. 'You need a hat if you're going to stay out in the sun, *mi gatita*. Excuse me for a minute.'

He headed off inside the stable, his long stride and two-metre frame seeming to strike sparks in the air as he moved. Aspen tried to feel annoyed at his high-handedness, but after last night and then this morning on his conference table it was hard to stay irritated with him over anything. It had been so long since she had felt this good.

So long since she had just enjoyed herself without the pressure of work and bills getting in the way.

So long since she had felt the freedom of truly being in charge of her own destiny.

And it was exhilarating. She grinned to herself. Almost—but not quite—as exhilarating as feeling Cruz move inside her body. She smiled again. Almost as exhilarating as feeling his mouth on her breasts, between her legs.

As soon as she had *that* thought liquid heat turned her insides soft and her smile widened, because now that she recognised the sensation she could actually feel herself growing moist. She glanced around surreptitiously, just to make sure no one else could see that she was turning herself on.

Her newly awakened desire was like a runaway train. And while part of her knew she should probably try and put the brakes on it, another part of her wanted to roll around in it like a cat in the sun.

Mi gatita. His kitten.

Aspen rolled her eyes. She shouldn't get so much joy out of the pet name but she did.

Her cell phone beeped an incoming message and she snatched it out of her pocket, hoping it was her uncle returning her call. Earlier she had left an excited message on his answering machine, informing him that she had raised the money they had agreed upon for her to buy The Farm. She wondered if he had got it yet and whether he was surprised, wishing she could have told him in person. Unfortunately a trip to England was not in the cards for her in the next twenty-five hours. Although, seventy-two hours ago she would have said a trip to Mexico wasn't, either.

Checking her phone, she saw it was just Donny, informing her that he'd organised for Matty, one of the local teenagers who attended her riding school, to relieve him for the day. Aspen quickly texted back to tell him to have a great day off with his family.

Family...

That sounded so nice.

'Catch.'

Cruz's voice broke her reverie and Aspen looked up just in time to grab the bundle of clothes he had tossed at her and to see a smirk on his handsome face. 'What's this?'

'You're my new groom. How soon can you change?'

Aspen didn't miss a beat. 'Five minutes.'

'See Luis over there?' Cruz pointed with his free hand towards the players' area.

'Yes.'

'Meet me there in two.'

Aspen felt deliriously happy. She reached out and grabbed

his arm as he made to walk past, a thrill of excitement racing through her. 'You're really going to play?'

He paused, cocked his head. 'You wanted to see poetry in motion, didn't you?'

Aspen shook her head, smiling at his cockiness.

It was dangerous to feel this much happiness because of a pair of jeans and a shirt, but it wasn't that. It was the man.

She'd fallen in love with him, she realised with a sinking feeling.

He must have sensed her regard because he turned and met her gaze.

'One minute left,' he drawled.

Totally in love, she thought, and she had no idea what to do about it.

He was in love.

The thought gripped him by the throat in the middle of the game just as he was about to make a nearside forehand shot and he nearly fell off his horse and landed on his behind. Fortunately years of training and a horse that could play blind saw him come out of the offensive strike still in the saddle.

He pulled up and let one of his team members carry the ball to the goalposts.

He couldn't be in love with her. It was impossible. He didn't want to be in love with anyone. Not yet. It wasn't part of his plan.

Surely it was just the exhilaration of being out on the polo field again that was sending weird magnetic pulses to his brain? The sense of fun he hadn't felt in far too long?

He glanced towards the players' area and his eyes effortlessly zeroed in on Aspen standing beside one of his players. She wore his Rodriquez Polo cap and her flyaway blond curls billowed out at the sides. She'd put on his team colours and she looked curvy and edible as she clapped her hands wildly.

The horn went, signalling the end of the game, and Cruz trotted towards her almost hesitantly.

Unaware of his thoughts, she beamed up at him. 'You are such a show-off. Congratulations on the win.'

He returned her smile. She was gorgeous. Gorgeous and smart and funny and hot-headed. And, yes, he was in love with her.

Other players thumped him on the back and congratulated him and he could hear the commentators waxing lyrical about his statistics and his comeback—not that this *was* a comeback, more a hiatus in his normal working life—but he wasn't really paying attention to anything other than Aspen.

He hadn't had any idea that he was falling in love with her but now that he had acknowledged it, it made perfect sense. Probably he had always loved her.

And he couldn't wait to tell her because last night and earlier, when he should have been concentrating on work, she had looked at him in such a way that he was confident she felt the same as he did.

Not that he would tell her here. He'd do it in private. Maybe over an elaborate dinner. He smiled, already anticipating the moment.

Aspen took Bandit's reins and he dismounted. 'That last goal was simply brilliant.'

'I thought so.'

He readjusted his helmet and Aspen automatically pushed some of his hair out of his eyes. 'You need a haircut,' she admonished.

He stilled, his gaze holding hers. 'I have something I need to tell you.'

'What is it?'

'Not here.' He shook his head. 'I promised Ricardo I'd

check in with the Chinese delegation I have apparently
neglected all day. How about we meet back in the suite in
thirty minutes?'

'This sounds serious.'

'It is. Here, let me take Bandit back to the stables for
Luis to get her cleaned up.' He mounted and reached down
for the mallet Aspen was holding for him. Instead of taking it he gripped her elbow, raised her onto her toes and
kissed her soundly. 'Very serious.'

Aspen watched Cruz canter back towards the stables,
her fingers pressed to her throbbing lips.

'Now, that was really touching.'

Aspen swung around at the sound of a mocking voice
behind her. For a moment all she could do was stare
blankly, her mind frozen as if she'd just been zapped.

'Chad,' she finally managed to croak out.

His smile was charming and boyish. 'One and the same,
babe, one and the same.'

CHAPTER ELEVEN

HOPING CHAD WAS just an apparition, Aspen blinked rapidly and then gave a sharp gasp as her vision cleared and she saw him properly. 'What happened to your eye?'

He fingered the puffy purple skin of his eye socket. 'I ran into your *boyfriend*. Didn't he tell you?'

Yes, he had, but he'd neglected to say that he'd done anything but talk to him. A warm glow spread through Aspen's torso. As much as she abhorred violence, the fact that Cruz had reacted on her behalf did make her feel good. Special.

'Are you okay?'

'Do you care?' he sneered.

'Of course.' Memories flooded in, preventing her from saying anything else. The unexpectedness of seeing him causing her heart to beat heavily in her chest.

He stood before her, the typical urban male, with his designer haircut, stubble and trendy sportswear. She knew it took him hours to achieve that casually dishevelled appearance, and that he'd always hated the fact that she didn't pay more attention to her own appearance.

'Can't you straighten your hair sometimes? It's a mess.'

'I didn't expect to see you so far from Ocean Haven.'

His words snapped her attention back to him and slowly she started breathing properly again.

'I'm…here on…business.' She stumbled over the words

and furtively looked around for Cruz. Then she felt angry with herself. She was no longer the naïve eighteen-year-old girl who had mistaken friendship for love and had thought that wealth was synonymous with decency. She didn't *need* Cruz to protect her. She didn't need any man to do that.

'Some digs,' Chad continued, looking back at the hotel. 'The stable boy has come a long way.'

'What do you want, Chad?'

'To say hello.'

'Well, now you've said it, so…'

'What?' He held his hands wide as if in surprise. 'That's all you're going to say?'

'We haven't spoken for a long time. I don't see any point in changing that.'

'What if I do?'

Aspen felt her mouth tighten. 'I believe Cruz told you not to come near me.' And she hated pulling that card.

Chad's lip curled. 'See, Boy Wonder would like to think he controls everything, but he doesn't control me. Does he control you, Assie?'

Aspen's mouth tightened. There was no way she was playing mind games with her ex-husband again. She'd done that enough when they had been married.

'Goodbye, Chad.'

She turned on her heel, intent on walking away from him. but it seemed he had other ideas.

'Aspen, wait.' He jogged after her. 'I didn't mean to upset you.'

'No?'

'No. I wanted to apologise to you, actually.'

Aspen stopped. 'For…?'

'For being such an idiot when we got married. I was in a bad way and—'

Aspen held up her hand like a stop sign. 'Don't, Chad.' She knew his game. She had heard his apologies a thousand times before. Usually they amounted to nothing. 'It doesn't matter anymore.' And amazingly it didn't. Cruz had seen to that.

Cruz who was *nothing* like Chad. Cruz who was proud, but gentle. Cruz who was smart and masterful and possessive. And it thrilled her. *He* thrilled her. And she couldn't wait to see him. Maybe even to tell him that she loved him if she had the courage.

She looked at Chad now. Really looked at him. He couldn't hurt her anymore and it made her feel a little giddy.

'Chad, I'm sorry, but I don't want to see you or talk to you. Whatever you have to say is irrelevant.' She smiled inwardly as she borrowed one of Cruz's favourite expressions.

'I just want to be friends, Aspen, put things behind us.'

Aspen felt petty in refusing him, but he had hurt her too much for her ever to consider him as a friend. 'I'd like to put things behind us too, but we can't ever be friends, Chad.'

'Because of *Rodriguez*?' Chad sneered. 'He won't want you for long. His heart belongs to his horses and nothing else.'

Aspen shook her head. This was the Chad she knew too well.

'Is it serious between you?'

'That's none of your business.'

'You're in love with him.' Chad spat on the ground. 'You always were.'

'I wasn't. I thought I loved you.'

'But you didn't, did you? It was him all along. I told your grandfather. That night.'

Aspen frowned. 'It was you who sent him out after me?'

'I watched you chase him like one of his fawning groupies. Did you have sex with him? Your grandfather would never say.'

God, this was awful, but Aspen wasn't sure if she was more appalled that he had talked to her grandfather so intimately about her or that he was talking to her about it now.

'Why do you hate Cruz so much?' She couldn't help asking.

Chad shrugged and stared at her mulishly. 'He was an arrogant SOB who never saw me as competition. He never took me seriously except where you were concerned.'

Aspen gave a sharp, self-conscious laugh. 'And there I was, thinking that you wanted Ocean Haven.'

Chad shook his head. 'I didn't. But he did. And he's won that too, I hear.'

An uneasy sensation slipped down Aspen's spine and she told herself to ignore him. To walk away. 'What is that supposed to mean?'

He looked at her like a hyena scenting a wounded animal. 'Boy Wonder bought The Farm. Not literally—unfortunately—but... You didn't know?'

Aspen knew better than most not to listen to anything Chad said, not to place any importance on his words, but she couldn't make herself leave. Not with her mother's cautionary advice that if something looked too good to be true it usually was ringing loudly in her ears.

'How would you know anything about the sale of The Farm?'

'My daddy wanted to buy it. He had high hopes of swooping in at the last minute and picking it up for a song.'

Aspen's head started to hurt. 'Well, it's not true. Cruz hasn't bought Ocean Haven. Your father has his facts wrong.'

Chad shrugged. 'I guess the guy brokering the deal is the one who has it wrong. My father did wonder when he heard Rodriguez had paid more than double the value of the property.'

More than double?

Aspen felt a burning sensation in the back of her throat. 'Yes, I'd say he's wrong. Excuse me.'

She pushed past Chad, only to have him grab her arm.

'He's not worth it, you know. You can't see it, but he won't hang around for long.'

Hardly in the mood for any more of Chad's snide comments, Aspen turned on him sharply. 'That's not your business, is it?'

Chad reeled back and covered the movement with a disbelieving laugh. 'You've changed.'

'So I've been told.'

She said the words automatically but Aspen knew that if there was any truth to Chad's words then she hadn't changed at all. Because if Cruz had bought The Farm out from under her it would mean that she had fallen into the same trap she had in the past—wanting the love and affection of a man who wouldn't think twice before walking all over her.

Telling herself to calm down, she stabbed the button on the lift to the penthouse and used the temporary access card Cruz had given her.

Chad had admitted that he hated Cruz, so this could just be trouble he was stirring up between them. But how would he know it would cause trouble? He couldn't. No one knew about the private deal she had struck with Cruz. No one but her knew that this morning Cruz had promised her he had decided not to buy Ocean Haven.

Calm, Aspen, she reminded herself, desperately trying to check her temper.

When the lift doors opened her eyes immediately fell on an immaculately dressed woman who looked like a supermodel.

For a minute she thought she was in the wrong suite, but deep down she knew she wasn't.

'I'm sorry...' She frowned. 'I'm looking for Cruz.'

'He's in the shower,' the woman said.

Was he, now?

Aspen swallowed down the sudden feeling of jealousy. The woman was dressed, for heaven's sake. 'And you are...?'

The woman held out her hand. 'I'm Lauren Burnside. Cruz's lawyer. Would I be right in assuming that you're Aspen Carmichael?'

The fact that his lawyer knew of her wasn't a good sign in Aspen's mind. 'Yes. Would *I* be right in assuming you're here about the sale of Ocean Haven?'

The lawyer's eyes flickered at the corners and an awkward silence prevailed over the room. 'You would have to ask Cruz about that.'

Cruz, not Mr Rodriguez, Aspen noted sourly. How well did this woman know him? And why did the thought of this woman running her hands all over Cruz's naked body hurt her so much?

Because you love him, you nincompoop.

Aspen moved to the side table beside the Renoir and placed her hands lightly on the wood-grained surface. Memories of the last time she had stood in this exact position, with Cruz behind her, kissing her neck, murmuring tender words of encouragement to her, lanced her very soul. Yes, she loved him—and that just took this situation from bad to completely hideous.

'His heart belongs to his horses and nothing else.'

Chad getting inside her head did nothing to stave off her temper either. But still she tried to convince herself that she didn't know the facts. That she wouldn't jump to conclusions as Cruz had done about her eight years ago.

'Lauren. Aspen!'

Aspen turned as Cruz entered the room. Pleasure shot through her at the sight of him fresh from the shower in worn jeans and a body-hugging white T-shirt.

He smiled at her.

She looked away, but he had already transferred his attention to the other woman.

'You have the contracts?'

'Right here.'

Aspen turned and leant against the side table, blocking all memories of the intimacies they had shared, blocking the pain of his betrayal, her foolish feelings for him.

'They would be the contracts to finalise the sale of my farm?' she said lightly.

Cruz's eyes narrowed and Aspen knew. She *knew*!

'When were you going to tell me?'

Her casual tone must have alerted him to her state of mind because he didn't take his eyes off her. 'Can you excuse us, please, Lauren?'

'Of course. I'll leave the contracts on the table.'

She threw Cruz an intimate glance and Aspen felt her cheeks heat at having witnessed it.

'So, here we are, then...' Aspen strolled across the room and stopped beside the urn of flowers on the dining table. She stroked the soft rose petals and thought how impervious they were to the fact that she felt like hoisting them up and hurling them across the room.

'Yes. And to answer your earlier question I was going to surprise you over dinner.'

Surprise her? Aspen's mouth hit the floor and her temper shot through the roof. *Surprise her!*

'Dinner? *Dinner?*' She laughed harshly. 'You filthy, gloating bastard.'

'Aspen—'

'Don't.' Disappointment coalesced into rage and she just needed to get away from him. 'Don't say a word. I don't want to hear it. I don't want to hear anything from you. I hate you.'

She whirled away and would have walked out of the room—no, run out of the room—but he was on her in a second.

'Aspen, let me explain.'

'No.' She shoved against him and beat her fists against his chest in her anger. 'You tricked me. You lied to me. You told me you weren't trying to buy Ocean Haven any more but you were.'

'Dammit, Aspen.' He bound her wrists in one of his hands but she broke loose and tried to slap him. 'Stop it, you little hellcat. Dammit. *Ow!* Listen to me. I left a message for Lauren to pull the pin on the sale but she didn't get it,' he said, breathing hard.

As suddenly as her rage had swept over her it left her, and Aspen felt deflated and appalled that she had hit him. She *hated* violence. 'Let me go, Cruz,' she said flatly.

He frowned down at her. 'It's the truth.'

Aspen sighed and pushed away from him, feeling shivery and cold when he released her. 'It doesn't matter.'

'Of course it matters.' Cruz moved to the table and picked up the wad of paper Lauren had left behind. 'Look at this.'

Aspen glanced at it warily. 'What is it?'

'As soon as I found out that your uncle had accepted my offer I had Lauren organise the immediate transfer of the deeds into your name. It's all here in this contract.'

'What?'

'That was what I was going to tell you over dinner.'

Aspen frowned. 'So you're saying our deal is still on?'

Cruz glowered at her. 'Of *course* the deal is not still on. I don't expect you to pay me back. I'm giving you the property.'

'You're giving…' She shook her head. 'You mean lending me the money to buy it?'

'No, I mean giving it to you.'

'Why would you do that?'

'Because this way you have security.'

'Security?'

'You would have been bankrupt within the year if you'd borrowed all that money.'

Scowling, she moved away from him. 'That's not true. I have a great business plan to get Ocean Haven out of trouble and—' She stopped as he shook his head at her as if she didn't have a clue.

'Aspen, there's no way you can carry that kind of debt and survive,' he said softly.

His words registered in her brain as if she was sitting at the back of a large lecture theatre and trying to read off a tiny whiteboard. 'So you're just giving it to me?'

'It's just a property, Aspen.'

It's just a dress.

It's just her self-worth.

Just her *heart*.

'I don't want you to give it to me,' she said.

'Why are you being so stubborn about this?'

Why? She didn't know. And then she did. For years she'd thought that all she wanted was security, but really— really what she wanted was validation. Trust in her judgement. What she wanted was to know that she could direct her own future. Her way. But somewhere in the last couple of days Cruz had become the centre of her world. Just as both her grandfather and Chad had been at one stage.

Hadn't she once pinned her hopes and dreams for the future on both of them and been let down?

She shook her head. 'I don't want it that way.'

'What way? *Hell!*' Cruz raked a hand through his hair. 'I don't see what the problem is.'

'I want to do it my way.'

'So do it your way,' he almost roared in frustration. 'Debt-free.'

'I would have thought you of all people would understand,' she said, completely exasperated. 'You hated that your mother didn't trust you to do things your way when you were a teenager.'

'This is not that same thing.'

'It is to me.'

'You're being stupid now.'

Aspen rounded on him. 'Do not call me stupid. I had one man put me down. I won't take it from another.'

'*Dios mio*, I didn't mean it like that.' He turned his back on her and then swung back just as quickly. 'Aspen, I'm in love with you.'

Aspen wrapped her arms around her chest as if she was trying to hold her heart in. Was this some backhanded way for him to get Ocean Haven? She stared at him, her emotions in turmoil, a terrible numbness invading her limbs.

'You're not.'

Cruz swore. 'I've just spent over two hundred million dollars on a property I'm prepared to give you. What would you call it?'

'Crazy.'

'Well, it is that…'

'What would you buy me for my birthday?' she asked suddenly.

Cruz frowned. 'Your birthday is…two months away.'

'You have no idea, do you?'

'How is that relevant?'

It was relevant because she knew if he presented her with an envelope full of cash it would break her heart. It was relevant because if he really loved her for who she was he *would* have some idea.

His eyes narrowed on her face. 'What is this? Some kind of test?'

'And if it is?'

A calmness seemed to pervade his limbs. 'You're being ridiculously stubborn about this. I'm giving you everything that you want. Most women would be on their knees with gratitude right now.'

Aspen wasn't sure if he meant sexually, but the fact that she thought it startled her. She wanted to be on her knees in front of him. She wanted to do all sorts of things to his body until he was as out of control as she was. But that wasn't right. His power over her was so much stronger than Chad's. Or her grandfather's. If she stayed, if she accepted his *gift*, she knew she would do anything for him. Would accept anything from him. And that scared her to death. She would be completely at his mercy and a shadow of herself. A woman seeking the approval of a man who didn't listen to her. It wasn't how she wanted to live her life. Nor was he the type of person she wanted to share her life with. Not again.

'I don't play those games, Aspen,' he warned.

'And I don't play yours. Not anymore. Goodbye, Cruz. I hope you never run out of money. You'll be awfully lost if you do.'

Thankfully the lift doors opened just as she pressed the button, but it wasn't divine intervention finally looking out for her. Ricardo was inside. His wide smile of greeting faltered when he glimpsed her expression and a stilted silence filled the space between them as she waited for the lift doors to close.

Once they had, Ricardo turned to his brother. 'What was that all about?'

Cruz let out a harsh laugh. 'That was Aspen Carmichael making me feel like a fool. Again.'

CHAPTER TWELVE

EXACTLY ONE WEEK to the day later Cruz sat on the squash court beside his brother after a particularly gruelling game. Both of them were sweat-soaked and exhausted and Cruz relished the feeling of complete burnout that had turned his muscles to rubber.

His phone beeped an incoming message and since he was right there he checked it.

Frustration warred with disappointment when he saw that it was from Lauren Burnside. Well, what had he expected? Aspen Carmichael to send him a message telling him how much she missed him?

Right. She'd rejected him. How many ways did he need to be kicked before he got the message?

'Now the woman sends me a text,' he muttered.

'Who?'

'My lawyer.'

Maybe if she'd dropped in he would have taken her up on her offer to get up close and personal with his abs. He wouldn't mind losing himself in a woman right now. Smelling her sweet floral scent with a touch of vanilla. Winding his hands through her tumble of wild curls. Hearing her laugh.

'You're muttering,' Ricardo said unhelpfully.

That was because he needed to visit a loony bin so that he could undergo electroshock therapy and once and for all convince his body that Aspen Carmichael was *not* the woman to end all women. Bad enough that he'd thought he had been in love with her. That he'd told her.

He clamped down on the unwanted memory. It had been a foolish thought that had died as soon as she'd walked out through the door. A foolish thought brought on by an adrenaline rush after the polo match.

Feeling spent, he scrolled through Lauren's text. 'Idiot woman.'

'I thought she looked quite smart.'

'Not Lauren. Aspen.'

'Ah.'

Cruz scowled. 'This is not a dentist, *amigo*. Close your mouth.'

Ricardo smiled. 'Are you going to tell me what she'd done now?'

'According to Lauren, she's signed Ocean Haven over to me.'

'Shouldn't you be happy about that? I mean, isn't that what you wanted?'

'No.' He ignored the interested expression on his brother's face. 'I don't want anything to do with that property ever again.' Scowling, he punched a number into his phone. 'Maria, get the jet fuelled up and cancel any meetings I have later today.'

'I thought you just said you didn't want anything to do with that property ever again?'

'I won't after I handle this.'

'Ah, *hermano*, I hate to point out the obvious, but this didn't end so well for you last week.'

Cruz picked up his bag and shoved his racquet inside. 'Last week I was too attached to the outcome. I'm not now.'

Aspen was in a wonderful mood. Super, in fact. Her chores were almost done for the day and all that was left was to bed Delta down in her stall. Now that the polo season was over there was less pressure on her and Donny to have the place ready for Wednesday night chukkas and there were fewer students. That was a slight downside, but Aspen found that as winter rolled around the lessons veered more towards dressage, with her students preferring to practise in the indoor arena rather than get frostbite in the snow.

Pity about the leak.

'Or not,' she said, to no one in particular. Roofs and their holes, walls and their peeling paint, fences and their rusted nails were no longer her problem. And she couldn't be happier.

'Ow!' Aspen glanced down at her thumb and winced. 'Damn thing.'

She looked at her other fingers with their newly bitten nails. When had that happened? When had she started biting her nails again? She hadn't since she was about thirteen and her grandfather had painted that horrible-tasting liquid on the ends of them.

Rubbing at the small wound, she picked up the horse rug she planned to throw over Delta and headed for her stall.

Delta whickered.

'Hello, beauty,' Aspen crooned. 'I see you've finished dinner. Me? I'm not hungry.'

Which was surprising, really, because she couldn't remember if she'd even eaten that day.

'Who needs food anyway?' She laughed. Who needed food when you didn't have any will to live? 'Now, that's not true,' she told Delta. 'I have plenty to live for. Becoming a vet, a new beginning, adventure, never having to see Cruz Rodriguez ever again.'

She leant against the weathered blanket she'd tossed over Delta's back. He'd told her he loved her but how could you love someone you didn't know? And she'd nearly convinced herself that she had loved him too.

'It's called desire,' she informed the uninterested mare. 'Lust that is so powerful it fries your brain.'

But she wasn't going to think about that. Had forbidden herself to think about it all week. And it had worked. Sort of.

Aspen took in a deep breath and revelled in the smell of horse and hay and Ocean Haven. Her throat constricted and tears pricked at the back of her eyes, her energy suddenly leaving her. She would miss this. Miss her horses. Her school. But things changed. That was the only certainty in life, wasn't it?

'The man who now owns you is big and strong and he'll take care of you.' Delta tossed her head. 'I'm serious. He loves horses more than anything else.'

'Is that right?'

Aspen spun around. Stared. Then swallowed. Cruz stood before her, wearing a striking grey suit and a crisp white shirt. 'What are you doing here?'

'I think you know why I'm here this time.'

She straightened her spine. 'Boy, that lawyer of yours works fast.'

'She should. She's paid enough. Now, answer my question.'

Aspen straightened Delta's already straight blanket over her rump. Better that than looking at Cruz and losing her train of thought. 'I would have thought it was obvious. You bought Ocean Haven so it's yours, not mine.'

'I told you that was a mistake,' he bit out. 'The whole thing happened while I was playing polo.'

Aspen shook her head. 'You really expect me to believe that?' she scoffed. 'That supermodel of yours wouldn't blink without your say-so.'

'Supermodel?'

'We *are* talking about the brunette who happened to know you were in the shower, aren't we?'

Cruz narrowed his gaze and Aspen stared him down. Then he smiled. A full-on toothpaste-commercial-worthy smile. 'I've never slept with Lauren.'

'Like I would care.' She jerked her head. 'Mind moving? I'm tired of you blocking my way. No pun intended.'

Cruz continued to smile. 'None taken.'

But he didn't move.

'You're right about Lauren acting under my instructions,' he began. 'Unfortunately they were my *old* instructions. My *new* ones were caught up somewhere in cyberspace when her firm's e-mail system went down.'

'I don't care. I'm moving on.'

'Where to?'

'I don't know.' She shrugged. 'Somewhere exciting.'

'And what about your mother's horseshoe?'

'It's gone.' She'd cried over that enough when she'd returned last week. 'And before you ask I don't know where and nor does Donny. When I came back last week it wasn't here.' She sniffed. 'I'm taking it as a sign.'

'A sign of what?'

His voice was soft. As gentle as it had been the night she had told him about Chad. It made a horrible pain well up inside her chest. 'A sign that I've put too much store in The Farm for too long. I thought I needed it, but it turns out I needed something else more.'

He stepped closer to her. 'What?'

'It's irrelevant. You know what *that* means, don't you, Cruz?'

Unfortunately he ignored her blatant dig. Blast him.

'Try me.'

'No.' She moved away from him and fossicked with Delta's feed bucket. 'I've discovered that I do have some pride after all, so…no.'

Cruz grabbed the feed bucket and took it out of her numb fingers. Aspen accidentally took a deep breath and it was all him. When he took her hands she closed her eyes to try and ward off how good it felt to have him touch her. She swallowed. Yanked her hands out of his.

'I'm going to finish my vet course and take an internship somewhere, start over,' she said quickly.

Not taking the hint that she didn't want him to touch her, he slid his hand beneath her chin and raised her eyes to his. 'Start over with me?'

Aspen jerked back. 'I didn't know you were looking for a new vet?'

'I don't mean professionally and you know it,' he growled. Then his voice softened. 'I've missed you, *mi gatita*. I love you.'

'I—'

'You don't believe me?' He blew out a breath. 'Kind of ironic that a week ago it was me who didn't believe you, wouldn't you say?'

Aspen's chest felt tight. 'No. I wouldn't.' Nothing seemed ironic to her right now. More like tragic.

Cruz pushed a hand through his hair and Aspen wished he was a thousand miles away. So much easier to deny her feelings when he wasn't actually right beside her.

'I know you're angry, Aspen, and I don't blame you. I thought I knew about human nature. I thought I had it all covered. But you showed me I was wrong. After your grandfather kicked me out I vowed never to need anyone again. I saw money as the way to ensure that I was never expendable. I was wrong. I understand why you didn't want me to give you The Farm now, and if you want we'll consider it a loan. You can pay me back.'

Aspen felt a spurt of hope at his words. But that didn't change their fundamental natures. She couldn't afford to be in love with him. She'd become needy for his affection and he'd do it again. At some point he wouldn't listen to her and they'd be right back where they started. Better to save herself that pain now.

'I can't.'

'I know you were hurt, Aspen. By your grandfather's expectations, by the lucky-to-still-be-breathing Anderson. Me. But I promise if you give me a chance I won't hurt you again.'

Aspen shook her head sadly. 'You will.' Her cheeks were damp and Cruz brushed his thumbs over the tears she hadn't even known she was shedding. 'You won't mean to, because I know deep down you're kind-hearted, but—' She stopped. Recalled what she had said to Delta. He *would* take care of her. But could she trust his love? Could she trust him to listen to her in the future? Could she trust that she wouldn't get lost in trying to please him? 'I'm not great in relationships.'

'Then we really are perfect for each other because I'm hopeless. Or at least I was. You make me want to change all that. You make me feel human, Aspen. You make me want to *embrace* life again.'

Aspen's nose started tingling as she held back more useless tears.

'I know you're scared, *chiquita*. I was too.'

'Was?' She glanced at him.

Cruz leaned towards her and kissed her softly. 'Was.' He gave a half smile and reached inside his jacket pocket. He pulled out a small red velour pouch. 'You asked me last week what I would get you for your birthday and I had no idea. It took me a while, but finally I realised that I was imposing my way of fixing things over yours.'

Aspen gazed at the small pouch he'd placed in her hand.

'One of my flaws is that I see something wrong and I want to fix it. My instinct is to take care of those around me. The only way I knew how to do that without getting hurt was to remain emotionally detached from everything.

But no matter how hard I tried I couldn't do that with you. You fill me up, Aspen and you make me feel so damned much. You make me want so much. No one else has ever come close.'

Aspen's mouth went dry as she felt the hard piece of jewellery inside the pouch. She'd guessed what it was already and she honestly didn't know what her response should be. She wanted to be with Cruz more than anything else in the world but the ring felt big. Huge, in fact. Oh, no doubt it would be beautiful, but it wouldn't be *her*. It wouldn't be something she would ever feel comfortable wearing—especially with her job—and it was just one more sign that they could never make a proper relationship work.

'Open it. It's not what you think it is.'

Untying the drawstrings with shaky fingers, Aspen carefully tipped the contents of the pouch into her hand.

'Oh!' Her breath whooshed out of her lungs and she stared at a tiny, delicate wood carving of a horse attached to a thin strip of leather. 'Oh, Cruz, its exquisite.' Her shocked eyes flew to his. 'It's just like the ones I saw lined up on your mother's mantelpiece. You *did* do them for her, didn't you?'

'I did,' he confirmed gruffly.

Studying him, she was completely taken aback by the raw emotion on his face and her lips trembled as her own deep feelings broke to the surface. 'You *do* love me.'

Cruz cupped her face in his hands and lifted her mouth to his for a searing kiss. 'I do. More than life itself.'

'Oh.' Aspen clutched Cruz's shoulders and welcomed the fold of his strong embrace as the hot tears she had been holding at bay spilled recklessly down her cheeks. 'You've made me cry.'

'And me.'

Aspen looked up and found that his eyes were wet. She

touched a tear clinging to the bottom of his lashes. 'When did you make this?'

'During the week. I couldn't concentrate on anything and my executive team were just about ready to call in the professionals with white coats. I have to say it took a few attempts before my fingers started working again.'

Aspen clutched the tiny horse. 'I'll treasure it.'

'And I'll treasure you. Turn around,' he commanded huskily.

Aspen let out a shaky breath, happiness threatening to burst right out of her. She clasped the tiny horse to her chest as he gently moved her hair aside and tied the leather strap around her neck. Then she turned back to face him.

He looked down to where the horse lay nestled between her breasts. 'You do know that in some countries this binds you to me for ever?'

Aspen smiled. 'For ever?'

'Completely. And in case you're at all unsure what I mean by that I have something else.'

He produced a small box and Aspen knew this time it would be a ring. She also knew that no matter how ostentatious it was she would accept it from him, because she knew it had come from a place of absolute love.

Smiling, she opened it and got the third shock of the day. Inside, nestled on a bed of green silk, was the most exquisitely formed diamond ring she had ever seen. And by Cruz's standards it must have seemed—

'It's tiny! Oh, I'm sorry.' She clapped her hand over her mouth. 'That came out wrong.'

Cruz grimaced and slid the beautiful ring onto her finger. 'It wasn't my first choice, believe me, but I knew if I got you anything larger you'd think it was impractical.'

Aspen laughed and flung herself into his arms, utter joy flooding her system at how well he *did* know her. 'I love it!'

Cruz grunted and then lifted her off the ground and

kissed her. 'I'm getting you matching diamond earrings next, and they're so heavy you won't be able to stand up.'

'Then I'll only wear them in bed.' Smiling like a loon, she rained kisses down all over his face. 'Oh, Cruz, it's perfect. *You're* perfect.'

'So does that mean you're going to put me out of my misery and tell me you love me? Because I know you do.'

'How do you know that?'

'You called my lawyer a supermodel.'

Aspen pulled back. 'You think I was jealous of her?'

'I hope so. Now, please, *mi chiquita*, say yes and become indebted to me for the rest of your life?'

'You'll really lend your wife money and let her pay you back?'

'If she ever gets around to telling me that she loves me I'll let her do whatever she wants, as long as she promises to only do it with me.'

'Yes, Cruz.' Aspen nuzzled his neck and basked in the sensation of safety and love that enveloped her. 'I love you and I will be indebted to you for the rest of my life.'

Cruz touched the tiny horse that lay between her breasts. 'And I you, *mi gatita*. And I you.'

* * * * *

A sneaky peek at next month…

MODERN™

INTERNATIONAL AFFAIRS, SEDUCTION & PASSION GUARANTEED

My wish list for next month's titles…

In stores from 17th January 2014:

☐ A Bargain with the Enemy – Carole Mortimer

☐ Shamed in the Sands – Sharon Kendrick

☐ When Falcone's World Stops Turning – Abby Green

☐ An Exquisite Challenge – Jennifer Hayward

In stores from 7th February 2014:

☐ A Secret Until Now – Kim Lawrence

☐ Seduction Never Lies – Sara Craven

☐ Securing the Greek's Legacy – Julia James

☐ A Debt Paid in Passion – Dani Collins

Available at WHSmith, Tesco, Asda, Eason, Amazon and Apple

Just can't wait?

Visit us Online

You can buy our books online a month before they hit the shops! **www.millsandboon.co.uk**

0114/0

Special Offers

Every month we put together collections and longer reads written by your favourite authors.

Here are some of next month's highlights— and don't miss our fabulous discount online!

On sale 7th February

On sale 17th January

On sale 7th February

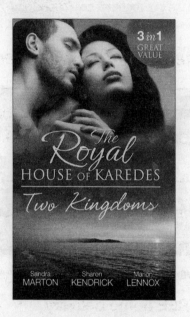

Discover more romance at

www.millsandboon.co.uk

- ❤ WIN great prizes in our exclusive competitions

- ❤ BUY new titles before they hit the shops

- ❤ BROWSE new books and REVIEW your favourites

- ❤ SAVE on new
  Mills & Boon

- ❤ DISCOVER

PLUS, to chat a
get the latest ne

- �f Find us on face
- 🐦 Follow us on tw
- ❤ Sign up to our